P·S

Starting with non-fiction, ~~~~
hundreds of articles and s~~~~
JJ Despain. In 2001 she b~~~~
career with *The Doctor D*~~~~
Medical Romance, *Nurse* ~~~~
and with more than 20 novels to her credit she has
enjoyed writing ever since.

Traci Douglass is a *USA TODAY* bestselling author
of contemporary and paranormal romance. Her stories
feature sizzling heroes full of dark humour, quick
wit and major attitude, and heroines who are smart,
tenacious, and always give as good as they get. She
holds an MFA in Writing Popular Fiction from Seton
Hill University, and she loves animals, chocolate, coffee,
hot British actors and sarcasm—not necessarily in that
order.

Also by Dianne Drake

Tortured by Her Touch
Doctor, Mummy...Wife?
The Nurse and the Single Dad
Saved by Doctor Dreamy

Sinclair Hospital Surgeons miniseries

Reunited with Her Army Doc
Healing Her Boss's Heart

One Night with the Army Doc
is **Traci Douglass**'s debut title

Look out for more books from Traci Douglass
Coming soon

Discover more at millsandboon.co.uk.

BACHELOR DOC, UNEXPECTED DAD

DIANNE DRAKE

ONE NIGHT WITH THE ARMY DOC

TRACI DOUGLASS

MILLS & BOON

First Published in Great Britain 2018
by Mills & Boon, an imprint of HarperCollins*Publishers*
1 London Bridge Street, London, SE1 9GF

Bachelor Doc, Unexpected Dad © 2018 by Dianne Despain

One Night with the Army Doc © 2018 by Traci Douglass

ISBN: 978-0-263-93368-0

MIX
Paper from
responsible sources
FSC C007454

This book is produced from independently certified FSC™ paper
to ensure responsible forest management.
For more information visit www.harpercollins.co.uk/green.

Printed and bound in Great Britain by
CPI Group (UK) Ltd, Croydon CR0 4YY

BACHELOR DOC, UNEXPECTED DAD

DIANNE DRAKE

MILLS & BOON

To a real-life cowboy I met on a lonely ranch road.
Thanks for the inspiration!

PROLOGUE

MATT ROLLED OVER in bed and looked at her. She was still sleeping, and so beautiful in her sleep he wanted to stay another night with her. That wasn't his life, though. As tempting as Ellie was, and she was the most tempting woman he'd ever met, he didn't get to have that kind of involvement in his life. In fact, he'd planned everything to fit him the way he wanted—no strings. It was easier. People didn't get hurt.

Still, that graceful form under the satin sheets next to him was so hard to resist. And it wasn't just the physical intimacy that had been good. They'd talked. Dined. Danced. Things he'd never done with a woman before. And Ellie was so easy just to hold, to be near.

The first night, he'd assumed it would be fun and games, she'd be gone by the time he went to sleep, and he would never see her again. But that's not what had happened. They'd stood on the balcony for a while, looking at the beautiful Reno lights, laughing at silly things, talking much longer than he'd expected to. And the night had passed so quickly. In fact, by the time they'd gotten around to what he'd assumed would take only a short time, the sun had already been coming up and he'd been wondering where the night had gone.

Then Matt had watched Ellie, off and on that day, always having an excuse to be near her. It was a convention and medical conference after all. The hotel ballroom was filled with various displays of new medical products and pharmaceuticals. Somehow, the ones that had seemed to catch his attention had always been near her booth. And while he'd tried not to be obvious about watching her, Ellie had caught him at it a time or two, leaving him with a blush on his face and a shrug on his shoulder. Much the way a schoolboy with a crush would act.

But those looks she'd caught—they'd led to a second night, one with much less talking and much more passion. In fact, she had already been in his bed when he'd gone back to his room, having bribed a maid to let her in. And that night it had been like two desperate people clinging together at the end of the world. In some ways, that's what it was. The end of their little world as, in three days' time, he'd be back in a hospital in Mosul, putting pieces of injured soldiers back together. That's who Matt was. And that was his world. Not this one.

Still, as Matt buttoned his shirt and headed to the hotel room door that second morning he wondered if something like this, someone like Ellie, could ever have a place in his life. It was a nice dream, but in his experience dreams didn't come true, and it was all he could do to make it through his reality.

Someone like Ellie deserved more. But he was a man who had nothing to give.

Opening the door quietly, so not to disturb her, Matt stepped into the hall, took one last look at Ellie before he shut the door, then leaned against the wall for a moment, watching the hotel maid making her way slowly down the corridor with her cart. By the time she reached this room, he'd be on a plane to Hawaii, and from there a military transport back to Iraq.

CHAPTER ONE

"I DON'T KNOW what to do with him," Matt McClain said, looking down at the little tow-headed boy in the firm grasp of his second cousin, or half-cousin, or whatever it was that related them distantly.

Sarah Clayton held the boy's hand like she was holding on to a dog that was about to get away. Tight, and with a purpose. But not friendly. There was nothing friendly *or* nurturing in her. Nothing compassionate. Nothing to indicate she cared at all for the kid. "The same thing you think *I'm* supposed to do with him. Only I'm not going to do it. I took care of your sister those last two weeks, and I've had him with me ever since. But you're here, and you're more blood to him than I am so, he's yours. Besides…"

She held out an envelope—one that had been sealed, opened then sealed again. "Janice left you this."

He opened it, and looked down at the shaky handwriting—the handwriting of a dying woman. A lump formed in his throat and he turned his back to Sarah as he read it.

Dear Matt,
If you're reading this, that means the cancer has finally beaten me. The doctors said I was too late for treatment, but that's been my life. Too late for ev-

erything. It's called non-Hodgkin's lymphoma, and I'm sure you know all about it since you're a doctor.

Yes, I know you're a doctor. Heard it from a man in the casino where I was working. He was drunk and saying all kinds of crazy things...things that didn't make sense. His name was Carter, I think, and he said he was a doctor. I don't know if that's true, but he was going on about his buddy Matt, from Forgeburn, who saved his life. Great doctor, he called you. And I'm sure you are.

Matt stopped reading for a moment and took a breath. Carter Holmes had been his best buddy since med-school days. He'd sustained almost fatal injuries and, yes, he'd saved his life. "Do you know how long Janice was in Vegas?" he asked Sarah, without turning to face her.

"For a while, I think. She told me she moved around a lot. Changed her name so your old man wouldn't find her. Said she was always looking over her shoulder to make sure he wasn't coming after her."

Matt clenched his jaw, not wanting to read any more but knowing he had to.

I don't blame you for not sending for me, Matty. We were both kids. Neither of us knew what to do. But I did wait until I couldn't stay there anymore. You were gone, Dad left me behind, and even though I wasn't even fifteen I knew I had to leave there, too.

I spent a lot of time going from place to place, never settling down. I was afraid to. Afraid I'd get too comfortable someplace and let my guard down. So I always moved on. Funny thing is, all those years I was running I guess Dad had died right

*after he left Forgeburn. At least that's what Sarah
said. Guess neither of us had to run away, did we?*

Matt turned to Sarah. "He's dead?"

She nodded. "They found him in one of the canyons.
They think he'd passed on quite a while before one of
the cowboys stumbled on him. He was living like he always did, they said. Hoarding trash and drinking his life
away. Folks around here said it was the drink that took
him. Didn't really care to find out."

Matt shut his eyes. So many wasted years he and Janice had had when they could have stayed together. But
they'd become two kids out on their own, in a world they
didn't know. He'd found his salvation in the army. But
Janice... Matt turned away from Sarah again, before she
could see the tears brimming in his eyes.

*I did one good thing, though, Matty. His name is
Lucas. I don't know who his father is, and there's
no sense looking. But he's a good boy—the only
thing I've done right. I want you to take care of him
for me. Make sure he has better than what we did.
Do for him, Matty, what you couldn't do for me.*

That was where the letter ended. No last words, no
signature. "Is this all?" he asked Sarah.

"It was all she could do to get that on paper. She went
to sleep with the pen still in her hand and she didn't..."

Matt nodded as he looked across the sandy expanse
at his sister's grave. A few mourners were still there—
maybe five or six and he wondered who they were and
why they had come. Forgeburn had never been a real
home to them. All it had ever been was the place from

which they wanted to escape. "Why did she come back here?" he asked.

"Because she wanted to contact you, but she wasn't up to it. And I was the only relative, even though I live a good fifty miles from here."

"So, Lucas," Matt said, once he'd regained his composure and turned around again to face Sarah. "You've got kids. You know how to take care of them. I don't. And I'm still on active duty. I have to report back in two months." He'd been granted emergency family leave to come and make arrangements for Lucas, but those arrangements didn't include keeping him. That thought had never crossed his mind as he'd assumed Lucas was already settled in with Sarah. But apparently not. "And I'm scheduled to go back to Iraq later this year. How, in all of that, does he fit in?"

"Look, Matt. I kept him until you got here, just to be nice, but this is where it ends. Janice named you as his legal guardian, the social worker from child services has seen to the legalities of it, which makes him your responsibility, not mine. So adopt him yourself, or find someone else who wants him—it's your decision. And I don't mean to be unreasonable about this, but my husband doesn't want him. We've got enough to handle without adding another child to it. So…" She shrugged. "Take him. Or get rid of him. Either way, I'm out of it."

Take him. Just like that. Take a nephew he hadn't even known he had until he'd received word his sister had died. Matt wasn't opposed to family responsibility. In a lot of ways, he liked the idea of honoring the obligation, even in a family like his. A mother who had left when he'd been five. A sister who had—well, ended up back where she'd started. A dad who apparently had died without notice. But Lucas—he needed his chance. He hadn't asked to be born into the McClain family. It's just what he'd got. Still, kids didn't belong in his life. He'd planned it like that. No kids, no obligations. *Obligations*—for a moment the image of Ellie flashed through his mind. If ever there'd been a time when he'd come close to taking on an obligation other than his career...

"Look, Sarah, give me a couple weeks to figure it out. Can you do that much?"

Sarah shook her head. "Sorry."

Well, she wasn't giving him many options. For a career military surgeon, always going in one direction or another, moving from place to place and in his case combat zone to combat zone, there was no room to care for a child. In fact, he didn't even have a place to call home, and kids needed a home, and stability. They needed someone there all the time to raise them. They needed what he and Janice had never had.

"All I can say, Matt, is I know you've been doing good for yourself, despite the way your daddy treated you. I'm glad for you. But I can't take Lucas. So, like I said, I've already contacted child services, they know the situation, and the paperwork's started. So he'll go to a group home until they can find a family who'll take him in, unless you do. As for adoption..." She shrugged. "Can't say what'll happen there. He's a cute kid. Doesn't talk, though. Not a word." She leaned in and whispered, "Don't think he's very smart."

"Probably because he's traumatized from everything that's been happening to him," Matt snapped. Then he looked down at Lucas, who was sucking his thumb. He had a ratty old blanket tucked under his arm, and he wore a pair of sneakers that were clearly several sizes too large. All Matt could think was he was so vulnerable. And scared. Matt knew what it was like to be vulnerable and scared. Knew exactly what the kid was feeling... like his whole world had just collapsed. Matt couldn't blame Lucas for not wanting to talk. There had been many times in his own young life when he hadn't wanted to talk either.

"Hope it doesn't mess up your life too much, Matt," Sarah said, then turned and walked away, leaving Matt standing alone in the cemetery, holding on to Lucas with one hand and a bag of clothes with the other. And with no idea what to do next.

"Do you eat hamburgers?" he asked Lucas, who looked up at him with wide, frightened eyes. The kid needed more than a hamburger. Matt knew that. He needed words of reassurance. The promise of a home. A hug. Right now, though, he was equipped to buy him a hamburger. That's all.

Did kids his age eat hamburgers? Matt's medical training told him yes. But his parenting training—well, there was none of that to draw on. No kids in his life, no kids in his future. No home. No wife. He thought back to that morning when he'd left Ellie sleeping and walked away. Too bad he couldn't go back and stay there. It had been nice. No worries. No past. No future. Just that moment in time. Unlike this moment in time, when his only goal was a hamburger, or anything else a two-year-old would eat.

"I need to do what?" Ellie Landers looked at the ultrasound, and didn't see anything particularly distressing. She knew how to interpret what she was seeing. Her brief time in nursing had taught her that much. And what she saw right now looked perfectly normal.

"Rest more. Eat better. Reduce stress. Cut back on work. You know, the simple things."

She did know, but she wasn't sure why all this applied to her. Dr. Shaffer had just told her the baby was healthy. She was healthy, too. So why the precautions? "But there's nothing wrong with me. You said so just a few minutes ago." Now she was worried.

"Your blood pressure is on the high end of normal. You're at risk for gestational diabetes partly because of your age and partly because your mother has diabetes. And you're chronically tired."

"Because I work eighteen hours a day." Ellie liked Doc Shaffer. He'd been her mother's obstetrician, now he was hers. Medically, he had a great reputation. Personally, he was just plain kind. He'd never asked her to explain the pregnancy. Not that there was much to explain about a two-night fling at a medical conference. All that, plus he had a great heart for his patients and treated them with respect and dignity no matter what the situation. As someone in the medical field, Ellie appreciated that. As a patient, she was glad to have it.

"Cut it back," he said, leaning forward across his desk, looking over at her across the top of his glasses. "You're thirty-four, Ellie. You live a busy life and drive yourself harder than anybody I've ever seen, except your mom. And I don't want you having complications with this pregnancy."

Thirty-four and owner of one of the fastest-growing medical illustration companies in the world. Something she'd built from the ground up. "But you think I could be at risk?"

"You could be, if you don't slow down—which puts your baby at risk."

Her baby. It was strange hearing that, because Ellie had never really thought of this life she was carrying as *her* baby. It was a baby, possibly someone else's baby, depending on whether or not her fling wanted to be a daddy.

But *her* baby? Hearing that gave her a maternal jolt she hadn't expected. It wasn't enough to make her change her mind to become a single mom, but it did make Ellie more aware of the baby she was carrying.

"Look, I'll cut back on the hours. Eat better. But I'm not going to go home, kick my feet up and watch old movies for the next almost five months. I have to work. My company needs me, and I need it."

"You're just like your mother. Do you know that?" Doc Shaffer leaned back in his chair, typed something into his computer, then shook his head. "She was as driven as you are. And as stubborn."

Ellie Landers wanted to smile at the comparison, but she couldn't as she didn't want to be like her mother and didn't want to be compared to her either. "And look how successful she's been. She owns one of the largest technology companies in Nevada." And she'd raised a child as a single mom. Well, mostly in absentia. But she did get the credit for hiring the right people to take care of her. All this was something Ellie wasn't prepared to do.

Children needed a real family, a parent or parents who didn't hire someone to take their child to the playground, who didn't pay for the most qualified caregivers but, instead, took responsibility for that care themselves. Family dinners, stories at bedtime. That's what children needed—what Ellie had never had, and what she wasn't able to give. Not with her job or her chosen lifestyle. That's what Ellie had learned from her own upbringing and what she carried with her every day of her life. That kind of life wasn't meant to be her kind of life.

Still, the dream of it—home, family. Husband. It was nice. But so ethereal it made Ellie sad. So that's where she stopped because the rest of the dream was so vague.

But the husband was not. Since Reno, she'd had a vision of him. Even more now that she was carrying his baby.

"Whatever the case, stop at Reception on your way out and schedule your next appointment. I'd like to see you back in six weeks as a precautionary measure. Also, I've written you a prescription for prenatal vitamins, and the name of a good physical therapist should your back spasms continue."

"I don't need a therapist for backache and I already take vitamins. I started the day I found out I was pregnant."

"Which is good. But the ones I'm prescribing have more iron—you're a little anemic, and they also have much more folic acid than anything you can get OTC, because you need folic acid. It's for the healthy development of the brain, eyes, cells and nervous system."

"I know," Ellie said. "Remember, I worked in obstetrics?" She'd been a good nurse, but nursing hadn't suited her the way she'd hoped it would. Maybe because it required nurturing in abundance, and she didn't have a speck of it in her. She had been good at the procedural aspects, but had lacked the genuine human touch that was also needed. Ellie could see her shortcoming, and she'd honestly worked to correct it because she loved medicine, but there had always been something missing. She couldn't define it, couldn't describe it to her supervisor when she'd resigned from her job.

And now, ten years later, she still couldn't define what that lack was other than she simply didn't have a nurturer's instinct. But she'd found her niche—medical illustration.

Ellie had always loved drawing and was pretty good at it. Had won a few childhood awards. Turned it into her minor course of study in college. So when she'd read that it was an expanding field with growth potential, she'd jumped at the chance to be part of it, anxious to combine her love of medicine with her love of drawing. Of course, more education had been required. Two additional years of study on top of the four she'd had in nursing school. In those two years, however, she'd gone from not only wanting to be an illustrator but wanting to build her own company. And it was also exciting. Even now, she had no regrets.

"Yes, I know you were a nurse—for about a minute— then you moved on. *Remember that?*"

"And those charts of fetal development you have hanging on the wall in your waiting room..." She smiled. She'd done them. And she'd illustrated numerous medical texts. Plus, they were doing medical videography now.

Doc Shaffer laughed. "Point taken. You've made a name for yourself, but that name must cut back on her hours, and get more rest. You work too hard, Ellie, and while I'm an advocate for women getting on with their lives when they're pregnant, your life is a little over the top. In other words, baby needs some rest."

Rest—that she would do. Even though she wasn't going to keep this baby, she did want to give it every advantage she could coming into this world, and keeping herself healthy was the start of it. "So, is that all you want? Or would you like another pint of blood?"

Doc Shaffer chuckled. "You know what I want, and at the rate you're going, that's a big order."

"Then I'll do better," she promised. And she would. While Ellie didn't want the responsibility of raising a child, not with her fear of turning out to be the kind of mother hers was, she certainly didn't want to put this baby at risk. She'd made her choice the day her dipstick had gone from blue to pink, and nothing had changed since then. She'd tell Dr. Matt McClain he was going to be a father and give him the option to raise their baby. Or she would opt for adoption, if he didn't want to. It was all straightforward. Ellie owned a business and that was her life, all she wanted. Real babies, boyfriends and husbands were not needed.

So all Ellie had to do now was tell someone who'd expected a couple of casual days of fun at a medical convention that casual had turned into commitment. *If that's what he wanted.* He'd seemed like a nice guy. A little distracted. But kind. And polite. Really good looking... traditionally tall, dark and handsome, and rugged. Dark eyes, wavy black hair, rugged. Built like she'd never seen another man built.

Just thinking about him now gave Ellie goose-bumps. The way he'd looked those couple of nights when she'd let go of her self-made business-first rules, let her hair down and lived in a fantasy that had never happened in her reality was still with her. He'd hung on in her mind long after Reno. From time to time she'd even caught herself distracted by a daydream of him. A leftover feeling she couldn't explain and didn't want to explore. Then the reality of those days had crept in, about six weeks later.

And now, well—all Ellie had to do was the figurative baby-in-a-basket-on-the-doorstep thing, and hope he'd take that basket in. It was his baby too and not only did he have the right to know, he had the right to be a daddy, if that's what he wanted. Or be involved in the adoption process, if *that's* what he wanted. Either way, she'd know what was going to happen soon. Ellie was glad he was out of the military now and back home, because from here she was headed straight to Forgeburn, Utah.

"It's not a traditional medical practice," Dr. Donald Granger explained. "But you know that since you're from here. Most of it's a cowboy practice now, and that's about as tough as it gets. Then you've got some of the canyon resort areas with tourists who need medical care occasionally. And we do have some locals in a couple little spread-out towns. There's a pretty fair patient base—enough to keep one doc busy.

"If you need help, the clinic in Whipple Creek will usually send someone out for a day or two, but you've got to keep in mind that you're the only real medical help within a hundred miles in any direction. So what you'll be getting is a practice that stretches out for more miles than any practical medical practice should have to, house calls that'll take up half your day for something minor—and, yes, house calls are part of what the people here expect—and the cowboy trailers—good luck finding those.

"It's a hard life, son. But a good one. People will appreciate you more because access to you isn't easy for many of them. And there's no one to rely on but you, which develops stamina. And courage. Lots of courage."

"If it's so good," Matt asked, "why are you giving it up?" He had qualms about taking over a GP practice, even if only for a little while because being back home came with all kinds of bad memories, and he was afraid those might surface at the wrong times and prevent him from doing his best. Plus, he wasn't a GP. That was another big drawback. In fact, the only good thing was that it would keep him busy, and he needed that. Lucas was a great kid, but spending every minute of every day together wasn't good for either of them. They both needed some separation from time to time.

"I've been doing it for fifty years, as you know, since I took care of you when you were little. And these old bones aren't rugged enough anymore. Also, I've got grandkids who don't even know me. So it's time for me to move on, to rest the weary bones and play with the grandkids."

"You do realize I'm only going to be a temp here. Once the situation with Lucas gets straightened out, I have to report back to duty. They've given me two months, which is the time I've accrued for regular leave. So you'll still have to keep looking for someone to buy you out."

"Or close the practice for good if I can't." Dr. Granger held out his hands. They were knotted with arthritis. "These hands can't do the job anymore, Matt, or I would carry on. I wouldn't want to see this place go without a doctor, but most of the young docs coming out of medical school want something better than what I've got to offer, and the older docs who have had something better now want something simpler. Practicing in Forgeburn doesn't just take love for the work, it takes love for the work *here*."

That would never happen. Once child services had a good placement for Lucas, he'd be gone. Being here was only a matter of circumstances, and Matt wasn't staying because he wanted to. He was staying for Lucas. "So, when do you want me to start?"

"Are you sure about this, Matt? Do you really want to do this?"

"No. But, I'm not staying here for me. The army has me and I'll go back as soon as I can."

"And that little one you're looking after?"

"Lucas is a good kid, and I'm going to make sure I've found the best situation for him before I leave. If that means staying here for longer than I'd wanted, that's what I'll do because I don't want him growing up the way I did. You know how it was with Janice and me, Doc—and no kid deserves that."

"But you came through it, Matt, and look at you now."

Yes, just look at him. The man who knew nothing about kids as temporary guardian of a child he couldn't raise. Kids needed much more than anything he had to offer. In fact, as it stood, Matt had nothing to offer whatsoever. His life in the army didn't mix with domesticity in any form. "But my sister didn't, which is why I have to do what I'm doing. I owe it to her to do this for Lucas." Even though he was sure Janice's intention had been for him to keep the boy. But that wouldn't work out.

"Well, OK, then. How about starting right now? Oh, and talk to Betty Nelson about watching Lucas. She's a retired teacher. Really good with little ones. I couldn't recommend anyone better than her."

"I'll do that," Matt said, thinking back to his grade-school days. Betty Nelson had been his teacher for a year. She'd paid for his lunch, and Janice's, when he hadn't had money—which had been pretty much every day. And she'd made sure that he'd had his school supplies even though his dad had refused to pay for them. She'd be a perfect babysitter for Lucas, and Matt was keeping his fingers crossed she would do that. "I'll definitely talk to her."

So now this was where he put on his stethoscope and stepped into a completely different life. For a little while. That's what he'd keep telling himself—for a little while.

But what if he couldn't find a good situation for Lucas? Could he walk away from him knowing he was leaving Lucas where he, himself, had been left so many times during his own childhood?

No, he didn't want to think about that. Didn't want to think into the future. Reality, here and now, was good enough. Always had been because it's all he'd ever been able to count on. Getting by, moment to moment.

Sighing, Matt held out his hand for the keys to the

clinic. This was for Janice, he reminded himself. For Janice and Lucas. It didn't make things easier, but it made him feel better. It's what he had to do—that's the thought that ran through his mind for the next few hours as he prepared himself mentally to be part of Forgeburn again.

The clinic was small, just as he remembered it. One underwhelming exam room with basic outdated equipment, a minor procedures room, a shared public and staff bathroom, a small reception area and waiting room, which seated only six people, and a tiny, knee-hole office. But it did have a nice storage room attached to his office, larger than he would have expected, with a window at the rear of it overlooking a rock formation in the distance.

A playroom for Lucas when Betty Nelson couldn't watch him? Switch to a Dutch door for security, add carpeting—it was a thought. One that didn't go away as he walked around the outside of the small white cement building that stood alone in the middle of a cracked asphalt parking lot, surrounded by sand, dirt and a lot of cacti.

The next closest structure, a small, nineteen-sixties-style hotel was, with a lot of squinting, within eyesight. There really was no upside to the medical office, nothing nice or pretty or comforting, but the house he'd also be getting as part of the deal was definitely an upside. Modestly large, fairly new, with a nice pool and beautiful canyon view. A squared-off adobe-style with an open floor plan, large kitchen—he used to love to cook—and a *casita* with in-home or private access. Not that he needed a *casita*, since he didn't anticipate anyone ever coming to visit him. But at least it gave him an option.

"This is where we'll be staying," he said to Lucas the next day as they explored the outside area together, to make sure the pool was completely secured and safe, grateful Doc Granger's one indulgence in life had been his house. It would be a good place for Lucas. Comfortable. Safe. "How about we go take a look?" He'd wanted to carry Lucas, but Lucas was often resistant to that, unless he was tired. *A child with determination*, Matt thought.

Lucas's reaction was to turn his back to Matt and stare at a little brown and blue skink darting into a rock garden at the edge of the patio. It was trying to get away from prying eyes. Sort of what Matt felt like doing, to be honest. "Well, if you're not interested in looking around today, we'll be back tomorrow when we move in. Plenty of time for exploring then."

Especially since Doc Granger had already vacated the place. Except for the furniture, which was staying with the house, all the personal touches were gone. And Matt had an idea Doc Granger was, right now, playing with grandkids. Which meant Matt was totally on his own here. It wasn't an unsettling thought, but it wasn't a comforting one either, since he knew so little about his new responsibilities. Well, live and learn. He'd make the best of it, like he was making the best of being a temporary dad.

"You ready to leave?" he finally asked Lucas, who'd gone over to the rocks, looking for the skink. Of course, Lucas didn't answer. Neither did he take Matt's hand when Matt extended it to him. Instead, he took an extra-firm hold on the ratty old blanket he carried with him everywhere, and trailed along next to Matt. Never too close, but never too far.

There were two cars in the parking lot. Actually, one car and a pick-up truck. And there was little to indicate this was a medical clinic except the weather-beaten sign at the edge of the parking lot that read: "Medical Clinic". Followed by an emergency phone number.

"Well, this is it," Ellie said. It had become her habit to talk to her baby. While she was only just past eighteen weeks along, and babies in the womb didn't start hearing until around twenty-three weeks, she liked the connection. Felt that, on some level, it would help her baby's development. So she talked.

"Not what I expected. For some reason, I'd guessed your daddy to be...better established." Of course, they'd never really talked about such things. They'd talked about other things, especially that first night—medicine, college days, the convention—but never about their own realities. That had been part of keeping it from becoming too personal. Of course, that hadn't worked out, had it?

Ellie glanced down at her belly as she stepped out of her car. It wasn't exactly flat now, but loose-fitting cargo pants and an oversized white, gauzy shirt still concealed the obvious. Not for much longer, though, as her naked profile was that of a woman with a bulging belly. But right now her baggy clothes kept her condition a secret from her co-workers—she didn't want to answer all the questions—and from Matt as well, until she found the right moment to tell him.

What she didn't want was for him to open the door to her and see her belly right off. Why shock him like that? It wouldn't be right.

Also, she wanted to reassure herself he was someone she wanted to raise the baby because Reno hadn't been about real life, whereas this baby definitely was. So Ellie wanted to know, see more, before she let Matt know what had happened. She'd thought about how to handle the inevitable the whole way here, and hadn't come up with a real solution yet. Time would tell, she supposed as she entered the building, only to discover a completely empty waiting room. No patients, no receptionist. Just chairs and a desk.

"Well, it's clean," she whispered, as she wandered down the short hall leading to the exam room, looking for signs of life. "Anybody here?" she finally called out.

Ellie listened, heard noises coming from the room marked "EXAM" and moved a little closer. "Hello?" she called out again.

This time there was an answer. "There is, and I'll be with you in about five minutes. Please, take a seat in the waiting room."

She recognized the voice, of course. Nice, smooth. Very sexy. A voice worthy of goose-bumps that were, co-incidentally, already running up her arms. "Thank you," she called back. It was closer to ten minutes, though, before a young woman, who wore khaki shorts and worn hiking boots, wandered down the hall and out the front door, sporting an elastic brace on her left arm. And it was another couple of minutes before Matt appeared in the waiting room, with a little boy at his side.

"Ellie?" he said, frowning at first then slowly giving a broad smile. "I—I didn't expect to see you here." He took quick steps in her direction, then stopped before the predictable embrace "How have you been?"

She stopped as well, suddenly feeling uncertain about what she was doing here. "I've been fine, Matt. I was va-cationing nearby, and thought I would stop by to see you. If you don't mind."

"Mind? Absolutely not. I...um... I'm glad to see you," he said, obviously surprised and a little off kilter.

This was so awkward. She felt it. He felt it. But she was here and now she had to go through with her plan.

Well, maybe not this very moment. But in a while. "I'm glad to see you, too. I wasn't sure if you'd want me to look you up, but I took a chance and..." Ellie took two more steps in Matt's direction, but too quickly as her head started spinning, spinning as the hallway slowly descended into darkness. Her last words before she toppled into his arms were, "My baby..."

CHAPTER TWO

NOTHING SEEMED ABNORMAL. Ellie's blood pressure was a little high, but not outside normal. Her pulse was fine. So were her reflexes and her heartbeat. She'd come to before he'd had a chance to do anything more than a cursory exam and had stopped him.

Right now, she was sitting up, sipping water. Fully alert. Offering no explanation for anything. And he didn't buy that she was here vacationing. She wasn't the type to vacation. Maybe travel for work but not for pleasure. Especially to a place like this. So, did she want to take what they'd started to the next level, even though they'd agreed to keep it casual?

The thought of that caused Matt's heart to skip a beat, even though he wasn't a next-level kind of guy. The idea of it did intrigue him, though, because he'd had that thought a time or two, then dismissed it as impractical. It couldn't work. They lived in different worlds. But it had been a nice thought for those few moments.

"You mentioned something about a baby, so I checked your car and…" He shrugged. "No baby."

"I call my car my baby," Ellie said, not looking at him.

He didn't buy that either. But he wasn't going to pressure her into telling him what she wanted because Ellie was direct. She'd do it in her own good time. "Well, your car's fine."

She didn't respond. Just nodded and kept on sipping.

"So, you said you're vacationing here?"

Ellie nodded again.

"In Forgeburn, where the population is in negative numbers?" This was getting more and more interesting, and he couldn't wait until she told him the truth. Which she would because Ellie wasn't a very good liar. It was showing on her face and in her fidgety hands. Normally, she was straightforward. At least, she had been in Reno. Yet this side of Ellie—it didn't fit what he knew of her. Which really wasn't much, come to think of it.

"You said the scenery here was beautiful, so I decided to check it out for myself."

"During the off-season when the resorts aren't operating at full capacity? Funny, I would have taken you for someone who'd want all the amenities."

"Is the little boy yours? Because he looks exactly like you," she said, obviously trying to avoid what she'd come here to say—or do. "I don't remember you saying anything about having a child. Or a wife. Do you have a wife, too?"

Was she really here to see him again? The thought crossed his mind but didn't stay there. Because Ellie had vehemently denied wanting a relationship. Which he'd been glad about. So why now, when he was on leave, had she turned up? And how did she even know he was on leave? Or where he'd be? "I've never married. And Lucas… He's my nephew, and I'm temporarily his legal guardian."

"Nephew?"

"My sister died, which left her son in my care, temporarily."

"Why not permanently?"

"I'm in the army. Single. Get transferred a lot because I'm a surgeon who likes to see action, as in battlefield. It's not a great combination for raising a kid as a single dad."

"You haven't retired?" Ellie asked, looking puzzled.

"No. I'm going back as soon as I fix the situation with Lucas. Hopefully, that'll be inside two months. So, how did you find me? How did you know I was in Forgeburn?"

"Part of my job is research. You were easy to track once I got to the right department in the army, and they connected me to your superior officer, who was very helpful."

It wasn't that simple for most people, and for a moment Matt admired her ability to not only find his superior officer but get him to tell her just where, on leave, he was. "But they neglected to tell you I was coming back?"

"They probably figured you'd tell me when I caught up to you."

"Well, you've caught up to me, and I'm wondering why."

"Like I said, a vacation. Oh, and I'm so sorry about your sister. It can't have been easy on you or Lucas."

"It hasn't been, and I appreciate your sympathy for my sister. She was a good sort who never really got a break in life." What was Ellie up to? It bothered Matt, not knowing. But what bothered him even more was how glad he was to see her.

This wasn't at all what she'd expected, and she wasn't sure which way to go with it, especially since Matt had made up his mind about what he was going to do. Get rid of Lucas then go back to the army. Which meant everything she'd hoped for when she had been told he'd gone home was up in the air. Ellie had assumed he was out of the army. He wasn't. And she'd hoped he would be settled enough to want their baby. Again, he wasn't. Also, he didn't even want Lucas.

So where did that leave her? Basically, at square one again. Pregnant without a plan. Except she would tell him and still give him the opportunity to raise his child. That was only fair. "Well, I need a room. The hotel down the road is a little…dated. Is there someplace better?"

Matt chuckled. "Like I said, the best places aren't running at full capacity yet, and the rest of the smaller places—I'm not sure you'd like them. Especially since I know, for a fact, you prefer satin sheets."

Satin sheets. Yes, she'd loved the feel of them, and the feel of him next to her as she'd enjoyed the soft caress of both the sheets and Matt. "I'm not really concerned about sheets, Matt. I just need some food, then bed…" For her pregnancy first, but also for her because she was tired. She needed to put her feet up, close her eyes and give both her and the baby at least ten hours of down time. Maybe more, if she could.

"If you go down the road, about five miles in the opposite direction, there's a place called Red Canyon Resort. It has nice rooms, decent amenities. Since it's early in the season, you shouldn't have trouble getting a room. But if you *do* stay…"

He stopped, paused for a moment, and that hesitation of a frown she'd seen on his face when he'd first seen her a little while ago returned. Only this time it didn't transform into a smile. She hoped he was glad to see her. In fact, she'd thought he was. Now she wasn't so sure.

"If you do stay, there's not much to do unless you like hiking or rock climbing," he finally continued.

"I'll manage," she said, scooting to the edge of the exam table, feeling a little more discouraged than she had before. Of course, she'd never been totally optimistic about asking him. That would have been foolish, given the circumstances. But she'd hoped. Right now, though, some of the hope was disappearing—because of Lucas, because of Matt's military commitments, because he was more rigid than she remembered him being.

"Before you go, I'd really like to get a better look at you. Something caused you to faint, and I don't know what it was."

"I was tired from the drive. Hungry. Probably a little dehydrated. Once I get a room, I'll eat, drink plenty of fluids, get some rest, and I'll be fine." Ellie scooted a little more until she was at the edge, then stretched until her feet were on the floor. As soon as she stood, though, she wobbled, and Matt was right there to catch her. Again.

"I think before you go checking into anywhere, I'm going to take you someplace to get something to eat. And drink. Your skin doesn't pass the pinch test, so I think your biggest problem right now is dehydration. Are you diabetic, by any chance?"

"Nope. Just had a physical yesterday, as it turns out. Blood tests were good."

"No kidney disease?"

"I'm fine, Matt. My doctor told me I needed to get some rest, which is why I'm here."

"You live in Reno. You could have driven an hour over to Tahoe and checked into a world-class resort to rest there, instead of driving six hundred miles through the desert to rest here. If rest is what you're really after."

"Right now, it is. I don't suppose there'd be a cab out here I could call. I don't think I'm going to be able to drive."

He doubted she'd even make it to her car. "Look, Lucas and I were headed home when you came in. How about you go with us, I'll make sure you get plenty of liquids, and I'll fix us a good dinner? Then later we'll see if you're in any condition to check into a hotel."

Matt took Ellie by the arm and steadied her to the floor again, but instead of letting her attempt to walk to his truck he swooped her into his arms and carried her like he had that first morning, when she had been looking out the window and he had been looking at her—with a longing that hadn't been quenched. He'd swooped her into his arms then, and had watched the satin sheet slither to the floor as he'd laid her naked body down on the bed, and laid his naked body over hers. Thinking about that, even now, caused her to shiver.

"This is very chivalrous of you," she said, without protest. Ellie still liked being in his arms, still liked the feel of him pressed to her. Matt had the power to knock her completely off track, and she couldn't let that happen. Couldn't let the thoughts of how good they had been together seep in. Couldn't let the thoughts of how nice it was to be in his arms, yet again, seep in either.

"I aim to give the best medical care I can, under the circumstances." Matt looked over at Lucas, who was occupied with a toddler version of a video game. "You ready to go home?" he asked.

Lucas picked up his video toy and his blanket, and went directly to Matt's side, the way he always did. Then fell into exact step with Matt, the way he'd only just started doing. "He doesn't talk yet," he explained to Ellie as they walked through the parking lot. "He's lived in some pretty rough circumstances for a while and he's a little delayed, but he's bright. Understands everything. Very observant of everything around him. Just not talkative.

"He will, when he has something to say. Guess he

just hasn't had anything to say yet." She wiggled into the passenger's seat, while Matt strapped Lucas into the toddler safety seat in the crew cab, and within a minute they were on their way to what Matt had dubbed Matt Casa. She still wasn't sure what to make of any of this, but one thing was certain—she did like the way he took care of Lucas. Liked it very much. And the way he took care of her went far, far beyond like.

What had she been thinking, taking that ten-hour drive in one long stretch, stopping only a few times for breaks? Well, a little rest, a little water, a good bed under her back for the night, and she'd be fine. But this sure wasn't the way she'd wanted her first meeting with Matt to go. Seriously, fainting into his arms? Ellie doubted she could have made a more dramatic entrance if she'd tried.

Anyway, telling him about the baby would keep until tomorrow, when she was rested. Yep, back to the plan, but only a modified version of it since she already knew Matt's intentions. No Lucas, no family commitments. But would that include his own child as well? Maybe something about bringing his own child into the world would mellow him, or cause him to change his mind. Ellie wasn't counting on it, though. But she wasn't ruling it out either.

Right now, though, she was going home with Matt. Not part of the plan but so far nothing else had been either. "Since you're obviously not working as a surgeon out here, what kind of practice do you run?"

"Well, I suppose you could call it a family practice or a general practice. The doc who had it before me called it a cowboy practice, and I think that works. Bottom line, I'll get to treat everything as long as I'm here."

As long as he was here. Suddenly, Ellie felt discouraged and disappointed. She'd wanted him to want their baby—it would have been the perfect solution. But there was no solution now. At least, not one she could think of. The thought of that brought tears to her eyes—tears Matt would never see as she turned her head to the window and pretended to be caught up in night-time stars.

"You have two choices. There's a *casita* adjoining the house and it has everything you'll need if you want to sleep there tonight. Or you can stay in one of the guest bedrooms. Your choice."

"How about the *casita*, since I don't feel like climbing stairs? My legs are a little stiff from the drive. Back's a little achy, too."

"Does your doctor know what you did?" Matt asked, leading Ellie through the hall to the entry to the *casita*— a nice little one-bedroom house with a small kitchen and a reasonably large living area. Traditionally, a *casita* was used by a family member or long-term guest. Or tonight, his two-night fling in Reno.

That was an odd question—out of the blue asking her doctor's opinion. Did Matt suspect she was pregnant? Quickly, she looked to make sure her belly hadn't puffed out a few inches and she hadn't noticed. But that wasn't the case. Underneath her baggy cotton shirt, it showed. But not with the shirt on. Whatever the case, she approached her answers cautiously because she was too tired and discouraged to address anything other than sleep tonight.

"No. I really don't have to account to anybody for anything in my life, and that includes my doctor. And before you ask, he would have advised against the drive until I was on vitamins with iron for a few days. Low-grade anemia. Nothing serious. But, like I said, I make my own decisions, and I decided to come to Forgeburn for a holiday."

"As you've said," Matt stated. He opened the door to the *casita* then stepped aside. "Well, whatever the case, it should take me about an hour to fix something to eat, so in the meantime I'd suggest you rest. There's a nice patio outside, and there's the bedroom...your choice."

"You really don't have to do this, Matt. I'm used to taking care of myself. The Red Canyon Resort would be fine."

"You look run-down. I wouldn't call that taking care of yourself."

"I work hard. Travel a lot. My business is growing, and I've got some amazing opportunities coming up. Also, like I said, it's low-grade anemia. All that earns me the right to look run-down. But a good night's sleep will work wonders."

He knew better, though, because he was beginning to suspect. "Well, then, dinner's in an hour. And I don't remember. Are you a vegetarian? I seem to recall you might be."

"I am," she said. "Hope that doesn't put you to any trouble."

"Nope. Because all I have here are chicken nuggets and hot dogs, neither of which are very good."

"Not healthy for Lucas either. Or you, for that matter." With that, she entered the *casita* and shut the door behind her, leaving Matt to stand in the hall staring at—nothing. He was staring at nothing. Until a tug on his shirt tail reminded him that Lucas needed to be fed, bathed and put to bed before anything else happened.

Matt sighed as he sat on the veranda, looking up at the stars. It was a beautiful night. Clear. And the view from this house was stunning. Growing up here, he'd never thought anything about the area was stunning. Not the scenery, the people, the wildlife. Especially not the cramped, rundown house trailers he'd grown up in, where his dad had got the bed, his sister the sofa, and he had been welcome to any spot he could find on the floor that wasn't cluttered with some sort of rubbish. Trailers in a rubbish lot, parked and ready to go for scrap.

He'd escaped that when he'd been sixteen. Had run away to Las Vegas, promising Janice he'd send for her as soon as he could. Well, that had never happened and now all he had left were bad memories of bad times, and a little boy who served to remind him of how he'd broken his promise to Janice. It wasn't a very good legacy, but he'd been able to put some of it aside in the army. Or, at least, justify it to himself. Too young. Too inexperienced in the world. Yeah, whatever.

And his promise to himself about never coming back to Forgeburn for any reason—fat lot of good that had done him because here he was. Maybe he deserved to be here, if only to remind him of what he could have become. Or what Janice could have become if he'd kept his promise. "Care for a margarita?" he asked Ellie, who sat down at a patio table across from him.

"I don't drink," she said. "Water's good, though."

"I seem to recall a couple of mojitos in Reno. But if you don't drink now…" He shrugged. "Water, vegetarian—that sounds like a mighty healthy lifestyle."

"We all make our choices, I suppose. My mom's diabetic and my dad, well, I never knew him because he was a number in a sperm catalogue. Someone with the right qualities to produce a good baby."

"That's what your mother told you?"

"We Landers women are very—forthcoming."

"And it doesn't bother you, knowing you were…"

"You can say it. I was the product of my mother's egg and her donor of choice. Now, about that water…"

He was stunned by how casually she took her parentage. It was simply a matter of fact, move on. He didn't know whether to admire it or pity it. "Well, I did find a few healthy things in the fridge and put a couple of salads together. Lots of *pico de gallo*, avocado, cilantro, corn, tomatoes—that sort of thing. I didn't add the jalapeños because I wasn't sure you could do spicy."

"I do spicy just fine, as long as it's not *too* spicy."

Matt stood. "Well, let me go get dinner, then."

"Lucas is in bed?" she asked.

"Asleep before his head hit the pillow." He took a few steps toward the veranda door then stopped but didn't turn to face her. "Is it mine?" he asked, quite simply.

"Is *what* yours?"

"The baby. I'm assuming it's mine, or otherwise you wouldn't be here." Matt blew out a long, anxious breath. "You *did* come to tell me I'm going to be a father, didn't you?"

"I did."

He nodded, his composure perfectly intact, then went into the house, leaving Ellie sitting alone outside. Once he got in, however, his passive demeanor gave way and his knees nearly buckled under him. In fact, it was all he could do to make it from the dining area just inside the door to the kitchen, which wasn't more than about twenty steps. And with every step he took he fought to push it out of his mind. Willed himself to not think. Forced himself to pick up the salads, pour Ellie a glass of water and make that long trip back outside to her. Not that he'd be able to eat now. Just the thought of food almost caused him to gag.

"I made some tortillas to go along with the salad," he

said, sitting back down, deliberately not looking at her, even though he knew she was staring at him.

"Are you always this cool under pressure?" she asked.

"When you work in a battlefield, you have to be cool."

"But this isn't a battlefield, Matt, and you're not working."

"No, I'm not. But what I *am* doing is trying to figure out where this conversation goes from here. It's a first for me."

"How about something where you're very excited about becoming a dad. Or you're very angry. Either one would be a start."

"But I'm not excited. Not angry either. I'm just… stunned. That's big news and I need some time to let it sink in."

"I'm not here to pressure you," Ellie said. "But I didn't think this kind of news should be dealt with over the phone, which is the real reason I'm here. I came to tell you in person. So, any initial thoughts…reactions?"

He poured himself a glass of margarita, took a long drink, then finally looked at her. "Numb. I'm numb. And shocked. And confused." He took another drink. "So, now it's your turn. Tell me how *you're* feeling."

Ellie actually laughed. "At first, pretty much the same way you are. I didn't plan this, Matt. We used protection. I know you mentioned that the condom had slipped but I wasn't fertile—at least, I shouldn't have been. I mean, having a little fling in a hotel with a stranger isn't me. I've never done that before. Then to have this happen as a result…" She shook her head. "It certainly changes things, doesn't it?"

It did, and he wasn't anywhere close to being ready to think about them. First things first. He had to come to terms with a baby—*his* baby—coming into this world in what he estimated to be about another twenty-three weeks, give or take. "So, should I ask the obvious? Are you sure it's mine?"

"You were the first man I'd been involved with in over four years, and there's been nobody since. But, if you need proof, we could have tests…"

This discussion was too rigid. It was as if they were talking about something impersonal, like what kind of tongue depressors to order. But damn. Matt didn't know the etiquette or protocol for this kind of situation, if there was such a thing. "No. I don't need proof." He trusted her. Even though he didn't know Ellie that well, something about her made Matt trust her. Maybe because she was—different. Very honest, very open. He'd found that an attractive quality when he'd met her in Reno.

This is what it is, Matt. No strings. Only a diversion for a night. Can you handle that?

It was especially attractive as no one in his life had ever been open or honest with him. *Going for a walk*, his old man would say. *Be right back.* Except right back often turned into two or three weeks. *There'll be food on the table tonight, son. I just got paid.* Except the only thing on the table was an empty booze bottle.

So, yes, he appreciated her honesty. Now more than before. "I believe you. So, what's the bottom line here, Ellie?" It occurred to him he didn't even know her real name. Was Ellie short for Eleanor or Elizabeth or Elena? And did she have a middle name?

"The bottom line is I came to Forgeburn to see if you want to be involved in this. It's your child, too, and you have every right to be a father in any way you want."

"You don't mince words, do you?"

"Like I said about the Landers women… Anyway, I knew after I passed out you'd probably suspect something like this. Especially since we were just a fling. So why bother pretending it's anything other than what it is? We took the first step together in creating this child, I took the second step in coming here to tell you, so now the next step is yours."

"As in financial obligation? Because I don't have a lot. I'm military, not private sector. But I'll certainly do my part."

"I was thinking something a little more substantial than that."

Matt swallowed hard. Something was coming, and it wasn't going to be good. "Define more substantial."

"Well, I'm not going to raise this baby. I don't want to be a single mom the way my mother and grandmother both were. The women in my family lack maternal instinct, and this baby wasn't in my plan. But I want to make sure he, or she, gets the best possible start in life. After that, I'm going to step aside because my life won't accommodate a child, and I don't want to raise a child the way my mother raised me—with tutors and nannies. Which is what would happen, given my involvements. Children need more than that, more than I had, and I don't have what they need. I'm smart enough to realize that. So, for starters, no abortion. We created this child, and it deserves a chance at life. Even though I'm only eighteen weeks along, I feel...an attachment."

Ellie paused for a moment, and her eyes went distant. Maybe to a place where she was holding the baby or singing it a lullaby. That's where Matt's mind was for that instant. The two of them, huddled together with their baby, looking so happy. But the image disappeared, to be replaced by an image of a battlefield surgery, and the blood, the distant gunshots. "So, if you've ruled out abortion..."

"The reason I'm here is to ask you if you want to raise

the baby. Take full custody, let me pay *you* child support, and allow me to step away from it. At least, that was my intention before I knew you were still in the army, so now..."

Matt swallowed hard, again. He knew what was on the other end of that sentence. Because if he didn't, she'd give the child—his child—up for adoption. How was it that just a few simple weeks ago his life was set? He knew where he wanted to be, and what he wanted to be doing. And now he had not one but two children who were both on the verge of being given up. Damn, what was he going to do about that?

CHAPTER THREE

"IT COULD HAVE been worse." Ellie dropped down on her bed and eased out a sigh. She was tired, and she was a little worried that she'd fainted. But Matt was a good doctor, which made her feel better. At least for now. But in the morning?

Sleep didn't come as easily as she'd hoped it would, though. For the first half-hour she tossed and turned, and willed every thought out of her mind. Which didn't work. So she punched the pillow for the fifth or sixth time, and thought about what a nice place this would be to raise a baby. Nice house. Beautiful landscape all around it. And she didn't mind the isolation. In a way it soothed her, held back the pressures.

Another time, another life, this might have been the kind of place she would have chosen for herself. Just the three of them, or actually four. Taking hikes in the desert together. Going for adventures near some of the old Anasazi pueblo ruins she'd seen on the road coming in. Maybe buying a couple of horses and learning to ride. Such an idyllic life, but that wasn't her life. Giving Matt the opportunity to raise the baby then going back to her business was. And it was on that note, the one that was always familiar, Ellie finally went to sleep.

* * *

Who to talk to when there was nobody to talk to? That's what his life boiled down to. Nobody. No old friends here anymore. Anybody Matt would have considered a casual friend was still in the army and somewhere overseas. It was disconcerting, realizing exactly how alone he was, but make no mistake. He was alone here. But, damn, if ever there was a time he needed to talk, it was now.

He thought about Carter Holmes, his old partner back in Kandahar. Top-notch surgeon, maybe even better than Matt, and Matt considered himself pretty damned good. They'd walked the walk for several months, had partnered as well as any two docs could, and had become close—the kind of closeness that could only happen on the battlefield. They'd seen things together, done things together than no person should ever have to see or do. And had come through it.

Except Carter's coming through hadn't been all that great. He'd taken some shrapnel, it had been touch and go with life for a while, and had come out with some PTSD working against him.

Lucky for Carter, he'd had a good woman waiting for him back home. That lucky son of a— And that's where Matt assumed he was now. In her arms, pulling his life back together. Which meant Carter didn't need to hear about Matt's problems. Not now. In a way, he envied Carter what he had, though. It was something he couldn't foresee for himself, but it was…nice. A settled life. Stability. Someone to love who loved him back. Nice dream, but not his dream.

So, once again, nobody to talk to. Normally, it didn't matter. Right now, in the wee hours, it did.

Blowing out a frustrated breath, Matt took a quick look in at Lucas to make sure he was OK, then went outside to the veranda. Sat down, stared up at the moon. Listened to the far-off howl of a wolf. No one howled back at him either.

"Pregnancy requires proper nutrition," Matt said, chopping sweet cubanelle peppers into the skillet.

He looked good. Nice jeans, nice T-shirt. Rugged. But not rested. Her fault, she was sure. Ellie felt bad for that as she hadn't wanted any of this to be disruptive. Of course, what had she expected? *Hi, remember me from a few months back? Well, I'm your baby mama now.*

"And my nutrition is good. Nothing to worry about there," Ellie said, sitting down at the kitchen table, pleased that he was taking care of her. No one ever had unless they had been paid to. This was strange—but nice.

"What does your doctor have to say about that?" Matt asked, turning away from the counter to face her. He wiped his hands on a cloth towel and slung it over his shoulder.

"He's fine with that part of my pregnancy."

"Is there anything you haven't told him yet?" he asked, crossing over to the refrigerator. He pulled out a wire basket of fruit and sat it down. "Because, as your attending physician…"

"He knows what he needs to know," she snapped, then instantly regretted it. Matt didn't need her mood—and, yes, she did have mood swings. That was the worst part of pregnancy so far. But to swing on Matt—he was trying to be the good guy here. The one in the white hat. While she was the stranger who had come riding in to interrupt his life. "Look, I know I'm not supposed to have it, but coffee…"

Matt shook his head. "No caffeine. And while I probably don't have the right to tell you that, remember you're the one who came to me with this…well, it's not a problem. Children aren't problems. But it's a situation. And because half that situation is mine, I do get some say."

She liked the forcefulness. Smooth yet firm. And sexy. Not that a woman in her condition had any business looking at sexy anything. Or did they? Ellie honestly didn't know if those kinds of feelings stirred during pregnancy, and she sure wasn't going to ask Matt, since he was the one stirring them. Maybe she'd ask Doc Shaffer when she got home. Or just ignore everything.

"You do," she conceded. "You're right about the coffee, too. I have moments of weakness, though. Don't give in to them, but sometimes they do surface."

Matt prepped the fruit and dumped it into a juicer, then tidied the kitchen. He said nothing for the next couple of minutes. Not a single word. And Ellie felt awkward, since she'd envisioned long talks with him and forging some sort of bond. But with his back to her, there was nothing to do other than sit and wait until he turned around and either gave her the smoothie or decided to talk. "How do you know I don't have a fruit allergy?" she finally said after the silence just got too much for her.

"Well, first off, since you see me preparing fruit, I'd assume you'd tell me if you did have an allergy. Also, that first night in Reno, when I was ordering late-night room service, you told me you were healthy. Weren't allergic to anything."

"You remembered that?" Ellie was surprised that he had since that was such a small detail in the scheme of everything else that had happened between them. Surprised, but pleased. Did that mean he might have thought about her since then? Or was she reading too much into something that really didn't matter?

"Had to. Didn't want to order something that would

result in an EpiPen later. Didn't have one with me either."
Matt turned and handed her a tumbler of the fruit drink.
Then smiled. "I also remember that you're a left-side-of-
the-bed person, almost to the point of an OCD problem."

"It's not that bad," she said, blushing. Was he flirting with her?

"Yes, it is. But it didn't matter because I can adjust to
any side of the bed, the floor, a cot, a trench or foxhole..."
He shrugged. "And I have, on all of them."

"Because of the army?"

"Because I spent my childhood sleeping on the floor,
or anyplace else I could find that wasn't covered with
my old man's..." Matt stopped. Turned back to the sink
to rinse the blender.

"Your old man's what?" Ellie asked him.

"Rubbish," he said. "My old man's rubbish. He found
it on the street, in alleys, in trash bins, and carted it
home then dumped it wherever he could. Including the
spot on the floor I would have cleared the night before
so I could sleep."

"You slept on the floor? In filth?"

"Filth, rodents, bugs." He turned back round to face
her. "That's what squatters and beggars do."

Ellie didn't even know what to say to that and judging from the cold expression she saw in his eyes now,
she thought it best not go anywhere near it.

"When did you go to the store?" she asked, hoping to
change the conversation to something not quite as explosive as his childhood seemed to have been. "Because
last night you didn't have any of this." She held up her
smoothie.

"This morning, on my way to take Lucas to his babysitter—Betty Nelson."

"Is she good?" Ellie asked. "My mother always went

through a lengthy interview process to find my nannies and tutors, but there were a couple of them she hired..." She cringed, thinking about the mistakes her mother had made finding good child care on several occasions, and wondering if she herself would have what was necessary to find the right adoptive parents for the baby. What if she made a mistake, the way her mother had done occasionally? The difference was her mother had fired her mistakes. She, on the other hand, would doom the baby to a lifetime living with the mistake she could make. It was a sobering thought and a frightening one.

"Betty's great. And the best part is she's flexible. I can take Lucas to her any time, day or night. She doesn't mind."

"Then you're lucky."

"I am, but I'd rather keep him with me as much as I can. Probably something to do with not ever having a real parent myself. At least, while Lucas is with me, I can be a real parent."

A temporary parent, she thought. Could Matt not see what would happen when another parent was found for Lucas? It was going to crush that child. Already her heart was breaking for that little boy. But it wasn't her place to say anything, so she didn't. "Well, sometimes having a real parent isn't all that it's cracked up to be. I did, and it didn't work out so well for me. Anyway, I think I'll take this smoothie with me—which is delicious, by the way—go take a shower, then maybe we'll have time to really talk about what we're going to do."

"Sorry. I have a couple of ranch calls to make this morning. Nothing strenuous or too far way, if you'd care to ride along with me," Matt said, cracking three eggs into the skillet, then dropping in some stick butter and a handful of vegetables he'd cut up earlier—cubanelle peppers, onions, mushrooms. "If you feel like you're up to it."

"A ride? Maybe that's a good way to start slowing down. I'm not used to doing things at a leisurely pace, so since you think I'll be OK…" Ellie shrugged. This wasn't what she'd had in mind but she was the intruder here. The choices weren't hers to make. Which was unusual, as in her real world all the choices *were* hers. Every last one of them. Yet right now, letting someone else step in was nice. It was almost like being on holiday. No worries. No concerns. No decisions.

Except… She placed her hand on her belly and felt a kick. The very first one. It caught her off guard because it hadn't happened before. But it was a good, sharp kick, and she gasped.

Immediately, Matt was at her side. "What?" he choked out, dropping to his knees, automatically taking hold of her wrist to take her pulse.

But she guided his hand to the spot where she'd felt the kick and smiled. "First kick," she whispered, amazed that she was suddenly on the verge of tears over something so ordinary. She was, though. Her lips were trembling when the second kick came, with Matt's hand pressed to her belly, then her tears started. Damned hormones.

"Strong one," he said, a look of amazement coming over his face. "And this was the first time?"

She nodded, sniffing back the tears. "She's been very quiet up until now."

"She?" he asked, refusing to move his hand from her belly. "You already know?"

"Not really. I've just assumed…"

Finally, he pulled away and stood. "With a kick like that, it's definitely a boy. Strong one. He's going to come out ready to play football." He backed away, saw that the scramble he'd been fixing had burned, and dumped it in the garbage.

"Women can be as strong as men," Ellie said, not quite ready to go take her shower now. Somehow, being connected here as a family of three seemed comforting. Cozy. It wouldn't last long, though. Everybody was caught up in a moment—and the moment would be over in a blink, and life would be back to where it had been. It was a complicated place to be in. But for now the fantasy of something she'd never had was settling over her, making her feel mellow. Would she ever have that? Or would her life be as it was now—all work, all the time?

"Sure they can. I've worked with some amazing women who were as strong as any man. But it still felt like the kick of a little boy to me."

Ellie laughed. "Wishful thinking, Doctor?"

"Not particularly," Matt said. Then suddenly that moment was over. His face darkened to almost a scowl and the look in his eyes went distant. "Look, I'd like to be out of here in thirty, if you're still interested in coming. My goal is to be back here by noon, grab Lucas, and see a couple of the locals this afternoon. After that, I do have one call later today, not out on a ranch. Shut-in who needs her medicine. You're welcome to come along on that, too, if you wish, since I promised Lucas we'd go to the Roadside for pizza afterwards." With that, he tossed the used dishtowel on the counter and headed toward the hall.

"Bring yourself some water. It can get hot out there. Oh, and two conditions. Let me examine you before we go. You showed up here exhausted and dehydrated and passed out yesterday, so I want to see if anything's off this morning. If it is, I'm going to suggest you go back to bed. Second, if you go, you sit. Nothing else. OK?"

"Are you saying pregnant woman aren't capable—?"

"No," he interrupted. "I know exactly what pregnant women are capable of doing. But since you haven't allowed me a good look at you, and I have an idea you're not going to, I just want to be careful. And it wasn't that long ago you passed out so, since that pregnancy is also mine, I don't want to take any chances. All I want to do, Ellie, is take care of you and the baby while you're here."

She did understand his concern because she was concerned as well. But being fussed over so much—she wasn't used to it. Her life was about taking charge, doing everything on her own. Then suddenly to turn part of herself over to someone else, even if only for a little while, was difficult. Went against her natural grain. But her life, right now, wasn't only about her, was it? It was also about the baby, which made it about Matt as well.

"I appreciate your concern," she said. "And I apologize if I seem…put off. I'm not. In fact, I'm grateful for what you're doing. I know my being here isn't easy for you, especially with the news I brought. So whatever you think you need to do…"

"How about we take this minute by minute?" he said. "I've got more going on than I ever thought I'd have, and for me it's mostly about improvising in the moment." Matt chuckled, finally lightening up. "Being in surgery wasn't as complicated as what I'm going through here. At least there I knew what to do. Here I haven't a clue, and it's a challenge I don't have a solution for yet."

"Well, get your stethoscope ready. I'll be back down here for my exam in fifteen minutes."

Ellie glanced back at Matt before she walked down the hall to the *casita*. He was heading toward the stairs, walking very rigidly. She'd never seen anyone so rigid before. But like he'd just told her, this situation was a challenge. She hadn't meant that to happen but, realistically, she should have expected it. Maybe she had, subconsciously. Because he was acting the way she would have, given the same circumstances—reluctantly. In her business world she didn't like reluctance, didn't deal with it too well.

But this wasn't her business world now, and she was beginning to see a side of life she'd never seen before. Matt was sacrificing a lot, staying here for Lucas. And here she was, asking him for an even greater sacrifice, then not being as cooperative as she should when he wasn't giving her what she wanted. She had to do better, and not just for the baby's sake. For Matt's as well. She genuinely cared for him. He was an honorable man, stuck in a very tough place. She'd seen that honor in Reno. But now, seeing him in this situation, she admired him. He was holding it together better than she would have.

Had she known him better when she'd made her decision to come here, she might not have come. But she was here and now, for the first time since she'd learned she was pregnant, this pregnancy wasn't just about her. She had to keep that in mind.

Matt looked in the dresser mirror and imagined a hundred tiny wrinkles had popped up around his eyes since yesterday. He wanted to kick something, or punch it so hard it smashed the bloody hell out of his knuckles—anything to make him feel something other than numb. But that's all he felt right now. Numb. Trying to be civil. Trying to hold it together—but not even sure *what* he was trying to hold together.

Six weeks ago, a soldier had been brought in on a stretcher, massive trauma below the waist. One leg gone above the knee, one leg hanging by a thread. No blood pressure to speak of. Massive bleed-out without the necessary replacement in store. Everything had been wrong with him. He shouldn't have lived. But he had.

They'd put in their time, not with much optimism, done everything humanly possible to save him, and while they'd sent him out with extensive damage, *they'd sent him out*. Miracle. He recalled celebrating that one with his colleagues. The ones who had been off duty had partied hard all night while he'd simply sat back, grateful another mother would have her son coming home. It was a feeling that always overwhelmed him.

Another soldier came through the door a few days later—had a little headache. They'd put him at the end of the list because he'd walked in on his own, was alert, joking, said all he needed were a couple of aspirin and he'd be good to get back out. Except ten minutes later he was lying dead in the entry hall. Healthy, to all outer appearances, and nothing wrong. But a bullet had ricocheted off his helmet, hadn't so much as touched his skin. Yet the impact had caused a brain bleed. No miracle there. And it hadn't made sense. Sometimes nothing did. And that had been the one he'd gotten drunk over. Had kicked a hole through the wall. Gone outside and screamed into the night for the uselessness of it all.

He felt like screaming now, being back in Forgeburn. Taking over a medical practice, even if only temporarily. Raising a child, again temporarily. Then finding out about his own child.

Matt wouldn't scream, of course. Or get himself drunk the way he had over the soldier with the headache. So that left feeling numb, and maybe that wasn't such a bad thing after all. He could just go through the motions, step by step, until something happened. Or until he knew what to do. But, damn—he wanted to kick something anyway. Which he did. The trash can sitting next to the dresser.

Funny thing was, it had no effect on him. Nothing satisfying, nothing stress-busting. In fact, he felt foolish, which was just one step above feeling numb.

Now all he had to do was go for stupid, and he'd have the perfect triple. Why? Because she'd been here no longer than the blink of an eye and he was already having… feelings. Sure, in Reno he'd had feelings. But he chalked them up to what had been happening in the moment. They'd been good. No denying that. And he'd enjoyed her company. Sitting around talking and relaxing—it was something he never did. But with Ellie it had felt right.

Now, though… Matt took one last look in the mirror, not even sure he recognized the man looking back. "How could you even think about her that way?" he asked himself as he threw on a respectable, doctor-like shirt. "She was just someone to suit your mood. Someone convenient." Except, even as he said the words to his reflection, they stuck on his tongue, bitter and disgusting. Ellie wasn't like that. He'd known that from the start. So why was he trying so hard to convince himself otherwise now? "Because she scares you, McClain. Because she's *not* like the others."

That was true. She wasn't. But why did that make a difference? "Because you're stupid. Bingo! Triple."

The only problem was, caring for Ellie in any capacity didn't really make him feel stupid. It made him feel… alive. She was nice to look at. No denying the attraction. It had hit him hard and fast the first time he'd set eyes on her in Reno. And it hadn't been just her beauty that had attracted him. It had been her confidence. And the way she'd dealt with the people who'd stopped by her display. Everyone had been important to her. Everyone had received her beautiful smile. Even the ones he'd seen pestering her for something other than information about her services.

His keen attraction aside—and it was difficult putting it there—now that he was getting to know Ellie even better than he had after their two nights, he liked what he was discovering. Sure, she was stubborn. And used to having things her way. But that's what had made her successful. She was smart, too. The best part was, even though she might be resistant to his suggestions at first, she listened to reason. She wanted what was right for their baby and for that he loved her.

In the romantic, happily-ever-after sense? Admittedly, that had popped into his mind a time or two, even as far back as Reno. But common sense always took over. *It couldn't work.* As harsh as that seemed, it was true. Neither of them wanted *that* kind of relationship. No romance, they'd both said. Of course, they'd both said one night only, and look what had happened to that. Still, those two nights in Reno may have been the best nights of his life, but that's all they had been. Two nights in his life. Two nights like he'd never known before. Probably would never know again.

"OK, ready for your physical?" he asked Ellie, on his way down the stairs. She was dressed in a pair of loose-fitting khakis and a white cotton blouse meant to hide the baby bump. But now that he knew it was there, it was obvious to him.

"If you insist," she said, sounding surprisingly calm. "But I'm not undressing."

He chuckled. "Maybe that's something we should have considered a few weeks ago."

"As I recall, you weren't complaining," she said, holding out her arm as he wrapped an old-fashioned manual blood-pressure cuff around it.

"Soldier on leave first time in over a year. Surrounded by pretty women at a convention. What can I say?" He pumped up the cuff, listened, then deflated it. "What's your norm?" he asked.

"About one-ten over mid-seventies. Why?"

"Because, like yesterday, you're a little high. Still in the normal range, but high for your normal."

"Which really doesn't mean anything," Ellie defended.

"Says who?" he asked.

"I was an obstetrics nurse. I know these things."

Matt bent down and assessed her ankles and lower legs. "And I'm impressed by that how?"

"Do you work with obstetrics on the battlefield?"

"Sometimes."

"But it's not your specialty?"

"Never claimed it was. Where I work…let's just say I'm a jack-of-all-trades. I take whatever's thrown at me." From the very best of it to the very worst.

"Well, obstetrics *was* my specialty, and…"

He stood back up and took a penlight to examine her eyes. "And you're an illustrator now. Correct?"

"And videographer," she said, tilting her head back for his exam.

"Which doesn't exactly put you in the mainstream of current medicine," he said, clicking off his light then next examining her hands.

"Actually, it keeps me right in there since I'm the one who's doing the media that med students, residents and even fellows are studying. You, too, if you stay current with the journals. So I would say that makes me more current than most doctors."

He prodded her fingers for a moment then looked directly at her. "Guess that's a field I don't know much about. You'll have to tell me more when we have time.

Now, give me your physician's contact number. I want to talk to him before I turn you loose to do something crazy."

Ellie looked instantly alarmed and her face drained of nearly all color. "What's wrong?" she sputtered.

"Nothing that I can see," Matt said, instantly regretting his lack of bedside manner. "Look, I'm sorry for being so—abrupt. I've never had a bedside manner, never had to. My patients come and go faster than you can imagine, and I rarely get to speak to them. My work is concentrated solely on getting the problem in front of me fixed. So I know sometimes I come on too strong and—"

"Strong? *You come on too strong?*" She held out her wrist. "Take my pulse and feel what your coming on too strong has done to me. That kind of bedside manner out here isn't going to work, Matt. I don't know battlefield medicine. Can't even begin to imagine what it's like out there for you, and I'm not going to judge you for your abruptness. But you're not out there right now. And I don't mean to be critical, but you really do need to concentrate on being…personable."

He chuckled. "Personable?"

"Friendly. Smile. You know, the way you were in Reno."

"Ah, yes. Me in seduction mode."

"Which worked," she said.

"Apparently. Anyway, do you always try to fix things like the way you're trying to fix my bedside manner?" he asked.

"Yes. It's what I do. Most people would call it second nature or something like that, but for me it's my first nature. I have a lot of people working for me around the world and I have to make sure everything stays fixed all the time." She smiled sheepishly. "I guess I was the one coming on too strong, wasn't I?"

"Look. We're in an awkward spot here. You know it, and I know it. We're both nervous. I'm not sure either one of knows what to do, or even how to go about starting to figure it out. It's going to take some time to get it all sorted, so how about we just make the best of it for now? Maybe be friends?"

"Sure, friends," she said.

Seeing the sudden look of sadness come over her, Matt walked over to her and wrapped his arms around her. "We'll get you through this, Ellie. Not sure how but, I promise, you're not alone."

"I'm always alone, Matt. And I didn't come here because I wanted someone to take care of me." She sniffled. "I really wanted to do the right thing."

"I appreciate it. Not sure what to do with it but, for what it's worth, I really do appreciate it."

Ellie sniffled once more, then pulled away from him. "You've got appointments, and I'd like to go, so if you need to call my doctor in Reno…" She brought up Doc Shaffer's number on her phone and handed it to him. He took it then wandered down the hall for some privacy. Three minutes later he returned. "Gestational diabetes?" he asked.

"Not diagnosed, no symptoms. My mother had it, and she's a Type-One diabetic, so naturally he's worried about me. Which is why I'm spot on nutritionally with everything I need to be. It's not a condition, Matt, until it is. So far, I'm good." She brushed the last of her tears off her cheeks.

"But you didn't tell me."

"Tell you what? A list of everything I don't have?"

"He said you were as stubborn as they came."

"But did he say I'm healthy enough to go out on this ride with you?"

"He said, and I quote, 'She'll do what she wants to do. I told her to go home and rest for a day but, apparently, she took a ten-hour drive and passed out in your exam because she wouldn't even stop long enough to buy a drink. That's who she is.' Which tells me that you're a royal pain." He said it with a smile on his face because under different circumstances he was sure he'd like the challenge of her. Right now, though, it worried him.

"I'm determined, Matt. There's a difference. What I do has a purpose. Being a royal pain is simply for fun and pleasure."

He chuckled. "So, this is how it's going to be?"

She smiled back at him. "How about I work on *my* bedside manner, too. Although you didn't complain about it in Reno, did you?"

His response was to groan. "Like I said, you're along for the ride *only*. Nothing else." Words easier said than done. He knew that. Knew that, with Ellie, he had a whole new level of headache to add to the ones already stacking up on him.

The first few miles took them down the highway. Smooth road. Beautiful scenery, with all the cacti in bloom. Ellie had read that this was such a good bloom year that all the vibrant colors were visible by satellite. She didn't doubt it. While Reno was on the edge of the desert, this was different. More remote. More raw. Wild. Stunning in a way she'd never expected, given that she'd never been here before. "It's amazing," she said, finally settling in, still feeling the tingle of Matt's touch as he'd examined her. She rubbed her arms briskly as the goosebumps reappeared simply from the memory. "Prettier than any garden I've ever seen."

"You chilly?" he asked.

"Nope," she lied. "Just enjoying the scenery."

"Well, the spring colors were one of the few things I liked when I lived here. That, and all the rocks and canyons where you could climb."

"You liked to climb?"

"Still do. Just haven't had the opportunity for, well— since I moved away. Did have some training in the army, which wasn't much of a deal considering all the real climbing I was used to."

"Maybe when you're here, you'll be able to get some in." She looked off in the distance at the red rock that seemed to be jutting out of nowhere. What would it be like to be able to simply go up the side of it? In her life, there had never been time for activities or athletics or anything like that. She'd had meal time, and tutoring time, play time, reading time, bedtime. On the weekends, but not too often, she'd been granted mother time, maybe an hour or two when she'd been allowed to tag along with her mother on appointments. But never time to simply go climb a rock or look at pretty flowers.

So maybe Matt didn't have the best of it here—she really didn't know that story, or maybe he'd been so overwhelmed he hadn't known how to look for the best of what he'd had. Whatever the case, she was enjoying the ride, enjoying the image in her mind of him climbing up one of those gigantic rocks.

"I hope so. Although I'll be out of shape."

"You look in pretty good shape to me," she blurted out, even though she hadn't meant to.

"Army life will do that to you. But if I keep up my cowboy medicine for long…" Matt sighed heavily. "They'll probably have to put me back through some basic training before they let me back out on the battle-field again."

"You really do want to go back to the battlefield? I've consulted with several military medical personnel who couldn't wait until their rotation was over. All of them said the work got to them, so many casualties and things that couldn't get fixed. And the gunfire in the distance. Or never knowing when the hospital might come under siege or they might have to evacuate. It was a consistent story, Matt. And here you are, totally the opposite. So why?"

"Because somebody has to do it, and I can. I do well under pressure. And I can shut out pretty much everything but what I'm doing at the moment. I got used to doing that when I was a kid. My old man yelled a lot. I learned to shut him out and concentrate on something else. Guess it carried over with me to the military." He slowed the truck, then made a right-hand turn onto something that once might have been called a road. Today it was barely a path with some gravel. Winding for miles. No end in sight. The sign at the turn-off read only "Tolly Ranch Road."

"Tolly?" she asked. "They give these roads names?"

"Nope. Tolly is my patient. His trailer is at the end of the road. Only one out this way. So the names you see on the roads are actually the names of the people who live on them. Normally, it's one person or family per road."

"And these roads are how long?"

"Sometimes eight, maybe ten miles."

"With no one else living on it."

"No one, and nothing. It's deserted out here, Ellie. Lonely. Barren."

"Why do they stay?"

"Open grazing for their cattle. They don't have to own

the land. They can lease it from the government, and the cost is a fraction of what they'd have to pay to buy it and pay the taxes. The stipulation is they must have a base from which to operate, and since they don't own the property they won't build on it because, technically, what they might build there would belong to the government as it's on government-owned property. Hence the cowboy trailers. They're not permanent. Rundown, yes, since they're not permanent residences and usually just a place to sleep for the night. But they serve their purpose."

As they proceeded down Tolly Ranch Road, Matt slowed the truck to almost a crawl. It was only precautionary, as the road wasn't bumpy like many of them were. "This is a pretty good road—Doc Granger left a road evaluation with each patient chart, so I'd know what I might be getting myself into. Some will be truck-worthy, others I can take a motorcycle, and some may require a horse. This is one of the better ranch roads, but just in case, there's a pillow in the back you can use if you need to support your back. And if it gets too rough, tell me."

"Thanks," she said, grabbing hold of the pillow because, yes, she was starting to have back spasms. She'd had them before—nothing serious. And these, right now, weren't too bad. But just in case... "As long as what I do doesn't put the baby at risk, everything's fine."

"*Our* baby," he reminded her.

That it was. *Their* baby. And the sound of it wasn't so bad. In fact, she rather liked it. Of course, that wasn't going to happen, not in the real sense. Still—she shut her eyes and for a moment envisioned a pink, frilly nursery. Pretty little-girl clothes hanging in the closet. Stuffed animals and dolls everywhere. And a music box with a ballerina spinning and spinning and spinning inside, like the one her nanny had given her, and her mother had taken away because it had been too foolish for *her* child.

For a moment, a melancholy mood slipped down over Ellie and she was sitting in a rocking chair in that nursery, holding her baby. But her mother's words came back to haunt her—*too foolish*. And the image disappeared. But was it foolish? Nothing inside her told her it wasn't, but nothing inside her told her it was either. She liked the dream, though. It made her feel contented in a way nothing else did.

"So, how far off the road is Tolly?" she asked, opening her eyes and trying to concentrate on the scenery.

"We go just a couple miles on this road, then we take a cut-off back about another five. Are you *sure* you're OK?" he asked, slowing the truck even more as a black-and-white cow wandered to the side of the road and simply stood there, looking at them. Ellie grabbed her phone and took a picture before they proceeded. "Maybe this wasn't such a good idea, bringing you with me," he continued.

"Like I said, I'm fine. Glad to get out and see all this. I never have time to just…look."

He smiled. "You know, if you weren't pregnant, we'd be out on my motorcycle."

"Might be fun, if you don't mind the weather. Me, I like my air-conditioning and creature comforts. Nice sound system, contoured seats, a little extra lumbar support. But that's not you, is it? You get along differently."

"See those abandoned house trailers over there?" he asked, slowing even more as they passed a small community of about thirty or forty abandoned structures sitting off by themselves. They were all falling down, rusted, looked as if they hadn't seen true care or maintenance for a couple decades.

"Yes. Why?"

"That's sort of a dumping ground for cowboy trailers that have gotten too rundown. They drag them down here and leave them. It's a small patch of private land and they pay the owner a dumping fee. He scraps what he can, sells parts, does some recycling. It's also where I come from. Lived there from the time I was ten or eleven until I left home when I was sixteen—one trailer or another. Lived in a storage shed a couple miles from here for a year before that, and in the back of my dad's car even before that. That's the difference between your world and mine, Ellie. Yours had air-conditioning and creature comforts. Mine didn't even have running water. In fact, we were merely squatters moving from trailer to trailer, always hoping for one that didn't have a leaking roof or holes in the floor."

"From what you'd said, I knew it was bad, but I didn't know how bad," Ellie said, taking one look at the trailer dump, then turning her head. She couldn't picture Matt there. Or anyone. "How did you get by?" she asked.

"Any way we could. Didn't always have food, but there were people who'd see me or Janice on the street and invite us in for a meal. Plus, we got handouts at the diner. And when we were in school, there was always a hot meal."

"But the other things—clothes, bathing."

"We took what we could, wherever we could get it. People gave us hand-me-downs. We could bathe in the sink at the gas station." Matt's face betrayed no emotion. Not a flinch, not a frown. "It's what we knew."

"But didn't you also know how other people lived?" she asked, looking for a sign of some feeling yet not seeing it there.

"We did. But we also knew who we were—the two kids who lived at the dump. I got along, but Janice…"

There it was, a quick softening in his eyes. Then a flash of pain. Now, more than ever, she understood why Matt was being so particular about Lucas. He didn't want him to end up here, the way his mother had. "Did she ever get out?" Ellie asked.

"For a while. We didn't keep in touch, so I don't know the details other than she started here then ended here."

That flash of pain again. Ellie's heart broke for him. He carried the guilt of his sister, probably had done ever since he'd been a boy. She laid a hand on Matt's forearm and gave him a squeeze "I'm sorry about…"

He laid *his* hand atop hers for a moment, then pulled it back, and sped up once they were past the little settlement. She was too stunned by his honesty to know how to respond, so she simply looked at the road ahead, thinking about their differences and similarities. He'd come from nothing while she'd had everything. Yet they both grown up so—alone. No one to care, no one to comfort them. And here they were now, with a child on the way, wondering what was best for him or her. Better than either of them had had—that's what would be best.

But wasn't that really just giving up their child to someone they could only hope would provide better? Her ideas about adoption were changing because being around Matt made this whole situation feel more real. Before, it had been an intellectual issue—her safe place. Always deferring to what she knew best.

Except that's not what she was doing here. Something was turning around in Ellie. Her convictions were weakening. The intellectual was giving way to the emotional, try as hard as she could to stop it. But she couldn't, and she wasn't going to blame it on being hormonal. She also wasn't going to admit that to Matt, because she wasn't ready to acknowledge these new thoughts to herself yet.

"How did that happen?" she finally asked. "How did you end up living like that?"

"No mother. An old man who didn't work but loved what he found in the bottom of a booze bottle. No one who cared whether two little kids were fed, or clean, or went to school." Once they were out of sight of the run-down clump of trailers, he turned onto the next road they came to.

"And the owner didn't say anything?"

"The owner was required to have someone on the property. He sure as hell didn't want to be there, so he used my dad's name in exchange for letting my dad have free access to whatever piece of rubbish trailer he wanted to stay in for a while. And I'm not telling you this because I expect pity, or any other kind of emotion from you. It's so you'll understand why I'm not giving you what I'm assuming you'd hoped would be a fast decision about the baby. I don't make fast decisions. Had too many of those made for me over my life, and they didn't always turn out well. In fact, *most* of them didn't when I was younger."

This wasn't the way she'd wanted this conversation to go. Wasn't at all how she'd expected it to happen. "You know, Matt, when I came here I thought since you were in a medical practice, that you'd left the military, or I wouldn't have even…"

The truth be told, she'd never really given herself over to the possibility that Matt might not want things to work out the way she did. Of course, that was the way she lived her life, ran her business, always got ahead. Ellie assumed herself into what she wanted, then worked hard to get it. Just like she'd assumed Matt would want to raise his child. Except she was pretty sure he didn't, and there was nothing inside her that wanted to work hard to make it happen.

For whatever reason, Matt was bringing out a softer

side to her she'd never seen before. And that new side clearly didn't want her to do what she normally did. "I don't want to tear up your life," she said simply.

"I never thought you did," he said. "I had a right to know, and be involved. I'm glad you didn't take that away from me. Not sure what to do with that right, though, because if you do go through with your own plans not to raise our child, it puts me in a tough spot."

It's your way, Ellie. Only your way. You don't need anybody else. Grow up and be a strong woman on your own. You don't need a man to prove anything to or about.

Her mother's words, her mother's sentiments. But her mother was so wrong. In fact, Ellie felt anything but that strong woman she'd been raised to believe in. And all because she was seeing something she hadn't expected to see—a man she simply hadn't expected. One who'd literally risen from the ashes. A man she was glad was the father of her baby. "Look, I don't want to pressure you into anything, Matt. That was never my intention. I'm a straightforward businesswoman in everything I do, and I couldn't have done otherwise with our situation."

"I appreciate your honesty, but you have to know the honest side of me. I'm going back into the military. Back to being a battlefield surgeon, as I've mentioned. And I can't do that and be a single father. The only reason I'm here now is to make sure Lucas ends up in the best situation possible. I owe that to my sister. The plan was that we'd always get out of here together. The agreement was that the first one to get away would save up until there was enough money to bring the other one along. I was the first one out. Had a few dollars—not enough to get us both out but enough to get me to Vegas. Unfortunately, it took me longer than I thought it would, and by the time I was in a position to help her, I was in the military, finally doing something with my life. And she'd given up waiting. I lost track of her, then got sidetracked with my military duty as well as going to school…"

Matt paused, took a deep breath and let it out slowly. "Bottom line, I got my life, she got cancer and died. So, that's where I am right now. Doing for my sister what I should have done a long time ago, and didn't. Which may make me look like the perfect person to raise our baby. But I'm not. I'm only fulfilling a promise I didn't keep by making sure Lucas gets what Janice never had—a good life. I'm sure that isn't what you want to hear, but I can't be any less honest with you than you were with me. I know you came here looking for a full-time daddy, but it's not me, Ellie. I'm sorry."

Now she was discouraged. Even on the verge of tears. Hormones again? Maybe, maybe not. But just for a little while she'd hoped—well, it didn't matter what she'd hoped, did it? A home and family. That proverbial house with the white picket fence. She'd seen that for a moment with Matt in Reno, and while that life was never her plan, every now and then she'd caught herself wrapped up in that daydream. With Matt, because he wasn't the kind of man she typically dealt with. They all had agendas, while all she could see in Matt was honor. More now than before. But she was wrong about that plan of hers, where he would raise their child and someday, in some small way, maybe even include her in their child's life.

Disappointed in a way she hadn't expected to be, Ellie slid down in the truck seat, readjusted the pillow, punched it, folded it, punched it some more, and when she couldn't find a way to make it comfortable, she opened the truck window, threw it out, and spent the last minutes of the truck ride fighting back the hormonal overflow she would not let him see. Not one burning drop of it.

CHAPTER FOUR

ELLIE WAS FIGHTING SOMETHING, and it frustrated Matt to know he was the cause of it. He hadn't meant to do that, hadn't meant to just blurt out everything. But he had, and there was no going back now. She wasn't going to get what she'd come here for and, for some reason, even though he'd caused her mood, what he wanted to do was pull off the road and simply hold her in his arms. Protect her. Comfort her.

It wasn't a reaction he'd normally have after being so blunt, but Ellie was different, and she caused different feelings and emotions in him. Because of the baby? Maybe. But also because of her. She seemed like she was always at odds with something in her life, and that was a very tough life to lead. He'd lived it himself for a long time. But he'd found his way. Had Ellie, though? She claimed she had with this business she owned, but he wasn't so sure because she seemed so exposed to things that hurt or discouraged her. And fought so hard against them.

He'd seen some of that in Reno—she had tried to be so serious even when they'd been in bed. Fighting hard not to show pleasure, even though it had shown through when she'd let down her guard. He smiled, thinking about that first night and her bravado—*I'm ready when you are,* she'd said as she'd stood across the room from him, practically hiding behind the armoire. He'd wanted to see her step away from that armoire but with respect to her shyness he'd turned off the lights and waited until she'd slipped under the sheets next to him. She hadn't been tentative then, as he'd expected her to be. In fact, she had been wild, like no other woman in his life had ever been.

The second night had caught him off guard. Ellie had been in his room in bed, waiting, when Matt had come back from the convention. No guards up this time. But they'd talked first. Mostly about insignificant things—at least, insignificant as far as they were concerned. Which had been when he'd discovered he really liked Ellie. In fact, if his situation in the army hadn't been so difficult, he might have asked to see her again. But he hadn't because he was going straight back to the war, and he didn't need the distraction of worrying about the woman he'd left behind, or if she'd be there waiting for him when he finally returned stateside.

But that second morning Ellie had seemed different. Not subdued so much as thoughtful. Maybe even a little sad as she'd stood at the window, looking out, all wrapped up in the bed sheet, and had said, *It's too bad this can't be real life.* He'd caught a glimpse of a vulnerability, much like the one he'd caught their first night together when she'd hidden herself behind the armoire, and both nights he'd wondered how someone so successful and forthright in the business world could almost shrink away when she stepped out of it.

Now he saw that vulnerability again, and she didn't even seem to be trying to hide it. "Is there anything I can do? Anything at all?" he finally asked in desperation.

"I'm fine," she said, her voice on the verge of sounding sad.

"You don't look fine, and you're not acting fine." He stopped the truck, reached over the seat and grabbed hold of his jacket. "You can use this as a pillow until we... find the one you tossed out on our way back or buy another one."

"I don't need a pillow, Matt."

"Look, Ellie, I know what this is about, and I'm sorry. But I'm not the one, and it's better you know now because that will give you more time to figure out what to do." Damn, he hated this. Hated every bit of it. But his life wouldn't accommodate what she wanted.

"Us, Matt. More time for *us* to figure out what to do."

"Did you really expect to show up on my doorstep, tell me you've got a baby for me to raise, then walk away from it?"

"I don't know what I expected," she admitted. "But I guess that's close enough."

"Well, you're right about one thing. It *is* something we need to figure out together." He was beginning to feel as discouraged as she sounded because this baby was his responsibility as well as Ellie's. And that's the one thing he had to keep in mind—it was Ellie's responsibility, too.

Even so, as sad as she looked, he really did want to put his arms around her and tell her things would be OK. Somehow, though, he didn't think that would be an appreciated gesture. "This first stop, like I said, is Tolly. John Tolly. Chronic backache, according to his chart. He stays in his trailer a good bit of the time, and usually gets seen whenever the doctor—which would be me—can catch up with him. According to the chart, it's been going on for a couple of years, intermittently. He's not agreeable to therapy or medication. Any ideas?" Sure, he was grasping now, but anything to connect to her was good, because she seemed so far away.

"He could be sitting badly in his saddle," Ellie finally commented. "It happens. They get old. The leather wears one way or another, throws the body out of alignment."

Stopping the truck in front of Tolly's trailer, Matt grabbed his medical bag and hopped out. "How would you know that?"

"Did a video about a year ago that featured uncommon ailments in a variety of workers who spend their lives outside, doing hard labor. Crooked saddle was one of them. It gets you in the lower back mostly."

"And the cure?" he asked, totally impressed.

"Either have the old saddle straightened—there are people who specialize in that—or get a new one." She rose up, looked at the old trailer sitting just in front of her, then slid back down in the seat. "Tell John Tolly a crooked saddle can be bad for his horse, too. Same thing—it gets them in the muscles." With that, she laid her head against the back of the truck seat and closed her eyes.

It wasn't much, Matt thought as he crossed the dirt expanse from the truck to the trailer, where John Tolly was standing outside, waiting for him, but it was a start. It had drawn her out of her slump for a moment or two. And she'd just made what could be a major diagnosis seem like she was simply telling a children's story.

Once upon a time there was back ache. "Check the saddle," said the nurse. And the doctor did. The nurse was right. The saddle was crooked. Then the cowboy was cured, and everybody was happy.

Everybody but the nurse, and for that he did feel bad.

"So, how long have you had backache this time?" Matt asked the old cowboy, after an exam of the usual—vital signs, joints, reflexes—but everything normal for a man who'd lived a hard, sixty-three-year life. "Because, according to my charts, it's been going on for a couple of years, with no relief."

"Old age, Doc. It's creeping up on me. What can I say? It happens to the best of them, and I sure as hell don't come close to the best of them." He pulled up his shirt for Matt to have a look at his back, and winced when Matt applied a hard thumb to John's extensor muscles.

"Trouble getting up from a standing position?" Matt asked, continuing his exam.

"Sometimes. But I manage."

"And lifting?"

"Can't lift as much as I used to but, at my age who can?" He winced again when Matt singled out his obliques and applied pressure.

"And you've been taking..." Matt grabbed his tablet and tapped the cursor, sending up the part of John's chart for medications. "Nothing at all"

"Don't like pills. Won't take them," John said, sitting up on his bed and buttoning his shirt. "Told that to the old doc, telling you the same thing. No pills. No shots."

"And I don't suppose you'd finally consent to physical therapy? Maybe some tests at the hospital?"

"Had some tests. They were negative. And the nearest place to get therapy is a hundred miles from here. How many times a week would you suggest I drive that, Doc? How many times a week would you suggest I neglect my cattle to go get my back rubbed?" He pushed himself off the bed, ever so slowly, then headed to the front of the trailer. It was a one-room deal. Bed at the back, small kitchen area at the front, a seating area near the center where there was barely enough room to sit.

Very compact and, to Matt, very claustrophobic and filled with bad memories. "How often are you out on the range?" he asked, typing some notes into his tablet trying to ignore the resemblance of this trailer to the ones he'd lived in. It was difficult, though. Everything surrounding him brought back bad memories...memories he'd have to put aside to do this job.

"Out for three, then here for two. But when I stay here, that's not to rest. It's to get myself ready to go out again. Try to get myself back to my real house a couple days a month, when I can."

What a hard life, Matt thought as he slipped his tablet into his medical bag, then pulled out some vials as well as a sample container. "Mind if I do a few tests?"

"Help yourself, but what you're looking for isn't there. The other doc took samples every time he was out here and all he could prove was that, except for a bad back, I'm healthier than a sixty-three-year-old man has a right to be."

"Still got a job to do, John," Matt said, as he took blood samples, then labeled them when John went to render up that other sample. Several minutes later the men walked outside together, but Matt stopped short of the truck, glad to get out of the trailer before he started breaking out in a cold sweat, and noticed the horse tied to the fence not too far from the trailer. "You still go out on a horse?" he asked. Some still did. Many did not. All-terrain vehicles were taking over the aspect of being a cowboy as often as not.

"Every chance I get. Some of the ground isn't fit, but a good bit of it is, so I do it the old-fashioned way."

"Would you mind saddling up for me?"

"Any reason why?" John asked, frowning.

"Something someone told me about crooked saddles. They can cause backache. Ever heard of it?"

John shook his head. And as he did so, Ellie stepped into view. "It's not common," she said, "but it happens often enough that there are saddle specialists out there who can fix most saddles, if they're not too badly out of alignment."

"Well, the one I've got is older than dirt," he said, extending his hand to Ellie. "John Tolly, ma'am."

"Ellie Landers," she said.

Matt noted that her face was pleasant now, the scowl gone. The rigid body had disappeared. This was the Ellie he'd met that night. The one he'd taken to immediately. "Ellie's a friend, and a very good nurse, out for the ride with me today."

"Can I offer you something to drink, Ellie? I have some fresh tea, cold water—or I can make you some lemonade."

She held up her water bottle. "I'm good. But thanks."

"Well, then, guess, I'll mount up and see if I've got that crooked saddle thing going on." With that, John wandered over to a shed that was better built than his trailer to get his saddle.

"You feeling better?" Matt asked.

"I get these—I suppose you could call them hormonal surges. They make me emotional, and not in a good way. Sorry about your pillow, by the way."

Matt chuckled. "I'm just glad it wasn't anything important."

"So, do you think it's his saddle?" she asked.

"Your guess is as good as mine. He's been seen for his back for quite a while, and nothing turns up. I'm hoping it's something as simple as he's sitting skew. Any other guesses? Or videos that might give a clue?"

Ellie rubbed her hand along her own lower back. "Nope. Just sympathy pains."

"Your back hurt?" he asked, suddenly concerned.

"Not really. Just a little twinge now and then. Nothing

to be concerned about. My doctor said a lot of pregnant women suffer back pain, and I suppose I'm one of those."

But she wasn't showing that much yet, and the additional weight of the baby wasn't pulling on her spine. So, unless she was subject to back pain as a rule, this seemed off. "And you didn't tell me?" He wasn't sure what to do now. Take Ellie back to the house where she could rest, or continue to his next appointment? If he took her back, it would put him off his schedule for the rest of the day, and he wouldn't have time for Lucas later this evening. But if Ellie was having problems…

"Like I said, many pregnant women get aches and pains, Matt. I'm fine. And, trust me, I'm not going to do anything to put this baby at risk. You have my word on that."

"You didn't have back pain before you were pregnant?"

"No. In fact, I ran every morning and worked out four times a week to keep myself in shape. Like my doc back home told me, it's just part of the process."

A part that had him worried. "Are you sure you're OK, because I could—?"

Ellie laid a reassuring hand on his arm. "I'm fine. Promise."

Matt still wasn't convinced. Of course, he didn't know if that was coming from a doctor's point of view or a nervous father's. A father's point of view—in a way, he liked that. So far, this baby wasn't all that real for him. He knew it existed, that Ellie carried it. But the idea of being a father to—him or her—hadn't sunk in, other than knowing it wouldn't work out in his life. Lucas deserved better. His child deserved better. *His child*…

A check of John Tolly on his saddle was all it took for Matt to conclude that his saddle was the cause of his pain.

"You're sitting way off to the left," he said, checking the view from both sides then the rear. "Which means that until you get it fixed, or have a new one made, take your truck. And it probably wouldn't hurt to get a lumbar support cushion for that."

"You saying my bones are getting too old to work?" John asked, as he climbed down off the saddle.

"I'm saying your equipment is too old. Get it fixed or replace it, give it a month then call me for another appointment." If he'd even be here in another month. He'd heard a couple of his buddies were going back over to Afghanistan—he wanted to ship out with them. There was an opening and it was his, if he got his home situation straightened out. But that was the big question, wasn't it? Could he get his home situation straightened out? Especially in only a month?

Sighing, Matt helped Ellie situate herself back in the truck, then he climbed into the driver's seat. "Maybe you should be the one running the medical practice out here instead of me."

"Hard to do when the people would expect more than a camera or a sketch pad."

"So, what made you change—well, not careers so much, since what you do is medical? But direction. I know your company's successful. I looked it up on the internet. Didn't you like nursing?"

Ellie settled into the seat as they set off down the dusty road. "Actually, I loved being a nurse. But it wasn't the kind of responsibility I wanted to take on. Probably because I didn't believe I was good enough. Whatever the case, that's the way my life has always been—finding one thing but looking for something else, someplace where I fit in better. So I was looking around at various options, given the education I already had, and medical illustration caught my attention. I'm an artist—at least as a hobby. Put that together with my medical background, and it just seemed to suit me. I'd still be in the medical field but I'd be doing something that took into consideration other passions I had."

"So you simply started a company?" He'd read that, seen the high praise for how she'd built the company from the ground up and become a major competitor in her field in only a few short years. Even though it had nothing to do with him, it did make him proud of her.

"After another couple of years of education and a lot of extra study on running a business. It's a relatively small field but very demanding. Four-year undergrad degree in a science discipline, two more years on top of that in applied medical illustration. Some business education thrown in. I was late when I finally got to the table, but I worked hard and fast to get us up and going, and I landed my first significant contract within the first six months, and my first major contract inside my first year. All that allowed me to grow my business, which is what I've been trying to do every day since I started it."

Ellie shifted positions again, favoring her back. He noticed it, and it worried him. "So, you're a career woman, one hundred percent."

"Competing in a corporate world that's largely owned by men. It's a hard battle sometimes." She smiled, and her nose wrinkled. "But I usually win."

"From what I read, your services are in pretty high demand." Matt liked the confidence he was hearing in her voice. This was a side of Ellie he hadn't seen, and it fit her well. The way her blue eyes lit up when she talked about her work, the enthusiasm that emanated from her—it was sexy in a way he'd never thought sexy could be. Her sexiness was more than simply her physical attributes—which were very nice. It was a package deal. Intellect, ambition, competitive edge. She had it all, and another time, another place...

The second ranch call went quickly, and before Ellie knew it, they were on their way back to Matt's house. It was about a thirty-mile drive, which wasn't all that long unless your back was spasming off and on, like hers was. "Matt, what do you know about relaxin?" she asked, as he slowed to avoid a pothole.

"Not a lot other than it's a hormone that lets the ligaments in the pelvic area relax, and the joints to loosen up in preparation for the birth process. The problem is, relaxin can also cause those ligaments to loosen too much, which causes back pain. Sometimes muscle separation. Is that what you think your back pain is coming from?"

"Maybe. I looked it up on the internet and it just made me wonder if I have some kind of imbalance."

"Well, relaxin isn't usually considered a complication unless there's an abundance of it. Has your OB/GYN checked that?"

"He's done routine blood counts but that's all."

"Well, how about I order in what I need for the test and we'll see if that's what's causing your pain? Because if it is..."

Ellie knew the rest of what Matt was going to say. An over-abundance of relaxin put her at risk for a miscarriage or an early delivery since her body was in the delivery mode due to the relaxin. "If it is, I could be in trouble."

"Which is why it's better to check it now, before we do anything else."

"Thank you," she said.

"What for?"

"For saying we. It makes me feel less alone in this. And less worried."

"You're not alone, Ellie. I may not be good for much else, but I'm not going to let you do this all by yourself." Which meant—well, he'd cross that army bridge when he came to it. Right now, his only concern was Ellie.

CHAPTER FIVE

ELLIE DROPPED DOWN onto her temporary bed in Matt's *casita*, not so much physically worn out as emotionally battered from the back-and-forth she was playing with herself. She'd been quite set in what she'd wanted when she'd arrived here, and every hour since seemed to have eroded bits and pieces of her resolve.

She was discovering how much she cared for this isolated man. He was the handsome, daring prince of every little girl's dreams, and he was the steady, noble man of most women's grown-up dreams. Certainly, he was the dream she'd fought against for a lifetime. And, no, that wasn't a hormonal surge leading her in that direction.

She'd watched him re-stitch a cowboy's dirty old wound this afternoon, taking care to get it clean and stitch it as neatly as he could, considering how the cowboy had first stitched it himself with regular thread and a sewing needle. It had been infected. Matt had given him antibiotics. It might require another open-up and a second good cleansing. Matt had made an appointment to meet him in ten days. The cowboy had initially been grumpy and resistant, only giving in to a doctor's exam at the insistence of his wife. But when they'd left, he had been laughing with Matt, recalling his own army days and inviting him back for a meal any time he was in the area.

Then Ellie had spent two hours in clinic with him, watching a handful of people come and go. All locals with simple complaints, all made to feel special by Matt's way. He wasn't overly friendly. He definitely kept a professional distance, was quite obviously trying hard to improve his bedside manner, and he was succeeding in making them feel the way she was feeling now. That was a gift she thought Matt was only now discovering in himself. Maybe it was the gift that had initially attracted her to him that night in Reno because for her to have done what she had with a stranger—that wasn't her. Not at all.

Whatever the case, Ellie was glad to be back here. Glad to hear Matt and Lucas playing in the other part of the house. The little boy still hadn't talked, but the way he automatically clung to Matt's hand and tried to walk the way Matt did, in long, deliberate strides, touched her heart. Everything about the special uncle-nephew relationship touched her heart, which made her long for the same for their child. And, perhaps, for her?

Of course, she was emotionally sloppy right now. Another time, another situation and none of this would have phased her. At least, she didn't think it would. She was a businesswoman who belonged in the business world. That's where she fit. Where she was comfortable. Although she wasn't quite as connected to that life as she had been yesterday. That would change, though. After she left here. After she got back to normal.

"Well, we have some dinner choices," Matt said, poking his head through Ellie's open *casita* door.

"Anything's fine with me," she said, lifting her head off the pillow only to see Matt *and* Lucas standing in her doorway, same exact pose, with Lucas imitating Matt. "I'll even eat a little meat protein, if you think I need to."

"I'm not going to compromise your eating sensibilities unless I have to. Right now, I don't have to. But it's not about the food. I've thrown some various things together for a picnic. So, what's up here is where, exactly, we're going to have that picnic. My suggestion is the patio. Lucas wants to go up to the flat. You get to decide between the two."

Ellie sat up in bed. "First, what's the flat?"

"It's an area up the path from the house, a short hike away. If you're rested enough, it should be easy. And the view is amazing—it looks out over the valley. It's beautiful at sunset. Lucas likes to go up there, take along some toys and play in the rocks."

"And he told you that's where he wants to go?"

"Not in words. But in the way Lucas tells me other things he wants me to know."

"Which is how?"

"Mostly by being observant. I asked him where he'd like to picnic, and he looked up at the flats. It's in his eyes a lot of the time. You just have to understand what his eyes are saying."

Eyes so much like Matt's that Lucas could easily be mistaken for his son. Would *their* child have those same beautiful eyes? Ellie hoped so. "Well, if you think I'm good to go, and that's where Lucas wants to go…" She scooted to the side of the bed, ready to stand.

"It's up to you, Ellie. Only you know how you're feeling."

Down in the dumps, emotionally. That was how she was feeling. "I'd like to see the sunset." And she wanted to spend time with Matt and Lucas, pretend they were a family. If only for a little while.

"Seriously, this is the walk a lot of doctors would prescribe for mild exercise. And if you have any trouble, you've got two big, strong men there to help you. Isn't that right, Lucas?" Matt asked, tousling the boy's hair.

Lucas looked up at Ellie for a moment, then switched his attention back to Matt. The little boy adored him so much. It was obvious to her, and it had to be obvious to Matt as well. Matt's decision to have him adopted—was that breaking his heart, because she knew it would break Lucas's heart once they were separated. And *their* baby—would she or he, in some unexplainable way, experience the pain of separation the way Lucas would? The way *she* would?

Suddenly, Ellie didn't feel so good, and all she wanted to do was go back to bed, pull the covers up over her head and blot out everything. Pretend she wasn't here. Pretend she wasn't carrying Matt's child. Pretend her life was the same as it used to be. Pretend. A nice place to go, but you couldn't stay there. Not when you were falling in love with your baby, and maybe also falling in love with your baby's father. There was nothing pretend about that.

"What I need is two big, strong men to lead the way, since I don't know where I'm going," she said, sitting up then tying on her hiking boots—boots that Matt had stopped and bought her earlier. Had he done that because he'd planned walks with her, not just this once but afterwards? He'd bought her a nice hiking jacket, too, with big pockets. The thought that he might want her to stay gave her an unexpected jolt. Would she stay if he asked her?

"I think we can manage that," Matt said, scooping Lucas up into his arms then walking through the door, stopping for a moment to face Ellie. "Are you sure you're up to this?"

What she wasn't up to had nothing to do with this walk, and she wasn't sure she could even define it. Or wanted to. But being so physically close to Matt—well, she'd felt that way before, which was why she was here now. Only this time there was an added bonus. She was getting to know him.

It was probably a good thing her mother had taught her that a competent woman didn't need a man because in knowing him, even a little, she was beginning to see just how wrong her mother was. Which allayed many of her fears that she was too much like her mother. She wasn't. Realizing that, she took the deepest breath of relief she'd ever had. *She was not her mother.* Ellie needed...the things her mother had told her she never would.

"Point me in the right direction, and I'll beat you there," she said, feeling like she could explode, she was so relieved. Yet taking care not to brush up against him. Because, even in her condition, she was getting a little goose-bumpy being so close.

"Up the path, then curve to the left. Follow that until you come to the divide and stay left there until you come to the big flat rock. You won't miss it because it blocks the path and to keep going up, you have to climb over it."

"But we're not climbing?" she asked.

"Nope. The rock is our destination. When you get past it the landscape gets too rough for a woman in your condition."

He laughed, and Ellie almost melted at the deep throatiness of it as she sat down on a little rock to rest for a moment.

Matt stopped at her side, sat down with her, and took her hand. And that's when her goose-bumps rioted.

"Hell, it gets challenging to me" he continued, "and I've got some pretty good experience in rock climbing."

"Sounds like it could be fun," she said, trying to ignore the feelings coming over her. Maybe it was the air or another swing of hormones, but she felt...flushed. And in the good kind of way. From excitement or happiness. Or maybe because Matt was holding her hand. "Maybe I'll try to learn some time." She hoped to hear him offer to teach her, but he didn't. Instead, he dropped her hand, sprang up and went dashing off after Lucas, who had decided to toddle his way on up the path ahead of him. "Well, so much for that," she whispered to her baby, then likewise stood up and toddled on.

"So much for what?" he asked from ahead of her.

"Rest time," she lied. "We've got one very anxious little boy who wants to keep going."

"Well, he's not going far because our destination is only about a hundred yards from here." He stopped and held out his hand to take hers. "Need me to carry you?"

Simply sweeping her up into his arms would have been nicer, like he'd done in his office, but an extended hand was nice, too. So she took it, not sure if he was extending friendship or more. Somehow she wanted more. "Maybe on the way back down," she said.

"Were you ever married, Matt?" Ellie asked abruptly, midway through the fruit salad he'd prepared.

Her question came out of the blue and nearly choked him. "Why?" he sputtered.

"Just curious, that's all."

She'd been quiet for a while. He'd assumed it was because the walk had worn her out. But now he wasn't sure. "Never really had much interest in it. I did have a short-term thing when I was in medical school, but what we both realized was that I wasn't committed enough to the relationship, and she wasn't patient enough to deal with me. It took us about a year to come to that conclusion, and no hearts were broken when we both walked away from it."

"Did you keep yourself apart from her?" She reached for a stalk of celery to dip in the guacamole. "The way you try to do with, well, everybody."

"Do I?"

"I haven't been here that long, but I don't get the sense that you want to fit in."

He didn't, because he wasn't going to stay. So what was the point? Matt had tried fitting in the first time he'd lived here. Had tried hard. Got ridiculed or ignored. Even by social workers who were too overburdened to see what had really been going on in his family. He and Janice had gone to school. They had been clean. And had been fed—not often by their father, but fed nonetheless.

On paper, it looked fine. In reality it had been horrible. And the worst part—no one had listened. Matt had just been the kid who'd lived in the dump no one bothered with. So shutting them out before they shut him out—it was his habit. Had been as a kid, in many ways it still was. Which was why he liked being a battlefield surgeon. The noise was too loud, the need too great, and no one shut him out.

"In a lot of ways I don't. Life has never worked out for me except in the military, and that's the world in which I'm accepted. I'm good there, and I don't need anything else." Brave words that he wasn't sure he believed so much anymore. Especially with these feelings of wanting Ellie to stay. He'd come close to asking. But if she agreed, then what? How could he adjust his life to that, and would it be fair to expect her to adjust?

It was a nice thought, though. But one he couldn't let out because she was so vulnerable right now and he was afraid he could tip her in a direction she'd regret later.

"Have you ever wanted something different? Or tried to get it?"

"To what end?

"I don't know. Maybe to see if there's something bigger and better you're missing."

"Have you ever tried?" he asked.

"One night, in Reno," Ellie said, then turned her attention to the salsa and chips. "That turned into two."

Matt was dumbstruck. He didn't know what to say. Because those Reno nights had been his own stepping away from what he had been. "Why all the questions?" Matt finally asked, as he sat down next to Ellie but in a position to keep an eye on Lucas. "I don't mind telling you about me because there's not much to tell. But why are you interested?"

"Maybe because we share a baby. Or because I want to get to know the man I let my guard down for. I don't do what we did, Matt. That's not me. I don't need a man in my life, and I've done well on my own without one. But, like it or not, for a little while you're in my life, and I want to know who you are. So far, you haven't been very forthcoming."

"Because you *still* think I should be the one to raise the baby?"

"Well, I guess that's a subject for debate now that I'm gaining some insight into you. At first, you were my plan. My only plan. But now—let's just say I'm not going to pressure you about any of this. What you do is your decision, and I have too much respect for you to try and change it."

"What about your backup plan? You've got one now, don't you?

Ellie shook her head, then smiled. "Normally, my first plan works, so I rarely ever have to resort to a backup plan.

"So why not you as your backup plan? Why don't you want the responsibility of raising the baby?"

Ellie's smile disappeared, replaced by a deep scowl. "Because the women in my family don't do it well. We're not…maternal. Because I know what I'm good at and—" She felt the baby kick, and was still amazed by the feel of it. The first kick she kept to herself, but on the second kick she reached for Matt's hand and placed it on her belly.

"Whoever's in there, kicking, needs better than I'd ever be able to do. I've got money, but it's not money a baby needs. A baby, or even a growing child, needs time and attention. He or she needs to have someone to count on every minute of every day. Someone to guide and protect him. Or her. Someone to be an example. I've spent a lifetime thinking I had to turn out to be like my mother, which I know now isn't the case. But what I also know is I don't have the broader picture I need to be a good mother. There's more to it than simply being where you need to be and doing what you need to do. That's not in me."

"Are you sure? Because where you need to be is right here, right now. And as far as doing what you need to do, you're doing everything possible to take care of your pregnancy. To me, that's perfect mothering." He left his hand on her belly for a moment, then pulled it back when the kicking stopped. "Are you sure you're totally set on your decision to give up our baby?"

"Right now, I'm not set on anything. Things are changing. I'm changing. All I know is I don't want to keep the baby and raise it with surrogates, the way I was raised and the way my mother was raised. A child should have a real home. One with a parent or two parents who put that child first. I can't do that, Matt. I may have the intellectual skills to see what a baby needs but I don't have the maternal ones."

Yet there she sat with her hand on her belly, a very protective gesture. And a very maternal one. "For what it's worth, Ellie, I think you're wrong," he said, taking a bite of the guacamole, and handing a small piece of chicken to Lucas, who gobbled it right down.

"You don't know me well enough to say that."

"In surgery, I make snap decisions that deal with life-and-death circumstances, and I'm damned good at it. I made a snap decision about you in Reno, and for what we had there, I was right about it. I'm right now as well. Maybe you don't see it, but I do."

"Think what you want, Matt. I can't stop you. And I probably can't convince you you're the one who's wrong. But the man I spent those two days with in Reno—he seemed like the type who would want to be involved. And that's why I'm here."

"I *am* the type who would want to be involved, and I'm glad you included me in this. But I can't be involved in the way you think I should be." He handed another piece of chicken to Lucas, then scooted in closer to roll the toy truck to him. "I don't belong in Forgeburn anymore. I barely got out of here when I was a kid, and I don't want to be back. Don't want to limit myself to what I would have been limited to if I hadn't gotten out."

"Then go someplace else. It's a big, beautiful world out there, and most of it's *not* a battlefield."

"Right now, I can't go someplace else. I have to stay here because Child Services are trying to find—" He looked at Lucas, then lowered his voice. "A good placement. I can't mess that up for him."

"And you don't consider yourself a good placement?" she asked.

"Not at all. Not for Lucas, not for our baby. You've got to understand, Ellie, I have a commitment. I've dedicated my life to it and I have no intention of looking for some way out of it. It's who I am. Nothing about that is going to change."

"You're so sure of that?" Ellie asked. She knew he was and maybe, for the first time, she understood what it meant to have that kind of dedication. Sure, she was dedicated to her work. But her work was ever-changing, possibly to suit her restlessness. And she was restless. Always had been. Nothing ever fit.

Nothing had ever seemed right, so she'd quit being a nurse and started being a medical illustrator. Added videography when the restlessness hit again, then photography. Taken on worldwide clients, run to Tokyo for a couple of months, then London for a while. There was always something driving her to do more, be more. But it was never enough. And here was Matt, a man who simply wanted one thing—to get back to his real calling.

It dawned on her that's what she lacked—a real calling. So how could she be responsible enough to raise a baby when she didn't even know where she was going?

But how could she expect Matt to give up his calling when he knew where he needed to be in life?

"As sure as you are that your life isn't going to change."

The problem was she wasn't sure. Her life had always been plagued with doubts about how she measured up, and nothing about that had changed. Even now, sitting here with Matt, she knew she didn't even come close to measuring up to him. He was a man who did great things and aspired to do even more. And she was a woman who aspired to what? A good plan? Living up to what her mother expected? Even the thought of that made her stomach churn. But it couldn't be denied. While she wasn't like her mother, the influence was still there, holding on for dear life.

You really don't want to raise this baby, do you, Eleanor? You're starting to succeed in life, and a baby won't fit your plans.

It always got back to that, didn't it? What would fit into her plans.

You need a plan, Eleanor. Always make sure you have a plan.

But right now she didn't. "Then we have a big decision to make, don't we?" she said, feeling crushed.

"Actually, right now we have a lot of food to eat. And I've got to finish feeding a toddler who's going to be asleep before the sun goes all the way down."

The setting sun. As beautiful as it was this early evening, and it was stunning, all she could see looked dismal. Dismal sun, dismal rocks, dismal everything. And right now the only thing Ellie wanted was to return to the *casita*, shut her doors and cry because she was desperately confused.

Matt was so unprepared for this. All of it. Lucas. Ellie. The baby. None of it fit in, yet it seemed to be taking shape right before him, and he didn't know what to do about it, especially since Lucas was becoming attached to him. Ellie had expectations, too. He knew that, and being around her, knowing what they were, made it tough on him. He cared for her. No denying that. And their baby— his feelings for *their* child were getting stronger by the minute. At first he had felt distanced from the whole thing. Knew it intellectually, but not so much emotionally.

Yet every time he looked at Ellie, strange new emotions welled up in him. Emotions he didn't understand. Not for her. Not for their baby. Could it be he wanted something he didn't yet understand? Something more than what he already had?

Matt shut his eyes for a moment and tried to picture

the four of them as a typical family. Surprisingly, the image came together so easily he blinked it away before it could sink in. No, he wasn't his old man, who couldn't hack it in that sort of life. That wasn't his fear. But being responsible for someone else or, in this case, three others wasn't in his make-up, and he'd proved that with Janice. And that had been such a simple thing. He'd been supposed to get her out of Forgeburn. That's all there was to it. Get her away from there. But he hadn't, and while there might have been justified excuses, he didn't accept them. So how the hell could he take care of three people when he'd already proved he couldn't take care of one?

Yet the more Matt tried surrounding himself with thoughts of returning to his army life, the only sure thing he'd ever had, the more they eluded him, being replaced by thoughts, even visions of him being needed elsewhere now. But life, for him, wasn't an easy thing to change. He didn't do well with detours and diversions because to climb out of the hole where he'd spent his childhood had taken a straightforward progression, no veering off anywhere. And he'd trained himself in that kind of rigid discipline. Had worked hard to achieve it, then lived it every day.

But now this was all about veering off, and it felt like he was so far off he might never get back to where he had been. And there was no straightforward progression here. Not with a toddler who needed more than he could give. And a woman who didn't know what she needed who was also carrying his baby. So, no, he wasn't prepared for this. Wasn't equipped for it either. But he also couldn't turn his back on any of it because, like it or not, this was all a part of his life. Maybe not life the he'd chosen for himself but definitely the life that was being chosen for him.

So why had he called Doc Granger simply to enquire how much buying out the practice and properties would cost? Was he really thinking in that direction, or had that been a moment of weakness? Truthfully, Matt didn't know. Didn't want to think about it either.

"Want more chicken, Lucas?" he called out as the confusion of his life swirled around in his head.

Lucas, who was fully engaged in playing "hands off the teddy bear" with Ellie, looked over at Matt but didn't reply. Matt took that to mean no, so he sealed the container of food and placed it back in the backpack.

"You want something else, Ellie?" he asked. What he really wanted was to start walking and not stop until he was back where he belonged. Except this was where he belonged right now. Right here, right now, doing exactly what he was doing. Duty-bound in a direction he could have never predicted. But was it really that bad? Or was he making it worse than it seemed because it scared him how easily he slipped into the flow of it?

"I'm good, thank you," she said, smiling over at him. "But I think Lucas might need a..." she grimaced "... diaper change. Do you have one in the backpack?"

"Sure do. We're into the pull-up kind these days."

"Ah, yes. The intermediate stage. So the battlefield surgeon is an expert on toilet training?" she asked, laughing as she took the diaper from him.

He chuckled. "No, but I'm learning. And I can do that," he went on. "Lucas and I have a system."

"Oh, I think we can manage. I used to be a nurse, you know."

"Probably a very good one."

"I got along."

And she did quite brilliantly with Lucas. In fact, it was amazing, watching the way he took to Ellie. Normally, he shied away from people. But for the last twenty minutes he'd been playing with her in a way Matt had never seen. And laughing. So far, he'd never coaxed much of a laugh from Lucas, but Ellie had, and he was a little jealous of that. Jealous of a natural ability with children she couldn't see. Or didn't want to see.

She needed to keep their baby, he suddenly realized. Until now, he'd believed her when she'd said she wouldn't make a good mother. But he didn't anymore and he wondered why, with the amount of maternal instinct she was showing with Lucas, Ellie didn't want to be a mother to her own child. To their child? What kind of fear did she hide that prevented her from seeing what he was seeing right now? And it did have to be a deep fear because, when Ellie let herself go, she was a natural.

It was his intention to persuade her to keep the baby, but first he needed to discover more about why she didn't want that. Maybe, after that, help her overcome it, or simply see in herself what he was seeing. "But you said it wasn't enough."

"Nothing ever has been. I have some pretty high standards to compete with, and it seems like every time I'm about to get there, the bar rises on me a little bit more."

"Why?" he asked.

"That's the way the women in my family are. Always upward."

"But what happens if you get to the place where you're happy and contented and don't want to leave?"

"That's just it. You never do. There's always something more. Something else to achieve. Ask my mother. Ask my grandmother. They'll both tell you that contentment is the same thing as laziness."

"But do you believe that?"

"What I believe is that I'm doing what I was born to do."

This was interesting. And insightful. No matter how good she was, where she was, it wasn't good enough. He did understand what it felt like not being good enough, but not like this. Or maybe it was all the same, just in a different version. "As in running this company you own? That's what you were born to do? Or is that just another stop-over until you find the *next* real thing?"

"You may think you're being clever, but you're not. I love what I do. But I could do more. Expand operations. Open more divisions. Go after bigger clients. Do something more in the technology line. There are a lot of opportunities out there, and I have to decide which ones are right for me because, yes, it's all about the next real thing."

"Is that *your* wish, Ellie? Or are you trying to live up to those other women in your family? You know, always upward?"

She hesitated to answer him, and Matt wished he could see the expression on her face, but it was too dark now and all he could see was her silhouette. A beautiful silhouette caught in the shadows. One he wanted to pull into his arms and simply hold because she seemed so vulnerable right now. No, she wasn't the staunch businesswoman at this moment. She was simply Ellie, and from the slump of her shoulders he could see a different person altogether. One who didn't have her plan to hide behind. One who was unsure.

"I suppose that *is* me," she finally said, after a long, deep sigh. "You know, like they say: the apple doesn't fall far from the tree."

"But what happens if you do?" he asked. "What happens if you see a better tree?"

"I did once, a long time ago. But I wasn't prepared to stay there because all I knew was what it had taught me. Unfortunately, life hadn't taught me to be independent somewhere else. In fact, all life had taught me was to grow where I was planted, so ultimately that's what I did. I didn't have experience outside of being who I was taught to be. And I was so carefully taught, I couldn't see past any of that.

"That's why I left nursing. It was my one attempt to find that better tree, but I didn't have the confidence I needed to stay there. I loved what I was doing, but I was also afraid of it, afraid of the mistakes I could make. There's no place in obstetric nursing for that kind of fear, so I went back to where my only true confidence was—the world my mother had prepared me for.

"I know my weaknesses, Matt, and I also know my strengths. For me, I find safety in my strengths, so I stay where I'm safe—as a woman who runs a growing business and knows her place there. No uncertainties, no lack of confidence. Anyway, I'm getting tired. Do you mind if we go back to the house?"

Sighing, Matt leaned back against a boulder and focused his attention on the valley below. It was too dark to see all the way to the bottom now. Kind of like his life. Too dark to see all the way to a resolution. But if he stayed here all night, morning light would bring a different view of the valley. A total view. One with new and different possibilities. If only he could share that with Ellie then maybe she, too, could see different possibilities for herself as well. And not just with the baby but with her whole life. To have so much, but to feel so small in its midst—he ached for her.

"It was a nice day," Ellie said, standing in the doorway of Lucas's bedroom while Matt put the boy to bed. "Different from what I normally do, and I enjoyed it. Thank you."

"You're not too tired or feeling any kind of…problem, are you?"

She smiled as he pulled the blanket up over Lucas and gave the sleeping boy a kiss on the forehead. "Spoken like a typical man. All your medical training aside, pregnancy is a normal condition. It has its rough patches since the body is constantly changing, but it's been happening since the beginning of time. I'm tired, which is to be expected, but other than that there's nothing to worry about." She watched him tuck Lucas's toys into the closet then take one last look at the child before he headed for the door.

Stepping aside to let Matt pass by, Ellie looked up at him as he pressed her back into the doorframe, then stopped and stood there, looking down at her. Was he going to kiss her? She wanted him to. Wanted to feel the tenderness he'd shown her in Reno, but instead of a kiss he simply brushed his hand across her cheek. It caused her breath to catch, though. And her pulse to quicken. All too soon he stepped out of the doorway and cleared his throat. "I think I'm going to turn in early tonight," he said, as he headed down the stairs. "Is there anything I can get you before I lock up?"

It was a dismissal. She knew that, knew the sting of a slap when it hit her. "No, I'm fine. Do you mind if I use your desk for a little while? I've got my laptop and I thought maybe I could catch up on some work." Her safety net. It protected her from everything, including the hurt feelings that were welling up in her for absolutely no reason. Because there was no reason to expect Matt would be comfortable with anything other than what they were—a two-night stand with consequences. Intimacy in any form simply wasn't on the table now, and he'd been making that clear since she'd arrived. Of course, she'd been doing the same, while hoping for something different, hadn't she? Why kid herself when romance had never been a part of their relationship?

Was it the hormonal thing again? Or was she developing different feelings for Matt? She wanted it to be the hormones, but she wasn't convinced. Being away from the *old* her, even for this short amount of time, was causing something to stir inside her. Something she'd put off, or never admitted that she wanted. In her other life, why bother? It was all cut and dried. But here, in this one—well, she didn't know. She just didn't know.

"Sure. Whatever you need. Internet connection is spotty, but it usually works. So help yourself."

Ellie watched Matt lock the front door then skirt her, taking care to stay as far away from her as possible as he crossed back through to check the patio door. "Fine. I'll just go get…" She took two steps backwards then turned and retreated down the hall to the *casita*, without looking back or saying another word. What was there to say after all? That she might be falling a little in love with him? That maybe the desires she'd always kept locked away weren't as locked tight as she'd thought?

She'd never had romance in her life—not until Reno. And Matt had romanced her. Treated her the way no one else ever had. Champagne, candlelight, soft music… Considering her first in everything they'd done. So, was that what she wanted? More romance from the only man who'd ever romanced her? Or did she want even more?

Instead of gathering up her laptop to work, Ellie took a quick shower and did what everybody else in the house was doing. She went to bed and hoped for fast, deep sleep. Because she didn't want to think about Matt. And being awake, that's all she could think about. Not in the practical ways she'd taught herself to do, however. But in ways that made her want Reno back.

"I sent it off with the local helicopter pilot so now we wait." Matt was referring to the tests to determine Ellie's relaxin levels. So far, she hadn't seemed anxious to leave Forgeburn, so he wasn't pressing her to do that, or anything else. They'd spent the early part of the morning simply coexisting. Not speaking much but getting along. She'd spent a good portion of her time online, working on her business while he'd got Lucas ready for the day.

Last night he'd wanted to kiss her, and he'd thought she might be receptive. At least, to him it had seemed that way. But what would that start? Another direction he couldn't go? Damn, what was he doing, letting himself get so tempted, knowing that even if he did step over the line, he could only take that single step and no more.

Was that fair to Ellie? Or even to himself? No. It wasn't. He was obligated to a life that had no place for domesticity or romance, and even thinking he could mix those with something else was risky because his focus had always been singular. So how could he get involved with Ellie and offer her something he didn't have to offer?

So many consequences from one little kiss that hadn't happened. But consequences be damned. Matt wished he'd gone ahead and done it anyway. Well, he hadn't, and there was really no reason to speculate about what might have happened. He'd had his chance, hadn't taken it and the rest was an empty point.

Matt wasn't like his old man, who'd shirked every responsibility life had given him. He knew that. But he'd gone to the opposite extreme, there really wasn't any give in him. It was black, or it was white. There was noth-

ing in between because in the in between that's where
he found his doubts and fears, and the terrifying nightmare that one bad move and he'd end up right back here,
not as the doctor but as the kid who lived in the dump. It
terrified him, thinking how easy it could be to take that
one wrong step.

It terrified him even more thinking that Ellie could be
dragged into all that with him. Some might look at her
as his way out, but he would never use her that way. And
while she could offer him a part of life he'd never had, he
could do the same. Only what she would offer would be
good for him and what he'd offer would be bad for her.
Which was why Matt kept to the straight and narrow.

Ellie deserved better, so did Lucas, the baby certainly
deserved better than the mire he'd never quite escaped.
Even with glimpses of what he could have if he took that
one step off the path, it wasn't enough to budge him. Not
for his sake and especially not for theirs.

Yet, in the distance, he could still see a different life.
Unfortunately, he was so stuck where he was, Matt didn't
know how to reach out and grab it. A simple kiss might
have been the start. Or it might have been the stumble
that started him on the descent. Which was why he hadn't
kissed her. He had been afraid where it would take him.
And, most of all, take Ellie.

"I appreciate that," Ellie said, without diverting her attention from her computer screen. "I'd feel better knowing what I'm dealing with before I make that long trip
back. That is, if you don't mind my staying for an extra
couple of days." She looked up at him for an answer but
her face was impassive. No expression. "Or I could stay
in that hotel down the road. That was always my first
option."

"The *casita* is fine," Matt said, picking up his medical bag. "Look, I've got some patients coming into the office in a while. I'm also going to keep Lucas with me this morning because the social worker has some prospective parents, and they're going to stop in for a few minutes. If you'd like to come with us, you're welcome. I have better connectivity at the office than I do here, so you might have an easier time working there."

She looked up, her face almost registering alarm. "They might want to adopt him?"

"That's always been the plan."

"But I thought..."

"What, Ellie? That this little slice of domesticity we're living might rub off?"

"Maybe—I don't know. Hearing you talk about it then seeing it actually happen—I guess I wasn't prepared for that."

Matt shook his head. "Sometimes reality bites, but my reality is a battlefield hospital full of casualties that need to be fixed. You've always known that."

"Just make sure you don't turn yourself into a casualty as well," Ellie said. "And I don't mean battlefield."

Then, just like that, she turned him off and launched into an internet conversation with a colleague.

Matt took his cue, held out his hand for Lucas, who grabbed it, and headed out the door. By the time the two of them reached the truck, Matt was kicking himself for not trying harder to get her to go with him. He didn't like leaving Ellie alone, even when she insisted she was fine. Maybe it was an overprotective reaction to her pregnancy, maybe it was about some different feelings for her stirring up in him.

Whatever the case, she'd made her choice, and he had to get over the idea that he was responsible for her. He wasn't, and she'd made it perfectly clear that's the way she intended to keep it. So, had her grumpiness this morning just been a by-product of anxiety over missing work? Something to do with her pregnancy? Or the kiss that had never happened? Had she wanted it badly enough she was still brooding over it?

Was she expecting kisses like they'd shared in Reno?

Which meant... He swallowed hard. "Well, Lucas, it looks like it's just the two of us today. You up for being my receptionist in the office?"

Of course, Lucas didn't respond. But Matt did notice that the boy was staring more intently at him than he usually did. Eyes open a little wider than normal. Expression a little more animated. Which was oddly discomforting. He loved this kid. It hadn't taken much, but he totally, hopelessly loved this kid, and what he was about to do... "Apparently," he said, as he strapped him to the infant seat in the truck, "one of us looks like he's going to have a good day." And the other one was already dreading the rest of it.

CHAPTER SIX

"Mr. and Mrs. Rigsby. They're outside. They'd like to have a look at Lucas."

Matt glanced up from his desk at Lucas's social worker, Mary Jane Snider, as trepidation knotted his stomach. Sure, this is what he'd asked for, but now that it was so close he wasn't as set on adoption as he'd been initially. But Lucas needed more than he could offer. And he owed it to Janice to see that Lucas got the very best. God knew, he'd failed his sister in doing that for her. And being a child, trying to raise a child, wasn't an excuse. To some maybe. But not to him. His sister had been his responsibility from the time he'd been five and she three, and that was the one responsibility in life he'd failed. He wasn't going to fail Lucas, though. "Good," he said half-heartedly. "Show them in."

He stood, went to the Dutch door play area connected to his office, and reached over for Lucas, who stood there with his arms up, smiling, waiting to be picked up. "Don't be afraid of all the people," he told the boy. "They want to be your friends." Try as he might, he could raise no enthusiasm in his voice.

"Remember me?" Mary Jane said, stepping forward to take Lucas from Matt.

Lucas's response was to draw harder into Matt's shoulder and bury his face. "He's not good with strangers yet," Matt explained. "It takes him a while to warm up to them."

"Any chance he'll warm up by the time I bring the Rigsbys in?" she asked, stepping back.

"Probably not."

"We could schedule for another time. Maybe by next week…"

Matt shook his head. "This is who he is. If they're interested in him, they'll have to accept it."

Mary Jane nodded, left the office, then returned a minute later with the Rigsbys—Mr. Rigsby with his hands stuffed into the pockets of a pinstriped suit, something no one out here wore, and Mrs. Rigsby with her arms folded across her chest. Neither looked unfriendly, though. Just indifferent. And older than he'd thought they would be. He doubted Mr. Rigsby would be able to teach Lucas how to climb a rock when the time came, due to his age. And Mrs. Rigsby—she seemed too nervous. Or out of place. Could someone like that nurture Lucas the way he'd need to be nurtured?

"This is Lucas," he said, making no attempt to get Lucas to look at them. "He's shy," he explained.

"Does he walk?" Mr. Rigsby asked.

"Yes, he does. But he doesn't talk, yet."

"Is he slow?" Mrs. Rigsby asked. "Is that why he doesn't talk?"

"He doesn't talk because he has nothing to say. And, no, he's not slow. More like he's just taking life at his own pace."

"Does his pace include toilet training?" Mr. Rigsby enquired.

"Not yet, but we're working on it."

"Any peculiar habits?" Mr. Rigsby continued.

"What do you mean by peculiar? He's two. Most of his habits could be described as peculiar."

"Just oddities," the man said. "Things you wouldn't normally expect to see a toddler doing."

Matt had no idea what other toddlers this age did, but nothing Lucas did seemed odd or peculiar to him. Actually, he suspected that hiding under that shy exterior was a bright little boy. The signs were there. Just not ready to bloom yet. "He has a pet skink he likes to play with in the rock garden," Matt said.

"A skink?" Mrs. Rigsby asked, shuddering.

"Lizard. Brown body, blue tail."

"The child has a skink?" Mr. Rigsby said.

Matt nodded.

"Well, that skink won't be coming with us if we decide to take Lucas in," Mrs. Rigsby said. "We don't have pets in the house, and the people who work for us—"

"People?" Matt interrupted.

"Well, right now we have a cook and a housekeeper. With Lucas coming in, of course we'd hire a tutor and a nanny."

Another time, another place, this might have sounded like a good idea. But he knew that was how Ellie had been raised, and saw the conflicts in her because of it. Certainly, the Rigsbys would be different from Ellie's mother but, still, the similarities—this wasn't what Lucas needed. None of it. What he needed was what neither Matt nor Ellie had had—people who would love raising him.

"I'm sorry," Matt asked. "But I'd hoped to place him with a family who was going to be personally involved with him."

"Which is exactly what we intend to do, Doctor," Mr. Rigsby said, his patience obviously brittle now.

"With hired help?"

"Because we only want the boy to have the best," Mrs. Rigsby said.

But what they offered wasn't the best. Maybe they couldn't see it, but he could, thanks to Ellie. "So do I," Matt said, taking Lucas back to his play area. "I'm sorry for wasting your time."

He went inside, shut the door, and sat down on the rug with Lucas to help him stack green and purple and red wooden blocks. This wasn't what he'd expected. In his mind, the adopting couple would have been eager and excited, full of wonderful plans for Lucas, anxious to bond as a family. Maybe even gushing over him a little bit. Maybe he was simply being too picky, but that was an ideal Matt had always had for himself when he'd been young. A real family, with eager, excited parents who were full of wonderful plans for him and Janice. Parents who were anxious to bond as a family.

He'd never had it, which was why he wanted it for Lucas. But Lucas would get it. He would see to that, no matter how many people he had to turn down to get to the right ones.

"Are you sure you know what you're doing? I could call them back..." Mary Jane said, leaning over the Dutch door.

"Yes. For a change, I really am sure."

It was well into the night when Matt finally dragged himself through the front door. Betty Nelson had come to get Lucas when he'd called her. He might have asked Ellie, but he hadn't had time to take Lucas home, and he certainly hadn't wanted Ellie making that drive until he was sure of her condition. So, after he'd called Ellie and told her he had an emergency, he'd called Betty, and she'd been there with open arms for Lucas in the blink of an eye.

He was blessed to have her as Lucas's babysitter. And Lucas did respond well to her. But, then, back in the day, when she'd been his teacher, she'd always been there for him, too, and she'd become one of the few examples in his life who'd shown him that there were good people in the world. Something he hadn't really experienced very much.

"Bad one?" Ellie asked, waiting for him just inside the door with a glass of fruit drink she'd made.

"Sorry I'm so late," he said, taking the glass she offered him, then heading for the big easy chair in front of the fireplace in the living room. "Not bad as much as it was tedious. One of the resort guests stepped over the safety fence to take a better picture and fell down a cliff. Not a huge one, thank God, but he busted his head open, and I had to help go down and get him.

"The local rangers weren't available to help, so it took me almost an hour to get the equipment I needed, then get to him, and another hour to stabilize him enough to get him back up. The first half of it wasn't so bad because he was unconscious, but when he started to come to, he wasn't very coherent, but he was *very* combative. With some help from the resort staff, we finally got him stabilized enough, and secured enough, to get him into an air rescue chopper."

Without thinking, Matt rubbed his jaw, then worked it back and forth. "I flew in with him to make sure he didn't get worse, which he didn't. But he's going to need surgery. The good news is he should be OK. The bad news is I feel like I've been put through hell."

"He hit you?" Ellie asked, bending to look at his jaw.

She cupped his head in her hand and turned it gently. "You're already bruising."

"I've had worse," he said, leaning his head back in the chair, closing his eyes, drawing in a deep breath and wincing.

"Where else are you hurt, Matt?" she asked. "And do you want me to go get Lucas?"

Matt shook his head. "I talked to Betty a few minutes ago, and she said he's already asleep for the night. She doesn't have a problem letting him stay there and, to be honest, with the way I'm feeling I really don't think I'd be very good for him to be around tonight." He tried to resituate in the chair and winced again.

"Shirt off, Matt," Ellie said.

"Sorry, not in the mood for *that*," he said, attempting as much of a grin as his sore jaw would allow.

"No joking around here. Take your shirt off. I want to see what's going on."

It was nice having someone care for him for a change. Usually it was the other way around. In fact, in his entire life he couldn't remember a time when someone else had ever offered to take care of him in any way. And while this was only Ellie getting ready to plunge into nurse mode, he was touched. "Not sure I can lean forward enough to do that, and I don't want to stand up. I'll be fine, but I appreciate the concern."

"And in the morning? When you have to function again? What happens then?"

"I do it without trying to groan too loudly."

"Shirt off, cowboy," she said, her voice unusually soft as she leaned over to unbutton it.

Truth was, Matt didn't want to see the damage because he feared he might have a couple of cracked ribs. So he shut his eyes as she exposed his chest, then held his breath as she ran her fingers lightly over it, fighting back the urges that had overtaken him so quickly with her before.

She'd laughed that night when she'd seen what she had caused, and so fast, then had shifted her attention to far better areas while he'd lain there, helpless to do anything but enjoy. And watch her. Loving everything he'd seen. And it wasn't like he was a starving man sexually. There had been times overseas… But her touch—it had aroused him so quickly he'd almost been embarrassed by his lack of stamina.

Yes, he remembered it well. Had thought about it too many times since Reno, because no other woman had ever caused that kind of response in him. Like the shiver that was running up and down his back right now. And the memories of her beautiful body atop his, underneath his. But he was fighting all that. Or, at least, trying to. So why not simply let it happen again? What would happen if he did?

For starters, he wouldn't be able to walk away from it this time. Because now Ellie came with commitments. And even though her touch caused thoughts of the two of them together, he had no right to think that. Still, in Reno, that touch had also compelled him to see her a second night when he'd vowed not to—the night when she must have gotten pregnant as his condom had…slipped. He'd told her, of course, but she hadn't been worried because it hadn't been her fertile time of the month.

Yet her touch had caused a big consequence from something that was meant to be transient, simply because he'd been unable to resist her. Was that what would happen again if he gave in to what he was feeling? Another big consequence? "Damn, that hurts," he choked, as she probed a little harder.

"Well, without a way to get you X-rayed, I can't say

for sure, but I'm not feeling anything that would indicate your ribs are broken. In fact, the bruising is a little lower than your rib cage, so the concern would be more about internal bleeding."

Even though Ellie wasn't feeling anything seriously wrong, Matt was, and it had nothing to do with his present physical condition and everything to do with the *what ifs* and *why nots* running through his mind. "Comforting thought," he muttered, finally looking down at himself. "He kicked me."

"Apparently. And more than once. How'd you let that happen?" she asked, while probing his rock-hard abdomen to see if she could detect any internal bleeding.

"He wasn't conscious. Then he was, and he was disoriented."

"Well, I'm not feeling anything distended so I don't think you've got a bleed going on. Where's your medical bag?"

"On the chair by the door. But you don't need to—" Too late. She was already off to get it, and he sensed a complete physical coming up. "I'm really OK," he shouted after her.

"You're really not," she said, coming back over to him, his stethoscope already out of the bag. "So we either do this upstairs in your bed, if you're up to climbing the stairs, or in the *casita*, since it's on this level. Your choice."

"What if my choice is to sit here, drink the rest of the fruit juice, then take a nap?"

"You can, but I'm still going to examine you, and if I have to do it while you're in the chair…" She pointed to her lower back, then smiled. "Don't give another thought to the idea that it could cause me back pain."

Matt chuckled at Ellie's attempt to blackmail him. It was cute. "OK, you win. You can play doctor."

"How about I simply *be* a nurse?"

He sighed, then pushed himself to the edge of the chair, realizing he hurt more now that he had only a little while ago. Ellie extended a hand to help him up, and he was grateful for it, both physically and emotionally. "I've been on the battlefield for almost two years in total, and nothing that's ever happened there comes close to what happened here," he said as he stood. "I think I'm getting soft."

Ellie laughed as she put a steadying arm around his waist. "Just felt your abs. Trust me, you're not getting soft. At least, not since Reno. Now, how about we just skip the stairs and go to the *casita*?"

"Sounds like a plan," he said, trying not to put any weight on her. She was, after all, pregnant. But tough. He liked that. Hadn't seen it before in the women he'd known, but this was one tough lady.

As they walked down the hall, Matt wondered what it would be like to have Ellie there all the time. It couldn't happen, of course. Neither of their lives would allow it. But the dream was nice. Cozy little family. Coming home to Ellie of an evening, and the two of them talking, or the four of them picnicking up on the flats. Lazy Sunday mornings, sleeping late—until the kids woke them up with their own plans for the day. Family meals. Yes, a nice dream, but Ellie would soon be going one way and he'd be going another. So what was the point of thinking about something that would never happen? "You want my trousers off?" he asked as they entered the *casita*.

"Wouldn't hurt. And I know you're not modest." She patted her belly. "Proof's right here."

He chuckled. "Would it be too much to ask you to undress me?"

"I did that once. Look where it got us. So take off your own trousers, get yourself situated, and I'll be back in a minute to take off your boots and socks."

"Where are you going?" he asked, as he undid the button on his jeans.

"To fix an ice pack for your jaw."

Matt watched her walk away, enjoying the view. Pregnant, not pregnant, any way he looked at her Ellie was a beautiful woman. Stunning. And the baby bump she was still trying to conceal under baggy clothes made her even more beautiful. Glowing as only an expectant woman could. He hoped that somehow, as her belly swelled even more, he'd be able to see that because he wanted to watch the changes.

Or would those changes serve to remind him later on that this couldn't be his life? That melancholy thought swept over him so quickly it felt worse than the kicks he'd taken to the gut.

"Just hold this to your jaw, and it would help if you got your jeans all the way off. One button isn't quite enough."

"Boots and socks, too?" he asked, trying to force a grin, even though the heavy thoughts of the inevitable weren't letting go.

"Might be a nice picture for one of my social media accounts," she teased, as Matt, with Ellie's help, stripped down then stretched out on the bed.

"Well, whatever you do, just be gentle," he said, closing his eyes, and not because he didn't want to see her. It was because he was trying to block out thoughts and images popping into his head that didn't have a place there. Thoughts and images of a different life for him. One he'd never had. One he wasn't even sure he understood. And one that scared him worse than being under fire on the battlefield did.

* * *

Matt did have a beautiful body. It hadn't been the reason for her initial attraction in Reno, though. That would have been his smile—so warm, curving into a sensuousness Ellie couldn't take her eyes off. She'd missed that afterward. Missed waking up next to him like she had those two mornings, with that smile. Missed going to bed with him like those two evenings, with that sensual smile. Now, when he did smile, it was full of worry and she understood why, but was there a way, other than seducing him, to entice his other smile back?

Along with his smile, everything else about Matt, as a man, was perfect. She'd admired it all in Reno. Boldly, openly for him to hear, just to please him. Then he'd moved—so smooth, so self-assured. And his hands—so strong and gentle. And his patience—maybe that was what had surprised Ellie the most about him. He'd been so bold going to his room, then, suddenly, when second thoughts and shyness had overtaken her, he'd waited, hadn't rushed her, hadn't ridiculed her. For that, she had almost fallen in love with him.

Then days later, when she had been back home, back in her same old routine, her dreams had been of Matt, and now, seeing him again—Ellie sighed, trying to get hold of herself. Letting herself be seduced by the memories wasn't why she was here. Still, seeing him undressed and sprawled across the bed…the memories simply wouldn't quit, try as she may to put them out of her head. But Matt was the substance of the most powerful, potent memories she'd ever had because he was the only one who'd ever found his way into the place she'd never allowed anyone to enter.

"Well, first let me listen to your chest. Make sure nothing's rattling around in there." Ellie had her listen, was convinced he was good, then went on to his blood pressure, which was perfect, despite the circumstances. Looked in his eyes, she saw nothing there, at least no popped blood vessels even though there was some swelling around his eye now. All while trying to keep her breath steady, keep her goose-bumps at bay, keep her fingers from wandering to places they had no business being. Places she had wandered to before.

Focus, Ellie told herself as she returned to his ribs. They still worried her, since there was no way to have a look at them. Suppose one had cracked? It could cause a fluid build-up, eventually lead to a collapsed lung. And he didn't necessarily have to show symptoms for that to happen. "I'm going to listen to your chest again, then go back over your ribs. I'm afraid I might have—"

Matt held up his hand to stop her. "Is this why you left nursing? Because you second-guessed yourself?"

"There was always so much at risk."

"And you didn't have the confidence to believe you were good enough to take care of it?"

"I was good in the academic sense when I was a student, but once I was on the hospital floor it all seemed too important."

"And what you're doing now isn't important?"

"It is important, but in a different way. While I was a nurse, the decisions I made were…costly. People counted on them, and what I did affected lives. You know, life or death situations. What I do now… My decisions are important, but in a different way. I make decisions, but the outcome isn't as crucial because I have fact checkers and art editors who nit-pick everything we produce. In the hospital, there was no one to come behind me to make sure what I was doing was correct."

"Is that the way you were raised? Always in doubt of

your decisions? Always with someone looking over your shoulder, nit-picking?"

"Not from the nannies and tutors. But my mother never thought I was good enough—at least, not as good as her—and she questioned everything I did or said. Always for my own good, she'd tell me. She would also tell me she was preparing me to take over her company someday, which wasn't what I wanted."

"Hence you chose nursing."

"Yeah. Medicine had never crossed my mind, but I wanted to break away from her, do something totally different with my life. Only what I chose didn't give me the confidence I lacked." Ellie sat down on the edge of the bed next to him.

"There was a baby—blue baby, actually. Not breathing. The mother was bleeding out and the whole medical team was focused on saving her. But they handed me the baby, and it was up to me to resuscitate him. I tried, Matt. I really tried. But he never did breathe. So in the end the mother lived but her baby didn't, and the look on her face when she found out... I resigned the next day because I did my best and I couldn't..."

And now he knew her deepest fear.

"Fix the situation?" he asked, reaching out to take her hand. "It happens, Ellie. There are patients we can't save. It's not easy, and sometimes it's so downright gut-wrenching that all you want to do is crawl off somewhere and cry. I know. I've been there too many times. And, yes, I've been the one who has crawled off and cried. But then there are the ones we do save. The easy saves. The hard saves. The miracles. And so many that fall in between. While they never make up for the ones we lose, the ones we save are the reason we keep trying."

"Except I didn't. I gave up. I couldn't save him and

I..." She shook her head. "I couldn't go through that again."

"I know it's a harsh reality to face, and I'm sorry it happened. But you didn't give up. At least, not your compassion or your love of medicine. You simply took a different route, sort of like what I'm doing now. It all counts. The bottom line is, Ellie, not everyone is cut out for every job. You weren't cut out for obstetrics, but that doesn't mean you're not cut out to be a mother. A mother's love and a nurse's duty are two entirely different things. A mother's love will always win over everything else. Including her fears."

Not that he'd ever had a mother's love, but in his ideal world that's the way a mother should be. A perfect mother would be... Ellie. If only she could see that. And not just for the baby's sake but her own.

"Except when you fail."

"But you didn't fail, Ellie. You were presented with a situation that wouldn't have turned out any differently for anybody else. But somehow you've got the idea that you've got to be better than everybody else or you're not good enough. Which just isn't the case. I looked at some of what you do online, and you teach people, through your work, to be better doctors and nurses. You inform patients about prescriptions and health conditions. You bring understanding and caution to a very scary time in a person's life, and that's important. What you do is important, Ellie. Who you are is important, no matter what you've been brought up to believe. And as far as my ribs go, no second guesses. You were right the first time."

"Can I at least wrap them?" she said, as a stray tear slid down her cheek.

"You can wrap anything you like," he said. "Except

I don't have a stretch bandage here. So it'll have to wait until morning when I open up the office."

"Just this once, indulge me. Let me go get that. I'm fine to drive, and I do want to make sure…"

He chuckled. "Keys are in my jeans. And if you're not back in thirty minutes, I'm coming to get you."

"Want me to text you every five minutes just so you'll know I'm OK?" She would have if he'd asked, even though it seemed silly. But having someone to care for her—if only for a moment—was nice.

"Just when you get there, and when you're leaving."

Matt smiled at her, and for the first time since Reno it was the smile she'd loved at the start. A smile that made all her doubts seem insignificant.

Fifteen minutes later Ellie inserted the key in Matt's office door, went inside and turned on the light. He'd said the supplies were kept in the closet in his office so she texted him and headed straight there, determined to make this a quick trip, found what she was looking for, texted him again, then headed straight out.

On the way, though, she paused to smile at the fax machine—a very old one. Old technology—it figured. She wondered, if Matt stayed long enough, whether he would upgrade. Then she remembered several different computers, tables and such she'd put into storage in her own company after they'd upgraded. She'd intended to donate them somewhere but hadn't gotten around to it. Would Matt benefit from some of what she had? She'd ask him, because, seriously, a fax machine…

Except the fax had a sheet of paper on it. Someone had faxed him. Without thinking about it, Ellie pulled it out, intending to take it to him since it might be important, and his odds of even coming to the office tomorrow were slim. And, yes, she looked at it. Not to be nosy but simply because it was in her hand. What she saw was her name at the top, as the patient, followed by her lab results.

Ellie's first impression was that had been a mighty quick turnaround. Then curiosity got the best of her so she looked at the results. Nothing had changed much from her last lab work. Except what was printed in red, which was the lab's indicator that something was wrong. It was her relaxin number, and it was above two. Halfway to three, actually. Her hands started to shake. That was more than twice the norm. Which meant *she was in trouble.* As was her pregnancy, and her baby.

CHAPTER SEVEN

MATT WAS SLEEPING by the time Ellie got back with the bandage, and she debated disturbing him. But if, by some chance, he did have a broken rib or two, he needed to have them bandaged. So she stood in the doorway of the *casita* for a moment, watched him sleep, with the sheet pulled up to his waist now and his bare abs exposed.

And with the lab results in her pocket. She knew she should tell him right off, but now didn't seem the time to bother him with any of this. Tomorrow would be another day, and the results would keep.

"Matt," she said, crossing over to the bed, "I've got the bandage." But he didn't answer, he was sleeping so soundly. She tried again, this time giving him a little nudge on the shoulder. The ice pack had slipped off his jaw and melted into a puddle in the bed near his face. "I really need to get this thing on you."

He opened his eyes slowly, attempted to smile up at her but winced then rubbed his jaw. "I think the bed might be a little wet," he said, sliding over enough to avoid the damp area. "Meant to get up and change the ice but—"

"The only thing you need to do is co-operate with me. I can change the bed after I've got the bandage on, then you can go back to sleep." Changing the bed with the patient still in it—one of her old nursing skills coming back. When she'd left the profession she'd had regrets but she'd never looked back. And here she was now, being a nurse again. Oddly enough, she was enjoying it more than she'd thought she would. Or maybe it was because she was taking care of Matt. "Sit up, and help me get it in place. Keep it snug, but not snug enough to hurt or do any damage."

"You've got a good bedside manner," Matt said as he struggled to help her with the bandage. Once it was in place, she slid her fingers between the bandage and his skin to make sure it wasn't too tight, and heard him gasp.

"Pain?" Ellie asked.

"Not exactly." Suddenly he reached up, pulled her face to his and kissed her. Gingerly. Tenderly. And only for a moment before he backed away from it. "Now, *that* hurt," he said, rubbing his jaw.

"Why, Matt?" she asked, stepping back from him.

"Why does it hurt?"

"No. Why did you kiss me?"

"Spur of the moment. Impulse. Giving in to being a man with a beautiful, kissable woman fussing over his body."

They weren't the words Ellie wanted to hear. Although she didn't know what she did want to hear. Maybe that he cared for her or was falling for her a little bit would have been nice. She stopped at that because anything else would have been too much wishful thinking and sad.

"That's not who we are," she said, moving back to the bed to fasten the end of his bandage in place, yet taking care to stay as far away from him as possible. "It wasn't in Reno, and it's not now." Although the kiss had been wonderful. She remembered his kisses, remembered so many other things from those couple of days. The laughing, the talking, wrapped in the sheet dancing and a little bit drunk. So amazing. In fact, almost too amazing for the likes of two people who didn't want commitment.

"Who we are is who we want to be."

"Who we are, Matt, is a woman who will be returning to the corporate world shortly, and a man who'll be returning to the battlefield. How do you make something like that work?"

Matt reached out, took hold of her hand and pulled her over to him. "By not being so rigid that we can't enjoy the moment and accept it for what it is. *Again*. Two people who are crazy attracted to each other, who made a baby together because of that, who are simply looking for the right thing to do." He forced himself into an upright position. "It's not rocket science, Ellie. It's simply us trying to be connected to something more than we already have." He patted the bed beside him. "Do you want to be connected? And I don't mean sexually right now."

"I do," she whispered, sitting down with him, then snuggling into his arms when he pulled her there. "But I don't think I know how, because I've never really been connected to anybody before." Except her baby, and that connection was growing inside every day.

"One step at a time, Ellie. That's the best most of us can do. One step at a time." With that he pulled her down into the bed, where they lay, still snuggled together. Connected.

It had been a painful sleep, but nice, having Ellie there with him. Matt had managed to take off her shoes, but hadn't wanted to wake her up as she had been sleeping so soundly he'd known she must be exhausted, so he'd left her in her clothes, then spooned in next to her, even though it had hurt, and had listened to her gentle breathing awhile before he'd dropped off to sleep himself.

Now, if possible, he ached more than he had last night. But it was worth it, waking up while she was still asleep, still immersed in a world without worries.

Cautiously, Matt rolled over then sat on the side of the bed for a moment, trying to catch his breath, before he got up and attempted the shower. But as he rolled, so did she, pulling up the cotton shirt she wore and exposing her belly.

It was surprisingly more rounded than he'd expected, even though he'd felt it before through fabric as their baby had kicked. Round and beautiful. But now, seeing it this way, stark and naked, it was hard to imagine that his child would come from this belly. *His child.* Tears sprang to his eyes and he couldn't claim them to be hormonal the way she did. But he was touched. Truly touched and overwhelmed by something as simple as a belly bump. It happened to women every day, but this was different. Matt *was* connected, for the first time in his life.

Matt swiped back the tears and attempted to stand. But his movements woke Ellie up, and she opened her eyes and smiled at him. "I really didn't mean to sleep here," she said, to his back.

He sniffed. "Did you sleep well?"

"Better than I have since, well, I don't remember when. So, are you getting up?"

"Need a shower before I go to work."

"You're not up for a shower yet, Matt. And in your shape, you can't work."

He felt her struggle to a sitting position behind him, but still didn't turn around to look at her. His emotions were still too wobbly for that. "Life goes on, Ellie. Sore ribs or not. People depend on me and they don't particularly care that I have things going on in my life that might stop me from seeing them. When you need a doctor, you need a doctor."

"And there's no one else around you can call? A locum?"

"Easier said than done. Resources are stretched thin, and Doc Granger said that nobody likes coming out here. He'd have to make a request weeks in advance when he needed someone to cover for him. And if he needed someone in a hurry, he'd send his patient to the clinic in Whipple Creek, which is a little over a hundred miles from here. So no. There's no one to cover for me right now, and I do have patients lined up."

"Have you thought about bringing someone else in to help?"

"Technically, this isn't my practice. I'm running it, not buying it. So that decision would have to be made by Doc Granger." He gave himself a push off the bed, stopped midway to catch his breath, then finally stood. Then, and only then, did he turn around to face her, and notice her shirt was pulled back down, covering her completely. "Which means off to the shower."

"Can I help you?" she asked, starting to scoot to the edge of the bed.

Normally, he might have jumped at the chance. He could almost feel her crammed into the shower stall with him, pressed to him, the two of them separated only by a slippery film of soap. But that wasn't for today. Probably not for any day. So as quickly as he could, he started walking toward the bathroom. "Nope. No help needed. Except afterwards, when I'll need help getting back into this bandage."

"Then maybe I'll go make us some juice," she said. "And please, leave the bathroom door open so I can hear you in case you need something."

"Sure." It was a fast agreement, brought on by the

fact that he was aroused again and he didn't want her to know. But this was how he'd responded to her in Reno, and he supposed she already knew this was how he was responding to her here.

The shower was difficult. More bruises were showing on his body now, and the spray of the water hurt. Everything hurt. And, as Matt discovered, getting out, drying off and getting dressed wasn't going to be easy. He was simply too stiff, too sore to move easily. But he did manage to make it back to the bed, where he sat naked, staring at nothing for what seemed an interminable amount of time, hoping his strength would return.

"Matt, you OK?" Ellie called through the *casita* door.

He wanted to say yes. Wanted to prove he was more than he really was at the moment. But in truth he wasn't going to be able to wrap the bandage again, let alone get his jeans, socks and boots on. "Good," he called back. "Getting dressed. It might take me a little while. I'm slower than I expected to be this morning."

She entered the *casita* with two fruit juices in hand, set them down and walked over to him. "How long have you been sitting there—naked?"

He looked down and realized he hadn't even bothered to cover himself with a bed sheet or towel. "Maybe ten minutes."

"And you didn't call me to help you dress?"

"Maybe I didn't want to admit I was weaker than I thought." He yanked the corner of the bed sheet across his lap.

Ellie laughed. "Men," she said, on her way back to the *casita* door. "You stay where you are, and I'll get you some clean clothes, then I'll help you get dressed. Oh, and as for the rest of your day, I'll cancel your appointments because you, Dr. McClain, get to spend the day sitting down with your feet propped up."

Matt wanted to argue, but Ellie was right. He was moved by how she observed him and how she wanted to take care of him. And saddened at the same time as he knew this connection was only temporary. They had separate ways to go, and soon.

Ellie really hadn't intended to spend the night in his arms, but it had been nice. She'd woken a couple of times and heard him breathe. Steady, strong, like she remembered from Reno. She recalled that after their first night together she'd wondered what it would be like waking up with someone like Matt every morning. In her mind, they'd be lazy about it. Linger together in bed as long as they could. Then make love. Shower together. Hate parting to go to their separate jobs.

In reality, that wasn't going to happen, of course. But Matt in his condition and she in hers—it was still nice. And now, as she went over his appointment list, making the various calls to cancel his appointments, she still couldn't shake the mellow feeling that simply sleeping with him had caused. It almost nullified the anxiousness over the lab report.

"Everything under control?" Matt asked, as he entered his home office.

"Called everybody on your list. Talked directly to three of them, left messages for two. And that ranch appointment—I did cancel that and told him you'd get back to him when you were up to the ride. I also gave him the contact information for Whipple Creek in case he wanted to make that trip."

"Which makes me a man of leisure today," he said,

dropping down into the chair across from his desk. The one Lucas usually sat in. "But I do have to go get Lucas."

"Taken care of. I called Betty and she agreed to keep him this morning. I'll pick him up after lunch." She'd gotten herself busy to keep from confronting the obvious, but now was the time. She had to tell him. "Um, when I was at your clinic yesterday…" She handed him the sheet of paper with the lab results.

He studied it for a moment, then looked up at her. "Why didn't you show me this last night?"

"I was trying to come to terms with it. And you were so tired I didn't want you taking on any more than you already had to deal with. My level is over two, Matt." She sniffled. "That puts me at—"

"I know what it puts you at," he said, standing then walking around the desk and wrapping his arms around her shoulders. "It puts you at a higher than normal risk for miscarriage or premature birth because relaxin, in the later stages of pregnancy, prepares the body for childbirth. But if the body is tricked into believing the rising levels of the hormone means it's time, it's done its job and got the process started, whether the pregnancy has gone full term or not… That's the clinical aspect of it. But the personal aspect is we're going to deal with it, together."

"How," she asked him, glad for the way he held her, and stepped in to give her support like no one had ever given her before. Normally Ellie was alone in dealing with problems, but now, having someone there to help her through…

"First by getting in touch with a friend of mine who specializes in high-risk pregnancies. Unfortunately she's in California, so I think the odds of you going to see her are zero because you're not going to be able to travel that far until you've been checked. And I'm not qualified to do that. But Susie—Dr. Susan Caldwell—can get us started in the right direction."

"And in the meantime?"

"You rest. Normally, I'd prescribe a healthy diet, but you already have that. You'll probably need an ultrasound and several other tests. But no travel for now. And no work. Until we know more, I'd also like to keep you isolated as much as possible. You know, colds, flu, those sorts of things. And we'll have to find you a doctor and a hospital that's set up to do a special care delivery, if that's what it comes to."

Ellie leaned her head against his arm. "It sounds like you expect me to stay here for the duration of my pregnancy, but I can't do that, Matt."

"Why not?"

"Because it was never my intention to disrupt your life. I intended to come and go."

"Making sure you and our baby are healthy isn't a disruption, Ellie. And what happens if you go back to Reno? Is there someone there who could help you through this?

"No, but I could hire—"

"A nurse? Is that what you want? Someone paid to take care of you, or someone who truly cares taking care of you?

"But I don't want to be your burden. Especially now that there could be complications," she said, swiping at her tears with the back of her hand.

"You're having my baby, Ellie. Taking care of you is no burden. It's what I want to do—*need* to do."

"What about going back to the army? You can't stay on leave indefinitely."

"I have two months of leave saved, which I'm about to use up. There are other things I can do instead that won't affect my standing. One would be vacating my contract and serving the rest of my time as a reserve officer. Then, when that duty is over, re-enlist. As long as it's for a justified family cause, there's no reason they won't let me back in when the time comes."

"You'd do that for me?" Knowing someone would make that kind of sacrifice for her caused her tears to flow even harder. "Put aside everything you want to take care of me?"

"Of course I would. Unless you push me away, I want to stay with you through your pregnancy."

But not after. While Ellie hadn't expected Matt to make that kind of commitment, part of her had hoped for it. The pregnant part probably. So once the baby was born and the hormones were doing what they should, would she still have these feelings and longings for Matt in a way she should never have? Or would they disappear, the way he would?

Ellie hadn't meant to break down the way she had. What she'd hoped was that she'd be emotionless when telling him, and he'd be emotionless when they had a clear-headed talk about what to do. Well, the best-laid plans on that one. She'd been emotional and he'd been supportive, which made her feel even more emotional. And now she was a wreck. A total wreck.

"What did she say?" Ellie asked anxiously, as Matt returned to the *casita* a few minutes later—the longest minutes of her life.

"Well, first, you're in good health, and that goes a long way in your favor. But because you're already at risk for pre-gestational diabetes, this could help it along, so with that we've got to be very careful. And you do need to be under the care of a high-risk specialist. There's no way around that. She's suggested two different ones, but the problem is one is about four hours north of here, and the other is about four hours to the south. It would be a long, rough drive either way, but she doesn't suggest road travel until you've been checked. Which means…"

Ellie shook her head. "Which means I'm in trouble."

"Which means a helicopter. The one that hand-delivered your sample to the lab. Cruz Montoya, the owner, will charter the chopper to take you to whichever place you choose."

"You've talked to him?"

He nodded. "He's a former army medic. Good man. He said he can make the flight tomorrow, and Susie called to check availability for me. The problem is, the doctor down south in Arizona can't see you at all this week. He's not in his office. But the one up north will squeeze you in immediately because she's a friend of Susie's. They went to med school together. Cruz said it's a forty-five-minute trip by air, and Susie thinks that will be safe, especially since I'll be there with you."

"You've been busy," she said.

"Because I'm highly motivated."

"But you're in no condition to fly," Ellie stated flatly.

"And you're in no condition for me not to fly. *You can't go alone*. Besides, this will be a good chance for me to get my ribs X-rayed, just in case."

Matt's voice was so emphatic it was almost cold. But Ellie knew he was worried. It showed on his face. "In case of what? Me knowing you need those X-rays so I won't back out of this exam? And what about Lucas?"

He chuckled. "You do have a devious mind, don't you, with your ulterior motive?"

"My mother always had ulterior motives. It comes naturally."

"But you're not your mother, for starters, and you're

not the kind of person who would automatically be suspicious."

"You're sure of that?"

"As sure as any man can be who sends a drink to the woman on the other side of the bar in Reno and ends up with her here in Forgeburn."

"OK, so maybe I'm stretching a little bit. But having more tests scares me, even though I know I need them."

"And I'll be right there with you, Ellie. Please, don't doubt that. Whatever happens, I'm with you these next few months, and that's a promise. And as for Lucas—I'm going to spend the rest of the day with him, and Betty will watch him tomorrow. In the meantime, Susie said it's OK for you to go about limited activities. If you feel tired, you rest. You can ride in the truck but no ranch roads. And easy walking is fine, as long as you don't do too much of it."

"Aren't we a pair?" she said, the discouragement so thick in her voice she couldn't disguise it. "Look, Matt, I appreciate this. And I'm sorry I brought it to your doorstep. If I'd known..."

"Would you have *not* told me about the baby?" he asked, sitting down on the bed next to her.

"It never crossed my mind not to. I'm a lot of things, and I know my ambition can get in the way of what most people would consider normal, but to not tell you, to simply come up with my own solution and carry it out..." She shook her head. "That's not me. My mother maybe. My grandmother definitely. But not me."

He slipped his hand into hers. "They're tough women, but not as tough as you."

"They *are* tough, but I don't want to be like that because neither of them particularly like men. I do...obviously. And both my grandmother and mother taught me that a strong woman doesn't need a man to complete them. Whatever a woman wants, she can do on her own."

"It's true. She can. If that's what she wants."

"I know it's true, but…" She shut her eyes. "But having a man in your life doesn't have to make you weak or needy. If he's the right man."

"Which was why you came to me. You were hoping I would be the right man to raise the baby the way a baby should be raised."

"I'm the genetic by-product of my mother and grandmother. Both cold-hearted women who didn't want children. Of course, that's what I was hoping for when I came here, hoping you'd raise our baby, and also to prove to myself that I'm not cold-hearted like they are." She ran her hand over her belly then smiled. "She's kicking."

"Or he," Matt said, as Ellie placed his hand on her belly. "Another nice strong one."

"I don't want to lose this baby, Matt. It wasn't my intention to have one, but I don't want to miscarry. This baby should have the best of everything, and while I'm not the one to give it to her, I do want her to have it."

"Which is what we're going to do."

Ellie hoped so, because the tougher this pregnancy got, the more she didn't want to go through it alone. And the only person she wanted with her was Matt. Even though his words were simple, they were encouraging. Made her feel better. Gave her the hope that everything would be fine, and she really needed that support because right now Ellie wasn't that strong woman she was pretending to be. She was merely a very scared woman, desperately trying to hang on.

"Look, since I'm allowed to ride along, why don't we go get Lucas and take him down to that little roadside café for breakfast—if Betty hasn't already fed him?"

"She hasn't. I called her after I called Susie, and Lucas was still sleeping."

"Then I'd suggest you put on some shoes…"

"Will you help me?" he asked, grinning.

"Men are so helpless," she said, grabbing a clean pair of socks, then picking up his boots.

"Is that your mother speaking?" he asked, returning her grin.

"Nope, that's me trying hard *not* to sound like my mother." She got the socks and boots on him in a matter of seconds, then headed for the *casita* door. "She's not my role model, Matt. Maybe for a while, when I was young, she was. But she's a pathetically unhappy woman, and I don't want to end up that way. I've worked very hard for many years, trying not to be my mother's daughter. And don't get me wrong. I love her like a daughter should. But she's not my friend, the way a mother should be. I talk to her occasionally, keep her updated on my life, but we live only twenty-five miles apart and we only see each other maybe twice a year. Her choice."

"And you're good with that?"

"I have to be. It's all I've ever known. So, how about we get going, although I'm not sure which one of us is more fit to drive."

"I'm fit," Matt said, following her through the house at a very slow pace.

"Yeah, right," Ellie said, holding the door open for him. "If you're even able to get yourself up into your truck."

He upped his speed, caught up to her, and slid his arm around her waist. "I'm able to do this, too," he said, as he pulled her close, then lowered his lips to hers. Ellie felt again the rush of excitement, not even thinking that she should pull away. More of this was what she wanted; what she'd wanted since Reno. That surging tide of warmth that rushed over her. The tingle that spread from her head down to her toes. And Matt's face. His beautiful face. Even though her eyes were closed, she could see it, every nuance. And wanted more. So she reached up and stroked his cheek, pulling him out of that moment, but just briefly, as he looked down at her and smiled.

"This is probably the worst thing we could be doing," he said, his voice so hushed she could barely hear him.

He was right, of course. But she didn't care. And as she twined her hand around his neck, pulling him back to her, he tilted her head up and kissed her, softly again but progressing to a shade of passion that made her cling to him like he was the only solid thing in her life. His unrelenting lips parted hers, causing her to press herself even harder to him—her, their baby, him all pressed together. And his demanding lips parted, drawing from her wild sensations she'd known only once before—with him.

It couldn't last, though. Not another second lest she be pulled even deeper into her confusion. So she backed away, the feel of him still on her lips. "What are we doing?" she asked, her voice nearly too breathless to carry her words.

"Damned if I know," he replied. His face was flushed and he was clearly aroused. "Probably something we shouldn't."

But how could something they shouldn't be doing feel so perfectly right? "I think we'd better get Lucas before we…" What? Made another mistake? Because nothing about this felt like a mistake. "…before Betty feeds him."

"Do you know how long I've wanted to do that?" he asked, not making a move to leave the house.

Ellie shook her head.

"Since the last time we did it in Reno."

"But we can't go back to Reno," she said, almost sadly. "That was another life. Two other people."

"Are you sure?" he asked, as he took her hand and led her to the truck.

No, she wasn't. And that was the problem, because the more she was around him, the less sure she was becoming about everything.

CHAPTER EIGHT

LUCAS WAS RAMBUNCTIOUS in the truck, kicking and trying to get out of his infant seat. It was like he'd been given an extra portion of energy in that single pancake he'd eaten for breakfast, and nothing Matt said or did on the drive back to the house would stop him.

It got to the point that Matt was forced to pull over and get out, then go back to the crew cab to see if anything was wrong. But there wasn't. This was simply Lucas in a good mood, laughing, playing and having fun.

"You don't suppose he understands what a pony ride is, do you?" he asked Ellie, while he pulled Lucas from the seat, rearranged him, then secured him back in. "I mean, he was right there when Betty mentioned taking him to her brother's ranch for a pony ride."

"I have no idea what someone his age understands. I have no experience with children. In fact, Lucas is the closest I've ever come to having any kind of relationship with a child, so I'm the wrong person to ask. But I will say he seems awfully bright. Maybe Betty explained what riding a pony was all about and now he's just excited to do it."

"Is that it?" Matt asked the child. Of course, Lucas didn't answer, but Matt did notice that his eyes were shining brighter than they had before. "Are you anxious for your pony ride?"

Lucas's response was to try wiggling out of his car seat again. "Well, as soon as we take Ellie back to the house, we'll see what we can do to get you on that pony." He shut the crew cab door, climbed back in the driver's seat and exhaled a deep breath. "I'm exhausted," he said, leaning his head back against the head rest. "I didn't know so little movement could produce so much fatigue."

"But you're going to go off and be daddy. That's a good thing, Matt. Lucas needs that in his life. Someone who puts him first."

"Well, today's not going to be a very good *daddy* day."

Ellie reached over and rubbed his shoulder. "If you're with him, that's a good daddy day. That's what he depends on now."

"Says the woman who knows nothing about children."

"Says the woman who didn't have a daddy or, in essence, a mommy."

Matt looked over at her sympathetically, saw the pain flash across her eyes. Understood it. Felt it just as deeply as she did. In so many ways they were alike, and while it was always said that a person did better with an opposite, it was nice to sit here with someone who could empathize totally with Lucas and him. In ways it was like they were a family—all three of them abandoned as children, no one who had ever truly cared.

When he'd been young, Matt had wanted a family. Sometimes he'd walk up and down the streets, stop at a particularly cozy-looking house and just stand outside, wandering what it would feel like, going inside and simply being part of that family there. But in the end, he'd always returned to wherever they were staying at the moment, always knowing what to expect. *Nothing*. That's all there ever had been. It was hard growing up that way, or even the way Ellie had because nothing was nothing, no matter how rich or poor it was.

But that wasn't going to be Lucas. No matter what he had to do, Lucas was going to be the lucky one. Still, the three of them—actually, the four of them as a family—made him long for something he'd wanted all his life but hadn't had.

"Well, guess we'd better get you back to the house and get Lucas to his pony," he said, pulling back onto the road.

"If I can find a place to sit and watch, I think I'd like to go with you two," she said.

Eyes forward and hands on the steering wheel, Matt smiled. Another moment of delusion? Yes, he could handle it. Because spending time with Ellie was becoming a habit—a very nice habit. One he could get used to.

It was lovely sitting in a chair, under a tree, watching Bert Connors lead the pony around the corral while Matt held on to Lucas for dear life, even though the boy was so secured onto the pony's saddle a tornado couldn't have blown him off it.

Matt was in agony, though. It showed in his every movement. But he wasn't going to let that hamper Lucas's fun, and that was another thing she loved about him: the way he put Lucas—and even her—first. She desperately wanted Matt to raise their baby and now she couldn't even imagine anybody else doing it. Didn't want anybody else doing it. But she didn't have the heart to disturb his life any more than she already had, so that was a wish she'd have to put away.

But another plan was forming. One that was trying to poke through as hard as she was trying to push it back.

Trying to ignore it. Trying to see herself in the future, doing exactly what she'd done before Reno. Except that image was beginning to blur.

"Care for a lemonade?" Francine Connors, Bert's wife, asked, holding out a glass for Ellie. "Just made it."

"I would love some," she said, bending forward slightly to take at. As she bent, though, she was hit with such a stabbing back pain that she gasped.

"You OK?" Francine asked.

Ellie leaned back in the chair, hoping the pain would go away, but it didn't. In fact, it got so bad that she doubled over and fell out of the chair to the ground. "Get Matt," she panted, scared to move, scared to breathe. This couldn't be happening. She had known it was a possibility but had never really considered that it would happen to her. Losing the baby... Tears slid down her face into the dirt, leaving small mud splotches.

"Ellie," Matt cried, dropping to his knees beside her. He took her pulse, turned her head to look at her face.

"Don't let it happen," she begged him, choking on her sobs. "Please, don't let this happen."

"We can take her inside, Doc," Francine offered. "To one of the beds."

"I don't want to move her just yet. Could you run to my truck and get my medical bag? It's in the back, in the crew cab." He glanced over at Bert, who'd taken full charge of Lucas, then pulled Ellie into his arms. "We've got to get you into a hospital," he said, taking the medical bag from Francine and immediately pulling out his stethoscope. He listened to her heart, then tried to listen for the baby's heartbeat, but since he didn't have the right equipment for that, all he could hear were normal stomach sounds.

"Francine, do you know Cruz Montoya?"

"Sure. Everybody knows him."

"Would you call him and tell him I have an emergency, that I need to get a patient to a hospital as quickly as possible. Ask him if he can fly us." He glanced down at Ellie's face again. Her eyes were shut but she was still crying softly. "Tell him stat. He'll understand." He handed Francine his phone.

While Francine made the call, Matt took Ellie's blood pressure. "How high is it?" she asked.

"Not that bad. Just the high end of normal, and that could be from stress as much as anything else. How bad are the pains?"

"Stabbing at first."

"And now?"

"Not as bad."

"Were they different from the pain you've had before?" he asked.

"I don't know," she said, glad he was there, glad for his touch, even though he was only examining her. "Why?"

"There can be a lot of different kinds of pain associated with a pregnancy. I'm just trying to figure out what's going on with you."

"You mean, it might not be..."

"I don't know, Ellie," he said, bending to kiss her on the forehead then pulling her even closer to him. "I just don't know."

"Cruz is on his way," Francine said. "He's going to land in the back pasture so she'll have to be carried out there. But he says he has a stretcher, so not to worry."

Matt nodded. "It might be a little rough," he told Ellie, "but I'll be with you and I'll take care of you." He looked up at Francine. "Lucas..."

"Don't worry about him. I've got six grandkids. I'm used to having little ones around."

"I appreciate that," Matt said. "I lived here when I was a kid, and I don't remember the people being so...decent."

"I remember you when you were a kid," Francine said. "Didn't know you, but everybody in these parts knew how bad you had it. Felt sorry for you. I'm glad you made something of yourself."

He nodded, as the sound of a helicopter drew his attention. "Ellie, I don't want you moving, if you don't have to. Cruz and I will do all the work and the only thing you have to do is relax."

"Relax?" she asked, trying to smile. "Doctors and their unrealistic expectations." Then she shut her eyes. The pain was subsiding, but her anxiety was not. She was more scared now than she'd ever been in her life. But Matt was there, and she trusted him to get her through this. She counted on him. Needed him like she'd never needed anybody, ever.

Cruz Montoya came running with an old army stretcher in his grip. Tall, handsome, dark, with black hair, he immediately dropped to his knees next to Matt and took Ellie's pulse like it was instinctual. It was. He'd been an army medic, a fact Matt was grateful for.

"She's got a hormonal imbalance that puts her at risk for miscarriage," he explained to Cruz. "That's why I'd asked for the lift to the hospital tomorrow. But back pains are one of the symptoms that indicates something could be going wrong, and she's going through that right now. I don't want her trying to move herself."

"Easy enough," Cruz said, laying the old canvas stretcher out. "You tell me how you want us to move her and we'll get it done." He looked down at Ellie and smiled. "I'm Cruz, by the way. Tour guide to paradise and occasional air ambulance."

Matt liked him. He seemed confident, and competent.

He'd only met him once before, when he'd handed over Ellie's sample, but that had been enough to know that Cruz was probably good at everything he did. At least, Matt hoped he was, because today he was going to be the one to get Ellie to the hospital.

"Let's roll her to her side, get part of the stretcher under her, then we'll lift her across it."

"Sure thing," he said, saluting Matt. "Did it just like that more times than I'd care to remember."

"You served in combat?" Ellie asked, as Matt gently rolled her to her side.

"Yep. Dispatched to Afghanistan the first time, then had a short stint close to Baghdad."

"Surprised we didn't run into each other," Matt said, as he settled Ellie down into transport position. "I was in Ramadi for a while, and had my turn in Afghanistan as well."

"I was evacuating injured de-miners—taking them to Bagram to get shipped out to a proper hospital."

Matt felt a connection to Cruz. They'd shared the same war, seen the same casualties. And both had ended up in Forgeburn. "Well, I think the evacuation we need to get on with now is Ellie."

"Which means you take her feet, I'll take her head." He smiled at Matt. "A superstition handed down to me from my dad. He did air rescue in Desert Storm. Said every time he was the one who took the head, everything turned out fine. No reason for me to break tradition."

"Hope you're right," Matt said, as they headed toward the helicopter. He hoped to God Cruz was right.

As they passed the corral, Matt waved to Lucas, who was now at the fence, watching what was going on. Bert was standing right behind him. "I'll be back in a little while," he said to the boy.

And Lucas waved back at Matt. "Bye, Daddy," he said.

"Matt," Ellie whispered.

"I know," he said, choking back tears. Damn it all. His baby was in jeopardy, so was Ellie. And Lucas was calling him Daddy. What was he going to do? What the *hell* was he going to do?

Dr. Anita Gupta smiled as she entered the exam room. "The good news is you don't have to stay. Nothing indicates you're having a miscarriage, and I'm actually leaning toward the diagnosis of severe muscle spasms. At least, for now. The bad news is, like Susie Caldwell said, you're going to have to see a maternal-fetal medicine specialist such as myself, or someone else of your choosing, every three weeks for the rest of your pregnancy, or even more if you start showing other signs of risk. Also, you must rest. I know you've heard that before, but the less you do, the better off both you and your baby will be."

"But everything's normal with the baby?" Matt asked. He was standing behind Ellie, who was still sitting on the exam table in her hospital gown, his hand on her shoulder for support. Both his own as well as hers. This wasn't the side of medicine he liked being on.

"While we didn't run a lot of specific tests, because they weren't indicated, what we saw leads us to believe everything is good. And I do know the gender of your baby, if you're interested."

Ellie twisted to look at Matt. "What do you think?"

"Sure," he said, trying to sound detached when he was anything but. Even though he'd been too nervous to check the gender when he'd looked at Ellie's ultrasound, now knowing that he could find out made the baby more of a reality than he'd expected. This was *his* baby and the idea that it would become somebody else's baby was hitting him hard.

Dr. Gupta looked to Ellie for her approval, and when she nodded, Gupta smiled even more broadly. "It's a boy."

Matt's eyes widened. "I have a son?" he asked.

"You do, Dr. McClain. Normal size, nothing to indicate problems with fetal development from what we could see. And I did have the radiologist look at it as well."

It stunned Matt, thinking in terms of his baby now having an identity. But he noticed Ellie wasn't reacting. There was no expression on her face. In fact, the look there was as cold as he'd ever seen on her. She was shutting this out. All of it. Trying not to make it personal. "Ten fingers, ten toes?" he asked, realizing he needed to be sensitive to Ellie's feelings but at the same time eager for the details for himself.

"Something like that," Dr. Gupta said. Then she addressed her next comments to Ellie. "With your back going bad, plus the stress of the trip getting you here, and I'm sure the worry over miscarrying, I want you to stick to light activity once you get back to Dr. McClain's house.

"You can drive short distances, take easy walks, go about normal chores if they don't make you too tired or cause your back to ache. There's always a fine line between allowing someone with a high-risk pregnancy to continue with daily life on a restricted basis, and sending them to bed for the duration. You're not near that line yet, and I want to keep it that way. So, please, use common sense. Like no lifting anything over five pounds, avoid using stairs as much as you can, no running.

"Oh, and no trips longer than what it takes to get you here to the hospital—by helicopter. Not driving. I don't want you on the road that long."

"What about working?" she asked.

"I hear you're a workaholic. That's got to stop. I'm going to limit you to four hours a day if you do it from home. Or Dr. McClain's home, if that's where you decide to stay. If you do go back to Reno, I'll set you up with a doctor there, but he'll probably restrict you to the same and tell you not to work from your office. I want you to have a safe, easy pregnancy, Ellie, and I want to see that son of yours born a happy, thriving baby."

Well, at least Gupta was giving Ellie some options, which was more than Matt had expected. Of course, those were daddy expectations. Not doctor expectations. Right now he wasn't sure what Ellie was feeling, but she'd be grateful that she wasn't being put on total bed rest once she got through the fright of fearing she was losing the baby. He was sure of that as she was the most determined, resilient person he'd ever met. "So we're good to go back to Forgeburn?" he asked, already texting Cruz to return.

"I don't see why not, unless Ellie doesn't feel ready. We could let her stay overnight and get rested."

"I'm fine," she said. "And I'd rather do my resting in Matt's *casita*."

Dr. Gupta held her hand out to Ellie. "It's been a pleasure meeting you, Ellie. I'll be happy to see you as your regular specialist, if that's what you choose. Or I'll make a referral to a colleague in Reno. He's very good. Either way, let me know."

"I appreciate that," Ellie said, the smile she returned to Dr. Gupta looking like it was forced.

"And you, Dr. McClain," Dr. Gupta said, extending a hand to him. "I admire the kind of practice you're attempting to run out there. It can't be easy, and I certainly wouldn't want to do what you're doing. So good luck with that. And in the future, if you run into another high-risk pregnancy, I'd certainly be glad to take the case. Or if there's any other kind of specialist you need, for *anything*, please call me. We're set up here for almost anything, and I'll be happy to connect you to the right person."

"Thank you," Matt said, deciding not to tell her his time in Forgeburn was limited. What difference would that make? Besides, saying that he was leaving was getting more and more complicated.

"I'll send the nurse in to help you dress, Ellie, then you can check out. Call me any time if you have questions or concerns."

Ellie nodded, but didn't reply. Instead, she slipped off the exam table, stepped behind the screened dressing area without waiting for the nurse, and reappeared only moments later, dressed. As she passed by Matt on her way to the door, she didn't look at him, didn't say a word. It was like they were total strangers.

"I'm sure Lucas will be glad to see us," he said, attempting to engage her in a conversation that wasn't about her pregnancy." But she didn't engage. She merely nodded and kept on walking. He followed, not sure whether to bring up the rear or step to her side.

He opted to step to her side, and he also opted to take hold of her arm, totally expecting her to shrug him off. But she didn't. She simply let him hold on through the check-out process, then to the cab outside that would take them to the airfield. "Are you OK?" he finally asked, once they were both inside, and the miles were ticking off on the meter.

"I don't know what I am," she replied. "Today's been... rough, and I feel so isolated."

"Because of Forgeburn?" he asked.

"No. Because of me. It's like I'm walking through this in a daze. Nothing is the way it should be and there's no simple solution to fixing it. Especially now that I know

I'm carrying a boy. Hearing Dr. Gupta say that makes everything too…real." Ellie sighed, and leaned her head against Matt's shoulder. "And I'm proving to myself that I'm not as strong as I've always thought I was. Maybe that's the hardest part of all."

Matt pulled her closer to him, enjoying the feel of her. "I'd gone out with the medics one day. The hospital wasn't under fire, but where I was headed was straight into the middle of it. I have this buddy, Carter Holmes. Great surgeon. A man I always counted on to have my back. He wasn't supposed to go out with me, but at the last minute he jumped on the truck, said he didn't want me out there alone.

"We were on this bad road that had already had the hell bombed out of it and Carter got motion sick, told the driver to pull over, so he could get out and, well, you can imagine what he did. Anyway, he got off the truck and I decided to go with him just to make sure he was OK. While we were out there, the truck got hit and everybody inside was killed. There was nothing we could do for any of them, it happened so fast."

He paused for a moment, took a deep breath, then continued. "Then we get shot at. I mean, we're doctors, not soldiers, and here we were in the middle of gunfire. So we looked for a place to hunker down. Found it under some rocks. Crawled in and held on.

"We were there for nearly thirty-six hours. There was fighting and gunfire all around us for two days and here we were, stuck under some rocks, no medical supplies, totally useless because we couldn't get out safely. It was a nightmare, knowing people out there might need us and we couldn't help. Listening to all that gunfire…

"For me, other than knowing I should be out there helping, it wasn't a big deal because I used to run away and hide from my dad all the time. Some of my hiding places were pretty bad. But Carter couldn't handle it. Like me, he was worried about the soldiers out there who might need a medic. It bothered both of us, but he started developing tics. Couldn't keep still. Wringing his hands. Nothing serious. Then he started mumbling and ranting, which eventually turned to screaming.

"I couldn't sedate him since I didn't have anything with me. Couldn't do anything except talk to him, and that didn't work out so well because he got to the point where he was past the ability to comprehend.

"Anyway, at the end of the first day he just got up and ran out in the open, right into the gunfire. Took a bad hit to his back, which nicked his right kidney. He was lying out there, screaming. I went after him, dragged him back to the rocks, hoping that we hadn't been spotted. But my buddy was literally dying in my arms, and there was nothing I could do except talk. Which was what I did until we were evacuated, because I was scared that if I quit talking, he'd die.

"And I felt so isolated. Nothing was right. Nothing was happening the way it should have. We had been going out for what was little more than some routine medical care, then to have all that happen... So I know where you are, Ellie, because I've been there. I was in that daze—in a situation there was no way for me to fix. And I was used to fixing things, the way you are.

"But you're wounded right now. Not like Carter was but in a sense it's the same. And the only thing I can do to help you is talk to you and take care of you the only way I know how. And listen, if you want to talk. Neither of us is in an easy place and, to be honest, all we have is each other. So don't shut me out. I'm going to get you through this the way I got Carter through it."

"He survived?" she asked.

Matt swiped at the tears that had run down his cheeks. He'd been scared in that cave, but not nearly as scared as he was now. Because this baby—it had to live. It was his child. A child he loved the way he'd never been loved. And it was Ellie, too.

"He did, but he struggles. The thing is, we all do, and we all need someone there to help us through it. Carter has a fiancée who's strong and loves him unconditionally. You and I, well, that's what it is. The two of us."

"Is this about me, Matt?" she asked. "Or only about the baby?"

"Both. But you shouldn't be alone. You need to be here, Ellie. Where I can take care of you. You need the support as much as I need to support you."

Still, he couldn't tell her that he loved her, that he might have even fallen a little in love with her in Reno, because the solution to that love wasn't easy, and it would put more stress on her than she already had. This wasn't about their jobs anymore. It was about them. With Ellie and the baby at risk, all he could think to do was support her and keep everything else away from her. Then later, after the baby was here, who knew what would happen? He sure as hell didn't.

But right now she wasn't making herself available. Even with her head on his shoulder, she was rigid. Reserved. Distant. Sighing, Matt leaned his head back against the seat, closed his eyes, then said, "I want you to stay, but the choice is up to you. If you go to Reno, so will I."

Those were the last words spoken until they reached the landing field. Then Ellie finally spoke. "I do want to stay. I think I did even before I got here."

But that still didn't solve the problem, because staying for a few months was one thing and what to do about their son was another.

* * *

Ellie was relieved, exhausted and now worried. She'd taken a big step, and it wasn't because she couldn't manage her pregnancy, even with its complication, back home. She simply didn't want to. Didn't want to be the one who didn't need anybody to lean on. She did need someone.

And that someone was Matt. He made her feel secure, made her believe that, with his help, everything would turn out all right. She'd never had that before and it was nice having someone else to go through this with her. Someone who could be strong when she wasn't. Or caring when she needed it. And she did need it, especially now that she understood what it was.

Because she loved him? Ellie was pretty sure she did. It hadn't taken long to fall, but she had. And, of course, it was an almost impossible situation. She had some time to figure it out, though, now that she was going to stay. Would that time do her any good? She didn't know. In fact, she didn't know his true feelings for her. Matt showed affection, said the right words, did the right things, but was that more out of his sense of duty, or was it genuine? Because if it was genuine…

"What about going back to active duty?" she asked him a few minutes later as she lowered herself onto the bed in the *casita*. "Have you worked that out?"

"That's not for you to worry about. I'm in good standing with the army, so I'm not going to have any problems making some changes."

"But I don't want to be the one to hold you back from your career." She lifted her feet onto the bed and dropped back into the pillows.

"You're not," Matt said, as he sat down on the edge of the bed next to her, then took her hand in his and stroked it gently. "And the only thing you have to worry about is taking care of yourself."

"But I worry about you, too, Matt. I put you on a detour you didn't expect. When the army told me you'd gone home, I thought… If I'd known you were still active in the military, I would have handled everything differently, without asking you to raise the baby. Being practical, the way I usually have been until now, I would have seen that you couldn't."

"Our son, Ellie. The baby is *our son*."

She was aware of that, but saying it out loud nearly broke her heart because the moment she'd heard it was a boy, she'd given him a name. Matthew. After his father. And she'd pictured little Matthew growing up with Lucas as brothers. The four of them together, as a family. "I know we need to talk about that, but I'm so tired. Maybe tomorrow?"

"Works for me, since I've got to get Lucas. I need some time with him. Especially since…" He swallowed hard.

"Since he called you Daddy?"

Matt shook his head. "Don't know what to do about that."

"Maybe you don't do anything and let it work itself out on its own." And again the image of a family of four popped into her mind.

"Well, however it works out, Lucas needs to be home. So…" He leaned over and brushed a light kiss to her forehead. But she snaked her arm around his neck and pulled him to her mouth.

She wanted that kiss. It wasn't right. It wouldn't lead to anything. But it was the only thing on her mind and she was, if nothing else, a decisive person. This was what she wanted. The kiss. To see his reaction. To go to sleep with Matt on her mind, and not all her worries.

But he pulled away before they'd really started. "That part of us is easy," he said. "Too easy. Which is why we shouldn't..." He shook his head and backed away. "Look, I'll be back in a while. Is there anything you need before I go?"

There was. But unlike the easy part of them, it was hard. Too hard.

"It should be a short day," Matt told Ellie the next morning as he came down for breakfast. She was already sitting at the kitchen table, helping Lucas eat his breakfast. Or more like playing with him as he did. "No one on a ranch, and only a handful of scheduled appointments. If any tourists come in, or I get an emergency call, that could delay me, but as it is right now I should be home shortly after lunchtime."

It was difficult facing her, after rejecting her last night. But he'd done what he'd had to do because both of them were playing volleyball with their emotions, and it wasn't getting them anywhere. He was especially worried about Ellie. She didn't need that kind of tension, which meant he was the one who would have to make sure things were slow and easy with them. For her good and, in a way, his own good as well.

"And you're taking Lucas with you?"

Matt chuckled, and patted Lucas on the head. "Us men need some bonding time. And Betty went to see her sister, so..."

"I could watch him."

"Or you could rest. Besides, he's too heavy for you to pick up, so for now this hombre is with me."

"You're probably right but, still, if you get in a bind, we could work something out."

"I appreciate that," he said. "But it's going to be tough

enough on him when he leaves, being bonded to me. I don't want him to have to go through the same thing with you as well." Even as he said the words, Matt hated them. But Ellie offered no stability on which to pin any hopes, dreams or expectations. And he couldn't allow that to enter Lucas's life. So, for now, he had to take care that he would be the only one to break the little boy's heart. Which broke his own heart.

"Anyway…" He scooped Lucas into his arms and headed for the front door, glad the pain from his injury had substantially subsided. "If you're up to it when we get through, I'll take you to lunch at the new resort a few miles from here. I want to get acquainted with the manager since I'll be on call for them. If you want to go."

"I might," she said, her voice unusually emotionless. "Call me before you make the drive back, so you won't make a wasted trip if I'm not up to it."

He didn't want to leave it like that, but he had to. Right now, he had everybody's best interests to juggle, and the most he could do was just separate them and see what happened. And pray something better *would* happen.

Opening her laptop and fighting back tears at the same time, Ellie wanted to attribute the tears to hormones, but she couldn't. Matt had hurt her, not letting her watch Lucas. She understood why, but that didn't make her pain any less. And that after his rejection the night before, which she also understood. Another thing she understood was that because of both rejections he was, most likely, planning on getting out from under all of it. Of course, that's what he'd said from the beginning.

Still, as her feelings about their baby had been changing, Ellie had hoped his were changing as well. But they weren't. She'd been hopeful, though. Not fully confident but hopeful. Yet here she was, stuck with new feelings and a different vision than she'd ever planned for herself. She wanted to keep her baby—a thought that had been running in and out of her mind since she'd learned she was pregnant, but wasn't brave enough to admit.

She wanted to raise him, see him grow up to be just like his father. And she would. She wasn't her mother. She *could* give her baby everything he needed and still do her job. It would be tough, doing it alone. But after she'd felt that first kick, and Matt had felt it, she'd known what she would do, even if her stubborn self wasn't quite ready to admit it yet.

Ellie loved this child with all her heart. Which was why she'd never considered abortion, and why she was so very careful in her choices now that she was high-risk. She thought Matt did, too. Or maybe he didn't. Maybe that was simply what she wanted to see in him when he couldn't see it in himself.

Whatever the case, no one was going to adopt this baby. In fact, she had a mind to adopt one more. Maybe they wouldn't be a family of four, but a family of three would be good. Her, baby Matthew and Lucas. Then Matt could have his life back without worries.

"Guess what, Matthew?" she said as she laid her hand across her belly. "We're going to be together, forever, just the three of us." Words that should have cheered her but somehow even made her sadder. Because she still pictured Matt there. He was in her mental image of a perfect family, and also in her heart. But he wasn't going to be in her real family, and that hurt her more than anything ever had.

CHAPTER NINE

Damn, he hated this. Not the job. Not even Forgeburn so much anymore. Being away from it for so long had changed Matt's perspective, and while he still didn't have that coming-home feeling, he was remembering how much he'd liked the area.

What he hated, though, was how he was going back and forth. He wanted to raise his son, and Lucas, yet he wasn't sure he was good enough. There was always that deep-seated fear of becoming his father in the back of his mind. And while it was never very prominent, he saw how Ellie struggled with the same thing, trying not to be her mother.

Neither one of them had been raised by good parents, and while he thought that should have forged a strong bond between them, he didn't feel that it had. The struggle was real, and ongoing. And there were now two babies in the balance.

"OK, Mr. Albright, let's have a listen to your chest." He placed a stethoscope on the elderly man's chest and heard bilateral wheezing, which was what he'd expected to hear from a three-pack-a-day smoker. "It's still emphysema," he said. "And like the last doctor said, you need to give up smoking."

"I need a tank of oxygen like you see all them people in the city toting around."

"Can't prescribe you oxygen while you're still smoking. Oxygen supports combustion, and if you decide to smoke while you're wearing your cannula, you could set yourself on fire. Give up the cigarettes and you'll get your oxygen."

It was a terrible solution, but the man had palsied hands, and that added to the recipe for disaster. If he missed his aim when going to light his cigarette, and he was wearing his oxygen cannula, well—Matt didn't even want to think about that. He'd treated too many burns on the battlefield. They were hideous and, in Mr. Albright's feeble condition, he wouldn't survive them.

"Take your aerosol treatments the way you've always done, and cut back the smokes. If you can't do that, and your breathing gets worse, we may have to talk about sending you to a rehab facility where they won't allow you to smoke, and they'll give you the oxygen you'll need."

"Not going there, Doc. You can't force me. And those aerosol treatments—haven't done one of them in months. They're worthless." He drew in a deep breath, wheezed out a cough, then scooted to the edge of the exam table. "As worthless as you are."

Matt didn't respond. Instead, he opened the exam-room door and watched Mr. Albright make his way out of the clinic. Some people simply wouldn't be helped, he thought as he returned to his cubby-hole office to make his notes.

James Albright, advanced emphysema. Heavy smoker—three packs per day. Bilateral sonorous wheezing. Clubbed fingers. Slight cyanosis both

fingernails and lips. At risk: cardiac complications,
pneumothorax, bullae. Possible signs of mental
confusion. Refuses aerosol treatments, refuses to
quit smoking. Doctor refuses oxygen due to feeble-
ness and high burn risk. Recommendation: long-
term care facility. Patient refuses to go.

"Stubborn old coot," Matt said to himself as he closed
the Albright file then took a peek in at Lucas, who was
playing a toddler video game. "I'll be right back," he told
the boy. "Just going next door to check supplies before
we leave." Which took all of five minutes.

"It's not right," James Albright shouted from Matt's
office as he emerged from the supply room several minutes later.

He'd come back, and Matt was *so* not in the mood to
argue with him. "What's not right?" Matt asked him as
he entered the office, only to find that Albright had made
himself at home and was sitting behind his desk, not in
front of it as patients were supposed to do. "And why is
the door open?" he choked, referring to the Dutch door.

"To let the kiddie in there out. He was calling for
Daddy, so I let him out to go find his daddy."

Matt's heart skipped a beat. "Did you see where he
went?"

"Why would I care? He's not my kid."

"Lucas," Matt called, running out of his office and
starting his search in the exam room. Then the public
toilet. Then the waiting area. But there was no sign of
him. "Lucas," he called over and over, rechecking the
same areas, as Mr. Albright stood and watched. "Are
you sure you didn't see where he went?" Matt cried desperately one last time.

But all Albright did was shrug.

"When did you come back in?" he asked, trying to control his temper.

"Turned around as soon as I got outside and came right back to tell you you're worthless."

Which meant Lucas had been gone at least five minutes or more. But where was he? Was there someplace to hide in the clinic he didn't know about? Someplace only a toddler could fit? Had he looked under the desk in the waiting room? Or in the cabinets in the exam room? That's where he had to be. One of those places. Matt chose the waiting room to begin another search, and this time he saw it.

The clinic door was standing wide open. Which meant— Dear God! He'd gone outside. That could be a good thing, though, Matt said to himself as he ran out the door. A child his size couldn't have gone far in that short amount of time. So, with a little hope returning, Matt ran to the parking lot, shouted Lucas's name, then turned in one direction after another, expecting to see him. But he didn't. So he ran to the other side of the building and did the same. Then to the road. And back to the clinic. By now, his panic had become so overwhelming he was shaking. Sweating. Nauseous.

"Lucas," he kept calling as Albright got into his truck and pulled out of the parking lot, not even offering to help.

And the clock ticked off another five minutes, which meant Lucas had been gone for ten.

Where could a toddler go in ten minutes? And where should he look? If he went in one direction but Lucas was wandering off in the opposite direction... Standing in the middle of the parking lot, Matt turned around in a circle one last time, looking everywhere. But saw nothing. He needed help. But he also needed to get out there and look. Maybe Ellie—she could call people.

"Ellie," he choked into the phone when she picked up. "Lucas is missing. I need help."

"When? How?"

"Sometime in the last ten minutes. One of my patients let him out of the playroom, and he wandered out the door."

"You've checked everywhere in the clinic?" she asked.

"Yes. He's not there. I've got to start searching away from the clinic. With all the rocks and canyons... What I need you to do is call people and ask for help. I need people out here, searching with me. Start with Francine and Bert. Lucas might be trying to get there for another pony ride. Maybe call some of the hotels and businesses and ask them to keep an eye out as well."

"Is there anything else I can do?" she asked Matt.

He wished there was. But putting her under even more stress scared him. "No. Just take care of yourself. And, Ellie, I'm sorry about—well, a lot of things." That was all he said before he clicked off and headed toward the dry river bed that was in view of the clinic. It was close, and it was as good a place to start searching as any. "Lucas," he called out in that direction. "Just stay where you are, buddy. I'm coming to get you."

He prayed those weren't empty words.

Everyone was called, search parties were being organized to meet at the clinic, Cruz was taking to the air, and she was about ready to jump out of her skin. Ellie paced the house, end to end, for about five minutes, then headed to her car. Maybe she couldn't get involved in the vigorous search, but she had to do something, and driving within reason was approved.

She looked at the clock on her phone and, by all estimations, Lucas had been missing for nearly an hour now. She hadn't heard back from Matt, so there was no optimism there. And among the people gathering for the search there were no trained search and rescue experts—just concerned residents. A group of rangers were coming in, but not for another hour. So there wasn't as much optimism as she'd hoped for there either.

Overhead, the sound of a helicopter went from soft to loud, and she looked up to see Cruz heading east, which would take him away from the clinic. Being so high, would he even be able to see someone as tiny as Lucas?

With a sigh and a prayer, Ellie climbed into her car and headed straight to the clinic to see what was being organized. Maybe she wouldn't be much help, but she'd feel better just being where the activity was. And maybe she'd catch sight of Matt somewhere along the way. She really needed to see him, to reassure him, to have him reassure her.

Ellie drove slowly along the way, looking up and down both sides of the road. Realistically, Lucas couldn't have come this far in only an hour. She was three miles from the clinic, the only one on the road—probably because everybody else knew what she'd only just figured out. Still, she looked. Saw cactus in bloom, lots of open space, a few cattle grazing here and there, a rundown cowboy trailer.

On a whim, she took the ranch road up to the trailer, glad it wasn't as bumpy as some, and stopped near the front door. She looked around, saw no sign that anybody was there, but she knocked anyway since it was open. No answer, though.

She decided to take one look around the trailer before she got back on the road, and halfway to the rear she ran into an old man who was tinkering with something in his shed. His rusty truck was parked off to the side, its door part open, its windshield so dirty she wondered how anybody could see out of it to drive. And his yard—it was so cluttered she had to watch every step lest she trip over something and fall.

"There's a little boy gone missing," she said. "Search parties are out looking. You wouldn't have happened to see him, would you?"

The man spun around, his face fixed in a dark glare, and stared at her for a moment. "What I see is a trespasser," he said.

"I'm looking for a lost child," she said emphatically. "Since you live near the place where he went missing…"

"Don't give a damn about lost kids," he hissed. "If the parents aren't smart enough to look out for them in these parts, that's their fault. Not mine. I don't want no part of it. So get off my property. Go look for your kid somewhere else." He turned his back to her and continued what he'd been doing, giving Ellie no choice but to leave. Stopping here had been a long shot anyway, since Lucas simply couldn't have come this far. She wouldn't have felt right if she hadn't stopped, though.

And what a rude man. He was the first rude person she'd made contact with in Forgeburn, but maybe he was just bitter about being past his cowboy days because he clearly was well past them. She sympathized with him a little, wondering how she'd feel if time and age had robbed her of who she was. And that man had been a cowboy. His saddle was resting on a sawhorse, exposed to the weather, probably not used in a long, long time. That's not the way she wanted to end up and now, more than ever, she knew she was on the right course, keeping her baby, adopting Lucas. But Lucas—dear God, she was so scared.

Back on the road, Ellie finally came to the clinic, where several people were still trying to figure out which way to go. She got out of the car, talked to a few of them, and nothing anybody said made her feel easier. The people here were well intentioned, but their searches were random. Even Ellie, who'd had no experience at this, could see that. "Has Matt been back to the clinic?" she asked Francine, who was setting out drinks for those involved. "I've tried raising him on the phone, but nothing goes through."

"Haven't seen or heard from him. Someone said he started at the dry creek bed over there..." Francine pointed to it. "But who knows which direction he went?"

"And he's by himself?" Ellie asked. Matt was still in no condition to do this. Granted, his injuries weren't serious, as confirmed by the X-rays he'd had while she'd been in the hospital, but they were still painful enough that she feared they might compromise him in some way. He was a soldier, though. Smart. Trained in rescue. He'd survived the battlefield, and keeping his friend alive while being shot at. That did give her hope, but she couldn't help worrying, nonetheless.

She loved that man. Loved that little boy. They'd changed her life in so many ways in such a short time, it had to mean she'd been ready to change and only waiting for the right one or, in the case, ones to do it. Matt and Lucas were the ones. And her baby. There was no doubt in her heart that they were the only ones. And now one of them was in such danger...

"Look, I'm restricted because of pregnancy complications, but I'm going to drive a little way out and see what I can see from the road. If Matt comes back, tell him I'm here but I'm taking care of myself. Will you do that for me, Francine?"

Francine took hold of Ellie's hand and squeezed it. "Of course I will, dear. But, please, watch out for yourself. The way Matt's eyes light up when he talks about you— he wouldn't want you taking chances. Not with yourself, not with his baby."

Ellie was surprised he'd told anyone about the baby. "He told you it was his?"

Francine shook her head. "No. But that day at the ranch when you keeled over—there was no doubting it. Especially with the way he was looking at you, and the way you were looking at him. Pure love I was seeing in both of you."

The way he'd looked at her—pure love. Those were the words that ran through her mind as she climbed into her car and headed down the road. Could Matt…did he actually love her? It was too much to hope for, too much to think about right now. Yet…

Matt glanced at his watch—yes, he was one of those who still relied on his watch and not his phone for the time. Lucas had been missing for an hour and a half, and he simply could not have come this far. He'd seen some of the people out looking, seen Cruz pass overhead a few times, but he was so damn discouraged he didn't know what to do.

Somebody should have found Lucas by now. A toddler on the loose couldn't have gotten that far, and because no one had spotted him that could mean— Matt didn't even want to think about all the rocks and canyons out here. Damn, he didn't want to think about them, but that's all that was on his mind—Lucas falling off a rock, or into a canyon, lying there hurt in a place where no one would ever find him.

Bye, Daddy...

Those words were on his mind. He *was* Daddy, wasn't he? To Lucas, to his own baby. Sure, maybe he'd tried to ignore that fact, or hide behind the complications, but he wasn't going to do that anymore. Lucas was in danger. Ellie was struggling to keep their baby alive and healthy. And here he was, always looking for a way out.

"Stupid," he said, as he trudged toward the road that would take him back to the clinic. There, he'd regroup and start over. And call Ellie. He needed to talk to her. Needed to hear her tell him that they'd find Lucas, that everything would be OK. Because on his own, he sure as hell didn't believe that.

When he got to the road, the only thing he could see was a distant car, heading very slowly in his direction. Someone out looking, he guessed, glad for the support from Forgeburn that he'd never had as a kid. It was a different community now. Or maybe he was different. Whatever the case, they'd come together for him and there were no words to describe his appreciation. So, could he stay here? Keep the practice, his son *and* Lucas, and stay?

That was the question he was contemplating when the car finally came close enough to identify. Ellie! Damn, she shouldn't be doing this, yet he was so glad to see her. "Ellie," he called running toward the car as it came to stop in a cloud of dust.

She was out of the car and in his arms in a flash. "Everybody's looking, Matt. More and more people are showing up to help."

"Are you OK?" he asked, unwilling to let her out of his arms.

"I'm fine."

"You know you shouldn't be out here."

"Where else could I be?" she asked. "I couldn't just sit at home and wait. That's not me."

"I know it's not you," Matt said tenderly, finally loosening his hold on her. "It's not going well. He couldn't have gone that far, and…" His words choked off. He couldn't say them aloud.

"We're going to find him, Matt. He's been out for a while. I'll bet he's probably crawled off into a shady spot to nap. It *is* his naptime, you know."

He tried to manage a smile, but it simply wasn't in him. "We, um—when we get Lucas back home, and we're all rested, you and I need to have a talk. There are some things—stupid things I've been holding on to, and I can't go on like this."

"Me, too," she said, brushing his cheek with her hand. "But right now how about I give you a ride back to the clinic? Francine's got some lemonade and other drinks going. You get yourself rehydrated, and maybe by then…"

"Maybe by then," he said, as he climbed into her car. Maybe by then, but probably not, because there was no optimism left in him. None at all.

"Are you sure you're up to it?" she asked Matt, as he prepared to go back out and join the thirty-five other people who were now engaged in the search. "Maybe you should rest a little while longer."

"Can't," he said, swigging on his third glass of iced water. "If Lucas is out there, that's where I've got to be."

"First, tell me exactly what happened. Tell me about the patient who let him out."

"He's a crotchety old guy. Has advanced emphysema and it's probably muddling his mind like it can do sometimes. He said he turned Lucas loose to find his daddy."

"OK, so maybe the guy has a problem. But did he leave the front door open as well?"

"Probably, since he'd just come through it."

Ellie shook her head. "Well, there's nothing we can do about that, but…" The rest of her words were drowned out by Cruz, in his helicopter, who circled once then started to land just off the end of the parking lot. Within a matter of a couple of minutes he was there with them.

"I'm a pretty good spotter. That was half the battle when I was rescuing in the army. But some of this area is so rugged I can't see as well as I'd like and, to be honest, I'm not as fast as I should be because of that. Didn't get as much area covered as I'd intended. Matt, would you want to come up with me for a while, so I can focus on the flying while you focus on the looking? I've been over every place I think he could have gone in the time he's been out there, given his age, but there are a few…" he swallowed hard "…less obvious places I want to get down into, and I can't do that alone."

Matt nodded. He understood. So did Ellie, as she fought to control tears that wanted to escape. The canyons, the rocks… She couldn't bear to think that Lucas might be— She reached over and squeezed Matt's arm. But neither of them spoke. She stepped forward and kissed him, though, before he went off with Cruz. And as the helicopter lifted into the sky, she went to Lucas's playroom in the clinic, sat down on the floor, and cried harder than she'd ever cried in her life.

Twenty minutes later, still racked with dry sobs, Ellie finally got up, then ran her fingers over the lock on the bottom half of the Dutch door. Matt was so proud of this room. A perfect solution for Lucas when he was at the clinic. She looked at the lock, hating the man who'd opened the door, even though there was a possibility that he had problems. But she couldn't help herself. Brain complications or not, he'd left two doors open, and now Lucas might be dead because of that. The unthinkable thought now in her mind, she wanted to cry again, but she needed to get back out there and do her little part, even though she was so limited, sticking only to the paved roads.

Sighing, and not caring that her face was still red and bloated, Ellie headed for her car, climbed in, then wondered which way to go. She'd covered everything she could near the clinic, but not the terrain where Lucas might have encountered the rocks and canyons. And Matt and Cruz were now flying over those. Plus, there were so many people going in so many directions…

Maybe she should go back the way she'd come. Maybe somehow Lucas was trying to get home. Although she doubted that since he was so young. But Ellie was desperate. She needed to be out there, looking. So, she headed back down the road toward home, passed the same cacti she'd passed a little while ago. Passed by the crotchety old cowboy's trailer… She got to about a hundred yards away, then jammed on the brakes. Crotchety? No. There was no connection. Could there be?

She looked up, saw Cruz's helicopter in the distance, dipping into a canyon, and she held her breath until it came back out. Looked back at the trailer, then put her car into reverse. OK, so he wouldn't be happy to see her again. But she had to go back. Ask one more time. Because—two crotchety old guys in Forgeburn? Sure, it could happen. The people she'd met here were nice, but that didn't necessarily mean everyone was nice. And the odds that Forgeburn had two old crotchety guys, or maybe even more, were high. She had to look again, though. One more try. Something was pulling her to do it. Something she'd never felt before. Something—maternal?

Whatever it was, Ellie walked straight to the back of the trailer, right past the sawhorse with the saddle, right past the rusty old truck, right up to the old cowboy, who was sitting in a yard chair now, his back to her. Huffing and puffing like he couldn't get his breath. Emphysema? Like Matt's patient. "Where is he?" she shouted at the man.

"Who?" he asked, not even bothering to turn to see who it was.

"The boy who's missing. Where is he?" She looked up as Cruz passed overhead, and jumped up and down, waving, hoping Matt would see her. But he didn't. The yard was too full of junk, she was too concealed. And the helicopter just kept going. "The boy you let out of his playroom at the clinic. Where is he?" She stepped directly in front of the man and repeated herself. "Where is he?"

"Don't know what you're talking about," he said. "Now get off my property, and I'm not telling you again."

"You took him," she hissed, and bent over to get closer to him. "You took him, and you'd better tell me…"

Her back caught, and she stood up. The pain was sudden and overwhelming, and she prayed it was only a back spasm, as Dr. Gupta had told her the other incident had been. Drawing in a deep breath, she let it out slowly, and as she did so she saw something through the dirty window of the old truck. It was moving. Then suddenly it was gone. She blinked, then walked deliberately toward the truck as she couldn't run. The pain was increasing with every moment. She had to look, though. Had to know…

Then it hit her. The truck's door was open. She'd noticed that before. Open the way he'd left the playroom door open and the clinic's door. Even his own front door.

An indication of his dementia, possibly. She wanted to hurry her pace, wanted Cruz to fly back over and spot her—but she was on her own now. This was up to her. "Lucas," she called. "Can you hear me?"

There was no response as she finally made it to the front of the truck. Then the side, and the open door. Where she found Lucas, sitting in the driver's seat, his hands on the steering wheel, like he was pretending to drive. "Lucas," she said, as the tears ran down her face. "I'm so glad to see you."

"Daddy?" he asked, looking over at her.

"I'll take you to him," she said, climbing into the truck and taking the boy into her arms. "He's been looking for you, and he'll be very happy to see you."

Lucas looked up at her, ever so innocently, then snuggled into her arms. And there they sat for the next several minutes as her back pains grew worse. But she had Lucas, and that's all that mattered.

"I'm right behind you," Cruz called, making sure his helicopter was secure before he followed Matt back to that old cowboy trailer.

Matt was already so far ahead, though, that he didn't hear. All he knew was that he'd seen Ellie down there, seen her signal. And the few minutes that had ensued before Cruz could set down had been the longest of his life. What was she doing there? Did she have Lucas? Was she in trouble? Too many thoughts tossed around in his brain as he pounded the dirt, running harder and faster than he ever had in his life, despite his injuries.

Finally, when he got there, he saw James Albright. Sitting in a chair. Coughing and wheezing. But no Ellie, and there was no way that Albright, in his condition, could have done anything to her. He looked toward the front of the trailer, saw her car, which meant—

"Ellie?" he called.

"Over here," came the response from an old truck sitting amongst all the junk.

Immediately, he was there, looking in the driver's side window. Then climbing in and pulling both Ellie and Lucas into his arms. "Are you OK?" he asked her.

"No," she said. "I'm not."

Matt studied the IV drip in Ellie's arm, then looked down at her. She was stable, the baby was fine. But this was the rest of her pregnancy. In bed. Resting. No work. No rescue operations. He took her hand and kissed it as he sat down on the edge of her bed.

"How's Lucas?" she asked him.

"Fine. No signs of trauma. I talked to the sheriff in the area who was assigned to investigate, and he thinks Lucas simply walked out of the clinic and got into Albright's truck, maybe thinking it was mine. Since Albright has a habit of leaving doors open, his truck door might have been open, making it easy for Lucas to climb in. There's a strong possibility that Albright didn't even know Lucas was there."

"Where is Lucas now?" she asked.

"On the back of a pony. A lot of people volunteered to watch him for a couple of days while I'm here with you."

"You don't have to stay, Matt. Lucas needs you now."

"So do you." He laid his hand on her belly. "And, so does our son."

"We need to talk about that," Ellie said. "Dr. Gupta's fairly optimistic that I can go to term, or near term. And she's approved the helicopter rides back and forth, since she'll be seeing me pretty much every other week now.

"But do you really want me to stay with you, because this isn't going to be easy. I think all I'm going to be allowed to do is chew and swallow, which means the burden of my care will be, well…up to you. And while I know you've promised to stay, is that really what you want to do? Because I've changed my mind about some things that will allow you to get back the life you want."

"Such as?" Matt asked, his face growing a little clouded with concern.

"I'm going to keep the baby. Raise him the way he needs to be raised. You don't have to be involved in that, since it's my decision and not yours. And the second thing—I talked to your social worker about Lucas a little while ago. I'm going to adopt him. I love him like he's mine, and I can't see him going to someone else. I'm pretty sure you'll approve me, because it's a good thing that the boys will be raised together."

"Want me to tell you about my plan?" Matt asked. "Because I have one, too."

Ellie shut her eyes and drew in a deep breath. "Is it going to break my heart?" she asked. "Because I really want the boys and me to be a family."

"Well, your plan is a good one, but it will be a perfect one if I'm included in it."

She opened her eyes, clearly startled. "What do you mean?" she asked cautiously.

"It starts with this—will you marry me, Ellie?"

"Because of the baby?"

"Because of you. You are the most engaging, hard-driven, optimistic woman I've ever known. I think I fell a little in love with you in Reno, and I've fallen the rest of the way in love with you here, in Forgeburn. Now I love you even more for wanting to adopt Lucas, but I think I've known all along I wouldn't give him up. I just chose to ignore the obvious because of, well, so many things. My past mostly. It's hard to move forward when you're so stuck in the past. Hard moving forward if you think you're going to be rejected, too."

"You thought I'd reject you?"

"Your plan was always about going back to Reno."

"Because your plan was always about going back to the army. What was I supposed to do?"

"Actually, we both did the same thing. We hid from our feelings, partly because neither of us wanted to be rejected the way we were when we were kids. And partly because it's scary changing your life so drastically when you've found it to be the safe haven you've never had before. I love you, Ellie Landers. And if part of that means moving to Reno with you, I'll do it."

"But I don't want to go back to Reno," Ellie said. "Part of my plan—the part I never thought would happen—was staying here, raising our boys together. But you were always so dead set on getting back to being an army surgeon, I thought I couldn't compete with that."

"You started competing with that the first time I laid eyes on you, only I was too stupid to see it. And while I haven't been consciously aware of how I was dealing with my feelings, getting rid of Lucas, not raising our baby, not getting involved with you the way I wanted to—that's all part of the way I cope. Maybe leaving Janice behind was, too. I don't know.

"But that's not who I want to be. That was the kid who lived in the dump. But I'm not that kid anymore. The one who always ran away. I'm the man who wants to be your husband, and father to our boys. The man who wants to stay."

"I would never hurt you, Matt. And leaving you—no. I didn't want to do that. Not after I saw who you were.

But my first reaction was how am I going to live the life I've been *trained* to live with a child? I took the easy way out. Dumped the decisions about what to do on you.

"But then…there was you. A completely different matter. Plus Lucas. A ready-made family for the woman who was so career-oriented she couldn't see anything else around her. I was hiding behind my career like you were hiding behind yours. Always telling myself I wanted, even needed bigger and better. But you, Lucas and our baby—that's what I need. All I need. That's my bigger and better, and I only came to realize that after I realized I wasn't my mother. My bigger and better isn't hers, and hers isn't mine."

She smiled. "And mine's so much better than hers will ever be. So, yes, I want to marry you. More than that, I need to marry you, and not because I'm pregnant but because we are a family—the four of us. We need to be together."

"Then will it be Reno or Forgeburn?" he asked, reaching over to brush a tear from her cheek. "Or someplace else, where we can start over?"

"We've already started over right here, in Forgeburn. This is where I want to stay. I'll keep my company. Just move the facilities here, if that's what you want. I like it here. Like the people here. And despite your bad memories, which I want to help you deal with, this is the place I want to raise our boys. The people are good. I love the desert.

"And when you give up your practice here to go back into the army, we can find another house or maybe buy this one—that is, if you want to stay here. If you don't, well, anywhere. I'll even go with you overseas when I'm allowed. I know some military families get to go. And the boys and I—we'll follow you when we can. And wait for you to come home when we can't."

"No following," he said. "I want my family to have stability. Besides, I'm only going to be gone a few days every month, working at a veterans' hospital. As a surgeon. Then the rest of the time I'll be here, as a GP."

"How?"

"Remember when I told you the army had options. My option was to vacate my contract and transition into the reserves to serve the rest of my active duty. I'll be in for a longer period of time but working only a few days at a time. So I've already started the process of buying the practice and the house from Doc Granger. Oh, and so you'll know, I wouldn't have let our baby be put up for adoption either. I fell in love with him the moment I knew you were carrying him. Just didn't want to admit it, like everything else I didn't want to admit."

"That first day when Lucas called you Daddy..."

"That's when I knew," he admitted. "Knew I was being stupid in so many ways. Knew what I wanted. Knew that it scared me to death. Knew that we were meant to be a family." He bent over and kissed her lightly on the forehead. "It won't be an easy life. I can't promise you much except my love."

"And a life I never thought I could have. That's what I've wanted, Matt. Like you, I didn't want to admit it because changing a life is so difficult, and I've had to do it so many times, trying to find out who I really am. Who I am, though, isn't so complicated after all. I'm the woman who wants to be part of her family. Wife, mother and, yes, career woman. With you, Lucas, Matthew—"

"Matthew?" he interrupted.

"That's what I've named him. I don't know your middle name but I want him to have that, too."

"No, you don't," he said, putting on a fake cringe.

"What is it?" she asked him.

"First, tell me your name. I don't have a clue what it is."

"It's Eleanor Landers, NMI."

"What's NMI?"

"No middle name. My mother believed middle names were useless, and being the practical woman she is she didn't give me one. And before you ask, she only named me Eleanor because it was convenient. It was the name of the nurse who helped deliver me. Apparently, my mother hadn't had time to choose my name, so when they asked her, she looked at the nurse's nametag and that's the name I got."

"Be glad it wasn't Brunhilde," he said, chuckling.

"Actually, I got lucky. I like my name. But, apparently you don't like your middle name?"

He shook his head.

"No secrets in this relationship, Matt. So tell me."

"Strandrew," he admitted.

"Strandrew? I've never heard of that." She lifted her hand to her mouth to cover a giggle. "Matthew *Strandrew* McClain."

"What can I say? I think my dad was drunk when he filled out the paperwork. I'm pretty sure it was supposed to be Andrew. At least, that's what I've always told myself." Her laugh was infectious, and he joined in.

"Matthew *Andrew*," she finally said. "I could get used to that. But you're right. *Not* Strandrew." She wrinkled her nose, just saying the name again.

"So, now that we've named our son, and you've accepted my marriage proposal, what's next?"

"Call the hospital chaplain, then happily-ever-after?"

"Definitely happily-ever-after," he said, stretching out

on the hospital bed next to her when she scooted over and patted the spot where she wanted him. "And would that begin with a kiss?"

"Or maybe a kick to the belly," she said, placing his hand on her belly.

"And a kiss," he said, leaning over but kissing her belly, as their son was still kicking inside her. "I think he knows he's the one who brought us back together, where we belong," Matt said when baby Matthew finally calmed down.

"I think you're right," Ellie said, scooting over a little more to cuddle in with Matt. "Now, how about a kiss for the mommy?"

* * * * *

ONE NIGHT WITH THE ARMY DOC

TRACI DOUGLASS

MILLS & BOON

To my precious Carma:

Thank you for watching out for me and this story
from across the Rainbow Bridge.

Until we meet again, love and miss you puppers!

CHAPTER ONE

"UNITS RESPOND TO trauma rollover. Motor vehicle accident. Hickel Parkway near Raspberry Road. SUV flipped several times, currently on roof. Three passengers involved—man, woman and young child. Man self-extricated, according to police. Woman and child trapped inside. Fire Rescue responding with Jaws of Life. Over."

"Copy. Unit A18 en route."

Dr. Jake Ryder replaced the receiver on the dashboard two-way radio, feeling the familiar buzz of adrenaline that always followed a call to arms pumping through his blood.

"Ready for action, Doc?" EMT Zac Taylor asked from the driver's seat.

"Always." Since taking over the Emergency Medicine Department at Anchorage Mercy Jake didn't get to spend much time out in the field, so this was a special treat. "I'll get things ready in the back."

While Zac steered them toward the accident scene Jake unbuckled his seat belt and moved into the rear of the ambulance. He grabbed some extra rolls of gauze and shoved them in his bag, then double-checked the batteries in his flashlight. His chief of staff's words from earlier that day were still echoing in his head.

"I know how you feel about the media, but this is Bobby's best chance at recovery…"

His best friend Bobby had saved his life once. Now Jake would return the favor.

There were no other options.

Even if it meant the possibility of revisiting the dreaded invasion of his personal life that had followed his Distinguished Service Cross commendation. That debacle was one of the reasons why he kept to himself these days. Other than Bobby and Zac, and a few other staff at the hospital, he wasn't really close to anyone. His ex and those reporters had really done a number on Jake back then, and now he had some reality TV doc ready to barge in and take over Bobby's case.

Exactly what he didn't need.

They swerved to a stop as Jake tried to picture this media darling doctor who would be waiting for him when he got back to the hospital. He'd never heard of this wunderkind guaranteed to be Bobby's medical savior. All he knew was what his ER staff had mentioned—that this traveling physician was all about the new and experimental, mainly at the expense of old-fashioned caring and compassion.

Not good. Not good at all.

Zac parked the ambulance, then leaned around the partition separating the front cabin from the treatment area. "Looks like a real zoo at the crash scene, Doc. At least the cops have the perimeter blocked off."

"Great. Let's roll."

Jake zipped up his pack, then pushed out of the rig with the heavy duffle slung over one shoulder. Sirens wailed and red and blue emergency lights blazed from all directions. One of the police officers gave them a rundown while they weaved their way toward the overturned vehicle.

"What happened?" Jake asked.

"From what the father told me, it was a moose," the officer said. "Ran out into the road and the guy swerved. Those SUVs are top-heavy, so the whole thing rolled under the strain. I asked him how many times, but he couldn't remember."

"Wife and kid still inside the car?"

"Yep. Both awake and talking. We've got a couple of guys trying to keep them calm."

"Awesome."

Jake slipped around the end of a fire rescue truck parked diagonally near the wreck, seeing the snowcapped peaks of the Chugach Mountains rising like sentinels in the distance.

"Any loss of consciousness with the father or the other victims?"

"He says no, but it's hard to tell."

The cop kept pace with Jake's longer strides.

"The kid keeps crying for his toy, poor guy. We've searched the area, but haven't found any stuffed sheep."

"Got it covered."

Jake patted the side pocket of his duffle. The thing in his bag wasn't a lamb, more like a cross between a giraffe and a dinosaur, but any port in a storm.

"Is that the dad?" Jake pointed toward a man huddled beneath a blanket despite the warm September night.

"Yep." The cop veered off toward the demolished car again. "I'll let you get to work."

"Thanks." Jake turned to Zac. "I'll check out the father while you assess the wreck."

"Sounds good."

Jake walked to the agitated male standing between a police officer and a firefighter. "Evening, sir. I'm Dr.

Jake Ryder." He set his pack on the ground near his feet. "I hear you had a run-in with a moose tonight?"

The guy, who looked about forty, and pale as death, nodded. "We're here on vacation and were out sightseeing. Next thing I knew this huge animal ran out in the road and everything happened so fast and—"

Recognizing the lingering signs of shock, Jake cocked his head toward the fireman and together they helped maneuver the father until his weight rested against a nearby squad car.

"Sir, help's here, and we're going to take care of you."

"What about my wife and son? Are they going to be all right?"

"The crew's working to get them out now." He proceeded to examine the man for any obvious injuries. "What's your name?"

"Mark. Mark Leonard."

"Okay, Mr. Leonard." Jake palpated the guy's head and neck before moving to his arms. "Tell me if anything hurts or doesn't feel right."

"I'm fine. I just want to see my family."

"Please let me finish this exam first." He crouched to check out the man's legs and discovered a nasty gash on Mr. Leonard's left calf. "Looks like you banged up your leg, Mark." He unzipped his bag and pulled out supplies. "I'm going to tape this up before we take you to the ER. Hold still. It might sting."

"Ow!"

The guy jerked away and Jake tightened his grip. The cut wasn't deep, but it was filled with gravel and debris from the accident. If not cleaned properly, it could cause a bad infection. Jake had seen more than enough of that on the battlefield.

The father scowled, a bit of his color returning. "What

the hell was a moose doing around here in the autumn? Don't they only come out in winter?"

"Rutting season."

Jake shoved the soiled gauze pads into a portable hazmat container, then unwrapped several fresh ones to cover the laceration before twining a bandage around the man's leg. Not perfect, but it would hold him until the Anchorage Mercy ER could suture the wound closed properly.

Talk of mate-seeking moose only served to remind Jake of the sad state of his own relationship status—or lack thereof. He wasn't completely pathetic. He was a healthy, red-blooded male after all. But these days he only engaged with women who knew the score, women who never expected more than a few pleasant hours between the sheets.

The firefighter beside Jake cleared his throat and brought him back to the present. He secured the end of the bandage around Mr. Leonard's leg with a metal clip, then straightened.

"Are we done?" Mr. Leonard tossed the blanket aside and tentatively put some weight on his injured limb. "Can I see my wife now? What about my son?"

"Stay here with the officers while I check in with the crew. Once they give me the okay, you can see them. All right, Mark?"

"Okay." The man's tense shoulders relaxed a tad. "Thanks for helping."

"That's my job." Jake packed up his gear again before joining Zac near the vehicle. "Dad's doing fine. What's happening here?"

"Mom says her arm hurts, and the boy is really frightened, but neither seem to have any serious issues. Remarkable, considering the shape of this SUV."

Jake stepped back and took his first real look at the

damage. Shards of shattered glass littered the roadway and the sharp smell of gasoline and burning oil stung his nose. The whole right half of the car closest to him was dented and twisted, making the doors impossible to open.

A small voice called from the busted-out rear window. "Where's Lamby? I want Lamby."

The little boy's plaintive tone pummeled Jake's heart and took him right back to his last day in the Kandahar desert: to the acrid stench of diesel and melting rubber clogging his throat and choking his lungs, to Bobby pulling him from the blazing village amidst a hail of gunfire. Jake was supposed to have been the one doing the rescuing, but Bobby had done the saving that day.

They'd been best buds since their first day of basic training—a friendship that had only strengthened over the years. Bobby was his rock, his shield, same as Jake was for him. He couldn't lose his best friend. Not after everything they'd been through.

As the memories crashed in—of other emergencies in far-off warzones—Jake slowly counted down in his head from ten to one, as his counselor had taught him, and the shadows gradually withdrew.

"You okay, man?" Zac thumped him on the shoulder, his expression concerned.

"I'm fine." Jake focused on the trapped family members. He'd always wanted kids of his own—always figured he'd get around to having them someday. Then time and circumstances and his career had slapped a quick kibosh on those dreams.

Jake battled the knot of regret tightening between his shoulder blades. Didn't matter. He was better off alone. Alone was safer. Alone was more comfortable. Alone didn't run off for a life in front of the cameras in glitzy, glamorous Manhattan.

He reached into his bag for the stuffed animal, then knelt beside the mangled car, clicked on his flashlight, and peered inside. Two huge dark eyes stared at him from the shadows. It was the child, still protected in his booster seat.

"Hey, buddy. My name's Jake. What's yours?"

The boy's bottom lip quivered and tears welled anew.

Jake hung his head. Here he was—a former special operations combat medic, trained to think on his feet with a hundred snipers poised to take him out at any second—yet all he wanted was to make this scared little boy smile again.

"Lamby's busy, but he sent a friend to keep you company. Want to meet him?"

"My son's name is Noah," the mother said from the front of the SUV, where she was secured partially upside down by her seatbelt. "He's four."

"Noah, my man." Jake held up the dino-giraffe. "This is Chewy. He'd like to come in and say hello...maybe sit with you until we get you and your mom out. Would that be okay?"

The little boy eyed him warily for several seconds before extending a tiny hand.

"Awesome." Jake passed him the stuffed animal, then turned his attention to the mother. "I'm Dr. Jake Ryder, ma'am. Are you doing all right?"

"My arm is killing me, and I've been pinned in this car for way longer than I ever wanted—but other than that, yeah. I'm fine, thanks."

The snark in her tone made him chuckle. "Do you recall what happened?"

"My husband swerved off the road to miss a moose, then glass shattered and flew everywhere and we were tumbling...over and over and over."

"Did you lose consciousness?"

"I don't think so."

"What about your son? Has he been awake the whole time?"

"Yes. I've been talking to Noah to make sure he stays calm."

"Excellent."

Jake shifted to survey the wreckage again. It looked like a bomb had gone off inside the car. He'd seen enough destroyed villages to know. Still, Jake and Bobby had been the lucky ones, coming home in one piece, without too many mental or physical scars from the war. Many others hadn't been so fortunate.

"Hey, Doc. Fire's ready with the Jaws of Life," Zac called from behind him.

"Ma'am, the crew's here to free you now." Jake started to retreat from the vehicle. "There'll be a lot of loud noise and some shaking, but I promise we'll have you both out soon."

"Thank you." The mom sniffled, her voice trembling. "Noah, sweetie? Remember the fireworks in July? All the loud booms?"

The boy nodded.

"It'll be noisy like that for a short while, but Mommy's right here with you, okay?"

"Okay." The little boy looked from his mom to Jake, the new toy clutched to his chest. "Bye, Jake."

"See you soon, buddy." Jake thumped his hand on the side of the car, then moved away as the firemen brought in the heavy equipment.

Moose!

Dr. Molly Flynn slammed on the brakes of her rented burgundy Range Rover and veered to the berm of this oddly deserted stretch of roadway. Well, deserted except for her and the behemoth creature standing twenty feet ahead. She shifted into "Park," then met the animal's startled gaze while fiddling with the onboard GPS once more.

Still nothing.

Molly shook her head and snorted.

"Go to Alaska," her executive producers had said last week. "A high-profile sports case is the best way to raise the ratings."

Normally she would've told them that her soon-to-expire contract clearly stipulated she got final say on all cases portrayed on her reality medical drama, Diagnosis Critical. But, considering she was on thin enough ice with the MedStar cable network, those ratings might be the only thing saving her career. And her career was all she had these days.

Besides, she'd earned this show, darn it. Built it from the ground up without any support from her father or her family. Now she'd do whatever was necessary to save it— even if it meant traveling to Anchorage, Alaska, a place that was a far cry from the hustle and bustle of Chicago.

She took a deep breath and stared at the lush forest around her. Maybe the middle of nowhere wasn't such a bad place to be after all. It might allow her a chance to escape the spotlight for a while.

Strange as it sounded, for a person who made her living in front of the camera, she'd always seen fame as a necessary evil. Curing the incurable, solving the unsolvable medical puzzles—that was her true love, the real driving force behind why she did what she did. In fact, the thought of being able to melt into the woodwork as she saved her latest patient sounded like pure bliss, if highly unlikely. Her network's syndication deals ensured that her show reached nearly every corner of the globe.

So much for privacy and anonymity.

Molly frowned at the digital clock on her dashboard. She'd been scheduled to meet with the chief of staff at Anchorage Mercy General Hospital twenty minutes ago, but her late-arriving flight, followed by the rental car's faulty GPS, seemed to have other ideas.

Add in the fact that the sun was setting over Cook Inlet, which was the opposite of where it had been when she'd left Ted Stevens International Airport at least an hour prior, gave her the sinking feeling she'd been driving in circles.

Overhead, an eagle swooped through the air, its low cries eerily haunting in the autumn evening. Despite her conundrum, Molly had to admit Alaska was lovely. Too bad she wouldn't have time to appreciate much of the gorgeous scenery, given her tight production schedule and the seriousness of her patient's case. Work came first, as always.

The male moose huffed and shook his mighty antlers before ambling into the forest on the opposite side of the four-lane road. Molly stared wistfully at the spot where he'd disappeared into the thick foliage, wishing she could find where she belonged so easily. Then her pragmatic instincts kicked back in and she focused on her current mission—find the hospital, locate her crew, save her patient.

Determined, Molly pulled back out onto the road and continued around a slight curve—only to slam on her brakes again. Now she could see why oncoming traffic had been virtually nonexistent. Judging by the array of emergency vehicles blocking all four lanes, there had been an accident.

As a licensed physician, it was her duty to assist when needed. Critics of her show always complained that she had the bedside manner of dry toast, but her real skill was as a diagnostician. And when she was working on a case everything else fell by the wayside—friends, family, romantic relationships. She'd sacrificed everything for her patients, and success was her reward.

A twinge of loneliness pinched her chest before she shoved it aside. The last thing Molly needed was a relationship. Especially since her last one had ended without warning. She parked on the berm, cut the engine, then blinked back the unexpected sting of tears as she walked around to the rear of the SUV.

Yes, maybe she did sometimes wish she had someone to share her life with. But, as her father had always said when she was a child, "Wishes are for fools. People like us seize what they want."

Trouble was, Molly had never felt like her father's kind of people. Or her mother's, for that matter. In fact there wasn't really a single member of her family, parents or sister, that she truly identified with. So she'd learned early on to live inside herself and bide her time. Now, though, it seemed she'd gotten so good at keeping her emotions bottled up she couldn't seem to show them at all—not even with the people she should. People like Brian.

She shook off thoughts of her ex and rummaged through the car for her emergency first aid kit. The pungent smell of spruce, mixed with a faint hint of fish and salt from the inlet, snapped her to attention.

Dressed comfortably for the nearly seven-hour flight from Chicago to Alaska, Molly didn't pay much attention to her appearance—jeans, sneakers and one of her favorite T-shirts that read, "Back Up. I'm going to try Science"—as she approached the nearby officer guarding the perimeter of the scene.

"Dr. Molly Flynn." She drew herself up to her full five-foot-four-inch height and held out her hand to the middle-aged guy. "Looks like there's an accident ahead. Do they require assistance?"

The cop looked her up and down, his expression dubious. "What are you, twelve?"

"Twenty-seven, actually, thanks for asking."

Molly adjusted her bag, undeterred. She'd put up with plenty of crap through the years because of her gifts. She'd graduated medical school at the ripe old age of twenty-four, with dual specialties in Immunology and Internal Medicine, but nothing made a girl feel less welcome and confident than having no friends and no one to sit with at the lunch table.

"Do I have to show my physician's license or are you going to point me toward the scene, Officer...?"

"Bentz." He sniffed and looked away. "The EMTs arrived a little while ago. Pretty sure they've got it under control."

"I see."

The man was dismissing her, but she was used to that too. Her mother had always been present, but aloof, and when her father had been home from performing amazing feats of surgical genius all over the world he'd only wanted to parade Molly around like some prize show pony instead of treating her like his beloved child.

"Molly, solve this impossible equation."

"Molly, impress my friends with another feat of mental acrobatics."

"Molly, earn my love by always doing what you're told, always being perfect, always performing, no matter what."

Her cell phone buzzed and Molly pulled it from her pocket, hoping for an update from her crew. Instead, all she found was the same dumb message that had been on her screen since before takeoff from O'Hare. The stupid text from her ex glowed brightly, its cheerful white background at direct odds with the dismal words.

I can't do this anymore.
Not sure you'll even notice I'm gone.

She resisted the urge to mic-drop the useless device into a nearby mud puddle and instead returned it to her pocket.

Looking back, she should've expected the break-up. Brian had always been complaining about her long hours and frequent trips, even though she'd been up-front with him about her demanding schedule from the beginning. And their blazing fights over the past few weeks had only served to resurrect painful memories of her father's indifference and cruelty when she'd been a child—the day he'd called her weak for crying over the death of her pet cat, the way he'd taunted her because she hadn't been able to make friends with the popular girls in her class, the night she'd graduated from medical school and overheard her father saying what a hopeless, awkward mess she was and how embarrassed he was to have her for a daughter because she'd been denied the membership of the Ivy League exclusive clubs and cliques her father had deemed necessary to mingle in his lofty social circles.

Even now those words gutted Molly to her core.

Brian, in the end, had pushed those same agonizing buttons, causing Molly to withdraw inside herself until they'd been basically nothing but glorified roommates. Still, she'd thought the year and a half they'd spent together rated more than a two-line text to end it all.

She guessed she'd been wrong about that too.

One more reason relationships were off her radar. Not even one-night stands. She preferred certainties to messy emotions, thank you very much. And, honestly, why bother when people left once you'd opened up and revealed your true, flawed self to them. Luckily, she wasn't likely to find a man who'd challenge those beliefs out here in Alaska.

Ignoring the lingering sadness in her chest, she concentrated on Officer Not Budging, still blocking her path. Intimidation was out of the question, given the guy had at least a hundred and fifty pounds on her, but maybe a healthy dose of mind-numbing logic would do the trick.

Whenever she felt overstressed or insecure, random facts always popped into Molly's head and out of her mouth. Blind dates, heated confrontations, heated situations of any sort, really. She'd ramble on and on about useless information until the poor victim's eyes glazed over and they wandered off in a fog of utter boredom.

Considering she was thousands of miles from home, hopelessly lost, and late for a potentially career-altering meeting, Molly couldn't get much more stressed. Plus, she'd done some light reading on the flight—facts and figures about Alaska, atlases, safety manuals, wildlife guides. Perfect for boring an unsuspecting cop to tears.

"Officer Bentz, did you know traffic fatalities in this state increased by twenty-six point eight percent from fifty-six in 2010 to seventy-two in 2011? Also, the percentage of statewide traffic fatalities related to alcohol-impaired driving decreased from thirty-four point three percent in 2009 to twenty-eight point six percent in 2010…"

Molly hid a smile. The man was fidgeting, his expression growing more uncomfortable the longer she droned. Soon the poor guy stifled a yawn and gazed skyward.

Chalk up another win for her near-eidetic memory.

"Most interesting of all…"

Officer Bentz looked at Molly again, his eyes as blank as his expression. "Go on ahead. I'm sure you can help with something. In fact, ask for Jake. He's with the ambulance crew tonight. He owes me one anyway."

"Thank you very much."

She turned on her heel and sidled through the maze of squad cars and fire trucks toward what she could now see was an overturned vehicle. During her emergency medicine rotation in Chicago, Molly had treated plenty of accident victims. That had been a while ago, however, and she'd been out of the ER trenches since signing on to do her TV show.

Fresh nerves and adrenaline quickened her steps and her pulse. Amidst the bright floodlights set up around the perimeter of the scene, Molly peered past the end of an ambulance in time to see a huge metal claw rip off a chunk of twisted debris from the SUV's side.

"Dammit." A man stalked over, his gray eyes sparkling with fury, his impressive build only adding to his imposing presence. "The cops are supposed to keep any rubberneckers away."

Molly looked around to see who he was scolding and realized, too late, that it was her.

"Get out." He stood at least a foot taller than her. And from the top of his dark brown hair to the tips of his black work boots the guy looked every inch the alpha protector. "Before you get hurt."

"I'm perfectly capable of taking care of myself."

She did her best to stand tall and forget about the fact this man was movie-star-handsome. Even with the beard. Molly had never gone for the lumberjack look before, but he made her seriously reconsider her life choices.

"The cop back there said I should ask for Jake."

His gaze narrowed. "Who told you that?"

"Officer Bentz." She pointed in the direction of her Range Rover. "I'm a doctor. Perhaps you've heard of me? I have a—"

"We're ready," said another guy. He was dressed in

an EMT uniform, African American, maybe midthirties, and was calling from near the crash site. "Time to quit flirting and start working."

Her gaze darted from the wreck to the scowling hunk before her.

Flirting? With me?

If glares and glowers were this man's idea of how to attract women, it was entirely possible she'd finally met someone who was worse than her in social situations.

"Excuse me."

Molly started to move around him, only to be stopped by his hand on her arm. Never mind the warmth spreading through her bloodstream, or the zing of awareness crackling like fireworks. Verbal sparring was one thing. Unwanted contact was another.

Outrage stormed through her and Molly tried to shake off his grip. "Let go of me."

"You need to wait over there."

The first responder pointed toward the area beyond the yellow crime scene tape, his rigid posture and stern expression obviously meant to wither any defiance. He was a man who was used to being obeyed—that much was obvious.

Molly squared her shoulders and glared. "And you need to remove your hand before I remove it for you. Permanently."

The man's eyes widened slightly and a hint of admiration ghosted across his features. Before Molly could dwell on it longer, however, he released her, crossing his muscled arms across his broad chest.

"Fine. Stay at your own risk. I have work to do."

With that, the hunk jogged back to the wreck and joined the other man inside the half-crushed SUV. Soon they'd removed a small boy from the front passenger seat, stabilized his neck with a brace, then slid him onto a waiting body board before repeating the same with a woman.

Reluctantly, Molly's curiosity about the daring rescuer blossomed. She watched him cuddle the child, coaxing a smile from the little guy, and a fresh pang of loneliness stabbed her—along with a lingering worry about ever finding someone who'd look at her that way.

Considering her relationship with Brian was DOA, Molly had grave doubts. For a woman brilliant in her profession, when it came to her personal life she was one big mess. Not that flirting at an emergency scene was appropriate, but she wasn't good at it anyway. She'd always been a wallflower—one more check in her Don't-Date-Much column.

"Gurney coming through."

Molly barely had time to keep her toes from getting crushed before the EMTs rolled past with the first victim. The two men hoisted the little boy up into the ambulance, then returned for the mother.

After they'd gotten the woman secured alongside her son, another man with a bandaged leg joined them in the back of the rig and the doors were closed. The hunk crouched near Molly's feet, gathering up scattered gear and shoving it into a medical bag. From her vantage point she couldn't help noticing how his tight navy blue T-shirt clung to his muscles and sinews and the way his black pants cupped his butt like a second skin.

Throat dry and head swirling, Molly panicked and said the first thing that popped into her mind—more random trivia. "Moose are herbivores and will casually devour seventy-three pounds of plant material a day in the summer. They like an assortment of shrubs, woody plants and aquatic vegetation; in the winter, their diet is more restricted."

She clamped her lips shut to prevent more useless facts from spilling out. Her father's voice echoed through her head, calling her pathetic. Worse, her last argument with Brian replayed in her mind like a bad song. The red flags were so easy to see now. She'd asked him to set a wedding date, to take their relationship to the next logical step, but he'd balked.

"Not everything's about logic. You solve everyone else's problems, but not your own."

The handsome first responder straightened and gave Molly a slow once-over. "Your facts are correct—except the bull that caused this accident wasn't looking for a meal. He was looking for a date."

Ah, right. She'd read about the mating season starting in late September in one of her pamphlets. Embarrassed heat prickled Molly's cheeks. Nervous, she smoothed a hand down her blond hair, still secured into two braids. Quickly she removed the bands at the ends of her plaits and ran her fingers through the stick-straight strands that wouldn't hold a curl to save their life.

The man's gaze followed the movement, the gray of his irises darkening to gunmetal. A throb of want started low in her belly, spreading like honey through her blood. It had been so long—too long—since a man had looked at her like that, and she found his arousal intoxicating.

"C'mon, Doc," the other medic said through the open door. "We got patients who need to be transported to Anchorage Mercy."

"Have a nice evening, ma'am," the hunk said, his stormy gaze flickering to her lips before returning to her eyes. "Be careful on the roads."

Molly stepped aside as the rescuer slung the medical kit over his shoulder, then climbed into the passenger side of the rig. The ambulance pulled away, maneuvering out of the tangle of vehicles blocking their path to the open roadway.

Hurrying back to the Range Rover, Molly started her engine, hoping to follow behind the emergency vehicle to her destination, all the while analyzing the new information she'd just gleaned. So he wasn't an EMT, he was a doctor. At Anchorage Mercy. Where they'd be working in close proximity.

Whoops. No.

Molly doused the sudden flare of excitement sweeping through her like wildfire. The last thing she needed was a rebound fling. Not with her career in the balance and her life in Chicago a shambles. Besides, she'd never chased after a man, never lived dangerously. At least not outside of the medical realm.

In the pursuit of a cure for her patients she'd tackle any challenge, take any risk.

In the pursuit of her own happiness? Not so much.

Still, one of the other reasons she'd chosen to do her TV show was to learn to listen to her gut. And right now her instincts were screaming that following that man and his ambulance represented her best shot at finding the hospital. So, Molly reasoned, this wasn't about a rebound relationship or a booty call with a hot doctor at all. It was about solving her next case and saving her show. She would worry about the rest later.

Squinting out the windshield through the gathering twilight, Molly realized she couldn't go through all the jumbled vehicles snarled in gridlock and still catch up to the ambulance, so she went around instead, driving her off-road-capable vehicle into the grassy gulley between lanes and past the still blocked section of roadway, then back onto the asphalt highway.

She might be late to her meeting, but if she was lucky she could still salvage this debacle.

CHAPTER TWO

"DR. FLYNN, I'M glad your producer was able to find a slot in the schedule for us."

The hospital's chief of staff grasped Molly's hand, his white hair and jolly blue eyes reminding her of Santa. He'd been kind enough not to mention she was an hour late. She was never late. Another lesson courtesy of her bully father. He'd always noticed any tardiness and the results had never been good.

"Your dad and I were classmates in medical school. How is he these days?"

Molly took the seat he offered. It seemed she hadn't quite outrun the looming shadow of her father after all. "He's currently in Beijing, conducting a training conference on the latest alternative techniques for closure of the open abdomen."

"Fascinating." The chief sat behind his desk and straightened his name plate. "Dr. David Carpenter" it proclaimed, in engraved gold letters. "And, please, call me Dr. Dave."

"Okay."

The cluttered room was the opposite of Molly's own pristine office back home. Amongst his papers and files were several family photos, in which everyone was laugh-

ing and cheerful. Smiles—genuine ones, anyway—were
rare in the Flynn family.

"What can you tell me about my patient, Dr. Dave?"

"Yes, yes. Of course." He searched through a stack
of charts on a shelf against the far wall then handed her
one. "His name is Robert Templeton, though he prefers
to be called Bobby. Thirty-one and a professional hockey
player for our hometown team the Anchorage Anoraks."

"Anoraks?" Molly raised a brow. "Isn't that a type
of jacket?"

Dr. Dave chuckled. "Yep. But it sounded cool so we
went with it."

"I see. Says here he's an enforcer. What exactly does
that mean?"

"It's not an official position on the hockey team, more
of a tough guy. He starts fights to protect the smaller guys
from taking the hits."

"Huh."

Molly had gone to a Blackhawks game in Chicago
once, with Brian, and had had to cover her eyes during the worst of the brawls. Even a year spent in the ER
hadn't prepared her for the copious amounts of gore and
raw testosterone. If her new patient regularly partook in
those kinds of brutal activities, it was no wonder he'd
landed in the hospital.

"What are his current symptoms?"

"He was initially seen through our outpatient clinic
for contact dermatitis."

She frowned. "How does a man go from a simple skin
rash to cardiac arrest?"

"Good question." Dr. Dave sat back in his chair. "The
treating physician gave him samples of diphenhydramine
to take before he left and the wheezing started shortly
afterward."

"He was allergic to the anti-allergy medicine?"

"It would appear so."

"Looks like they gave him point one cc of epinephrine to counteract his reaction to the antihistamine." She traced her finger down the chart documentation. "Could he have an underlying heart condition? A skin infection like cellulitis can cause a rapid pulse. Or perhaps inflamed blood vessels from vasculitis?"

"Nope. His CBC results were normal. No signs of an infection anywhere."

"Hmm." She flipped to the patient's labs, then went back to the history and the physical. "No food allergies? He's not taking any meds on a regular basis?"

"None."

"And he's been complaining of strange scents?"

"Yes. Says he smells cinnamon and cloves all the time."

"All right." Difficult cases were Molly's bread and butter. She took them as a personal challenge. "Can you please order a CT of his chest to rule out Churg-Strauss Syndrome? His bloodwork may have been normal, but inflammation of the blood vessels in his heart, lungs and skin would explain all his symptoms. Also, let's start him on a high-dose steroid therapy."

"CSS doesn't have a good prognosis, does it?" Dr. Dave asked, his tone concerned.

"For patients diagnosed and treated quickly the life expectancy is five years. Untreated, Mr. Templeton would have a year at most. Of course there's always the chance this isn't autoimmune-related."

"You're the expert, Dr. Flynn. I'll get these orders to the staff right away." Dr. Dave smiled—the kind of fond grin she'd always wanted from her own father but never received. "You look so much like your dad."

Molly clasped her hands atop the file on her lap. Looks were about the only thing she and her father had in common. Always active, Roger Flynn expected everyone around him to adhere to his hectic schedule. To him, Molly had always been too quiet and boring, preferring to stay home and read a good book rather than operate in the jungle.

"Would you like to meet your patient now?" Dr. Dave stood and moved toward the door. "I believe your crew's waiting for us outside Bobby's room."

"Of course." She followed him out into the busy hallway. "And, please, call me Molly."

"Okay." He pushed the button for the elevator. "All the staff assigned to Bobby have signed the required releases except one. I'm still working on him."

"Unfortunately anyone who doesn't sign the forms can't participate in the care of the patient from this point forward. My crew films whenever I'm present, to make sure we get an accurate portrayal of the process." The elevator dinged and they boarded. "Perhaps this person can be reassigned?"

"Right." Dr. Dave chuckled. "And perhaps polar bears will learn to tap dance."

Molly glanced up, surprised by his sarcasm.

"This particular physician is a close friend of Bobby's and can be…stubborn when it comes to people he considers family. I talked to him again, before you got here, but he hasn't budged on the publicity releases. I'm afraid he prefers to keep a low profile. Dedicated workaholic, really."

"I see." Molly crossed her arms, wishing she'd had time to unpack her lab coat and cover up her casual travel clothes. "Well, I don't know anything about this Dr. Ryder, or his reasons for not signing, but those rules come directly from the network. Besides, treating a close friend or family member is a conflict of interest."

"Oh, I'm still the patient's official care provider."

The elevator arrived on the fourth floor and Dr. Dave held the doors, exiting after Molly.

"But Bobby signed consent forms allowing Jake full access to his medical records when he was admitted, and granted him power of attorney in case he's incapacitated."

Molly waited while Dr. Dave walked on ahead to the nurses' station, to speak with a curvy Latino woman whose name tag read "Gladys."

"Our boy available?" he asked.

"Yes, sir, Dr. Dave. He's got company, though."

"Dr. Ryder?"

"Yep."

"Great." He turned to Molly once more, his smile broad. "You'll like Dr. Ryder. He's a brilliant trauma surgeon, like your father. The youngest head of EM in Anchorage Mercy history. Cut his teeth on combat rescues in Afghanistan…"

Molly only half listened from that point, her mind still snagged on Dr. Dave's earlier words.

"He's a brilliant trauma surgeon, like your father."

Great. Just what she needed. Roger Flynn, Version Two.

"Hey, Mol. About time you got here," said her cameraman Rob, coming around the corner with her show's field producer, Neal. "Thought we'd have to send out a search party."

"Funny." She smoothed her hand down her shirt, then asked Neal, "Everything all set?"

"Everything except the guy sitting in the room with the patient."

"Molly?" Dr. Dave stood with his hand on the door. "Ready to go in?"

"Of course." She turned to her crew. "Give me a moment."

Resolve steeled, she followed Dr. Dave into Bobby Templeton's room. Whatever this Dr. Ryder's issue was with being on TV, she needed him to get over it or get out. Perhaps all those years of dealing with her father had made for good practice after all.

"Bobby, this is Dr. Molly Flynn, from Diagnosis Critical. As we discussed, she'll be managing your case from this point forward." Dr. Dave placed a guiding hand on Molly's back and gave her a slight nudge. "Dr. Flynn, this is our local superstar—NWHL MVP Bobby Templeton."

"Hey." The burly guy gave her a small wave. "Honor to meet you. I watch your show all the time when I'm not training. My favorite episode was the one with the weird toe fungus." His gaze darted from her to the man at his bedside. "What's the matter, Jake? Tongue-tied around a beautiful woman?"

Dr. Dave smiled. "Dr. Flynn—this is Dr. Jake Ryder."

She turned, her polite smile freezing then falling. Dr. Ryder was the gorgeous rescuer from the accident scene. With her luck, she should've guessed.

He looked different now, dressed in scrubs instead of his navy and black EMT uniform. Not that the pale green material looked bad. Quite the contrary. With his stethoscope slung around his neck—no lab coat—he was transformed into a stoic professional, but she wasn't fooled. She'd seen glimpses of the passion lurking beneath his surface at the accident scene. In fact, just the thought of him rushing headlong into danger to save that little boy and his mother caused a fresh wave of giddiness to bubble through her.

But her attraction to him wasn't a good thing. It was a distraction she couldn't afford.

Molly swallowed hard against the lump in her throat caused by the tension between them. "Nice to meet you again."

"Again?" Dr. Dave asked with interest. "You two know each other?"

"I came across an emergency scene where Dr. Ryder was working on my way from the airport. He seemed quite…handy to have around." Molly rubbed her arm where Dr. Jake Ryder had grabbed her, her flesh still tingling from his touch.

"I should've guessed you were media."

The way he said the last word, like a curse, set her hackles rising. Common sense demanded she keep her head down, focus on work. Ignore this man who broke her concentration and keep her distance. Unfortunately he seemed to push all her buttons without even trying.

She met his sanctimonious stare directly. "What's wrong with the media?"

Instead of answering her question, the man looked back to Dr. Dave and exhaled sharply, his expression a mix of disgust and exhaustion. "Can we hurry this up, please? I'm coming off a thirty-six-hour rotation."

"Jake, please," Dr. Dave implored. "Dr. Flynn's one of the best in her field. You should reconsider signing those forms. Together, you two could make a fabulous team."

"No." He widened his stance, an immoveable wall of nope. "No releases. Not until I've seen for myself I can trust her."

It was the derision in his tone, Molly decided, that really got to her. She'd developed a thick skin over the years out of necessity, and could put aside almost any slight. Except one against her professional conduct.

Incensed, she stepped closer to the arrogant man, ignoring the heat of him penetrating her thin cotton T-shirt and the clean, soapy scent of his skin. Bad enough that she had to constantly prove herself to her father. She wasn't about to take the same crap from this pompous stranger—no matter how maddeningly attractive.

"My integrity isn't in question here, Dr. Ryder. Now, as per my network's guidelines, I must exclude you from Bobby's care unless you sign the required paperwork. I understand having the crew trailing your every step might be a headache, but—"

"You don't understand a damned thing, lady," he growled, his jaw set.

"Sorry, Dr. Flynn, but no one's touching me if Jake's out of the picture," Bobby added. "My prerogative."

Molly crossed her arms, all previous flutters of attraction for the handsome ER doc buried beneath a mountain of affront. She hated appearing so flustered, and cringed inwardly at the thought of how her father would judge her—letting her emotions get the better of her—but there was nothing to be done at this point.

"Then it appears we're at an impasse."

"Sure does."

Dr. Ryder mimicked her defiant posture and didn't give an inch. His gaze had gone positively flinty, and a small muscle ticked near his tense jaw, drawing her eyes to the hint of stubble shadowing his tanned skin.

"Why won't you sign the releases?" she demanded.

"Why do you think it's any of your business?"

His lips were pressed so tightly together Molly was surprised he could even get words out.

Dr. Dave coughed, the sound reverberating in the small room. "Jake, be reasonable. Dr. Flynn's a prodigy.

She graduated high school at thirteen. In addition to her medical degree she's earned two PhDs."

He cocked an eyebrow. "In what?"

"Art history and genetics," Molly said, her tone equally frosty.

"Then I'll be sure to call you the next time I need to know the DNA sequence for a Jackson Pollack painting."

"Unfortunately for you, Mr. Pollack didn't leave behind any DNA samples for testing. Although it might be possible to extract a specimen from his exhumed corpse, given the lack of oxygen and sunlight to denigrate the samples. In fact, the oldest actual DNA specimens hail from Greenland, extracted from beneath a mile of ice..."

Molly's voice trailed off as she took in the dazed stares of the others in the room and her heart sank. Not again.

"Right." Dr. Dave passed Bobby's chart to her on his way to the door. "I've got other patients to attend this evening. Jake, you'll have to leave if you won't sign the releases. We discussed this."

"I don't want to be on camera." Dr. Ryder scrubbed a hand over his face.

"Why not?" Molly asked again. "Perhaps if you voiced your concerns—"

"He just doesn't, okay?" Bobby rose to the defense of his friend. "Can't Jake be an off-screen consultant or something?"

The door opened and Neal stuck his head inside. "We need to get a move on, Mol. The network's called me five times already, wondering when they're going to receive initial footage."

Molly hated to admit defeat, but things were getting desperate. If a compromise would get this guy to agree to the network's terms then it was worth it—at least for now.

"Fine, Dr. Ryder. But you'll have to work around my

schedule. If I need access to Bobby you leave, no questions asked." Molly extended her hand. "Deal?"

He didn't move at first, and her hopes dwindled. Finally, Dr. Ryder grasped her hand, his voice sounding as reluctant as she felt. "Deal."

"Good."

Molly brushed aside the inconvenient flood of endorphins fizzing through her from his touch and handed him the patient's chart. She did her best work when she had colleagues with whom to brainstorm, and tonight she needed to bring her A game.

"Before the crew comes in, what's your assessment?"

Dr. Ryder thumbed through the pages, glancing at her with no small amount of suspicion. "Given the weird olfactory hallucinations, and the fact we've ruled out the other obvious choices, how about encephalitis?"

"The only elevated result on the CBC was a slightly higher than normal eosinophil level, which doesn't point to a brain infection."

Molly struggled to keep her voice steady. It wasn't the case that unsettled her. It was this man. He was too big, too masculine, too…everything.

Gladys came to check the patient's vitals. Molly wanted to question Dr. Ryder further, but his cell phone buzzed.

He pulled it from the front pocket of his scrubs, then scowled at the screen. "I need to get back to my department. Bobby, you're okay with all this?"

"Yep." The patient shifted on his bed, the plastic frame creaking under his muscled weight. "I'll call you if I need you, Jake. And don't hover. You just think you have to watch out for me because—"

"That's not why."

A look passed between the two men and the air in

the room seemed to vibrate with a secret silent understanding.

Then Dr. Ryder headed for the door, calling to her over his shoulder. "May I speak to you outside, Dr. Flynn?"

Still trembling slightly from a jumble of unexpected confusing emotions, Molly took a deep breath and followed him out into the hall. She hated being this overwrought in front of people, especially her new patient, but this issue between her and Dr. Jake Ryder needed to end. She wouldn't let him destroy her best chance to save her show, even if it meant putting up with his irritating sexiness for the duration of her shoot.

"What are your next steps?" Jake asked once they'd reached a secluded corner of the hall.

The words had emerged more harshly than he'd intended, given Dr. Flynn's slight wince, but he couldn't seem to help it. Bad enough that she'd walked around that accident scene looking like some Disney princess come to life—all big blue eyes and lush blond hair—making him itch to hold and protect her. The tightness in his chest intensified, though his frustration was directed more toward himself than anyone else. Even worse that the first woman he'd felt attracted to since Kellie's departure was the media star Dr. Dave had invited to collaborate on Bobby's case.

Irony at its finest, folks.

Trust wasn't something Jake gave freely. He'd been burned too badly in the past. The truth was, he had a hard time believing in anyone these days, except his Army buddies and his tight-knit circle of friends. Intimacy required vulnerability, and Jake didn't do vulnerable anymore. Besides, he was a successful trauma surgeon. With his crazy schedules and on-call nightmares it was difficult to meet people, let alone have any kind of life outside his profession.

That was the excuse he was going with anyway.

And maybe Molly Flynn was the best at what she did—if Dr. Dave was to be believed. That didn't excuse her impassioned speech about her sterling integrity—which, crazily enough, had only increased his foolish awareness of her as a woman. All he'd been able to concentrate on when she'd talked was her sparkling azure eyes and soft pink lips. God help him, he was in trouble here. Because she was Bobby's specialist and a TV sensation.

The last time he'd dealt with the press—after his commendation—he'd gotten way more than his fifteen minutes of fame. Worse, the glare of media attention had only intensified after his relationship with Kellie had fallen apart, with reporters poking and prodding into his wreck of a personal life like vultures at a roadside kill.

The last thing Jake wanted now was to delve into that shark-infested cesspool again, but he couldn't leave Bobby without an advisor in his corner. The guy had risked his own life to save Jake—literally. No way would he turn his back on him, no matter how uncomfortable the situation, and releases be damned.

During his time in Afghanistan he'd spent hours on the front lines, patching up men and women and ally civilians who'd given their all for their country. He'd enlisted initially for the experience, and to uphold the family legacy—his father had served as a Special Operations Pilot during Vietnam. But six years with the Seventy-Fifth Ranger Regiment had made his fellow soldiers Jake's surrogate family, his brothers and sisters. With them, he'd found a tribe of kindred spirits all addicted to danger and valor.

Day in and day out he'd vowed to protect every one of them with his life, if needed. The time had come to make good on his promise.

Rock—meet proverbial hard place.

"I've ordered a chest CT to rule out CSS," Dr. Flynn said, jarring Jake from his thoughts. "If you'll excuse me…"

"Wait." He pinched the bridge of his nose between his thumb and forefinger, doing his best to ignore the heat of her body wrapping around him, beckoning him closer. "I think we got started on the wrong foot."

"Yes, I think we did," Molly said, her gaze glittering with obvious irritation.

She wasn't going to make this easy. Then again, neither was he.

"Churg-Strauss Syndrome is a severe conclusion to jump to so quickly, isn't it?" he asked, puzzled.

Dr. Flynn sighed, the rise and fall of her chest causing the front of her T-shirt to hug her small curves. Not that he was looking. Nope. Definitely not looking.

"It's a remote possibility, yes, but it would explain all his symptoms. And I like to be thorough. Satisfied now, Dr. Ryder?"

Not by a long shot, sweetheart.

Sudden images of them tangled in his sheets, her long silky hair splayed around him, swamped Jake's exhausted mind. He backed away, alarmed. He'd just met her, for goodness' sake. Must be the lack of sleep. Had to be.

"Keep me posted on the results." Jake handed Bobby's file back to her, then headed for the elevators. "If you don't, I know where to find you."

The brief flare of awareness in her eyes made his own pulse kick higher. Apparently he wasn't the only one affected by this weird connection between them. Good thing she'd be on the first plane out of here as soon as Bobby had recovered.

All Jake wanted was an empty bed and peace and quiet. Unfortunately he still had about an hour of documentation to finish and a few patients either to admit or discharge before he was off duty for forty-eight blissful hours. Hours when he wouldn't have to see Dr. Flynn or deal with the odd blaze of emotions she stirred inside him, making him want to both kiss her and throttle her in equal measures.

It was crazy. And then there was that slight yearning that crept into her expression sometimes, like when they'd been standing in the hallway discussing the case—a hesitation that called to his inner protector. Dangerous, that, since it threatened those precious walls he'd built—the ones meant to keep his heart from getting torn out and stomped on again.

Honestly, it had been so long since he'd had a significant other he couldn't remember what it was like. During the last few months before Kellie had left him things had been so strained they'd just been going through the motions. Even so, the last thing he'd expected had been her accepting a network job in New York City without even discussing it with him. Blindsided didn't begin to cover how he'd felt at the time. How he still felt, in some ways.

Eighteen months had passed and it still hacked Jake off whenever he remembered. He'd thought they had something good together—something real, something lasting.

He guessed that just went to show what an idiot he was when it came to love.

Good thing he was brilliant in his career. Saving lives was what he did, who he was. Since his fiancée's abrupt departure Jake had thrown himself into saving his patients, into making their lives better. It helped him forget about the loneliness, the doubts. Doubts that if he hadn't been enough for Kellie, why should he believe he'd ever be enough for anyone else?

One more reason to stick with short-term flings.

No muss, no fuss, no commitment. No chance for heartbreak and disappointment.

Yeah, perhaps if circumstances had been different, and he and Molly had met at some bar on a lonely night, they might've shared more than a medical case. Jake might've let her get a glimpse of the man locked behind those staunch barriers…might've let that instant connection between them evolve into something more.

But not now. Now he'd consult on Bobby's case, be his advocate. That was all.

The elevator dinged and Jake climbed on board, ignoring the niggle of regret that bored into his chest.

Once he reached the first floor, he headed to his office near the ER and the inbox full of patient files awaiting his attention.

Yawning, he took a seat and grabbed the top chart, scanning the lab reports and papers inside before making his notations. Work kept him busy and sane. Work also kept him distracted. The constant hustle and bustle was part of the reason he spent so much time here. The other part was the fact that he didn't have much going on outside of this place.

Determined to stay on track, Jake worked his way through the stack of charts until they were finished, then grabbed his keys and did a final check on the condition of his patients at the nurses' station. Once that was taken care of for the night, Jake headed home.

He climbed behind the wheel of his truck and cranked the engine, squeezing his tired eyes shut. Bobby's words during that firefight in Kandahar were ringing in his head like a clarion call.

"We'll make it, bud…"

And they would No matter what trials and temptations Dr. Molly Flynn might pose.

CHAPTER THREE

"JUST PUT YOUR arm around it!" Rob yelled to Molly from behind a swath of thick rope. "Pretend it's that hot doc at the hospital."

She gave her cameraman a peeved stare. Had her attraction to Jake Ryder been that apparent? If Rob and Neal's smirks were any indication then, yes, it had. Ugh. She usually kept a tight lid on her emotions. One more casualty of her jet lag and post-break-up-from-Brian funk.

Fabulous.

Exhaling loudly, Molly did her best to snuggle up to the world's largest broccoli spear—weighing in at an astonishing thirty-nine pounds—and flashed a TV-perfect fake smile for the camera. The thing smelled like dirt and towered above her, its fanned floret casting ominous shadows. She'd read that Alaska was famous for its abnormally large produce, and here she was, within breathing distance of the proof.

"Perfect!" Rob gave her a thumbs-up while Neal texted on his phone.

Remarkably, they seemed to have good cell service out here—better than she'd had on her drive in from the airport the night before.

"I want to grab a corn dog before we head to the next location. Mol, you want anything?"

She shook her head. They'd set out this morning to capture some of the local flavor before her case took precedence. Bright and early, they'd packed up her Range Rover to explore all the area had to offer. After stopping at a diner for breakfast, and taking some exterior shots at the must-see spots in Anchorage—the modern curved sculptures outside the Z.J. Loussac Public Library, the gorgeous Native American exhibits at Rasmuson Center, the rustic quaintness of the Oscar Anderson House Museum, the city's oldest residence—they'd driven forty minutes north to the small town of Palmer and the Alaska State Fair.

She released the giant cruciferous vegetable and scanned the vendors there, selling everything from pretzels to enormous ice cream cones. The air smelled of sweet popped corn and deep-fried dough. Rob tottered off to get his corn dog and Neal linked arms with Molly, leading her down a path designated as "The Purple Trail" to buy something called a Doughnut Burger.

"C'mon. It's guaranteed to make you gain ten pounds." He gave her a wink and placed his order but she passed.

She tried to eat healthily, even while traveling. If she ever let herself go physically her father would be the first to comment, so it was safer to not go down that road to begin with—no matter how tempting at times like this.

After collecting his food, she and Neal took a seat at one of the many wooden picnic tables to wait for Rob. The two guys had been a couple since before she'd joined the network, though they kept their personal relationship out of the office.

"Are you sure you don't want a bite?" Neal asked.

Molly eyed the thick caribou steak patty between two slabs of grilled glazed doughnut, ketchup and mustard dripping down its sides, with trepidation. She could almost feel her arteries clogging. "Uh…no thanks."

"It's so scrumptious." Neal wiped his face with his napkin, speaking to her around a mouthful of food. "At least try a corn fritter with honey butter dipping sauce. They're delicious."

"I'm still stuffed from breakfast, really."

Molly pulled her phone from her pocket and zipped through her emails while Rob took a seat on the bench beside Neal and slid a plate in front of her.

"I got you a funnel cake, Mol. My treat." Rob grinned. "Extra powdered sugar."

Frowning, she stared down at the greasy confection. Its yeasty aroma was enticing, despite its odd look. She'd heard of these things, but never tried one herself. Tentatively she pulled off a tiny chunk and ate it. The treat melted in her mouth, releasing its sweet, rich goodness.

Eyes wide, Molly blinked at her smiling crew. "That's amazing."

"Told you." Neal winked, then nudged Rob with his elbow.

She gobbled down more of the sweet deliciousness before answering her buzzing phone without checking the caller ID, assuming it would be the hospital. "Dr. Molly Flynn."

"Hello, dear. Did you hear about Martha?"

"Yes, Mother."

Neal raised a speculative brow and Molly swiveled on her bench to face in the opposite direction. She and her older sister Martha weren't exactly close, but that hadn't kept Molly from escaping the dreaded Baby Aboard! email blitz.

"I heard."

"Then you'll help me plan the shower?"

"She's five months along." Molly squinted into the hazy morning sunshine.

"Never too early to plan, dear. Not if you want the best."

And of course Martha would have the best. She always got the best—from prom dresses to husbands.

"We need to reserve a room and order flowers. Pick a caterer and a cake maker too."

"It's a baby shower, Mother. Not a wedding."

A cute little girl dressed to perform in one of the fair's many shows waddled by and Molly smiled. She'd always loved children, but having her own someday seemed farther out of reach than ever. Mainly because of the belief her father had instilled within her every day of her childhood—that if people saw her true fallible self, her imperfections and quirks, they wouldn't love her, couldn't love her. So she hid behind her slick professionalism, her media persona, never letting anyone get too close to the truth.

"Speaking of weddings—how are things with Brian?" her mother asked.

The question hit Molly like a sucker punch. For a moment she considered lying about their separation, but her mother would find out soon enough—if she didn't already know. "We're taking a break."

"Break?"

"Yes." Molly reached behind her and grabbed the remaining huge chunk of funnel cake, shoving it in her mouth without thinking. "He's busy with stocks and bonds and I'm swamped with shooting in Anchorage for the next few weeks, so it's fine."

"I see." Her mother's tone suggested that she'd seen straight through Molly's crap. "You can't keep doing this, dear."

"Doing what?"

"Putting your personal life on hold. You're not getting any younger."

Exactly what she didn't need today. A baby pep-talk from her mother. When she was a teen, Molly had often wished she had the kind of parents that showed up in her favorite sitcoms. The loving, supportive variety, who never pushed their kids to do things they didn't want and loved them unconditionally for who they were. But real life wasn't like TV, and usually you just had to do the best with what you'd got.

Her shoulders slumped as the scent of fresh kettle corn drifted on the breeze. Molly's lifelong imposed restraint buckled under the pressure and she all but tripped over herself on her way to buy a bag. After all, she should experiment while she still had the chance, right?

Molly changed the subject while she waited in line. "What are my duties for the shower?"

"Decorations. And I'll see if your father knows anyone."

"For what?"

"For you. When will you be back home, dear?"

"I just got to Alaska."

Not to mention the fact the last thing she wanted was a blind date with one of her father's legion of devoted clones.

Molly paid and thanked the vendor then returned to the table with her popcorn. "I'm not ready to date anyone else yet. Besides, there's a colleague here who's giving me issues."

"Really? Is he attractive?"

"No."

Yes. All she had to do was picture Dr. Ryder's stormy gray eyes, his chiseled jaw and toned muscles, and molten heat spread outward from her core to sizzle through her bloodstream. It seemed the gorgeous man caused her problems even when he wasn't around.

If only he wasn't her new colleague.

If only...what?

No. That line of thinking was completely unaccept-able. They were working together. Molly was only here temporarily. Dr. Ryder treated her as if she harbored a deadly contagious disease. It was all so irritating and an-noying and incredibly intriguing.

Scowling, she shoved another handful of popcorn in her mouth. "What difference does it make? He's a nui-sance. Challenging everything I do, every order I give."

"Perhaps if you tried charm instead of your usual abruptness you might get further."

Molly checked her watch. If they were going to fit another location in before she went to the hospital, they had to get a move on. "I need to go."

"Thank you for proving my point, dear."

She felt her mother's disapproval like a slap.

"I'll call you next week with a list of supplies."

"Fine," Molly said, though the line had already gone dead. Talk about abrupt. Clicking off her phone, she turned back to her crew. "Have you guys decided on our last stop?"

"We have." Neal gave her his devious smile—the one that always warned of mischief ahead. "You ready?"

She tossed her trash in a nearby bin, then followed her crew toward the exit. "Can I at least get a clue where we're headed?"

"I talked to one of the ER nurses yesterday before you arrived," Rob said. "She's part of a volunteer moun-tain rescue group. They're practicing maneuvers today. Neal thinks it might be a nice way to segue into the local medical scene."

"Ready, Ryder?" shouted a man in an orange emergency jumpsuit.

"Ready!" Jake yelled back.

He was currently dangling off the north face of O'Malley's Peak, wind whistling, while his training-partner-slash-victim for this rescue was strapped to a body board.

"Victim's secure for lift."

He sagged into his riggings to wait, enjoying the stunning views from this vantage point. Bright autumn colors dotted the landscape as far as the eye could see, and the city of Anchorage gleamed in the distance. Most tourists cleared out of Chugach State Park this late in the season, leaving it to year-round locals like himself until the first snows hit. Then this place would be packed again, with ice-climbers, skiers and winter enthusiasts.

And, like clockwork, some of those weekend daredevils would do something ill-advised, requiring intervention. That was why he was here. Plus, volunteering for the Anchorage Rescue Team—or the ART—helped him keep his rescue skills sharp. And, particularly this weekend, he hoped the training might help him forget about a certain blond doctor who seemed to haunt his every waking moment.

Dr. Molly Flynn was proving to be a challenge. In more ways than one.

Inhaling the crisp mountain air, Jake distracted himself by double-checking both his harness and the one around his pretend victim, then tested the ropes and carabiners for strength. He'd scaled these peaks since his teens, knew every nook and cranny by heart. He and his dad had used to come here when he was in high school, just to hang out and relax.

Those carefree days seemed a million miles away now, with his parents off traveling the country by RV for three-quarters of each year, returning to Alaska only during the brief summer months. In fact Bobby was really the closest person he had left in Anchorage.

If I lose him…

Jake's muscles tightened with anxiety. The wind gusted harder and he grabbed the ropes near his victim's chest to steady himself. He wouldn't lose Bobby because he couldn't lose Bobby. Just as he couldn't allow himself to get involved with Dr. Flynn. It would be bad. Very bad. Besides, he didn't trust her—would never trust her. Kellie had destroyed his ability to trust.

"You trying to cop a feel, Doc?" Wendy Smith—fellow ART volunteer, an ER nurse at Anchorage Mercy and today's pretend victim—grinned up at him from the body board. "Been there, done that—not going back again."

"Shut up, smartass." Jake focused on the distant hazy peaks of Denali, doing his best to shake off his melancholy. He and Wendy had known each other since grade school. "You have a rare day off too, Clutch?"

"Don't call me that. I hate it," she said.

Half-Inupiat and all attitude, Wendy looked like a swimsuit model, swore like a drunken drill sergeant, and had grown up fast after her mother had passed away when she was only twelve.

Living with three older brothers and having a mechanic for a father had made her into quite a tomboy, and Jake often found her tinkering with cars when she wasn't saving lives in his ER. They'd gone out once, but the romantic sparks hadn't been there. They'd remained good friends ever since.

"And I could ask the same of you," she said.

"What?" He scowled. "I take plenty of time off."

"Right."

"I can't help it if my patients need me."

She gave him an exasperated look. "Whatever gets you through the night."

He squirmed a bit. Her comment had hit too close to home. Trouble was, his time-honored excuse wasn't getting him through the night anymore. Especially since a certain prickly and disturbingly pretty media star had arrived.

They were totally unsuited. Polar opposites on so many levels it wasn't even funny. His best bet would be to put her out of his mind and concentrate on Bobby's recovery. Except all it seemed to take was one thought of her and his blood burned like lit gasoline, sparking a primal rush of need he didn't expect or want.

Jake peered up toward the summit, waiting for the signal to start his ascent. Finally their new field commander waved, giving the all clear, and he started the slow pull-stop-readjust-pull-stop-readjust that would hoist them back to civilization. His muscles strained and the excess adrenaline clawing through his system began to burn off with the effort.

Undeterred by the fact that she was supposed to be comatose, Wendy continued to chatter. "I hear you're working with a celebrity."

"Excuse me?" Jake muttered a curse as a particularly stiff carabiner gave him issues.

"That fancy doctor from the television show. Hot stuff, from what the orderlies say."

Frowning, Jake maneuvered them around a rock ledge. For some reason the thought of other men talking about Dr. Flynn made him want to punch something. "Which ones?"

"Pretty much every straight single male working at Anchorage Mercy."

Wendy shrugged, causing the body board to sway precariously. Jake gave her a warning glare.

"The ones I talked to said they wouldn't mind showing her some Alaskan hospitality..."

Between the strong breeze and Wendy's observations, this ascent was becoming more treacherous by the second. The fact that Jake had stayed up far later than he should have researching Molly Flynn's credentials last night probably didn't help either. Nor did the fact that Dr. Dave had been right, dammit. Dr. Flynn was brilliant—but such overachievement came at a price.

In his experience, high intelligence like hers meant spending all your time with your nose stuck in a book, not connecting with people. One more difference between them—which only made his ever-growing attraction to her that much more baffling.

"Dr. Flynn's only interested in her case and her show—that's it."

"Real workaholic, huh?" Wendy shoved her hand in the pocket of her jumpsuit. "Sounds like someone else I know."

"I'm not a workaholic. I have other interests, hobbies. Look at me now."

"Yes. Dancing on a knife's edge is so relaxing, eh? Here."

Jake stared at the oblong ivory-colored object she held out to him. "What's that?"

"A carved walrus tooth—brings the owner luck."

He tucked it safely in his jumpsuit pocket, then worked the carabiners again. "Thanks."

"Any time. My brother Mike's got a whole tent full of them at the State Fair this year. Tourists love them." Wendy winked. "So, you going to ask this woman out or not?"

"Not," Jake said.

As they neared the summit the voices of the ART team grew louder—pretend orders were barked, pretend conversations with the hospital were called in by 911.

From this height, the valley below was even more breathtaking—golden fields, a few mountain goats foraging, the modern skyscrapers of Anchorage shining like golden monoliths in the sunshine, and the sparkling waters of the lagoon and Cook Inlet beyond deep blue and clear. The air zinged with the mossy scent of dead leaves and the cry of a red-tail hawk pierced the sky.

Multiple hands reached down to help Jake get Wendy over the edge of the summit, then assisted him in the last few steps to the top. Once they were both safely on solid ground Jake unhooked the ropes from his harness and felt the last of his pent-up tension dissipate.

Maybe Wendy was right. Not about asking out Dr. Flynn, but at least about getting to know her. After all, they would be stuck working with each other for the next few weeks. Better to be on friendly terms than at one another's throats the whole time. And perhaps the spark of rivalry between them would drive them both to solve Bobby's case.

Sparks…

In an instant his traitorous mind flashed images of he and Dr. Flynn creating an entirely different kind of fire, reaching new heights of passion between the sheets, their limbs tangled, his hands in her hair, his mouth on her skin, his name on her lips as he brought her to the brink of ecstasy…

Jake cursed under his breath and ran a hand through his wind-tousled hair. He had to stop thinking about Dr. Flynn that way. They were working on a case together. She'd be gone in a few weeks. He'd be stuck here alone. Again. It was too complicated.

Dr. Flynn was here for Bobby. He couldn't allow himself to go down that path again, to be vulnerable. He couldn't. Jake took a deep breath and scanned the area, spotting the ART vehicles, a burgundy-colored Range Rover, and a cameraman with his lens pointed directly at...

Oh. Hell. No.

He stalked over to where the woman foremost in his thoughts stood with her crew. "What's going on?" Jake demanded. "Why are you here?"

"Good to see you again, Dr. Ryder." Dr. Flynn's producer, Neal, extended his hand. "We've been out all morning getting exterior shots. One of your nurses gave us a tip about this practice drill today. We figured we'd take advantage of the beautiful scenery and the excitement."

"Must be fun...cavorting around while Bobby's in his hospital bed." Jake's gaze never left Dr. Flynn.

Color slowly flushed her cheeks. "I do not cavort and I'm on call with the staff twenty-four-seven." She gave him a cursory glance. "What's your excuse, Dr. Ryder?"

"This is my day off—not that it's any of your business." Jake had intended to be brusque, except the nearer he got, the more he caught Dr. Flynn's scent—light, floral, like sunshine and happiness. He clenched his fists at his sides.

This was ridiculous. He shouldn't want to touch her. And yet he did. So much it hurt. His fingertips itched with the crazy urge to stroke her skin, to see if it felt as velvety as it looked. His lips tingled with the insane need to taste her. His heart thudded, drowning out every other sound in the area but her voice.

Summoning every ounce of willpower he possessed, Jake stepped back, turning to Neal once more. "You said one of my nurses gave you a tip that we'd be out here today. Who?"

"Her." The cameraman, Rob, pointed. "Over there."

Wendy waved innocently as the ART crew trundled her off to the MediVac unit.

Jake stared at the departing chopper, perplexed. Wendy, of all people, knew of his aversion to the limelight—knew what had happened with Kellie and how he didn't want to get involved like that again. Why would she push him?

Scowling, he refocused on Neal. "If you have any shots of me your footage is useless. No releases, remember?"

"Don't worry," Rob said. "I shot around you."

"We don't want to get sued any more than you want your privacy invaded, Dr. Ryder," Neal said.

"There are worse things than having people want to get to know you better," Dr. Molly Flynn said, still not looking at him.

"Really?" Jake kept his distance and jammed his hands into his pockets, in case he got the overwhelming urge to touch her again. "And what might they be?"

For a brief second pain flickered through her gaze, so fast he would've missed it if he hadn't been watching her so intently. The edges of Dr. Flynn's lips tightened, causing his well-guarded heart to tug.

"No one knowing the real you at all."

Her tone held such sadness that Jake had to force himself not to ask more. Whatever the woman's issues were, he'd do best to steer clear of them. No good could come from forming an attachment to her. He had a busy life— no time for a relationship, and no time for what would surely be nothing but heartbreak in the end.

With a curt nod, Jake re-joined the rest of the ART team to help them pack up the gear, reminding himself for the umpteenth time of his goals for the next few weeks. He'd work with Dr. Flynn to consult on Bobby's case—always off-camera—and monitor his best buddy's progress.

Forget this awareness that flared brighter than a supernova. Forget this wayward attraction. Forget his raging pulse and the way the world came alive whenever she was around.

That was the best option. The safe option. The smart option.

Now, if Jake could remember those things whenever they were together, he'd be all set.

CHAPTER FOUR

TWO DAYS PASSED with no further sign of Dr. Jake Ryder, though Gladys had let Molly know he'd stopped by each day to see Bobby. True to his word, he'd avoided both her and her crew like the plague. And, given all the weird reactions he evoked inside her whenever he was around, that was fine. Also, considering the fact she hadn't made any real progress on the Templeton file, Molly didn't need any distractions.

All Bobby's tests had been negative. Even the chest CT had showed no vascular problems, so no Churg-Strauss. Good for the patient, bad for Molly—since she had nothing else to go on at present.

She slumped in the hard plastic chair in her tiny interim office and sighed. Cases had stumped her before, but never one like this.

Stretching her aching neck and back, Molly stared up at the ceiling. She hadn't slept much since she'd been here, which wasn't uncommon. New hotel, new bed, new noises to wake her every hour or so... About the time she got used to her surroundings it would be time to leave again and head home. But at least she hadn't received any more surprise phone calls from her mother. Or hurtful texts from Brian.

Molly yawned, then winced at the stiffness in her

muscles. Maybe she should've taken Gladys up on the second cup of coffee she'd offered earlier.

The familiar voices of her crew filtered in through the open office door. Today Neal and Rob were shooting filler scenes and staff interviews for the show, in between documenting the patient's many tests and visitors. All in all, the whole trip thus far had been a lesson in patience and persistence instead of the rousing ratings booster the network had envisioned.

Pushing to her feet and stretching, Molly was just about to head out and grab some lunch in the cafeteria when the overhead PA system crackled to life.

"Dr. Flynn to ICU Room 407, stat. Paging Dr. Flynn to ICU 407, stat."

That was Bobby's room.

She raced for the door. Nurses were pushing trays of equipment in the same direction and Molly broke into a jog. Rob and Neal were already waiting by the door when she arrived. She elbowed her way through the small crowd, concerned. Bobby had been doing fine when she'd checked on him an hour earlier.

"Stand back, please."

Molly shoved the privacy curtain aside. Bobby sat on his bed, arms crossed and face contorted with fear, huddled in a corner of the mattress, staring up at the ceiling in horror. She checked the monitors—his vitals appeared normal.

"He's delirious," Gladys said, shooing the other people out of the room. "Keeps mumbling about the enemy on the roof and people creeping through the walls."

Leaning closer to her patient, Molly put her hand on his arm—only to feel his whole body stiffen.

Bobby collapsed onto the bed, convulsing. "He's seizing!"

"What's going on?" Dr. Ryder yelled as he burst into the room. "I got here as fast as I could."

Molly waved him over to the bed. "Help me get him on his side."

He rushed over and helped turn his friend. "Whoa. That rash is new."

"What rash?" She frowned down at the red blisters covering the patient's left lower leg. "Gladys, is this his first seizure?"

"Yes, Doctor."

The patient's body relaxed and Molly released Bobby's weight onto the mattress. "Any signs of fever prior?"

"No, Doctor."

Bobby blinked open his eyes and seemed genuinely shocked to find them all staring at him. "Why's everybody watching me?"

"Everything will be fine, Mr. Templeton. Don't panic." Molly gave him her best reassuring smile. "You had a seizure. Do you remember anything about what happened?"

"No. All I recall is speaking to the nurse, then things got fuzzy."

"Okay." She took his file from Gladys. "I'll get to the bottom of this, I promise. Let the nurse finish checking your vitals, then we'll talk again."

Dr. Ryder swore and looked away, but not before Molly caught the deep worry in his eyes. It was the same concern burrowing deep inside her.

"I'm going to speak with Dr. Flynn for a moment and I'll be back," he told Bobby.

"Sure." Bobby tucked the robe tightly around himself again. "Just please someone find out what's wrong with me."

Molly exited the room, Dr. Ryder hot on her heels. Her mind raced with new information, quickening her steps.

"He was delirious right before you arrived. Talked about people being up on the roof and men creeping through the walls. Do you know anything about that?"

They entered her office seconds later and Dr. Ryder closed the door behind them. "I still think it could be encephalitis. Did you get a lumbar puncture?"

"I did. This morning. Waiting on results."

Molly took a seat behind her desk and opened the folder, not missing the fact that he'd avoided her question. But she had bigger problems to solve first.

"Those vesicles on his leg look like herpes."

"If it is herpetic encephalitis, then his immune system is severely compromised."

Dr. Ryder leaned over her shoulder, unlooping the stethoscope from around his neck and placing it on Molly's desk as he stared at his friend's chart. His warmth surrounded her again, carrying along with it a hint of the crisp outdoors, reminding her of their last meeting on top of O'Malley's Peak. He'd been angry with her for being there, but there'd also been a lingering spark of want in his eyes. Just like that first night at the accident scene. An answering need coiled tight inside her before Molly tamped it down.

"Steroids suppress the immune system, but not to this degree, so it can't be the medication." She called the nurses' station. "Gladys, start Mr. Templeton on IV acyclovir: twelve hundred milligrams every eight hours for the next ten days."

Molly hung up, then peered at Jake over her shoulder, resisting the urge to snuggle against him.

"The drug is relatively non-toxic. Empirical treatment is recommended by the ADA."

"No argument here."

"That's a first."

"Don't worry. I'm sure we'll find something to disagree on momentarily."

He winked, and her stomach fluttered despite her solemn intent to steer clear of him.

Dr. Ryder held Molly's gaze for a long moment, his lips so close that if she leaned in an inch more they'd kiss…

Dr. Ryder cleared his throat and stepped back, returning his attention to the file, a hint of color flushing his high cheekbones. His words emerged a bit huskier than before—another sign that she wasn't the only one affected by this powerful connection between them.

"The herpes diagnosis still bothers me, though," he said, rubbing his hand over the back of his neck. "Seems too easy. What about Lupus? Bobby said he felt better on the steroids. That could explain why."

"Except the treatment for Lupus would be more steroids, which we can't use if it's encephalitis." Molly forced the words past her constricted throat. "I'll…uh… make sure the network edits you out of those shots."

"Oh, yeah." His dark brows drew together, as if he'd only just now remembered her crew had been filming back in Bobby's room.

He licked his lips and she wondered if his mouth tasted as good as it looked. Molly lowered her gaze and clasped her hands tight in her lap. She'd never felt so turned on, or so torn. Her father would have a field-day if he could see her, acting like a hormonal teenager. Good thing he was thousands of miles away in China.

Dr. Ryder headed for the door. "I'll check in on Bobby later."

Perhaps it was the adrenaline still pumping through her system, or her complete lack of common sense at that moment, but Molly didn't want him to leave just yet.

"What did Bobby mean the other day when he said you felt like you had to watch out for him?"

"Huh?" Dr. Ryder swiveled to face her again, his expression guarded.

Dazed, Molly met his eyes and saw a deep loneliness and yearning to match her own. This crazy bond between them reminded her of a runaway train, rumbling headlong down the tracks toward what she feared was certain disaster. If she didn't move, didn't avoid it at all costs, it would sweep her right off the map...

Luckily Dr. Ryder stayed where he was, half in, half out of her office, allowing Molly to regain some semblance of control over herself. Whatever this was sparking between them was best forgotten. It was probably nothing. Except, given the way her heart jackhammered against her ribcage just from his nearness, it certainly felt like...something.

Flustered, Molly shook her head to clear it. "You two served in the military together, correct? Dr. Dave told me you've done several tours as a combat medic in Afghanistan and Bobby was on your security team. Perhaps—"

"I doubt our time in the Army is relevant." Dr. Ryder scraped a hand through his hair, his usually smooth movements agitated. "I need to get back to my ER. Let me know when those test results come in."

"Will do." She watched him leave, feeling oddly bereft—which was silly. They were coworkers, that was all.

To get her mind off the awareness still bubbling through her Molly got back to work, scribbling details of Bobby's new symptoms and treatment plan in his chart. But when she went to turn the page her movement was blocked by Dr. Ryder's stethoscope.

He'll need that.

She'd been on her way to the cafeteria earlier, so it

wouldn't be out of her way to drop it off. Not to mention she'd have a chance to observe him in his natural environment—maybe figure out what made him tick.

Decision made, Molly headed for the elevators, stethoscope in hand.

"Hey, Mol!" Neal yelled from the other end of the hall. "We need to get some follow-up footage."

"In a minute," she called. "I have to take care of a few things first."

Jake walked through the automatic sliding glass doors into the hectic ER, grabbing a chart off the rack and reading it while he headed toward Trauma Bay One. With the first days of October in full swing, and employee vacations galore, he found himself filling in more than ever.

Unwanted sexual heat still shimmered through his blood, and he wasn't sure if it was the mental rush of running diagnoses with Dr. Flynn or the flood of need that washed over him whenever he was around her. But if he hadn't moved away when he had, he would've kissed her. Would probably still be kissing her now, given the yearning thrumming inside him.

And that would be stupid. He barely knew her, let alone trusted her. Kissing Dr. Flynn would be a monumental mistake.

Jake took a deep breath and double-checked the name on the file before heading past the drawn curtain. "Hello, Ms. Murphy. I'm Dr. Ryder. What brings you in to see us today?"

The portly senior citizen pointed at the two EMTs standing near the corner of the room—Zac and a new girl from the local volunteer fire department named Stacy—and gave the pair a disgruntled look. "They made me come."

"They did?" Jake grinned at the paramedics. "What happened?"

Ms. Murphy reached through the bedside rail and clasped his hand, her voice a whisper. "You see, I had to use the restroom."

"Okay…" He glanced at Zac, who kept his expression blank. "Then what?"

"Well, I couldn't get up."

"Her knees buckled," Stacy supplied helpfully.

"Oh, hush. I don't know why I ended up in this place." The patient gave Zac and Stacy another dirty look before continuing. "Hey, Doc. You're handsome. You remind me of that guy in those superhero movies. What's his name? Captain somebody?"

"Thanks." Jake smiled. "I'll take that as a compliment."

"You should." Ms. Murphy batted her eyelashes.

Stacy stepped forward. "She became nauseated…vomited a little too."

"Okay." He jotted a few notes on the patient's chart. "When you were in the bathroom did you experience any chest pain, Ms. Murphy?"

"No."

"How about feeling like you were going to pass out?"

"Yes." The woman's gaze widened. "I suffer from sciatica. My back was killing me."

"I'm sorry to hear that."

More than likely it had been the patient's nerve issues causing her problems. Still, he needed to run the proper tests to rule out something more serious, like a stroke.

Jake sent Zac and Stacy on their way, then turned to Ms. Murphy again. "All right, I'm going to—"

"Oh, I'm sorry."

Jake's heart skipped a crazy beat as Dr. Flynn came around the curtain, his stethoscope in her hand.

"The nurse at the station said to come on in. You left this in my office."

"Thanks." The word creaked past his tight vocal cords.

All he had to do was take the stethoscope and let her walk away. Temptation avoided. Only he couldn't seem to do it—because he was a weak-willed idiot where she was concerned.

"I...uh...appreciate that."

His fingers brushed Dr. Flynn's as he took his stethoscope, sending an electric jolt of lust straight through him. He met her startled gaze and discovered an answering passion. Oh, boy. This was going to be difficult. Difficult because everything about her drew him in like a moth to a flame—her quirky shy smile, her focus on work instead of on the persona the network had built, her beautiful brain and the equally stunning package it came in.

Do not go there.

At least some part of Jake's rational mind still seemed to be functioning, sending up alarm bells. Dr. Molly Flynn was off-limits. He reminded himself why he was leery of the media, why he didn't trust his heart or his emotions, why he didn't want to get involved with anyone.

"Hello, there." The overt curiosity in Ms. Murphy's voice had Jake snapping to attention. "What's your name, honey?"

Dr. Flynn gave him a deer-in-the-headlights look, frozen in place. "Uh... Molly Flynn."

"I've got a granddaughter named Molly in New York. Come closer, so I can see you properly. Just look at that skin, Dr. Ryder. Creamy and smooth."

Pink color suffused Dr. Flynn's cheeks and Jake gripped the chart tighter, continued to advise the patient of his treatment plan.

"As I was saying, Ms. Murphy, I'll order some blood-work and a few scans to make sure there are no blockages or bleeding. If all those come back okay, then we'll discuss your living arrangements."

At eighty-four, the woman was at too high a risk to live alone if she was unstable on her feet. The last thing Jake wanted was to send the poor lady home only to have her return with a broken hip or worse.

While he jotted down orders for Wendy, Ms. Murphy tugged a hesitant Dr. Flynn closer. For someone who made her living in the public eye, Bobby's new physician seemed decidedly wary of attention—hardly the media darling Jake had expected. In fact, Dr. Flynn was different in a lot of ways from what he'd expected.

"You're not married, are you?" Ms. Murphy said, studying his colleague's ringless left hand. Jake did his best to stifle a grin at Dr. Flynn's obvious discomfort. "This handsome man is available. You two should—"

"I'm not interested in dating," they both said in unison.

Taking that as his cue to leave, Jake headed toward the exit—only to be halted by his patient's voice. "Wait a minute, Dr. Ryder. I just want to stretch my legs a bit…"

He swiveled to see Ms. Murphy teetering on her feet. The older lady swayed for a moment before falling forward—straight toward Dr. Flynn. She rushed forward at the same moment Jake dived, and they ended up locked in an awkward hug, with the patient sandwiched in between them like an overstuffed hoagie.

"This isn't quite how I pictured my afternoon going," Dr. Flynn said, her voice muffled by a face full of hospital gown.

"No?" Jake leaned around Ms. Murphy's side to meet her gaze. "Working in the ER, you come to expect the unexpected."

"I should have remembered."

"Ready on three?" he asked.

Together they managed to get the patient safely back into bed.

Afterward, shoulders stiff and neck sore, Jake stood beside Dr. Flynn at the end of Ms. Murphy's bed. If he'd had a hard time with the patient's bulk, he couldn't imagine the toll on Molly Flynn's petite frame.

"Are you okay?" he whispered.

A stray lock of hair had come loose from the tight bun at the nape of Dr. Flynn's neck. Before Jake could second-guess his actions he'd tucked it behind her ear. Yep. Her flushed skin felt like silk beneath his touch, and his wayward thoughts quickly transitioned to whether she blushed that beautifully in other…situations.

"I'm fine." She sidled away, avoiding his gaze. "Are you all right, Ms. Murphy?"

"I'm great, kiddo." The patient gave them both a saucy wink.

Considering the older woman's quick wits, Jake wouldn't have put it past her to fall on purpose. It seemed everyone was a matchmaker these days.

Ms. Murphy grinned. "Promise me you'll find yourself a nice man and have lots of beautiful babies, okay?"

Dr. Flynn frowned. "I'm focused on my career and…"

"Nonsense." Ms. Murphy scoffed. "You can be a doctor and a mother and anything else you want to be." Her gaze darted between the two of them. "Besides, with this fine hunk of superhero around you'd be a fool not to take advantage."

"Don't mind her, Dr. Flynn," Jake said, feeling an unaccountable urge to put her at ease.

"Under the circumstances, Dr. Ryder," she said. "I think you can call me Molly."

Given their rather rocky start, he hadn't expected that, and it knocked him off his game, making him stumble over his words. "Oh, right. Sure. And…uh…you can call me Jake."

"Go, love!" Ms. Murphy gave them two thumbs-up as a technician arrived to take her away. "Don't do anything I wouldn't."

The gurney rolled past and Jake gave Molly a quick side glance, finding that same piece of hair had slipped free to dangle against her cheek. Time slowed as he reached out to brush it behind her ear again…

"I need to go." Molly scurried from the room faster than scorpions in the Kandahar desert.

Go. Yep. Jake needed to go too. Go and get his head on straight before he did something insane like haul Molly into his arms and kiss her senseless.

CHAPTER FIVE

"A HYPERBARIC CHAMBER?" Dr. Dave said, his tone incredulous.

Molly stood across from him, with Bobby's bed between them and her crew rolling. They'd been at Anchorage Mercy for a week and a half and she finally had an inkling as to what might be wrong with her patient. Now, if she could just get the chief of staff to sign off on the testing, she'd have firm confirmation.

"Yes. It's a bit unconventional, but do you have one?"

"Well, of course." Dr. Dave frowned. "We keep one in the Burn Unit to aid in wound healing, but I don't see how that would help in this situation."

She walked around to stand beside the older man, lowering her voice to avoid waking Bobby, who'd managed to fall asleep at last. "Let's talk in the hall."

They exited the room and Rob followed with his camera.

"I received the patient's latest lab results early this morning," Molly said, once they'd reached a deserted spot near the end of the corridor. "He tested positive for herpetic encephalitis."

Dr. Dave winced. "I told that boy to be careful with all those groupies."

"Sexual transmission isn't the only way to transmit

the virus. And, regardless of how he acquired it, the results still point to one thing."

"Which is?"

"His immune system is severely compromised."

"Oh." Dr. Dave stared out the nearby window, then back at Molly again. "His file says we prescribed steroids early on..."

"Yes, but two doses of medication wouldn't cause something this bad." Dr. Dave's tense shoulders relaxed and Molly sighed. "I think we need to look at other possible diagnoses."

"Such as?"

"Mixed Connective Tissue Disorder. It explains most of his symptoms. It would also explain why the patient felt better while on the steroids, at least initially." She closed the file and took a deep breath. "That's why a hyperbaric chamber is our best and only option."

"I still don't see the link." Dr. Dave shook his head. "Sorry."

"The normal treatment for MCTD is corticosteroids, but we can't use them for obvious reasons."

Rob moved in closer for a tight shot.

"Therefore we need to treat him with something that modulates the immune system but doesn't suppress it."

"I don't know..." Dr. Dave paced the narrow corridor. "There's no established protocol for using hyperbaric treatments for autoimmune disorders and it's not without risks. What about oxygen toxicity or damage to his eyes or liver?"

"Those risks are minimal compared to the greater benefits of this treatment."

"Well, if you think it's the best way..."

"I do." Molly put an arm around Dr. Dave and led him

back toward the elevators. "Now, do you need to book the sessions with the Burn Unit or shall I?"

"And...cut!" Neal's voice echoed down the hall.

Dr. Dave made the necessary call, then turned back to Molly with a smile. "I have a surprise."

She held her breath. Surprises—in her world, at least—weren't good things.

"Your father will be in Anchorage this Sunday. Turns out he's been asked to consult on a transplant case up at Fairbanks General and he called me to say he's going to fly in here from Beijing, then drive north. He's looking forward to seeing you. We'll talk later."

Molly forced a smile and headed back toward Bobby's room.

My father. Here. In three days.

Nausea and dread knotted into a tight ball inside her stomach. He might be consulting on a case, but the only reason he'd stop in Anchorage would be to keep an eye on his disappointment of a daughter—plain and simple. Most likely because he couldn't stand the fact that Molly was breaking out on her own after all this time.

She was still stewing over her father's impending visit when Jake burst out of the nearby stairwell a few minutes later, his expression dark.

"Are you filming?" he asked.

"No. We just finished. Why?" She gave him a confused look. "What's going on?"

"We need to talk. In private."

"Follow me."

Molly took him into the small meditation chapel, finally releasing the breath she'd been holding. It had been nearly five days since she'd seen him in the ER, but his effect on her was still as potent. Her pulse sped and her knees wobbled.

"What's happening?"

"You can't give Bobby hyperbaric treatments."

Molly frowned. "How'd you hear about that? Dr. Dave only just called in the order."

"I've got friends in the Burn Unit." Jake rubbed his eyes, as if struggling for patience. "Bobby's a hockey player—a professional athlete. If the chamber damages his lungs, his career's over."

"But it's the best option at this point with MCTD."

Molly's annoyance levels rose along with her unaccountable awareness of this man's every move, his every touch, his every breath. Not to mention she wasn't used to having her orders on a case questioned.

He braced his arm against the wall beside her head and his masculine presence seemed to envelop her. It was enough to drive her batty. That and the fact that the guy seemed to have friends everywhere. Or spies. Either way, she doubted the bullet trains in Japan worked as fast as the rumor mill here at Anchorage Mercy.

Jake narrowed his gaze. "You don't even know if that's what's wrong," he said, his tone skeptical. "I saw the bloodwork. His ANAs were barely elevated."

"Bobby's still my patient, and I feel this is the best course of action." Molly tapped the toe of her shoe against the shiny linoleum, wanting to throttle him and cuddle him in equal measure. Which made no logical sense.

The stress over her father's impending appearance mingled with Molly's untenable, undeniable attraction to this irritating man who challenged her at every step and boiled over into simmering fury. How dared he question her methods? Distracting her with his looks and his charm and his potent, provocative…steaminess.

She matched his guarded pose and raised her chin defiantly. "What about his underlying condition?"

"There is no underlying condition."

"Oh, yes, there is."

Molly pointed out several lab results, which Jake brushed off as coincidental. God, he was the most infuriating male she'd ever met. To think she'd considered kissing him a minute ago. She'd rather kiss a toad at this point.

Exhaling slowly, to regain her control, Molly considered her options. She could continue arguing with him about this, which would only waste time and effort. She could concede to his wishes and forget about the hyperbaric chamber completely. Or she could compromise—strike a bargain that would only prove her point in the end.

"Fine. We'll try your treatment first. If there's no improvement by next week, we do things my way."

"Fine. All I want is Bobby healthy again."

"And what do you think I want? Don't you think I want him to get well?"

Jake stared at her, unblinking, his expression unreadable. For a moment he looked as if he wanted to say more, do more. His fingers curled and uncurled at his sides and his gaze flickered to her lips again before returning to her eyes.

"Honestly, I don't know what you want, Molly. That's the problem."

With that, he yanked open the chapel door and stalked out. Molly took a few solitary moments to calm her raging pulse before heading back to Gladys's desk. Her heart ached as much from their argument as from the passionate heat sparking between them.

Molly plunked Bobby's chart down on the counter, resisting the urge to fan her burning cheeks. "Change of plan for Mr. Templeton. Hyperbaric treatments are on hold. Instead, let's start him on forty percent oxygen until his O2 sats increase and prescribe him a non-ste-roidal anti-inflammatory."

Jake got the page on his way back down to the ER, his posture tense and his blood pounding as he leaned against the elevator wall.

Gunshot victim. ETA ten minutes.

He was on a much-needed break, meaning his team would only call him back in if the situation was dire. Work usually settled him, but his senses were rioting. And unfortunately he knew exactly what had caused it—or rather who.

Bad enough that each time he saw Molly these days all he seemed to focus on was her soft skin, her sweet, dis-tracting scent, her pink full lips. Lord help him. A man could drown in that mouth and die happy.

Focus, Ryder. Focus.

He spent too much time alone these days—that had to be the problem. Since Bobby had gotten sick, most nights when Jake wasn't in the ER he was at home, working on the never-ending renovations to his place. The truth was, he liked using his hands, and it felt good to make some-thing, to create something lasting. After all the destruc-tion he'd witnessed during the war, building felt pretty damned amazing.

Jake shifted his weight, pulling out his phone again to check for updates as the doors opened and he hurried to-ward his department. Wendy met him at the glass doors and walked with him into the controlled chaos of the ER, handing him a scrub jacket and hat as they headed for the ambulance entrance.

"What's the cause of the shooting?"

"Not sure yet," she said. "All we've got so far from the EMT crew is that the wound's in the left flank and the patient's breath is agonal."

Gasping for air meant dropping oxygen levels. Jake cringed. "Exit wound?"

"None the paramedics could find."

"Damn. We'll need to order a CT to locate the bullet."

He finished tying his mask just as the ambulance crew wheeled the patient down the ramp from the helicopter pad and into the ER.

"Give it to me," Jake said to Zac, jogging next to the gurney as they veered off toward Trauma Bay Two, a team of nurses and technicians following.

"Nineteen-year-old male, hunting accident. Single bullet hole in the left side."

"Okay." Jake waited while the patient was transferred to the trauma bay table then patted the kid's cheeks. "Sir? Can you tell me your name?"

Nothing.

He tried again, louder and more forcefully, pinching the guy this time as well. It seemed harsh, but they had to rouse him if they could.

"Sir? Tell me your name."

No response.

Nineteen was too young to die, and Jake refused to let it happen on his watch.

"All right, team, we need an O2 sat. He's not responding to painful stimuli; GCS is less than seven. Get ready to intubate for airway protection."

While one of his residents moved in to insert a tracheal tube, Jake continued his rundown of the patient's vitals.

"Agonal breathing indicates a lack of oxygen and a

seven on the Glasgow Coma Scale suggests a strong possibility of traumatic brain injury."

"We're in." The resident withdrew the bronchoscope and Wendy used the clear plastic tube to pump air directly into the patient's lungs.

Jake continued his exam. "Nothing in the axilla areas. Bilateral breath sounds. Only one visible wound in the left lower lateral chest wall. Blood pressure down to sixty-nine over forty-two. Okay, people. Let's move this to the OR. We need to find where that bullet landed."

While his team took the patient upstairs by elevator, Jake discarded his soiled jacket and mask in a nearby biohazard bin, then hustled to the stairwell. The kid had lost a lot of blood and his pulse was weak. Time was of the essence.

As he jogged upstairs memories of his time in the military swamped him. He'd joined right after graduating from medical school and proposing to Kellie.

She'd been two years behind him in college, so once he'd got out of the service after six years and returned stateside she'd been established at the local network affiliate as a reporter. She'd suggested putting off marriage a little longer, to let things settle and get back to normal after the media frenzy over his Distinguished Service Cross commendation. At the time, it had seemed like the right thing to do.

But the longer they'd put off the wedding, the more the relationship had started to unravel. Kellie had resented his long hours at the hospital and claimed he'd changed since the war. He'd disliked her newfound love of the spotlight and constant craving for attention.

In the end it had all gone horribly wrong.

Jake pushed out through the second-floor doorway

and hurried over to the prep area. It didn't matter. All that mattered tonight was saving this kid's life.

He scrubbed down with Betadine, then backed into the OR, arms bent and raised at the elbow to prevent contamination. A surgical nurse outfitted him in a fresh jacket and mask. The anesthesiologist finished administering the required dosage of sedative and Jake approached the operating table.

Talking through his actions always helped him stay centered and focused during complex cases. Bobby had used to tease him when they were out on desert rescues.

"You gonna save them, Doc, or talk them to death...?"

Today, hopefully, it would be the former.

He grabbed a scalpel from a nearby tray and made his initial incision.

"Okay, team. We don't know the location of the bullet. Three full-body X-rays found nothing." Jake glanced at the monitors and his own pulse stumbled. "We've got to locate the source of the bleeding and clamp it."

Trauma surgery required split-second decisions. Hesitation could mean the difference between life and death.

"The heart's unstable, and the left lung is compromised. Removing it is the only chance we have of saving him."

Jake hated taking such a drastic step on a young kid, but surviving with lowered lung capacity was better than the alternative.

The bullet had ricocheted inside the kid's body, tearing through tissue and complicating matters. It took another hour to complete the delicate surgery, but afterward the patient's blood pressure had stabilized and his pulse strengthened.

Jake stepped away, confident he'd made the right choice. "He's alive. Thanks, everyone."

Wendy followed him out of the OR.

"What are his chances of survival?" she asked as she pulled off her jacket.

"Too early to say." Jake disposed of his soiled gear. "I did what I could, but we still have no idea of the bullet's location. That CT's paramount, but we can't risk moving the kid again until he's stabilized, which could be several hours."

As he washed up and splashed cool water on his face, images of Molly standing toe-to-toe with him in that chapel, giving as good as she got, burned into his mind. Crisis had a way of making everything seem more intense, and between their earlier encounter and the dramatic surgery, Jake felt lucky he didn't have adrenaline poisoning.

It was a good thing he'd gotten away from Molly when he had, or there was no telling what might've happened. He might've cupped those lovely cheeks of hers and kissed her until neither one of them had wanted to argue anymore. He might've pressed her close and relished the feel of her curves against him at last. He might've fallen to his knees and begged for one night in her arms.

Lord, help me.

Jake dried his face with a scratchy white towel, then tossed it into the bin with the rest of the soiled items before rolling his stiff shoulders. "I'm going to the gym for the rest of my break. Keep me posted on the patient's status."

CHAPTER SIX

AFTER HOURS OF nonstop reviewing of medical journals for clues to her patient's condition, Molly blinked to clear the blurriness from her vision and finally admitted she needed a break. Normally this late at night she'd hit the workout facility at her hotel and then go to bed, but she didn't want to leave the hospital just yet. There were still a few test results pending for Bobby, and she wanted to wait until they came back before she left.

She recalled seeing an employee gym in the basement of the hospital, on one of her many trips to the cafeteria. Back home in Chicago she ran five miles a day and kick-boxed to stay in shape. Here, she sat in her tiny office most of the time and drank ultra-strong coffee. Stiff and achy, Molly pushed to her feet and grabbed her duffle bag from the corner.

Time to get her mojo back.

She took the elevator down to the brightly lit basement and followed the overhead signs to the staff locker room. After changing into a pair of yoga pants and a tank, Molly headed out into the gym area.

The whole place looked empty, except for one guy jogging on a treadmill near the back wall. He had earbuds in and his shirt off, clearly in the zone as sweat trickled down his tanned torso and toned back. He was in fantastic shape. Cute too, with dark, damp hair spiked around his head.

As Molly neared the short row of treadmills, however, her heart sank. It was Jake, jogging along, eyes closed, seemingly oblivious to her presence.

She tossed her towel over to the wall, then climbed aboard the only other treadmill machine, on the left of Jake's. Okay, fine. If she was quiet, perhaps he wouldn't even notice she was there.

Faint strains of music pumped from his earbuds, increasing her sense of security. With his volume that loud, Mt. St. Helene's could erupt again and he wouldn't know.

Except, as Molly set up her running course and pressed "Start," she couldn't seem to keep her attention from drifting over to Jake's reflection in the mirrors, her blood sizzling anew at the remembered feel of his fingertips against her skin, the scent of his skin, the deep rumble of his voice as they'd argued in the chapel.

Her gaze flicked down his body—all lean, corded muscle and sinewy strength. A tattoo covered his left bicep. She squinted. A caduceus, maybe?

Molly glanced up again and found him watching her, his expression wary. Uh-oh. He pulled out his earbuds and gave her a tiny half-smile. Or was that a frown? Hard to tell when all she seemed able to focus on was the bead of sweat gliding down the side of his neck and her sudden longing to lick that moisture, to taste the salt of his skin, to feel his alpha strength…

Alpha strength?

She grabbed hold of the sides of the treadmill to keep from tripping over her own feet as the machine picked up speed. Jeez, the stress must be getting to her more than she'd thought if she was resorting to purple prose about her colleagues. This wasn't like her. Not at all.

Getting on with her run, Molly did her best to focus straight ahead and not pay attention to the weight of Jake's stare burning a hole through her composure. Soon the treadmill speed increased yet again and the base tilted upward, and Molly soon lost herself in the bliss of her racing heart and her pounding feet and the illusion of glorious speed.

"Doing the mountain course, huh?" a deep male voice said, interrupting her fantasy.

Her runner's high vanished and her knees threatened to buckle beneath the satin timbre of his voice. Molly hazarded another glance over at Jake and saw his machine was at maximum incline. She pushed a bit harder to keep up with him, her competitive streak surging despite her shaking muscles and raging libido.

"Yeah. You too?"

He shrugged and looked away. "I have my own special course set up to match the one I run at Chugach on my days off."

"The state park where we filmed your rescue crew?"

"Yep. Been back there yet?"

"Nope." Once again her speed and trajectory notched higher and she pressed onward despite the burn. "I'm here for my patient, remember?"

Taking in some of the natural wonder of the Alaskan wilderness was on Molly's list of things to do, but only if it didn't interfere with Bobby's case. Work came first. Always. That was the way she liked it, right?

Her chest tightened and her breath puffed harder, her whole body tensing at the horrible sinking feeling that maybe it wasn't.

Maybe it's your father who only cares about his career, not you.

She swiped a hand over her sweaty forehead and

checked the timer. Five minutes left. She could do this. Sure, she'd blown past her ideal pulse-rate a long time ago, but what was a little heart attack in the name of success?

Jake's machine beeped and his treadmill gradually lowered to its original flat position before stopping completely. "Well, you know what they say."

Molly hazarded an annoyed stare in his direction, puffing. "No. Please enlighten me."

His slow grin nearly toppled her to the floor. Molly gripped the sides of her treadmill and closed her eyes. Seriously, she needed to get over her wanton infatuation with this guy before someone got hurt. Namely her.

"All work and no play..." Jake walked over to stand beside her machine "...makes Dr. Flynn a very dull girl."

Molly opened her mouth to respond, then hesitated, not wanting to reveal just how close to the truth he'd come. That was why Brian had left her. He'd claimed she was about as interesting as a trip to the DMV. Then again, she'd never really opened up to him, so she only had herself to blame. Her flawed, quirky, weird, dull, fallible self.

Her unlovable self.

Before she knew what was happening, her muscles locked and her feet fumbled. The machine beeped and two strong arms pulled Molly close, to keep her from face-planting on the gym floor. Slowly Jake eased her down to a sitting position, then crouched beside her, his expression a mix of concern and barely concealed amusement.

"Doing okay there?" he asked.

"I'm fine."

Her voice sounded shaky even to her own ears. Molly

kept her head bent between her knees to increase circulation to her fuzzy brain and to hide her embarrassment.

"I'm used to tougher workouts back home. Must be low blood sugar."

"Right…" No mistaking Jake's teasing tone now. "And here I thought you were trying to impress me."

"Impress you?" The words croaked from her parched throat. "I was not—"

"Here, Usain Bolt." He nudged her arm with a cold bottle of water. "Drink this."

Molly swallowed half the contents in two long gulps. As she drank she saw Jake doing the same, and felt a weird, all-consuming need to nuzzle the thudding pulse-point at the base of his neck.

Frazzled, she pushed to her unsteady feet and grabbed her towel. She still had at least an hour before Bobby's last set of test results were due back from the lab, but she couldn't stay where she was. Not with Jake looking like sex on a stick.

She headed to the far side of the room and a pair of punching bags strung from chains in the ceiling. After strapping on a pair of boxing gloves Molly pummeled one of the bags, zeroing all her anger, pain, and frustration into her jabs. There was one for her mother, for making Molly feel like a dried-up old prune. Another for Brian, for dumping her by text message and reinforcing her doubts about herself. And one final blow for her father, for always pushing her, always expecting the impossible, always treating her like she was never, ever enough.

"Hey. Take it easy, Bolt." Jake strapped on a pair of gloves too, then walked behind her bag to steady it. "You're a kickboxer as well, eh?"

"Yep."

Wham, wham, wham.

It should be illegal for a man to be that sweaty and still look that fine. She ignored the soft clenching in her core caused by his nearness.

"Best fighter at my gym."

"Why am I not surprised?" He shook his head as Molly landed a fierce roundhouse kick.

"What's that supposed to mean?"

"Nothing. You just seem a bit...driven."

"Really?" She stepped back and punched one glove into the other, her gaze narrowed. "You're one to talk. Bobby told me he can't remember the last time you took a vacation."

Jake stood before her, his black shorts riding low on his hips and showing off that delectable V of muscles that always drove her wild with lust.

"Bobby should mind his own business." He rubbed his nose. "Spot me, okay?"

He walked to the other bag and Molly held it while Jake threw some impressive left hooks and right upper cuts.

She attempted to make small talk to distract herself from his rippling muscles. "What's your ink?"

"Huh?" He scowled, throwing a fast flurry of punches.

"The tattoo on your arm. What is it?"

"Combat Medic logo." Jake glanced down at his bicep, then performed a perfectly placed crescent kick that knocked Molly back a few steps. "And watch what you say next. The guys and gals from my regiment are like family."

"Oh." The fierce protectiveness in his voice made her envious. She doubted her own kin would ever defend her so staunchly.

Molly recovered her balance with the help of his steadying hand, missing the pressure of his touch as soon as he let her go.

"I guess that explains why you and Bobby are so close."

"That's part of the reason, yeah."

He stripped off his gloves and tossed them aside. Molly did the same, then walked back with him to their towels and water bottles, silent, doing her best not to say something stupid and ruin the tenuous accord that had settled between them.

"I'm surprised you came here to Alaska," Jake said finally, after pulling a black "Anchorage Mercy" T-shirt over his head. The clothes helped, covering all that forbidden flesh. "Doesn't your network usually prefer more glitzy locations?"

"MedStar thought a sports star case would draw in more viewers, so here I am."

"That simple, huh?"

"That simple." Molly wiped her face on her towel then slung it around her neck, her nerve endings on high alert with him sitting so close. "Why are you so against the media?"

"I was raised to keep my head down and stay humble. Doing good should be its own reward. And I've had some bad experiences with reporters in the past."

Jake leaned against the wall beside her, his arm brushing Molly's and sending a fresh explosion of sparks through her system.

"So… Molly Flynn. Daughter of the famous Roger Flynn?"

She cringed, staring across the empty gym. "Yes."

"We spent a whole semester in medical school studying his suture techniques."

She gave a derisive snort and he narrowed his gaze, his expression thoughtful.

"Must be hard, living up to that kind of perfectionism."

"You have no idea." Head lowered, Molly poked the

toe of her running shoe into the carpet. "Everything in my household was performance-based. Everything."

"Ouch. I'm sorry."

"For what?"

Outside, the world might be pure chaos, but in here with him all seemed oddly private and safe. But cracks were appearing in the logical wall she'd built to keep him away—the one that told her touching him, tasting him, would be wrong. Jake was so close now that Molly could see the tiny flecks of gold in his stormy gray eyes, and all her practical ideas and reasons evaporated.

"For what must have been a tough childhood," he said, his voice gentle, husky as he leaned closer still.

She didn't move away. "It wasn't like I was abused or anything."

"No." His gaze lowered to her mouth. "But I bet you weren't nurtured either."

"Nurtured?" The invisible cord between them tightened, the word squeezing Molly's heart like an embrace. "N-no. I wasn't."

"Such a pity…" Jake frowned, his lips hovering over hers for a brief second before capturing them in a light kiss.

Warning bells clanged in the back of Molly's mind, telling her this was happening too fast. Telling her she'd only be hurt by this man who saw too much, who fought as fiercely for what he believed in as she did. But instead of pushing Jake away Molly twined her arms around his neck and pulled him closer, craving his taste more than she craved her next breath.

Jake groaned low and slipped one hand around her waist while the other cupped the back of her head as he deepened the kiss. Molly opened her lips, welcoming the gentle sweep of his tongue and his minty, sweet flavor. It was nice and wonderful and…

Over.

Cursing, Jake pulled away and grabbed the cell phone clipped to the waistband of his shorts, blinking down at the screen with a frown. "Sorry. I've got a critically ill patient in the ICU. He's stabilized enough to get a CT scan. They're taking him now."

Still woozy from the emotional hurricane raging inside her, it took Molly a moment to let the words penetrate her haze of lust.

Patient. Critically ill. CT scan.

Work. Yes. That's why I'm here.

Silence fell between them once more as they gathered their supplies. Kissing Jake had probably been a mistake, but Molly couldn't bring herself to regret it as Jake walked across the hall to the men's locker room.

After a quick shower and a change into a fresh set of scrubs, Jake made a beeline for the ER. Each time he licked his lips he still tasted Molly there—sugar and bright lemon, her flavor zinging through his veins like a narcotic. He'd dropped his guard, despite his resolve, and now he'd have to deal with the consequences. Like knowing that, instead of making him less distracted, experiencing even a tiny taste of her had all but guaranteed he'd never get her out of his head.

Which wasn't helpful at present. With a gravely injured patient, Jake needed all his wits about him.

He made a pit stop at Wendy's desk on the way to his office. "Any word from CT?"

"Let's see." She clicked a few keys on her computer. "Looks like they're finishing up with your patient as we speak."

"Thanks." Taking the stairs two at a time, he emerged into a bright hallway on the third floor moments later and headed to Radiology.

One of the techs waved Jake into the viewing room, then pointed at her screen. "Doesn't look good, I'm afraid."

She stood, and Jake sank down into her chair, staring at the glowing images. The bullet they'd been searching for was lodged snugly in the patient's brain. Right smack in an area critical for breathing. No amount of trauma surgery would heal that level of damage.

"Can you send these to me?" he asked, his attention frozen on the screen.

"Will do, Dr. Ryder. Sorry the outcome wasn't better."

"Not your fault."

Spirits heavy, Jake called Neurosurgery to have them confirm the dismal prognosis. Two hours later he led the patient's family into a private conference room and told them the heart-wrenching news. Doing his best to keep his emotions out of the equation, Jake answered their questions, deferring to the neurosurgeon when needed, and finally left when there was nothing else to say.

All his training for these scenarios never made them any easier. Bone-deep weariness and a gnawing sense of failure haunted him all the way back to his office. Thankfully his shift was done, because all Jake wanted now was the solitude of his home and his bed. He quietly packed up his stuff and left with only a mumbled farewell to Wendy.

Following a hot shower and a cup of soup for dinner, Jake slipped between his sheets. His eyes felt scratchy from fatigue, but as he drifted off that kid's arrival in the ER replayed in his head. Maybe if he'd done something different, if he'd gotten to the bullet sooner, if...

Slowly the hospital scenes dissolved into his last day in Kandahar...

"Area's secure. No snipers. Nothing suspicious. Ready for transport," Bobby had said as he'd helped clear a space for the helicopters to land safely and retrieve the wounded.

Jake had just finished hooking up an IV when the first bullet had whizzed past him. Next thing he'd known it had been raining ammo like hailstones.

"Get down! Keep the victims covered."

The enemy had seemed to be everywhere—on the roofs, in the walls, behind each corner. Choppers had swooped in and returned fire.

There'd been a village nearby—local civilians who'd been kind to the troops. One house had taken a direct hit, going up in flames while the people inside screamed for help. Without thought Jake had taken off across the battlefield. Behind him Bobby had yelled for him to stop, yelled for his men to provide cover, yelled as three soldiers had crumpled to the ground—dead.

Jake had successfully rescued the trapped family members, after seeing to his own troop's fallen warriors, when white-hot pain had seared up his leg. Dazed, he'd stared down at the wound in his thigh. Must've nicked the femoral artery, he'd thought dazedly, judging by the amount of blood.

It had been as if it was all happening to someone else. Then Bobby had been there, tying a tourniquet, hauling Jake behind a pile of scrap metal, saving his life as agony hacked through Jake like a machete.

"I—I need to h-help them. N-no m-man left b-behind..." Jake's words had trailed off as his world had gone cockeyed. The smell of gunpowder and the salty taste of fear had filled his senses and his consciousness had slipped.

The last thing he remembered was Bobby's words—"We'll make it, bud!"—and an earsplitting boom.

Eyes snapping open, Jake threw back the bedcovers and rushed to the bathroom to splash cold water on his face, swallowing hard against the bile in his throat. He took deep breaths in and out, in and out, until his thudding pulse slowed and his mind cleared.

Yeah. Maybe being by himself right now wasn't the best idea after all.

By the time he made it back to the bedroom and checked the time it was nearly 5:30 p.m. With his odd schedule he'd learned to catch a snooze whenever he could, but he'd not expected to sleep away most of the day. He sank down onto the edge of the mattress and rubbed his eyes. His favorite local pub would be open. He could grab a real dinner, have a drink. Be around people, life, laughter.

Decision made, he pulled on some clothes, then headed out.

The Snaggle Tooth Pub had always been his and Bobby's go-to hangout. People greeted him as he passed, no one commenting on his messy hair or haunted eyes.

"What can I get you, Doc?" the bartender asked as Jake took a seat on one of the stools.

"Pale ale, please."

"Sure thing." The guy returned with an icy bottle of cold brew and a menu.

Drink in hand, Jake swiveled to survey the room—cheesy retro décor and moose antlers covered the walls, and the tang of whiskey and greasy bar food filled the air. This pub had the best salmon nachos in town. He ordered a plate from a passing waitress, then took a long swig of his beer, feeling some of his tension abate.

Then the bell above the door jangled and in walked Molly. Jake swiveled away quickly, but not before he'd caught her eye. Images of their heated kiss swarmed in his overtaxed mind and his body responded before he could stop it. How had she heard about this place? Was she meeting someone here? It would be better if she was. Not because he didn't enjoy her company, but because he was coming to enjoy it more than he should.

"Is this seat taken?"

Molly's cheerful tone washed over him. He closed his eyes, knowing he should tell her yes even as he shook his head no and hazarded a quick side glance at her. Damn if she didn't look adorable, in jeans and sneakers and some silly green sweatshirt with the symbol for Pi on it, surrounded by the words "Too much gives you a large circumference".

Jake took another swallow of ale, feeling the alcohol swirling through his empty stomach and creating a nice buzz. In fact Molly looked almost as cute tonight as she had in those yoga pants in the workout room. Or in scrubs. Or that T-shirt that first night. Honestly, the woman would look gorgeous in anything.

Or nothing at all...

Jake coughed to clear the sudden constriction in his throat.

She ordered a glass of white wine instead of the frou-frou drink he'd expected. Kellie had always gone for those ridiculous glasses of fruit juice and fairy dust.

Molly's light touch on his forearm made the whole right side of his body tingle.

"I heard about your gunshot patient. I'm sorry."

"Thanks." The word emerged as more of a grunt.

"Bobby's doing okay, though," Molly continued, filling in for his silence. "I checked on him again before I left." She met his gaze, held it before looking away. "You were right."

"Excuse me?"

She frowned—something she always did when she was thinking. "About too much work making me a dull person. Did you know a new study shows a significant difference between being engaged in a task and being addicted to it?"

Yep. There went her brain again. He'd worked with a few guys like her in the military. Brilliant at what they did, but no social skills at all.

"You're saying I'm compulsive?" Jake took another sip of ale, realized he'd drained the bottle. "I'm the best at what I do."

"So am I." She toyed with the stem of her glass.

He couldn't help wondering how those graceful fingers would feel against his chest, his abs, lower still…

"I have a question for you. More of a proposition."

Her voice cracked a little and he felt the vibration clear to his toes.

Stick around, Bolt. I might have a proposition for you too.

Jake stared at the sticky bar top. That was the alcohol talking—loosening his inhibitions, pushing him to do and say things that were not in his best interest. Apparently one ale was more than enough for him tonight.

He flagged down the bartender. "Can I get a cup of coffee, please?"

"Sure thing." The guy grabbed a steaming pot and returned with a white ceramic mug.

"Anything for you, ma'am?"

"No, thanks," Molly said.

"Great. Your nachos should be out in a minute, Doc."

Once they were alone again, Jake stirred cream and sugar into his coffee, ignoring the burning weight of her stare.

"Will you take me to Dr. Dave's party?" Her question rushed out in a nervous tumble.

Jake froze. "What? Like a date?"

"No." Molly shook her head, sending a few tendrils of hair from her ponytail bobbing around her face.

He longed to reach out and run his fingers through them, but resisted.

"Not a date. More for protection."

"Protection?" He scrunched his nose. "Someone's put a hit out on you already, Bolt?"

She gave him a look. "No. My father will be there. I'd rather not face him alone."

Was it his imagination or were her hands trembling?

All his defending instincts roared into life. As a department head, he'd been invited to the dinner party Dr. Dave had announced he was throwing for Molly's father. Having a professional companion along would make things easier for them both. Still, he wanted to make sure he understood her reasoning.

"Why me? Why not take one of your crew?"

"Rob and Neal are busy with production. I already checked."

"Oh." He took a sip of his coffee. "You really don't like your father, do you?"

"Things between us are…strained."

Finally, he said, "Well, I suppose we could go together—as colleagues."

"Yes. Colleagues. That'd be great."

They sat there for a while, the silence between them growing heavier by the second.

"So, you and Bobby..." she said finally. "How did you guys become friends?"

Jake chuckled, staring down into his coffee. "We met in BCT—basic combat training at Fort Benning, Georgia. He and I went in as officers, because of our college degrees, but that didn't save us from eight and a half weeks of hell. In fact, I think it made it worse, because they were harder on us." Jake snorted. "Anyway, Bobby and I hit it off the first day. We had a lot in common, even though I was from Alaska and he was from the Midwest. My dad was a veteran—so was his. I was an only child—so was he. We both loved hockey and hated clowns."

"Sounds like a match made in heaven."

"Or hell! Bobby eventually had to drop out of Ranger School because of an inner ear problem. He went into the security forces and led the troop that traveled with my regiment. Trouble had a way of following him around even back then. Bobby loved playing practical jokes, and he thought it would be funny to pull a prank on our drill sergeant."

"Is that a good idea?"

"No."

"Yikes."

"Yeah. Of course I was such a cocky idiot that I went right along with his plan. In hindsight...? Big mistake."

"Uh-oh. What happened?" Molly sipped her white wine, her eyes adorably wide.

"We got drunk on leave, then snuck onto base and broke into the sergeant's barracks to booby-trap the shower. The guy was a huge Toronto Blue Jays baseball fan, so we filled the shower head with neon blue dye. When he turned it on it left him looking like a giant Smurf."

"Oh, no!" Molly tried to bite back her giggles and failed. "I'm sorry. That shouldn't be funny, but it is."

"Yeah. We felt pretty proud of ourselves—until the next day at roll call."

"Was your punishment awful?"

"In the long run, not so much. Half a day in the major general's office getting screamed at and a permanent warning in our files. But it sealed the friendship for Bobby and me. Later, on the battlefield—" He stopped himself, not ready to go further quite yet, after his awful day and the nightmare earlier. "Well, we stayed close over the years."

"That's great."

The hint of sadness in Molly's tone had Jake focusing on her again.

"All right. I've told you about me and Bobby. How about you share more about this scary father of yours? You said everything when you were a kid was performance-based. What exactly does that mean?"

She gave a small shrug. "If you didn't meet my father's standards you didn't exist."

"That can't be right."

"No, it's not right. But it's true." Molly sighed. "He was gone a lot with his work—which was good. Because when he was home he'd trot me out to show off for his friends. It was bittersweet, because those were really the only times I spent with him. I hated performing—hated all those people staring at me, judging me. But I did it because it meant I'd have my father's undivided attention and affection for those few precious seconds, even if it was all for show. Back then, I thought if I could prove to him that I was good enough, smart enough, he'd love me."

"My God…" Jake whispered, reaching for her hand. She let him take it, blinking hard. "It wasn't that bad, really. I had food, clothes, a pretty house…any toys or books I wanted. Nothing to complain about."

"Except love?"

"Except that."

"Wow."

Jake gazed around the bar, trying to figure out the most diplomatic way to ask what he wanted to. In the end he just said it, because he didn't know how else to phrase it. "Why TV, though? I mean, for a person who hates being the center of attention it seems like an odd career move."

She stared into the distance, as if deep in thought. "Originally I started the show as a means to prove to my father that I wasn't the failure he imagined. Then later, once Neal and Rob became my friends, it meant more. I truly do enjoy my cases, even if the travel and filming portions aren't my favorite. And I trust my colleagues to portray me in the best light." She lifted one shoulder and looked back at him. "Does that make sense?"

"It does."

The bartender brought a heaping portion of food and two plates.

Jake set one in front of Molly. "Would you like some? Best salmon nachos in Alaska."

"Oh…um…" She stared at the platter, her stomach growling. "They do smell incredible."

"They're fantastic."

Jake dished some up for her before digging into his own portion. The creamy cheese and salty chips went perfectly with the sweetness of the fish and the spice of the jalapenos.

"What do you think?"

"Really delicious."

Molly licked her lips, and all Jake could think about was kissing her again.

Luckily, she raised her wineglass and held his gaze, a question lurking in her eyes. "To colleagues?"

Her words echoed in his head.

I trust my colleagues...

The significance wasn't lost on him, and nor was the fact that her asking him to Dr. Dave's dinner party was a big deal—another step forward in their relationship. Jake hesitated only slightly before clinking his coffee cup against Molly's wineglass, not missing the slight flicker of guarded joy in her eyes or the matching twinge of hope deep in his chest.

"To colleagues."

CHAPTER SEVEN

"Do I LOOK all right?" Molly asked Jake.

Two days had passed since that night at the bar, and now they were poised before the beautiful carved front door of Dr. Dave's mansion, perched on a hillside of Anchorage's posh neighborhood of Coral Lane. The place was as large as her parents' estate in Oakbrook, though this house seemed much more inviting—at least until she remembered that her father lurked somewhere inside.

The same pulse-pounding fear of rejection and the sickening doubt she always felt in her father's presence welled inside her before she could stop it, choking her breath and making her palms slick. Molly was an accomplished physician in her own right, yet all it took was one pending encounter with her bully of a father to send her right back to the darkest, loneliest days of her childhood.

She smoothed her trembling hand down the front of her little black dress and prayed she looked sophisticated enough—the outfit was the only somewhat formal thing she'd brought. Jake looked marvelous in a suit, the scruff on his jaw adding a mysterious, wild edge. Seeing him out of his scrubs, dapper as Cary Grant in An Affair to Remember, did crazy things to Molly's already overloaded nervous system. So she tried not to look at him often. And failed. Miserably.

"You look beautiful," Jake said, his voice low and sincere.

Her stomach fluttered anew, this time from pure sweetness. Still, Molly had to be rational. This was a business arrangement. Strictly platonic. An evening between colleagues despite that soul-searing kiss they'd shared in the gym. Besides, getting involved with a man who lived half a world away would never work out. It would be foolish.

Too bad none of that seemed to matter a bit to her yearning heart.

Time to take the plunge.

Raising her shaky hand, Molly rang the bell. "Here goes nothing."

"You got this, Bolt." Jake gave her a little nudge with his shoulder and the shadows closing in on her seemed to recede slightly.

A stunning older woman with dark hair and a model-perfect figure, answered the door. "Hello," she said, her smile broad. "Always a pleasure to see you, Jake."

They embraced. Jake kissed the woman on the cheek, then placed a gentle hand on Molly's lower back, playing the part of doting date extremely well. So well, in fact, that if Molly wasn't careful she'd forget all this was pretend.

"And you must be Dr. Flynn." The woman extended a hand to Molly. "I'm Sara Carpenter—Dave's wife. I love your show, by the way. My favorite was Toe Fungus Guy."

"Thank you. That episode seems to be popular."

Molly stepped inside the house, thankful for the reassuring presence of Jake's hand guiding her forward. Sara took Molly's coat and hung it in a nearby closet, then led them down a short hall toward the sounds of a party in full swing.

The home was a perfect combination of rustic charm

and modern convenience—an Alpine cathedral, with walls and floors made entirely of caramel-colored pine and ceilings soaring at least twenty-five feet above them. Oriental carpets and dark leather furniture helped make the huge open spaces seem homier. At one end of a spacious great room sat a giant stone fireplace, flames crackling merrily inside.

Molly felt thoroughly charmed—until she spotted her father, standing to one side of the room, deep in conversation with Dr. Dave. The sound of her pounding heart thudded loud in her ears, drowning out everything else.

Hands clenched tight at her sides, Molly did her best to maintain a cool façade while hoping to avoid her father for as long as possible. With a polite smile, she turned to her hostess. "Your home is spectacular. I'd love to see the rest."

"Absolutely." Sara gestured toward the nearby hallway. "I adore giving tours."

"Since I've been here a million times, I'll just head over and chat with the other department heads," Jake said, backing away slowly. "Unless you need me, Molly?"

Though every fiber of her being screamed for her to keep him close by her side all night, she knew deep down that she needed to face this on her own. Besides, given the way her father had ripped Brian to shreds on a regular basis, Molly didn't want Jake to face the same fate.

She forced words out. "No. That's fine. I'll see you in a few minutes."

Molly followed Sara out of the great room and into a grand chef's kitchen, full of stainless steel appliances and granite countertops. "Wow!"

"Yes, it's a bit breathtaking, isn't it? We hadn't planned on going quite so overboard when we built the place, but Dave and I figured this is it. Might as well get what we want, right?"

"It's amazing."

Molly ran her fingertips along the edge of a counter, wishing she could lay her heated cheek against the cool stone for a while. A familiar buzzing had started inside her head and her dread grew. Random facts and inappropriate responses zinged like pinballs through her mind.

Please don't let me embarrass myself—not now.

"Martha would have an orgasm and die in here," Molly said, unable to stop herself.

Too late.

"I'm so sorry. I didn't mean that the way it sounded." Fresh heat prickled Molly's cheeks. "What I meant was my sister loves to cook and would really enjoy such a well-appointed kitchen."

"I understand." Sara burst out laughing. "As a fellow foodie, rest assured I had the same reaction my first time too. I think you and I will get along just fine."

Molly smiled back, her usual awkwardness disappearing with Sara's genuine friendliness. "I hope so. I tend to rub people up the wrong way sometimes."

"Really? Why?"

"When I get overly stressed or nervous I recite odd random facts." Just one more thing her father had made her feel bad about. "Or I say snarky, strange things."

"Well, I admire people who speak their minds—if it's done with kindness. And I'm sure your facts are fascinating. I can't imagine how a brilliant mind like yours works." Sara linked arms with Molly. "Come on. I'll show you the rest of the place."

They viewed several bedrooms and a master bathroom larger than Molly's entire apartment in Chicago. By the time the tour ended they were upstairs in a loft, overlooking the first level, and Molly felt almost calm again. From all the way up here her father appeared a bit less intimidating. But only a little.

Molly shuddered and refocused her attention elsewhere. In the crowd below Jake was working the room like a pro, shaking hands and laughing. He seemed so attentive, so genuinely interested in everyone in his life.

What she wouldn't give to have him feel that way about her too. Not that she was in his life, exactly—not permanently anyway. A pang of sadness ached inside her—which was absurd. They'd shared one kiss.

A heart-melting, steamy kiss…

As if sensing her gaze, Jake glanced up at Molly and waved, his crooked grin making her knees tingle. She waved back, sending him a goofy grin of her own.

"Are you married?" Sara asked.

"No." Molly gripped the thick wooden banister, wishing it was Jake's arm instead. Amazing how fast she'd come to rely on his support. "Recently single, actually."

"Hmm…" Sara pushed away from the railing and started downstairs. "C'mon. Let's get you something to drink before you see your father. He's been asking about you."

They returned to the kitchen and Molly chose a glass of Cabernet.

"Must be hard," Sara said, pouring a generous serving for Molly then recorking the bottle, her expression thoughtful.

"I'm sorry?" Molly sipped the rich wine. She'd not eaten since breakfast, and the next few hours would be difficult enough without getting tipsy. Not to mention she was on call for Bobby and having trouble controlling her reactions to Jake. No need to loosen those inhibitions any more.

"Having the illustrious Roger Flynn as your dad," Sara said. "That must be very hard."

Molly stared out through the expanse of window across from her. Streaks of gold, purple and indigo colored the expansive Alaskan sunset. She'd love to lie and say she'd learned so much from her brilliant father, that he'd supported her in her life and her career. That he hadn't reduced her self-confidence to zilch and then blamed her for being too shy and having no friends.

Instead, she said nothing at all. Just gave a sad little shrug.

"Ah!" Dr. Dave walked into the kitchen, shattering the silence and making Molly jump. "I wondered what had happened to you ladies."

"I taught you better than to skulk in corners, daughter of mine."

Roger Flynn strolled into the room, and Molly's oxygen seemed to evaporate. He looked the same as always—designer suit, perfectly styled silver hair, icy green eyes. Intimidating. Imposing. He gave Molly a quick air-kiss, not touching her, and her face ached from the strain of keeping her smile in place. In his assessing gaze, she saw judgment and disappointment. Par for the course.

"When do we eat?" Dr. Dave asked, oblivious to the electric tension in the air. "Molly, Orion's Catering makes the best pot roast this side of the Rockies. You're in for a treat."

She tore her attention away from her father's disapproving stare to focus on their charming hosts. Had her parents ever been that happy? Her stomach churned—not from hunger but from anxiety. Molly could barely remember her parents holding hands, let alone being affectionate with each other.

She swallowed hard around the lump of sadness in her throat. "It smells wonderful, Dr. Dave."

"Hey, Sara. Got any pale ale?" Jake strolled in, his gaze resting on Molly as he stepped closer to her side, his arm brushing hers as he whispered, "Everything okay, Bolt?"

The endearment reminded Molly of their heated kiss and warmed her from the inside out—not enough to thaw the frigid ice caused by her father's looming presence, but a start.

Craving his support, she pressed closer, aware of her father watching their every move. "Everything's fine, thank you, Dr. Ryder."

At Molly's use of his professional title, Jake cocked a brow.

"Jake, have you met our guest of honor?" Dr. Dave said congenially. "Dr. Jake Ryder—may I introduce Dr. Roger Flynn?"

The two men shook hands briskly, silently assessing each other in a blatant display of masculine bravado Molly had seen too many times to count around her father. It was like Wild Kingdom—except in place of the bull elephants or stallions there were alpha surgeons.

"Pleasure," Jake said.

"I'm sure." Roger Flynn knocked back the rest of his liquor, and regarded his younger rival with cool interest.

"Dr. Ryder's my Head of Emergency Medicine," Dr. Dave said with pride. "Finest trauma surgeon in the state of Alaska."

"Rather a tiny pond of comparison, isn't it?" her father said under his breath.

Jake's posture stiffened. "We're the largest level one trauma center in the region."

"Ryder cut his teeth in combat. Courage under fire," Dr. Dave continued on affably, as if a professional gauntlet hadn't been thrown down.

Molly was torn between wanting to see her father flayed alive for his insults and wanting to protect Jake from the man's cruelty.

"You both have that in common. The love of adventure, the thrill of danger—"

"Here you go." Sara passed Jake a bottle of ale, then gave her husband a Be quiet look. "Dinner will be ready shortly. Why don't you all go mingle?"

"Dr. Ryder," her father said, with all the friendliness of a frozen cod.

Once he'd left Molly exhaled and placed her glass on the center island. "I'm so sorry."

"About what?" Jake looked perplexed.

"About my father's behavior." She shook her head. "I'm glad he left before things got worse."

Jake still hadn't moved from her side, and he stared after her father. "He's…interesting. And pompous. But I saw far worse displays from the five-star generals and Pentagon bigwigs in Afghanistan. You want to talk egos? Go a couple rounds with those guys."

"Really?" Molly's breath hitched and the large kitchen seemed to close in on her. Oh, God. Not a panic attack, please. She squeezed her eyes shut. "You okay, Bolt?" Jake rubbed her back and leaned closer. "Is there anything I can do?"

"F-fresh air," she managed to gasp.

"Right. Excuse us," he said to their hosts, who had already moved toward the door, and then he slipped his arm around her waist and pulled her into his side. "I've got you."

Molly clung to him, appreciating his quiet strength and confidence. Brian had always mocked her panic attacks, claiming she only did it to get attention. Her father had always simply ignored them, considering them another unfortunate sign of Molly's weakness. Jake, however, didn't bat an eye, shielding her from the curious stares of the other guests as he guided her toward a secluded space off the main great room.

Gradually the pressure in Molly's chest eased and she sucked in a much-needed breath. A shiver ran through her and Jake held her tighter, his gray gaze concerned.

"We're almost there, sweetheart. Hang on for me, okay?"

"Okay." Molly gave him a small smile, her heart aching at the endearment. "Thank you."

"For what?"

"For being so nice to me. I'm not used to being coddled."

Jake got Molly settled on the window seat then crouched in front of her, lacing her icy fingers with his, stroking idle circles over her palm with his thumb, soft and infinitely tender. "After meeting your father, I'm not surprised. But we're in this together, right?"

"Yes."

His steady caress and the lulling deepness of his voice had her hypnotized. Molly leaned closer…so close she could kiss him again…

"Bolt?" he said, his voice huskier. "Do I need to take you into my ER?"

The mention of the hospital broke through Molly's haze at last and she blinked hard to clear her fuzzy head. It wasn't the wine. She'd only had a couple of sips. But Jake was proving to be more intoxicating than any alcohol.

"No," she managed to say at last.

Her hand was braced against his chest, feeling the thud of his heart beating in time with hers. She took another deep breath and the room around her expanded again, filling with the low hum of chatter.

She smoothed Jake's lapel and gave him a shaky smile. "I'm better. Thank you."

"Good." He grasped her chin between his thumb and forefinger and grinned. "Now, quit thanking me. You can make it up to me later, Bolt."

Jake took a seat beside Molly, his shoulder resting comfortably against hers. She had no idea how to repay him for such kindness, but the possibilities caused all sorts of naughty butterflies to shiver through her stomach.

"Dinner is served," Sara said from near the grand fireplace. "Please, come into the dining room and find your assigned seats."

Food was the last thing on Molly's mind, but thankfully Jake stayed steadfastly by her side at the table. Catering staff bustled around, filling water goblets and placing plates before each guest.

Molly took a tentative bite of the tangy arugula and tomato salad with a balsamic vinaigrette dressing as her father regarded her with cool assessment from across the table.

"Tell me about your latest case," Roger Flynn said.

After a quick glance at Jake, Molly relayed the medical details about Bobby while keeping his identity secret. "We're following a conservative approach to allow the patient's system time to recover."

"Conservative only produces mediocre results." Her father scoffed. "Where's your ingenuity?"

"Ingenuity isn't always what's needed in an acute situation," Jake intervened, his tone icy. "As I'm sure you understand."

"Ingenuity is what creates medical breakthroughs," her father said, his tone seething. "I would've expected more bravery from a combat veteran."

Jake tensed. "On the battlefield, my number one priority was to get the wounded triaged as quickly and safely as possible. Not to chase the next big innovation."

"Innovation saves lives." Her father's green eyes had frozen like Siberian emeralds. "Without pushing the boundaries, we never know how far we can go."

"I was raised to respect boundaries."

"More's the pity." Her father gave a dismissive snort. "Boundaries are your downfall."

"And your ego is yours." Jake glared at Roger Flynn, a muscle ticking near his tense jaw. "You don't have any compassion for anyone, do you?"

"I'm the top trauma surgeon in the world, Dr. Ryder. Compassion is a luxury I can't afford. In my world respect must be earned—as my daughter can attest."

Molly's heart plummeted. She could attest all too well to his stringent demands and lofty ideals, which she had never attained. She'd failed him again and again, always falling short of his impossibly high standards, of his dreams for what he'd wanted in a daughter. As an adult, she should be past caring, but it still stung.

Beneath the table, Jake took her hand. Molly hazarded a glance over at him, expecting to see a defeated man, scraped raw from her father's scathing insults. Instead Jake gave her a small half-grin and squeezed her fingers tight.

Confused, she started to whisper, "I'm—"

"I'm going to start keeping count of those apologies, Bolt. A few more and before long you're going to owe me more than you can ever repay." His grin widened. "Now, eat up."

Stunned, Molly continued to nibble on her salad. Brian had always cowered before her father's bully tactics. But Jake? Well, he hadn't backed down an inch. He'd defended her.

No one had ever chosen Molly's side before.

The waiter removed their salad plates and replaced

them with heaping portions of pot roast and grilled vegetables. The delicious sweet smell of tomatoes and carrots mixed with the rich aroma of braised beef had Molly's appetite returning.

She was about to dig in when her phone buzzed from inside her evening bag and her pulse tripped. She was expecting lab results on Bobby.

"Excuse me a moment."

Molly walked back into the living room, pulling out her phone and hitting redial as she wandered toward the windows. In the valley below the lights of Anchorage sparkled like diamonds, and she could almost picture herself building a new life in this rugged place…raising a family, making a real home here with Jake…

A technician answered, putting an abrupt end to her daydreams.

"Lab."

"Yes, this is Dr. Flynn. I got a message that my patient's results are in."

"Yes. Hang on a moment, please."

"What's going on?"

Jake came up behind her, the heat of him surrounding her. She held up a finger as the technician returned to the line.

"Dr. Flynn, Bobby Templeton's BUN and creatinine levels are rising. You said to call with any changes."

"Yes. Thank you." She ended the call, then dialed Gladys's extension. "How's Bobby?" she asked.

As Molly waited for the nurse to pull his records she turned to Jake.

"Hospital calling with results."

"Any change?"

Gladys came back on the line. "Mr. Templeton's lung

function is deteriorating, his fever's back, and that rash on his legs is spreading to his torso."

"Damn," Molly said.

"What?" Jake moved closer, his hand returning to her lower back.

She rubbed her temple as she relayed to him what she'd found out. "I'm afraid your treatment plan isn't working."

Roger Flynn had walked into the room as well, and was giving them both a disparaging stare. "I told you. Conservative methods won't yield—"

"Please, shut up!" Molly said before she could stop herself.

Eyes wide, she snapped her mouth closed. Before tonight she'd never had the gumption to talk back to her father. Perhaps Jake's attitude was rubbing off.

"How dare you—?"

"The lady said shut up!" Jake growled, cutting her father off again.

Molly finished with Gladys, then faced Jake. "What's your diagnosis?"

"Metabolic disorder?"

Jake looked as agitated as she felt, but Dr. Dave had been right. They did work better as a team. The rest of the room disappeared as they brainstormed ideas.

"Something genetic—mitochondrial, maybe?"

"Perhaps we should try my protocol? The hyperbaric chamber would force more oxygen into his blood, helping him to heal faster."

"No. I'm sorry, Bolt, but I stand by my decision. We need to avoid any treatments that could put Bobby's future career as an athlete at risk. Nothing wacky."

"Wacky?" After dealing with her father tonight, the word hit a bit too close to all the old insults that had been hurled her way as a kid.

"She's very smart, but a bit of a wacky mess when it comes to her social skills," her father had used to joke to his colleagues.

She stepped away from Jake, frowning. "There's nothing wrong with using a hyperbaric chamber."

"It's a bit unorthodox—even you admit that. I prefer the tried and true."

He reached for her hand again, his expression imploring, but she pulled away.

Jake's smile fell. "C'mon, Molly. I've seen your show. 'Unorthodox' doesn't begin to cover your treatment methods. If I allowed you free rein we'd have Bobby strung up by his toes with a voodoo priestess dancing around his room."

Snickers rang out around the room—including from her father.

Gone was the warm, fuzzy comfort she'd felt with Jake earlier. Now Molly felt only exposed, raw to the bone—the same way she had during those dreaded performances for her father as a child.

She stalked away from Jake, with her father's vexed glare forever burning in her mind. Coming here tonight had been a mistake. Inviting Jake as her date had been even worse. She'd opened up to him, let him see her most vulnerable side—had begun to think of him as her partner in this case, maybe more. She'd thought he was different…that maybe he might see past her flaws and care for her anyway.

But she'd been wrong.

Eyes stinging, Molly rushed toward the foyer. All she wanted to do was get back to Anchorage Mercy—back to her comfort zone, back to the one place where she felt competent and successful.

Ignoring the inquiring looks of the other guests, who'd

filed into the living room to see what all the commotion was about, Molly yanked her coat from the closet. "Thank you for the lovely dinner, Dr. Dave… Sara. I'm going back to the hospital to take care of my patient. I'll do my best not to try anything wacky while you're gone, Dr. Ryder."

Jake made his own quick farewells, then stormed after Molly toward her Range Rover. "Mind telling me what just happened?"

"Yes, actually." The lights on the vehicle flickered as she jabbed a button on her key fob. "I do."

Pulling open the passenger side door, Jake climbed into the seat, barely managing to get the door closed again before Molly revved the engine and took off down the long, winding driveway. He'd been in bombing raids friendlier than the vibe he was getting from her at this point—though her stress was understandable. Her father was a complete ass.

Still, Jake thought they'd handled things well tonight. He'd had her back—would've protected Molly against Roger Flynn or any other blowhard in that room. Bobby's case had brought them together, but tonight had made them a team. At least that was how he'd felt. He'd even found himself, against all odds, trusting her. More than he had anyone else in a long time.

The tension around her mouth now and the paleness of her cheeks bothered him, though. Hoping to regain some solidarity, he said, "Boy, your dad's a piece of work."

Molly swerved out onto the main road, tires squealing. "I don't want to discuss him."

"Pull over and let me drive." Jake gripped the dashboard as she passed another vehicle, switching lanes without signaling. "Please."

"What's the matter?" Molly glanced over at him and ran up onto the berm, bumping noisily before she merged onto the Seward Highway heading toward Anchorage Mercy, a wild spark in her eyes. "Afraid I'll go all wacky on you?"

"If this vehicle being wrapped around a utility pole is your idea of wacky, then, yeah."

"My driving skills are exemplary, thank you very much." Molly gripped the wheel tight, her fingers tapping out a rapid cadence. "Many more men than women die each year in motor vehicle crashes. Men typically drive more miles and engage in more risky driving practices, including not using safety belts and operating a vehicle while intoxicated."

"Speaking of alcohol—how much wine did you have?"

"A few sips." She gave him a withering stare. "But don't you prefer girls who drink pale ale?"

He sat back, exasperated. "Since when do you care what kinds of girls I prefer?"

"I didn't say I cared. I just—"

"What? Feel like prying into my private life?" Furious, he turned away. "Typical media."

"And we're rehashing that again." Molly jammed on the brakes as they approached a red light, screeching to an undignified halt. "Is that all you've got? Boo-hoo. The big, bad media's out to get me."

"You're one to talk. What was all that kowtowing to your dad in there, huh? What are you? His slave? No, wait. His irritatingly intelligent fact-spouter? Does he rent you out for parties?"

The angry flush in Molly's cheeks drained away and she lowered her gaze, her stiff posture slumping.

Remorse clunked heavily in Jake's chest. He'd gone too far. But damn if she hadn't pushed all his buttons.

Part of him wanted to get out of the vehicle and call a taxi. The other part of him wanted to pull Molly into his lap and kiss her until they both forgot about this disaster of a night—forgot about everything except the incredible chemistry between them.

The car behind them honked. The light had turned green.

Molly accelerated—slower this time. They traveled on in silence for several minutes, until she said quietly, "Why don't you like the media? The truth."

He sighed. "I received an honorable discharge in August 2011. The following February they awarded me and Bobby Distinguished Service Crosses for extraordinary heroism on the battlefield in Kandahar. With the stress of trying to assimilate back into civilian life with my ex and my new job at Anchorage Mercy, the added pressure the media put on our relationship was the final straw. The fact Kellie was infatuated with all the attention didn't help. Between my need for privacy and her need for the spotlight, it finally tore us apart."

"Oh." She looked at him, her eyes sad in the greenish glow of the dashboard. "I'm sorry."

"Didn't we agree you wouldn't say that anymore, Bolt?" He flashed her a half-hearted smile, then stared out his window at the lights of his Alaskan hometown. "Anyway, by the end I'd become isolated, and protective of my privacy. Kellie blamed me for all her problems and said I was holding her back. She ended up moving to New York for some big network job without even discussing it with me. The press had a field-day with that too, by the way. And I was totally blindsided by Kellie leaving. I'd trusted her. I'd thought the war had done a number on me, but I was wrong. Kellie's betrayal and those reporters screwed me up a hell of a lot worse."

"Yes, I can understand your resentment now." Molly concentrated on the road ahead, her expression contemplative.

"Tell me why you let your father treat you the way he does," he said, turning the tables.

"That's the way it's always been."

"Doesn't make it right."

"No." She shrugged. "But it makes things easier. His bullying only gets worse if I fight back or try to defend myself. I'm different than the rest of my family."

"How so?"

"Well, let's see… My mother is a socialite extraordinaire. My older sister is a junior Martha Stewart on steroids. And you've just experienced Superstar Roger Flynn, able to do amazing feats of surgery with a single bound."

"What about you?"

"What about me?"

"What's your special power? Besides the whole genius thing."

"That's pretty much all I've got." Molly gave a sad little snort. "That's why I'm such a big disappointment. I'm not beautiful. I'm hopeless in social situations. And I'm definitely not the kind of daughter Roger Flynn thinks he deserves. But my intellect's given me many opportunities, so I can't complain."

"Sure you can." Jake swallowed hard against the lump of remorse in his throat. "And I'm sorry for calling your methods wacky back there. I understand now why that touched a nerve."

She acknowledged his apology with a single nod.

The tension in the air lifted and Jake couldn't resist stealing another glance at her. It astonished him that Molly thought she wasn't beautiful. She was quite possible the most exquisite thing he'd ever seen.

At last they turned in to the Anchorage Mercy parking lot and Molly pulled up beside Jake's truck. They walked inside the hospital, heading for the elevators.

Molly punched the buttons, then took out her phone, frowning. "Is Bobby a heavy drinker or involved in any illicit drug use?"

"No. He's the biggest health nut I've ever met. You read the list of his supplements, right?"

"I did…"

The elevator dinged and they stepped onboard. Jake leaned a shoulder against the wall while Molly scrolled through the texts on her phone screen.

"None of them explain all his symptoms, though."

Dread pooled thick and heavy in his gut. "We have to do something. I can't lose him. He saved my life back in the desert. That's why he got his commendation."

They arrived on the fourth floor and walked over to Gladys's desk.

"Any more changes since we talked?" Molly asked.

"How was the party?" Rob said, coming down the hall toward them, Neal by his side. "Any juicy tidbits?"

Molly shook her head, casting Jake a quick glance before answering. "Nope."

"Too bad," Neal said. "Network says we need more sizzle."

"This is a medical show, not TMZ." Molly pushed past her crew and grabbed her lab coat.

Jake thought it was a shame she had to cover up the outfit, but he could see how it might be distracting, the way it hugged her curves in all the right places. Then again, he found just about everything about Molly distracting these days.

"Dr. Ryder," she said. "Can I see you in my office a moment, please?"

"Uh…sure." He followed her into the tiny shoebox they'd given her to use.

Molly closed the door and they were alone again. It would be so easy to lean in, to kiss her deeply, to show her she was more than her smarts, more than Diagnosis Critical, more than perfect enough for him.

Molly moved past Jake to grab her stethoscope and it took every shred of his inner strength not to pull her against him. She wore her hair loose tonight, and he remembered the feel of it when she'd leaned against him at Dr. Dave's house, all silky and soft. Making him imagine how he'd like to clutch those thick strands in his hands as he lost himself inside her.

As if sensing the erotic turn of his thoughts, Molly stepped back, her eyes glittering a bit too bright. "I know we agreed I wouldn't, but I want to make one final apology about what happened tonight."

"Accepted." Jake shuffled his feet. "I'm sorry too."

"For what?"

"For your father being a selfish, insufferable bastard."

"Oh, well." She frowned down at the floor. "We Flynns aren't exactly a model family."

He tipped her chin up with his finger. "You deserve better, Molly."

"Um… I've…uh…been thinking about doing some sightseeing while I'm here."

Her voice trailed off, and her cheeks were blazing so red Jake could practically feel the heat pulsing off them. She tended to ramble when she was nervous or scared. One more endearing thing about his Molly.

His Molly?

His mind snagged on that thought. "I'd be happy to show you around. When's your next day off?"

"Day after tomorrow. I thought I'd book a whale-watching cruise."

"I'm off then too." He smiled. "Let's do it."

She grinned back. "All right."

"All right."

Molly held his gaze for several moments, and the air between them vibrated with delicious possibilities.

She smoothed a hand down the front of her lab coat and gave a slight nod. "Great. Okay. Back to work. We're thinking some type of metabolic disorder?"

It took a second for the abrupt switch in topic to penetrate the fog of desire clouding Jake's brain. "Uh...yeah, I don't see what else it could be, given Bobby's history."

"Right." Molly yanked open the door and walked back to Gladys's desk, where she pushed aside the tray with a small teapot and a mug of brown gunk sitting on the counter and opened the patient's file. "Jake, look at these labs to make sure I'm not missing something."

Forgetting about the cameras rolling, he did as she requested, his nose wrinkling at the foul stench. "Jeez, Gladys. What's that crap you're drinking? Smells like dead rat."

"That's not mine." The nurse grimaced. "It's Bobby's tea. His hockey coach brings him in a batch whenever he visits. Nothing except herbs and water, but it stinks to high heaven."

Molly paused and picked up the mug, sniffing it. "Is there a box this comes in?"

"Yep." Gladys walked over to one of the trash bags awaiting pick-up and pulled out a torn foil packet. "Here."

"Yohimbe." Molly looked from the packet to Jake. "One of five pausinystalia evergreen species growing in West and Central Africa in lowland forests. The side effects include high blood pressure, increased heart-rate, headache, nausea, tremors and sleeplessness." She turned to Gladys again. "How often has Mr. Templeton been drinking this?"

"Not so much now, but at first he had several cups a day."

Molly faced Jake again, her smile dazzling. "That's it. This works by opening the lungs and increasing blood flow. If Bobby ingested this tea and then received an injection of epinephrine in the ER—"

"It explains his cardiac arrest." Awe and adrenaline rushed Jake's system. "We can take the heart issues out of the equation."

"Yes." Molly's gaze narrowed. "And all the rest of his symptoms point to a long-term severe allergic reaction. Which was the original diagnosis."

"Cut!" Neal said, shutting off the mic. "Perfect, Mol. Nice delivery."

Jake shoved his hands in his pockets. He'd forgotten all about her film crew. Molly did that to him—made him forget about everything but her whenever she was around.

"Don't worry. I'll make sure they edit you out," she said, her eyes never leaving his. "And I'll text you. With the details of the whale cruise?"

"Great." Jake backed away, feeling oddly reluctant to leave.

Molly bit her lower lip. "Goodnight."

"'Night." As he walked away, Jake couldn't remember ever craving a day off more.

CHAPTER EIGHT

BRIGHT AND EARLY Tuesday morning, Molly bounced on the balls of her feet outside the local superstore, waiting to board the bus that would take her and Jake to the Kenai Fjords National Park and their day of whale-watching.

"All right, folks," the driver said from near the door. "Everyone have your vouchers handy and watch your step. Thank you."

The small crowd of about thirty people shuffled forward. Most of them looked to be retirees, though there were a few younger couples with kids and a small quadrant of teens.

"Are you going to be warm enough?" Jake asked, eyeing her new candy-pink outerwear.

The man at the sporting goods store had sworn the high-tech fabric was guaranteed to fifty below zero. She figured the coat, plus her new hat and gloves, would be enough to ward off the chill of any passing glaciers.

Molly gave Jake a quick once-over as they neared the front of the line. He was decked out in sturdy hiking boots and thick plaid shirts doubled up over a taupe thermal Henley. He'd topped it all off with a brown canvas jacket and a black knit skull cap that made him look as if he'd walked straight off the set of Deadliest Catch.

Despite his bundled-up appearance, he was still distractingly gorgeous.

"I'll be fine."

Molly handed her excursion ticket to the driver, then climbed up the steps into the bus. Jake followed close behind, once again placing his hand on her lower back to guide her toward a pair of open seats. Even through the extra layers his touch sent sizzles of awareness through her blood.

"This work for you?" He pulled off his hat and shoved it in his pocket, then ran his hand through his disheveled brown curls.

Molly swallowed hard and looked away. They weren't even out of the parking lot and all she could think about was sliding her hands beneath those thick flannel shirts. "Yes, this is fine."

They sidled into their row and Jake raised the armrest in the middle to give them more room. Comfy as the seats were, Molly couldn't help brushing against him each time she moved, ratcheting her pulse higher as the driver pulled out of the parking lot and their trip got underway.

Exhaling, she focused out the window and struggled to get a grip. Bad enough she'd spent most of the night tossing and turning. After the way things had ended with Brian, Molly didn't want to make the same mistakes with Jake. Nor did she want to go overboard yet, even though she was passionately drawn to him.

"Welcome to Wild Frontier Whale-Watching Excursions," their driver said over the PA system. "We'll be out of Anchorage proper in a few minutes, folks, so settle in and prepare to see the most gorgeous scenery on earth. Have your cameras ready and have a wonderful day!"

"This is probably old hat for you, huh?" Molly said, glancing over at Jake.

"No, actually." He shrugged. "Workaholic, remember? I don't get out here often."

"Right." She watched the urban landscape change to thick green forest. "I was afraid you'd be bored."

"I'm lots of things when I'm with you, Molly, but bored isn't one of them."

His words ignited a fresh burst of excitement inside her.

As they rode along Molly snapped photos of the passing scenery while Jake read the copy of the latest emergency medicine journal he'd brought. About an hour into their trip a tour helper came around with complimentary cups of coffee and pre-packaged pastries.

"I'll pay you back for this," Jake said, unwrapping and devouring half his blueberry muffin in one bite.

"No need." Molly carefully removed her lemon Danish from the cellophane, then unfolded her paper napkin. "Breakfast is included."

"No, I mean the tour." He eyed her neatly prepared area with amusement. "You're tidy too, huh?"

"Is that a problem?"

"No, not a problem."

He gave her a slow appraisal, from the top of her head to the tips of her toes, now curled up inside her hiking boots. His gaze held an answering flicker of heat to match the growing inferno inside her. Her whole body seemed to tremble after his frank perusal.

"But these tours are expensive. I'll pay you back for my share, Molly."

"How about we call this payback for all my nonstop apologies last night?"

Light broke through the hazy clouds gathered near

the mountaintops and streamed through the spruce trees, highlighting more of the glorious late fall landscape. Rich scarlets and golds and deep, dark greens hugged the roadway.

Jake chuckled. "Yeah, okay. We can do that."

Molly hazarded another glance at him. "I'm just glad I got you out of the hospital."

"And I'm glad I got you away from your crew for a couple of hours."

"It's nice to have a break."

"It's been so long I've forgotten what it's like to just relax and enjoy a day off." He gave her a sad little half-smile, his tone holding regret mixed with a hint of guilt. "After Kellie left I threw myself into my career, made a lot of sacrifices to get where I am today. Sometimes I wonder if they were worth it—wonder if I'm in control of my career or if it's controlling me."

Without thinking, Molly took his hand. "I think about those things too. Especially when I see people my age getting married and having kids. My sister's pregnancy hasn't helped. Not that I'm not happy for Martha. I am. I just…" She sighed. "I always wanted children someday."

"Me too." Jake stared down at their entwined fingers. "But we've got plenty of time."

"My mother's fond of reminding how fertility drops off after age thirty."

"I just don't get your family." He frowned. "Both my parents are off traveling the US in their Winnebago, but they're always my biggest supporters. Through school, the military, the end of my engagement to Kellie—everything. Your family doesn't seem to be there for you at all."

"Like I said, I'm the oddball. I don't think they have a clue how to support me, so they just pretend I'm not there." Molly ate the last of her pastry. This was stepping into unknown territory. Brian had never liked to discuss anything unpleasant. "Tell me about your ex-fiancée."

"Kellie and I had known each other since high school. She was a cheerleader and I was on the football team, but we didn't start dating until freshman year of college. She was always volunteering for stuff…trying to get everyone to like her. I pictured us having a white picket fence kind of future."

"Sounds perfect." Molly's heart pinched.

"Obviously not perfect enough." Jake stretched his long legs out in front of him. "Considering she chose her career over me."

The driver's voice crackled over the PA system again. "Folks, if you look toward the right side of the bus you'll see some of the mudflats that make up the Turnagain Pass shoreline."

Molly took a couple more shots while Jake rested his head back against his seat and closed his eyes. She watched him through her lashes, hesitant. Talking about her abysmal break-up with Brian wasn't her favorite topic, but he'd shared about his ex, so it seemed only fair.

"I was seeing someone back in Chicago. His name was Brian."

Jake peeked one eye open and glanced at her, but didn't say anything.

"He was a stockbroker. Smart, educated, looked good on paper. In reality…? Not so much. At least not for me." Molly stared out at Cook Inlet. "Guess I wasn't the person he expected me to be. Story of my life." Her eyes stung again. "He broke up with me. By text message." She shook her head. "How pathetic does that make me?"

Jake gave her fingers a reassuring squeeze. "He's the pathetic one—not you."

"My family might say otherwise."

"The more I learn about your family, the more I'm starting to believe they're a bunch of idiots."

The conviction in his tone, coupled with the spark of understanding in his eyes, had Molly wanting to melt into a puddle of goo at his feet.

Jake smiled. "You're just...different."

"And if that isn't a nice way of saying weird, I don't know what is."

"Hey, I happen to like weird."

"You do?"

"Yeah..." He tugged her closer. "I do."

Molly snuggled into Jake's side and he slipped his arm around her shoulders, guiding her head down to rest on his chest. She did her best not to swoon while he stroked her hair.

"Tell me more about what it was like for you growing up," he said, his voice rumbling comfortingly beneath her ear.

"Being gifted isn't all it's cracked up to be." Molly started to pull away, but Jake held her in place until she relaxed once more. "My parents meant well, I suppose—always pushing, always demanding more, always criticizing—but I felt incredible pressure to achieve, to earn their love and respect. In a lot of ways I still do." She swallowed hard. "Sounds silly."

"Not silly at all. Justified." Jake massaged the nape of her neck, his voice both firm and protective. "Like I said, Molly. You deserved better. You deserve better now."

Hearing him defend her so ardently rekindled that deep yearning inside her. Maybe getting closer to him, if only for a little while, wasn't such an impossibility after all. "Okay..."

"Okay." He leaned past her to point toward the window. "Look. Sea lions."

Resisting the urge to close the tiny gap between them and kiss his cheek, Molly gazed out at the colony basking in the sun on the mudflats. "Cute!"

"Yeah. Adorable…"

Except Jake was looking at her, not the view.

"Welcome aboard the scenic wildlife cruise portion of your trip through the Kenai Fjords. My name's Captain Fred and this is my assistant Joe. We'll be here to point out interesting sights and to answer any questions you may have. Enjoy your day!"

The gruff-looking older man headed back into the ship's cabin to steer them out into the open waters.

Jake leaned against the rail beside Molly, feeling lighter than he had in years. He didn't share his past with many people, but with her it had felt right. He gripped the railing, his hands itching to touch her, stroke her, gather her close and hold her tight.

He stared out at the placid blue water, releasing the stress of the past few days. He'd had precious little respect for Roger Flynn before that dinner party, and after hearing Molly talk about her painful childhood he liked the guy even less. Her father might be brilliant in his chosen field, but his life outside of trauma surgery left a lot to be desired.

The irony wasn't lost on Jake.

If he wasn't careful he could end up heading down that same lonely path.

Several tourists nearby gasped as two dorsal fins slipped through the water about two hundred feet away—orcas, most likely. Jake pointed them out to Molly, but he much preferred to look at her. The wind had flushed her cheeks a delightful shade of pink. Her lips were parted. He wondered what would happen if he leaned in and kissed her again. Would she want more or push him away?

Jake cleared his throat and battled the erotic images flooding his mind, croaking out the first dumb thing that popped into his head. "Whales."

"Yes. Whales." Molly stared at the giant creatures as if in a daze, her voice drenched in awe. "Sea lions, puffins, Dall's porpoises, American black bear, snowshoe hares—and mountain goats too. They're all native species to this area."

"Thanks for another zoology lesson, Bolt."

She gave him a side-glance at his sarcastic tone and he grinned.

"Kidding. It's pretty here."

"It's beautiful."

Molly closed her eyes and inhaled deeply. All Jake could think of at that moment was her beneath him, arching, panting, crying out as she came undone in his arms.

"Almost makes me sad to leave."

Her words stirred something inside him. Deep down, his instincts told him he could find happiness with her and urged him to take a chance. Told him that despite their differences, and all the reasons why they shouldn't be together, things between them felt sort of…perfect.

"I'm sure Chicago's nice."

He gazed into the distance as Captain Fred moved them into the larger fjords. A noisy flock of squawking seagulls filled the air and the crisp scent of sea water stung his nose. Hazy clouds had blown in with the stiff breeze off the glaciers, frosty and bleak.

Jake hunkered down in his jacket and shoved his hands into his pockets. "There's got to be more things to do in the big city than what we have here."

"Oh, it's fine. If you like those sorts of things."

"And you don't?"

"I like the museums and the theaters, and walking down by the lakeshore in the summer. But I'm not really much of a party girl."

"No?" he said, his tone dripping with mock horror.

"Yes." Her lilting giggle shivered through him like chimes. "I know it's hard to believe."

"What do you do on all those long Chicago nights, then?" He shouldn't have asked, but he couldn't seem to help himself. "Besides curing the incurable."

"I read. A lot. And I work."

"Sounds like a rollercoaster of thrills."

She chuckled. "You're one to talk."

The wind whipped her pale hair around her face beneath that impractical flouncy hat. No way Molly wasn't cold in that jacket, no matter how much it had cost her—which was too much, based on the fancy designer logo stitched on the front. Besides, Jake could think of much better ways to keep her warm—like with his arms, his body, his mouth and hands.

"From what I've heard, all you do is hang around the hospital and pick up extra shifts," Molly said. "You even admitted on the bus you're a shameless workaholic."

"Hmm..." Jake looked at her again. She was lovely. Lovely and infinitely touchable.

Her smile widened as weak sunlight filtered through the overcast skies. "Thanks for sharing about your past."

"Thanks for listening."

Jake jammed the toe of his hiking boot against the deck of the ship. Now wasn't the time to let his libido take charge. They were just getting familiar with each other, exploring this connection between them, figuring out if they wanted to take things further, deeper. He found himself trusting her more and more each day.

"And thanks for talking about your childhood with me."

"You're welcome."

"Your secrets are safe with me, Bolt."

"As are yours with me. My lips are sealed."

She made a little twisting motion with her fingers in front of her mouth, like turning a key then tossing it away, and his stubborn thoughts zoomed right back to other things she might do with those fingers, with that mouth…

"Ladies and gentlemen, in the distance you'll see a group of humpback whales bubble-netting," Captain Fred announced.

Jake moved in beside Molly again, his arm resting comfortably against hers.

"Bubble-netting is a cooperative effort by a pod of whales. They work together to encircle prey fish such as herring into a ball with bubbles. Then they swim up through it and trap the fish in their mouths, expelling the sea water as they breach the surface."

On cue, two of the humongous whales arched over the surface of the inlet and spouted enormous plumes of water high into the air. The mist drifted on the breeze to drizzle down on the passengers.

Molly gasped along with the rest of the tourists, then clapped with delight, snapping photos with her phone before pointing excitedly. "Did you see that?"

"I did."

But Jake was having as much fun watching Molly's reactions as he was the whales. In fact if there hadn't been so many people around he would've revisited that passionate kiss they'd shared in the gym, maybe taken things a bit farther—removed that ridiculous hat and plunged his hands into her hair, slipping his fingers beneath her coat and…

"How about I take a picture of the two of you together?" asked Joe, the captain's assistant.

"Uh…" Jake looked over at Molly, who nodded. "Okay. Sure."

"Great." Joe motioned for them to move closer. "Put your arm around her waist."

Jake did as he was instructed, pulling Molly into his side as she slipped her hand beneath his coat to hook her finger through the belt loops on his jeans. His whole nervous system jolted from her touch.

"Cool." Joe adjusted the camera angle. "All right. Let's see a smile from the happy couple."

"Oh, we're not a—" they both started in unison.

Snap. Snap. Snap.

"Awesome." Joe handed Molly her phone, then slapped Jake on the back. "You're a lucky man. Take care of her."

I will.

Jake watched Joe walk away, somewhat stunned at his inner response.

Molly stood across from him, frowning down at her phone screen.

"What? Are they awful?" he asked, moving in beside her again.

"No." She shoved the device back in her pocket before he could see what was on the screen. "I'm just… It's nice being here with you today. Spending time with you."

Funny how much her thoughts mirrored his own.

"My shooting schedule and difficult cases don't leave me much time outside of work. That's another reason why Brian left," Molly said, leaning against the railing again, staring out to sea. "His text said he doubted I'd even notice he was gone."

"And do you?"

"What?"

"Notice he's gone?"

"Honestly? I haven't—not really." She laughed, short and sweet, then smiled. "I've been too busy. Thanks to Bobby and a certain Head of Emergency Medicine."

Jake's body warmed with affection and he moved a tad closer to her to block the harsh wind, a now familiar surge of protectiveness joining the simmering passion inside him.

"When I was growing up, my mom always said love can't be rushed. That if you stop searching it'll happen."

"She sounds like a wise lady."

The earnestness in her voice made his heart clench. His scores in the lasting relationship department might not be stellar, but at least he'd been there, done that. The fact that Molly hadn't, made those staunch barriers Jake had built around himself crumble even more. Yes, she was leaving soon, and maybe whatever happened between them could only be temporary, but that didn't mean it couldn't also be real.

"I have a suggestion," Jake said, before common sense made him rethink his actions.

"What?"

"How about I take you to dinner when we get back to Anchorage? A true date this time."

"I was going to go to the hospital and check on Bobby."

Jake pulled out his phone and showed her a recent message. "Gladys says he's stable and resting comfortably."

Molly chewed on her bottom lip. "Are you sure?"

"More than anything, Bolt." He put his arm around her and cuddled her close, unable to resist any longer. Against all odds, God help him, his walls were crashing down. "More than anything."

CHAPTER NINE

"I JUST HAVE a bad headache," Molly said over the phone to Neal, doing her best to keep the guilt from her voice.

She still couldn't quite believe she'd agreed to go to dinner instead of going to the hospital. Yet here they were, back at Jake's favorite pub, splitting another order of salmon nachos. The tiny rebellion both thrilled and terrified her.

"I'm going to sleep it off and be ready to go again tomorrow."

"Hmm…" Neal said, his tone concerned. "Maybe it's a brain tumor."

"It's not a brain tumor." Five years of working on a medical reality TV show had made her crew into hypochondriacs.

She peered through the glass doors of the small lobby. Jake caught Molly's eye and waved. With a sigh, she tugged at her long-sleeved black T-shirt, this one proclaiming Bacteria—It's the only culture some people have, then smoothed her hand down her faded jeans.

"Listen, I need to get off the phone."

"Are you losing consciousness?" Neal said. "I'll dial 911."

"No. I'm fine. I'm going to take a hot bath and a couple of ibuprofen, then go to bed. I've instructed the hospital staff to call me if there are any changes to Bobby's condition. Talk to you later."

Before Neal could respond Molly shut off her phone, then walked back through the doors, joining Jake as the server placed a large platter of nachos and two sodas on the table.

Molly slid onto the bench seat across from him, shoving her pink coat into the corner to make more room. "Sorry."

"Everything okay?" he asked. "Nice shirt, by the way."

"Oh, thanks." Her snarky tees were one of her favorite means of creative expression. "Some people don't get my sense of humor."

"That's one of my favorite things about you, Bolt." He winked and her heart did a flip. "Hand me your plate."

"Thanks again for dinner."

"My pleasure." Jake handed Molly a heaping pile of nachos, his long legs nudging hers under the table. "Is that enough for you?"

"Pretty sure this is enough for four people." She tucked her hair behind her ear and stared down at her plate, suddenly shy. "I had an excellent time today."

"Me too." He passed her a fork, his fingers lingering longer than necessary. "Let's eat."

She'd been hungry before, but the spicy smell of the nachos made her famished. They both dug into the food with relish. Minutes went by, filled with small talk and lots of crunching as they devoured the Mexican treat.

At last Molly took a final bite then sat back, stuffed.

Jake grinned over at her. "You have something in the corner of your mouth."

"I do?" She wiped her lips. "Gone?"

"Nope." He pointed toward the right side of his face. "Right there."

Molly tried again. "Did I get it?"

"No." Jake shook his head, then reached for her napkin. "Here—let me."

She leaned forward, meeting him halfway across the table. Her gaze fell to his mouth as his fingertip grazed her skin.

"There…" he murmured, with unmistakable desire lighting his eyes.

"Thanks," she whispered, not pulling away.

"You're welcome." Jake closed the tiny gap between them and brushed his lips over hers.

The sound of a throat being cleared broke them apart.

"Sorry, folks," their server said. "I'll just leave the check here for whenever you're done."

Jake sat back, one dark brow cocked. "I'm ready. How about you?"

Molly nodded, her frenzied response to him raging higher.

"Great."

He flagged down the server and handed over cash before leading Molly from the pub. They'd left her Range Rover at the supercenter and driven here in Jake's truck. Once inside the vehicle, he started the engine and cranked the heater, turning out of the parking lot and heading in the opposite direction from her hotel.

"Where are we going?" Molly asked.

"I thought I'd show you my house."

Jake took her hand again, and the gentle stroke of his thumb against her skin sent a frisson of need through her body.

"Sound good?"

"Yes."

She stared out the window beside her as they zipped through the nighttime traffic, heading out of downtown

Anchorage and into a residential neighborhood. He pulled into the driveway of a ranch-style home with lots of construction supplies stacked around the perimeter.

Jake cut the engine, then came around to help her out. "Excuse the mess. I'm doing some remodeling."

"No. It's great."

Molly's breath hitched as he kissed her against the side of the truck, the cold metal at her back at direct odds with the solid heat of Jake pressed to her front. She surrendered to the wonderful sensations storming through her—passion, affection, aching want.

At last he broke away, resting his forehead against hers. "I've wanted to do that again since that night in the gym."

"Me too." She smiled, tangling her fingers into the silky curls at the nape of his neck, her pulse thudding and her knees weak.

Molly wanted him so much she hurt. This wasn't like her. This wasn't logical. This wasn't like anything she'd ever experienced before and she was loving every single second.

"C'mon." Jake led her to his front porch, then fumbled to get his key into the lock.

The notion that he might be as affected as she was made Molly giddy with hope. He tugged her inside and flipped on the lights, removing his coat and his flannel shirts to leave only the Henley behind.

"Let me show you around."

The open-concept interior of the house was exceptionally tidy for a bachelor pad, if a bit sparse. Tools and construction equipment filled several corners, but the kitchen was finished and well-appointed, with gleaming appliances and granite countertops. The floors were hardwood, shining as if newly waxed. The smell of sawdust and fresh paint tickled Molly's nose as she gazed around.

"You're doing all this yourself?"

"Yep. In my spare time."

"Right… All that spare time, huh?"

"Yeah." Jake gave Molly a self-deprecating grin, heading toward a large double-sided fridge. "Can I get you anything? Water? Wine?"

She shrugged out of her coat and hat, draping them over the back of a folding metal chair. What she really needed to find was a place to plug in her phone. "Got a place I can re-juice?"

"Sure."

Jake led her down the hall and into a master suite, complete with king-size bed and a large walk-in closet attached to a luxurious travertine-tiled bath.

"Right there." He pointed to a spot on the nightstand.

"Great." Molly plugged in her device, then straightened.

The air crackled with sexual tension and her muscles were tight with need. She wanted to touch Jake, taste him, burrow beneath his rigid self-control and make him pant with desire. She'd never had this kind of amazing chemistry with anyone before and she longed to explore every facet.

As if reading her thoughts, Jake closed the slight distance between them, taking her hand. "I like you, Molly. A lot."

She rested her forehead on his chest, inhaling his comforting scent, and waited for the inevitable caveat that always followed such statements, whether from her father or Brian or any other man.

"Except you need me to work harder, or stop arguing, or—"

"No." Jake silenced her, placing his finger beneath her chin and forcing Molly to meet his gaze. "I like you. Just as you are."

Then he kissed her again, his strong arms pulling her close. His lips were demanding, yet gentle, and every cell in her body felt heavy and buoyant at the same time. Her head fell back as his mouth traveled down her neck to her pulse point and… Oh, my…

With Brian, sex had always felt a bit detached and, well…clinical. Now, though, Molly didn't know where to touch Jake first.

He took one of her fluttering hands, kissed her palm before placing it over his thudding heart, allowing her to feel just how much she affected him. His mouth returned to hers, deepening the kiss, tasting her, seducing her. His caresses grew hotter, more insistent, until he pulled away to stroke the hair back from her forehead.

She swayed closer and Jake cupped her cheek. "Do you want to go to bed with me?"

"Yes, please," Molly whispered, every nerve ending in her body poised on a precipice. "Are you sure you want to go to bed with me?"

"Oh, yeah, Bolt. I'm sure."

Jake smiled as he picked her up. Her legs wrapped around his waist and her arms went around his neck and she returned his kisses, hard and deep. His low moans only served to stoke her passion higher. She couldn't get enough. She had to have more of him…would die without him.

Desperate, Molly pulled at his clothes, needing to get closer to this beautiful man who made her feel beautiful too.

Tearing his mouth from hers, Jake kissed his way down the side of her neck as he laid Molly on the bed, then stretched out beside her. His hands seemed to be everywhere at once—touching, stroking, undoing and removing things. Her T-shirt was the first to go, followed in short order by his Henley, and then she reveled in the first brush of his naked chest against her skin.

Jake made quick work of her bra too, cupping her bare breasts gently, his thumbs circling their sensitive pink tips while Molly, emboldened, slipped her hand between their bodies to feel his rigid length pressed tight against the front of his jeans.

He groaned softly while she caressed him through the soft material. His breathing grew raspier and she kissed him again. At last, he rolled her beneath him and she looped her legs around his waist once more, craving the feel of his hard body against her.

"This first time should be special, but I want you too badly. It's been too long."

"I want you too." Molly flicked open the top of his fly, then snuck her fingers inside his waistband. The zipper crept down slowly, to accommodate her touch as she traced the outline of his erection through his briefs. "So much."

His breath caught and his gaze was searing, hot and demanding. "Keep that up and I won't last."

"Endurance is overrated," she said, grinning.

Quickly discarding the rest of his clothes, Jake lowered himself beside her once more, reaching between her thighs to stroke her wet folds. Gently, he thrust first one, then two fingers inside her, while his thumb circled her most sensitive flesh, preparing her.

She whimpered, arching hard against his hand. He seemed to know exactly how to touch her, how to tease her to the brink of ecstasy in no time flat. Her orgasm loomed closer, closer, and she buried her face against his shoulder as her first climax struck.

"I've got you." He held her until her body quieted against him, then smoothed her hair from her flushed cheeks. "Good?"

"Amazing."

Molly pressed Jake down onto his back, straddling him. She wasn't a vixen, by any stretch, but she had to see him, touch him, taste him. In control, she grasped the hard, hot length of him, draping her hair over his chest and hips as she leaned forward and licked his skin, savoring the salty flavor.

"My turn…"

Molly's warm breath and tongue against his aching flesh was almost Jake's undoing. Then she engulfed him in the wet embrace of her mouth and he damned near passed out. He slipped his fingers through her silken hair while she pleasured him with her lips and tongue, but soon his need grew too strong to deny.

Unable to wait any longer, Jake rolled over, pinning Molly beneath him as he kissed a slow descent down her body, stopping along the way to pay homage to her delightful breasts, then nuzzling her navel before traveling lower.

She was everything he'd ever wanted and more. All creamy soft skin and dreamy soft sighs.

Gently he licked once, twice, over her heated core, making love to her with his mouth, only stopping when she'd reached her second climax. Then, at last, he kissed his way up her body until he settled atop her again.

Molly laced her fingertips in the hair at his nape, her bright blue eyes glittering with passion. An involuntary shudder ran through Jake at the soft caress. She reached for his hard length again, but he placed a restraining hand atop hers.

"Stop, or I won't last more than a few seconds." He nipped her earlobe. "And I want this to last forever."

Levering himself up on his elbows, Jake grabbed a condom from the nightstand drawer and smoothed it on before entering her in one long thrust. Molly moaned, the sound low and laced with satisfaction. Buried hilt-deep, he stilled, savoring the exquisite sensations.

"You feel amazing, sweetheart. You are amazing."

"S-so are you," she whispered, her gaze locked with his as he began a slow, steady rhythm, driving them both closer to the brink.

He loved the sexy catch in her voice. The way their lovemaking seemed to chase all coherent thought from her brilliant mind.

Molly ground against him, increasing the delicious friction. "Please...don't stop."

"Never."

He moaned as she clutched him closer, riding out the waves of another orgasm. Unable to deny himself any longer, Jake slipped his fingers through hers, his senses overwhelmed by her passion, her...everything.

Soon a familiar tightness filled his groin, signaling his looming release. Jake drove into Molly one last time before his body went whipcord-tight, a deep groan tearing from his lungs. He murmured her name again and again, lost in an endless avalanche of endorphins and pleasure.

As the intensity ebbed and drowsiness overtook him he rested his head in the valley between her breasts. He felt boneless, weightless, yet heavy as concrete, sated beyond belief as she toyed with his hair.

She always smelled like citrus and sunshine.

Like home.

He wanted to stay inside this heavenly private universe and never come out. This was what he'd searched for and never found—this closeness, this connection, this trust. He struggled to keep his heavy-lidded eyes open, not wanting the moment to end.

Eventually Molly's breathing evened out into the pattern of sleep and Jake rolled to his side, spooning her against him beneath the covers before drifting into slumber.

CHAPTER TEN

MOLLY WOKE BEFORE dawn and looked over her shoulder at the man snoozing beside her. Jake Ryder was one sexy beast. No doubt about it. In fact she couldn't stop admiring the gorgeous corded muscles in his strong arms, the design of his tattoo visible on the tanned perfection of his left bicep. Couldn't stop admiring the chiseled lines of his back as he hugged the pillow beneath him, admiring the way his torso formed a perfect V down to his slim waist, then dipped into his lower back.

She eyed the covers. If he moved slightly those sheets might reveal the tight globes of his butt too.

Molly grinned like a dope as she stared up at the ceiling. What a spectacular night.

She was no blushing virgin—she and Brian had lived together, after all—but the difference between him and Jake was like sun and shadow. Brian had never been one to take the lead—or to take his time. Jake had no problem being an alpha male—in the sack or out. And yet he'd taken all the time in the world to make Molly feel exquisite. The things they'd done to each other had been hot and sexy and…well…sweet.

Memories of him came: his dark curls sweaty and his cheeks flushed, his muscles shaking from tension and release as he collapsed beside her and murmured endearments into her hair. Her insides fluttered just from thinking about it.

Then her phone buzzed from the nightstand and her bubble of sublime happiness burst.

Yesterday, out in the wilderness, it had been easy to forget about reality. But now the world seemed determined to crash in at every turn, chipping away at the tiny utopia they'd created.

Molly rubbed her eyes and groaned. Coffee. She needed liquid energy before she could face the world again.

Carefully she slipped out from between the sheets and used the bathroom before tugging on her clothes and then fumbling her way down the unfamiliar hall. There were only a few hints of the coming dawn in the sky, so it must still be super-early. She stumbled into his kitchen and clicked on the lights, squinting into the brightness as she searched for the necessary supplies to make a pot.

Once finished, Molly tiptoed back into the bedroom to grab her phone and charger, then returned to the kitchen, where she scrolled through what appeared to be a gazillion messages from her crew, asking her to call in immediately. Man, a girl takes one day off and everything goes nuts.

After a resigned sigh, Molly dialed Rob's number. "Hey, it's me."

"Have you seen the announcement?" her cameraman asked, his voice a tad panicked.

"What announcement?"

"Promise me you won't look until you get here."

"Seriously?" Molly sighed heavily, leaning her hip against the island and tapping her stockinged toes against the chilly hardwood floor. "Is Neal there?"

"He can't come to the phone."

"Why not?"

"He's on a conference call with Les Montgomery and—"

"The head of the MedStar Network?" Molly straightened, her pulse kicking a notch higher. "About what?"

"Hang on." Murmured voices echoed through the line before Rob returned. "Just get to the hospital as fast as you can—okay?"

He hung up before she could respond.

Crap.

Molly walked into the living room to tug on her boots and clicked on the lights there too. Rob tended to be a bit of a drama queen when it came to network gossip, so she wasn't going to freak out quite yet about his urgent request for her to get to Anchorage Mercy stat, but she did want to return soon anyway, to check on Bobby.

After tugging on her footwear, she spotted a group of photos on one wall, near the windows. The first showed a young Jake—maybe four or five—with a man and woman she guessed were his parents. The man had the same dark hair and gray eyes and the woman shared her son's devilish grin.

Next was the same group shot, but all of them were older, in front of a large RV. This time Jake held a gorgeous brunette in his arms. From the besotted expression on his face and the way his lips were pressed to the girl's cheek, Molly guessed this had to be the infamous Kellie.

The third picture showed Jake again, handsome and serious in his dress uniform. And was that the President, pinning a gold medal on his chest? He'd briefly mentioned receiving an award for his service in the Army but nothing like this.

Molly moved on to the last photo. This one had to be his beloved regiment—a group of about twenty men and women. Jake and Bobby were near the middle of the back row, easily the tallest guys in the group. Jake's eyes sparkled with mischief and one side of his mouth was curved in that sweet smile she was quickly coming to know.

To know and love…

Pulse thudding, Molly raised a shaky hand to her face. She liked Jake—much more than was probably wise. They were compatible in many ways, but had she fallen for him?

The sound of footsteps echoed behind her and she turned to find Jake leaning against the doorframe. His broad chest was distractingly bare above a pair of worn sweatpants that hinted at far more than they concealed.

"What's going on?" he asked, his voice sleepy and deliciously rough.

Her phone buzzed again and Molly squinted down at a text from Neal.

Get in here. Now.

Right. Work. She thumbed in a quick response.

On my way.

"Is it Bobby?" Jake moved closer, rubbing his eyes before glancing down at her screen.

"No. My crew. Something's going on with the network." Molly shut the device off, doing her best not to stare at Jake's amazing torso on full display. At the muscles she'd love to stroke and kiss and nuzzle all over again.

Get your head back in the game, Flynn.

She exhaled and looked away. "I need to get back to the hospital."

"That's too bad," Jake said. "I was hoping we could spend time together this morning."

Me too…

A "ding" issued from the coffeemaker and the rich smell of fresh-brewed coffee filled the air. They walked into the kitchen and Jake poured them each a large mug. Toes curled and eyes lowered, Molly sipped her brew and struggled to express how much last night had meant.

With Brian, she'd always gone to work early, maybe leaving a small note on the nightstand, asking him to pick something up for dinner. Quick exits made for fewer awkward conversations about things neither of them wanted to discuss.

But with Jake Molly wanted to talk about all sorts of things—birthdays, favorite colors, favorite foods, if he rooted for the Cubs or the White Sox. Go Cubbies. With Jake she cared—much more than she was ready to admit. Of course it didn't help when he stood there, rumpled and perfect and nice and naughty all rolled into one.

Jake watched her over the rim of his coffee cup, his gaze far too perceptive.

Beneath his scrutiny Molly's analytical mind kicked in again, blaring with all too familiar warning bells.

Slow down, step back, assess and strategize.

While her heart demanded the opposite.

Cuddle. Snuggle. Ravish. Repeat.

Flustered, Molly set her half-finished coffee on the counter and inched toward the hallway. "I…um…should get going."

Not the most eloquent parting words, but considering the war going on inside her she'd been lucky to say anything coherent.

"Right." Jake put his mug aside as well, following her. "About last night…"

Uh-oh. That statement was never good.

Molly held her breath, not sure she'd survive if Jake said what she feared he might say—that what they'd shared had been a mistake instead of the best, most emotionally moving experience of her life.

The realization of her true feelings for Jake sent shockwaves through Molly's system. She'd promised to stay safe, stay unattached, stay un-entangled, and here she was in—

Nope. Not saying that word.

Nope. Nope. Nope.

But her rebel thoughts refused to cooperate, flooding her mind with fresh images of them in his bed, touching, tasting, lost in each other in the darkest hours before dawn.

Adrenaline mixed with the ache in her chest and Molly stumbled backward, darting a glance at Jake and then instantly regretting her decision. His firm lips were quirked into that sexy little half-grin as he crowded into her personal space with one dark brow arched.

"No need to panic, Bolt. I only bite when asked."

Stunned into silence, Molly watched as he placed one hand on either side of her on the doorframe, his chest brushing against her with blatant seduction. She bit her lip and stared at his tanned throat. If she rose on tiptoes she could nuzzle that spot below his ear...the one she'd discovered made him shiver.

Her phone was buzzing, buzzing, buzzing and her mind was distracted. Her anxiety skyrocketed. She blinked hard, unwanted facts clogging her mind before they tumbled out in a torrent of embarrassment.

Cue awkward rambling in three...two...one...

"Contrary to popular belief, penguins do not live at the North Pole, or anywhere in the northern hemisphere, including Alaska. Also, Magellanic penguins are monogamous and have the same mates for life."

Jake's gaze flew to hers and Molly's heart raced like a hamster on a wheel.

Please don't make fun of me. Please don't make me feel like an outsider. Please.

"Um…wow. Okay." His eyes narrowed. "Are you telling me you enjoyed last night?"

"I…uh…" Feeling totally exposed, Molly rushed to the living room to gather her things before barreling for the front door. She paused halfway out on the porch. "I'll see you at the hospital."

She left before Jake could respond.

It would've been a movie-perfect departure too—except she'd forgotten he'd driven last night and her Rover was still back in the supercenter parking lot.

Fabulous.

Breath frosting in the early-morning air, Molly trudged back to the front door and found Jake waiting, arms crossed and smile patient. "Can you give me a ride to my car?"

"Be with you in five minutes, Bolt." His tone was laced with mirth.

The wait, at least, gave Molly time to gulp down the rest of her coffee and sort through her emails.

Jake joined her in his living room with ninety seconds to spare, having showered and pulled on fresh jeans and a black crewneck sweater. As he bent to shove his feet into his boots she couldn't help staring one last time at his marvelous physique. The man was gorgeous and wonderful, and the fact she'd spent the whole night with him still seemed a bit unreal.

"Ready?" Jake asked, slipping on his coat.

"Ready." Molly nodded, doing her best to regain her mental equilibrium.

She was back on duty. Time to think of Bobby and her career. Time to put her needs and wants second.

They walked out to his truck, which was covered in the thin layer of frost that had formed during the wee hours. Jake cranked the engine while Molly grabbed a scraper to brush off his windshield. Soon they were on their way, rumbling down the road as the heater struggled to warm them.

This early, it seemed wildlife was everywhere. She'd not paid much attention the night before, but Jake's property abutted the Chugach National Forest. Trees towered overhead and a large hawk swooped amongst the boughs, hunting for a meal. She even spotted a fox with kits darting through the foliage.

"This place is amazing," she said, pulling out her phone to snap a few shots.

"I love it." Jake smiled. "Alaska's home. Can't imagine living anywhere else."

Molly suppressed a pang of sadness. Yet another reason she should check her feelings at the door and just enjoy last night for what it had been. A one-time occurrence. A fling. She had a career in Chicago. Jake had deep roots here in Anchorage. Long-distance relationships never worked. And hadn't Brian complained he never got to see her as it was?

She was still mulling this over as they pulled into the supercenter lot and Jake parked beside her Range Rover.

Molly unfastened her seat belt and grabbed the metal door handle, feeling its icy chill through her gloves as she hesitated, unsure what to say. "Um… I had a wonderful time."

Jake nodded, staring at the shopping center beyond. Only a few determined bargain-hunters were heading out this early in the morning.

"Maybe we can have lunch together later? To talk?"

His rough, deep voice made her knees go weak again. Yes. "Maybe. Depends on my schedule. Text me and I'll let you know."

Molly started to climb out—only to be pulled back into the truck and against Jake's chest. His soft lips found hers and he kissed her deeply, leaving them both breathless. He smelled of soap and shampoo from his recent shower, and when he lifted his head, his pupils were dilated, nearly obscuring his stormy gray irises.

Molly bit her lip and Jake tracked the tiny movement, frown lines forming between his dark brows. She pressed her palms against his chest and forced herself to move away, before she ended up surrendering to temptation.

"See you later."

"Yeah," he said, his voice husky. "See you later, Bolt."

Jake waited until she'd gotten the Range Rover started, and was still waiting when Molly pulled out of the lot and headed toward her hotel. His image grew smaller and smaller in the rearview mirror as her uncertainty grew and grew. She should turn around. She should go back. She should call her crew and tell them she'd be there when she was ready.

Molly kept driving. Her career and her patient were waiting at the hospital. She needed to shower and change and then get back to work. Lives depended on her skills, her genius.

Last night had been a singular fantasy, a brilliant one-time dream.

The sooner Molly remembered that, the better.

Jake sat for a long while after Molly left, just thinking. He wasn't due back at the ER for several hours and his thoughts, along with his heart, seemed jumbled.

Last evening he'd allowed himself to let go with Molly, to feel more, both physically and emotionally. By trusting her, he'd allowed himself to be vulnerable. He'd never imagined he'd get to that point again after what had happened with Kellie, but he had—a hell of a lot faster than he'd expected too. The time he and Molly had spent together these past few weeks had allowed him to see past her hard candy shell and vice versa. He'd glimpsed the real woman beneath her professional persona—a woman with wants and needs, a past and a future. A woman who was smart and interesting and well-spoken.

And, yeah, a bit quirky too. Loveably quirky.

He chuckled at the memory of her penguin outburst. Funny thing was, Jake had taken an online test once, in a college freshman Psych course, to find out what animal best fit his personality. Turned out he was indeed a penguin—witty, meticulous, intelligent, inscrutable.

Yep. That about summed him up.

After starting the engine, Jake headed back toward his house again—only to step on his brakes as a family of Canadian geese waddled across the main roadway. While he waited for the feathered pedestrians to move past, Molly's remark about penguins mating for life swirled in his brain. Why had she chosen that fact to spout? Was she interested in forever with him?

He sighed and accelerated once the geese had passed— only to stop at a red light.

Nah. Molly couldn't want a future with him. She had her TV show, a busy career. The last thing she'd want was to live out here on the wild frontier.

Besides, last night was a one-time deal. He'd gone into this knowing full well what he was getting into. To wish for anything more would just be courting disaster, no matter how spectacular those hours with Molly in his arms had been. No matter how scorching the sex or how funny and smart and fascinating she was. That was no reason to go off the deep end and get his heart broken again when she left.

Right?

Jake passed a slower moving car before signaling back into his lane, feeling that ache of indecision returning. Dammit. He'd hoped to sit down with Molly and talk this morning before heading into work, maybe figure out how to handle this thing between them—have a chance to make sure that they were on the same page, that he wasn't missing something important like it felt he was.

As he turned down the road leading to his house once again Jake decided to let it rest. He'd text her for lunch later, just as he'd said. Then they'd meet in the cafeteria and discuss things rationally, objectively. Hearts and emotions uninvolved.

CHAPTER ELEVEN

By THE TIME Molly reached the hospital the churning unease in her gut was threatening to boil over. The fact that there were multiple emergency vehicles blocking the front entrance didn't help either.

She pulled over to the curb and got the attention of one of the police officers to let her through. "What's going on?"

"Grizzly cub slipped through the automatic doors. Momma followed her baby inside, causing a ruckus," the officer said, tipping his hat when she flashed her physician's badge. "No worries, Doc. No one was hurt, and the conservation officers have the bears tranquilized and caged. We'll be airlifting them to a safer location away from the city soon."

Molly shook her head. "Never had that happen back in Chicago."

"I should hope not." The cop grinned and waved her through toward the physicians' parking area. "Have a good day, Doc."

"Thanks."

Molly pulled around the building and into a spot, then hurried to the fourth floor. The elevator doors opened to reveal Neal and Rob, looking nervous.

"All right—what's going on?" she asked as they all

headed for her office. "If the network's canceling my show, please tell me. I can handle it. This was the last episode on my current contract anyway."

"No, Mol." Neal closed the door behind them. "They're not cancelling your show. You want the bad news or the worse news first?"

"Bad."

"Okay. They're giving your father a show of his own."

"What?" The world seemed to tilt on its axis and Molly slumped into her chair, coat half-off. All those years of work to escape him, and now he was taking over her territory. "His own show? On my network?"

"Yep." Rob looked pained. "And there's more."

"More?" Shock had made Molly into a parrot.

"They're giving him the prime spot right after Diagnosis Critical."

"I'll be my father's lead-in?"

"Don't think of it like that, Mol." Neal winced. "You're already established and you have a loyal, if small, audience base. Nothing's going to change."

Nothing would change?

Everything would change if Roger Flynn joined the MedStar Network.

Molly swallowed against the rising bile in her throat. Losing her show because it had failed on its own merits was one thing. Having it forced into cancellation by her own father would be beyond awful. Forget fumbling and flailing in front of his small group of assembled guests at their house when she'd been a kid. This time her epic fail would happen on a global scale.

Molly hung up her coat, then took her seat again, the news still refusing to sink in. Gone. The sweet refuge of her show, the years she'd spent building it, growing it, sacrificing her time and effort and any semblance of a normal life. All gone.

"Trust me, Mol. This isn't the end of the world." Neal placed a hand on her shoulder. "I bet this hoopla will blow over and things will get back to normal soon."

"This is not going to blow over."

Molly knew her father. For him, things were all or nothing. Roger Flynn wouldn't be satisfied until he was number one on the network, no matter who he had to crush along the way—including his own daughter.

"I need to think about things for a moment. Alone."

The two men exchanged a look and her heart sank even further.

Eyes closed, Molly braced herself. "Fine. Tell me the rest of it."

Rob cringed. "Well…about that footage."

"What footage?"

"The footage of Dr. Ryder we've shot over the weeks—the stuff the network was supposed to edit out. It got leaked."

"Leaked?" Molly frowned. "To who?"

"The world." Rob glanced over at Neal. "Snippets turned up on the Internet."

The enormity of the situation engulfed her, seizing the air in Molly's lungs. "Jake could sue us. He never signed the releases."

He trusted me.

Molly clutched the edge of her desk to keep herself from crumpling. "Who leaked it?"

"The network blames one of the interns," Neal said. "And their attorneys are going to use implied consent as their defense, since Dr. Ryder knew we were filming and stayed anyway."

"That's flimsy, at best," Molly said, her voice quiet.

Jake had trusted her. That was huge, after everything that had happened with his commendation and with Kellie. Sorrow squeezed her chest tight. The future of their relationship was now solidified. Once he discovered the truth he'd never want to see her again. And rightfully so.

But she wasn't ready to let him go yet, not when she'd just found him.

Neal pulled off his baseball hat and scrubbed a hand through his graying hair. "If it's any consolation, the clips are popular. Hit the number one search spots on the big search engines and social media sites."

"No." Molly covered her face with her hands. "It's really not."

"We're sorry, Mol," Rob said, head lowered. "If there's anything we can do…"

"I know," she mumbled, and her crew left the office at last.

This was going to require some major damage control and Molly honestly had no idea where to start.

She needed to pull her contract with the network and make serious decisions about her show. She needed to check in on Bobby and make sure he was doing all right this morning. She needed to talk to Jake and beg his forgiveness, even though none of this was really her fault. But she was sure Jake wouldn't see it that way. It was her name, her face on the show. It had been her in his bed—her he'd trusted. Therefore, this debacle was her responsibility.

In the end, overwhelmed and frozen with fear, Molly sat and stared at the blank wall, wondering how a day that had started off so beautifully could crash and burn so fast.

After eating a quick breakfast and checking his emails, Jake headed to Anchorage Mercy. The traffic light turned green and he made a right toward the hospital—then halted as a line of departing squad cars blocked the main entrance.

A conservation truck pulled up next to him and the driver waved. "Had some bears in the lobby again, Doc. Got 'em out, though, no problem."

Jake nodded, appreciating the update, and waited until the rest of the traffic had cleared. At last he looped around to the back of the hospital and pulled into the spot beside Molly's Range Rover. He felt a sudden, yearning ache around his heart and…damn. Maybe sleeping with her hadn't been such a brilliant idea after all—not if he felt this attached to her, this fast.

After cutting the engine, Jake climbed from his truck and braced himself against the brisk wind. Their torrid night had stirred up all kinds of emotions—happiness, confusion, joy, fear. All those feelings had mixed together now, into a scary sludge inside him that made him wary as hell. He kept reminding himself that this wasn't the past and Molly wasn't Kellie. This was a new situation, with new rules, a new outcome.

The tension inside him didn't abate.

Maybe it was this whole thing with Bobby. He just wanted his best bud healthy again.

Jake swiped his physician's badge at the door, then headed inside. Technically, his shift wasn't scheduled to start for another hour, but he was sure another stack of paperwork awaited. Besides, he figured being at work would keep him from dwelling on what had happened with Molly last night—how she'd felt wrapped tight in his arms, how she'd made those delicious tiny gasps as he'd licked and kissed every single inch of her…

Wendy ran toward him down the hall. "Dr. Flynn's

been trying to contact you. Bobby's heart-rate is irregular again."

Frowning, Jake pulled out his cell phone. The battery was dead. Normally he plugged it in each night like clockwork, but he hadn't followed his normal routine the previous evening.

Damn.

Jake sprinted upstairs and rushed into Bobby's room. Molly was checking his vitals while her crew filmed from the corner. Neither Neal nor Rob would meet his gaze. Jake thought that was weird, since he'd thought they'd become friendlier over the past few weeks, but he couldn't worry about them now. Not when Bobby's life was at stake.

"What's happening?"

"No idea. The tachycardia came up without warning," Molly said. The heart monitor beeped loud then went flat. She checked Bobby's pupils. "Start CPR and get a defibrillator stat!"

While Molly pumped air into Bobby's lungs, using an oxygen mask and bag, Jake started chest compressions. His best friend couldn't die. Not here. Not now. Not like this. Not after what they'd survived together back in the desert.

"Hang in there, buddy. Stay with me."

"Cart's here," Gladys said, shoving the machine up to the bedside.

"Get ready to shock him," Molly said. A sharp whine sounded as the paddles charged. "Stand back."

She jolted Bobby's heart with the electric current and his large body jerked. The monitor blipped. Stopped. Blip-blipped again. Grew stronger and more regular. Jake exhaled loudly as Molly set the paddles aside.

"Okay. We have a pulse. Gladys, start him on oxygen and watch him closely."

Jake took a deep breath to calm his own racing pulse, then followed Molly out into the hall. "I don't understand. Bobby was fine earlier."

"Could be residual effects from the yohimbe." Molly washed her hands in a nearby sink, not meeting his gaze. "But I won't know until his latest bloodwork comes back."

His earlier surge of adrenaline evaporated, leaving a trail of confusion and restlessness in its wake. Jake wanted to decompress, deconstruct, dissect all that had happened with Molly, but she was acting distant and distracted. Yep. Something was definitely up.

His wariness grew. And as her crew trundled out of Bobby's room, Jake pulled her aside. "Listen, Molly. I—"

"I'm sorry, but I—I can't do this right now."

Her voice had turned brittle, broken. Because of him? Because of what they'd shared last night?

The ache of tension inside Jake intensified, his doubts deepening. Maybe this whole thing about penguins and monogamy and a possible future with her was just a pipe dream. Maybe he'd been wrong too trust her so quickly.

That's your past talking.

"I'll keep you posted on the patient's condition." Molly headed for the elevators and gestured toward her crew to follow. "C'mon, guys."

Jake headed back to his ER alone, feeling decidedly unsettled. After what had happened with Bobby, and with Molly pulling away the same way Kellie had just before the end, he was left feeling even more on edge.

CHAPTER TWELVE

THE NEXT DAY one thing was abundantly clear.

Molly couldn't tell Jake about the leaked footage—
at least not as she'd originally planned. Never mind that
the network's attorneys had expressly forbidden her to
say anything. Truth was, she didn't know how to explain
what had happened—didn't have the first clue how to
apologize for a betrayal that would most likely destroy
any bond they might have formed that night in his bed.

Not to mention that since making love with Jake Molly
had discovered all sorts of uncomfortable, unruly, un-
explored emotions jostling and poking inside her like
sharp needles. Part of her couldn't suppress the flush of
happiness each time she remembered their incredible
lovemaking. But another part felt a deep twinge of guilt
over the same.

Perhaps if Molly had stayed here at the hospital—
not gone on the whale-watching cruise, not spent the
night with Jake, Bobby wouldn't have taken a turn for
the worse.

Until recently work had always come first. Now,
though, for at least that one day and night, she'd decided
to put her own wants and needs first and perhaps that
hadn't been wise. Her father's censorious voice kept ringing through Molly's head, deriding her for allowing her

emotions to gain the upper hand, ridiculing her because she'd failed to remain cool, aloof, unfeeling.

But those few hours in Jake's arms were the first time Molly had felt truly alive in...forever.

And once she told him about the leaked footage it would all be over.

Molly wasn't sure she could survive squeezing herself back into the tiny box her family had put her in for her whole life—not when she'd finally experienced such blissful freedom with Jake.

My Jake.

Her heart ached and her head hurt and the whole mess left her sad and off-balance.

She finished going over Bobby's chart notes and lab results again while Gladys checked the patient's IV. Rob and Neal stood in the corner, catching all the details for digital posterity. At least Bobby had bounced back again, now awake and alert despite the previous night's episode.

"Man." Bobby scooted up in his bed amidst a sea of tubes and monitor wires. "Can't believe that tea caused all my problems. I thought it was just some health supplement."

"Supplements are chemicals too, Mr. Templeton." Molly jotted down a few reminders for the staff, then closed his file. "And the tea didn't cause all your problems. It only added an additional symptom that masked the underlying disease process."

"Come again? I thought you said the heart thing was unrelated?"

"It is."

"I'm confused."

Rob moved closer to get a dramatic close-up of Bobby and Molly.

"The cardiac arrest you experienced the first time

in the ER and again last evening was directly related to the yohimbe in the tea. Now that we've taken it out of the equation, and the chemical is leaving your body, we can concentrate on the real cause of your problems. Allergies."

"Allergies?" Bobby wrinkled his nose. "You mean like hay fever?"

"There are many types of allergies, Mr. Templeton. It will take time to narrow down the specific irritant responsible for yours. But because this allergy has gone untreated for so long, it's likely moved beyond simple watery eyes to a full-blown systemic issue. Your body's natural defenses have been compromised, diminishing your ability to heal. Those same defenses may have also caused damage to your organs."

"But I was tested for allergies a long time ago, Doc." Bobby gripped the sheets tighter. "Nothing came back positive. I don't want to be a human pin cushion. Needles aren't my favorite."

Molly raised a brow. For a man who regularly participated in mayhem on the ice, it seemed silly for him to fear a few epidermal scratches. Then again, most phobias weren't logical.

Take her fear of her father. In her mind, Molly knew she shouldn't let the man bully her anymore. She was a grown adult, more than capable of defending herself. But deep in her heart Molly still felt like that same scared little girl who had longed for her father's approval and love. Which was a wasted effort because he'd proved time and again that the only thing Roger Flynn loved was himself. His takeover of her network was only the latest in a long line of selfish acts.

"The good news is you'll have a few days to decide, Mr. Templeton." Molly scowled down at the orders clipped to the front of Bobby's chart, shoving all disturbing thoughts about her father aside. "It's too soon to test you at this point. The results would show false positives due to your high reactivity."

"I'm radioactive?" Bobby looked stunned.

"Not radioactive. Reactive. It means the antigen levels in your blood are too high to give us accurate results at this point. So we'll stabilize you, isolate you from all possible allergens, and give your body time to recuperate before proceeding."

"Uh…okay. How will that work?"

"We'll put you in a clean room," Molly said, glancing up at him.

Bobby surveyed the space. "This one looks pretty spotless to me."

"No. A clean room is sterile. Even the air is filtered to prevent any outside contamination. It's the only way for us to find out what's really causing your illness." She smiled and laid a hand on his arm to reassure him. "Visitation will be limited to a glassed-in area, where people can talk with you through special vents, unless they're wearing full protective gear."

"It'll be like a prison, then?"

"Think of it more as a spa. With lots of time to reflect. Maybe catch up on your sleep."

Bobby exhaled loudly. "All right—if it's the only way I can get better. The new season starts in a few weeks and I need to get in fighting shape by then or we've got no chance at the championship."

"Oh." She looked over to see her crew shaking their heads in despair. "Right…"

"Dr. Flynn?" Gladys peeked her head around the door. "Dr. Ryder's here to see you."

Her heart did a little somersault. "Thank you. I'll be

right out. Do you have any other questions for me, Mr. Templeton?"

"No. Thanks."

"And, cut!" Neal said.

Rob lowered his camera and the two men followed her out of the room. Molly veered toward the nurses' station, then stopped abruptly at the sight of Jake bent over the counter. Heat unfurled within her again before she tamped it down.

Molly took a deep breath and handed the file to the nurse. "The orders for Mr. Templeton are inside."

Jake peered back at her over his shoulder. "Hey."

"Hey." She resisted the urge to fidget under his stare. "What are you doing?"

"I'm on a break and decided to check on Bobby."

He looked far more tempting than a man should be allowed to in faded green cotton as he read the file over Gladys's shoulder.

"A clean room?"

"It's the only way to confirm what's causing Bobby's allergic reactions."

"Agreed."

"Wonders never cease." Molly headed for her office.

"I know, right?" Jake chuckled, walking beside her. "Tell me when they're ready to move Bobby and I'll help get him situated."

"Are you expecting problems?"

"No. But he'll put up a fight when you try to take away his essentials."

"Essentials?"

"TV. Sports Illustrated."

"Hmm…" Molly stopped at her office door, facing him. "I never really considered it before, but it will be hard, being so isolated and alone."

"Uh-oh." Jake narrowed his gaze.

"What?"

"Be careful, Bolt. I think your empathy's showing."

"I have empathy. A great deal, in fact."

His words hurt more than she cared to admit. She'd been working on improving her bedside manner and had thought she was getting better. Jake could've helped her with that. He was so good with his patients, so caring and concerned.

Too bad he'd hate her once he found out about those leaked clips.

Shoulders slumped, Molly tucked her hair behind her ear. "I've already explained to the patient that it's only for a short while."

"Is everything okay?" Jake asked, his expression concerned. "Not just with Bobby."

"Of course." She forced a smile, swallowing the words that needed to be said. "Why?"

"You seem troubled." Jake took her hand, his thumb stroking her knuckles and driving her to distraction. "We never really discussed what happened between us the other night. Want to have dinner with me later and we can talk?"

Her heart pinched at his earnest tone. She wanted to... oh, did she want to. But she'd already agreed to another conference call with the network attorneys, and if she had dinner with Jake she'd be tempted to tell him about the network's mistake, and then all this would be over and she'd be banished back to her cold, emotionless box.

Jake must have mistaken her silence for refusal, because he let her go, his smile fading and a glint of hurt flashing in his eyes. "If you don't want to go, just say so, Bolt. No big deal."

"No, no. It's not that." Her nervous babbling started.

"I just need to see how things go today with my meetings, and I'm sure your schedule is nuts too, and I don't want Bobby to be alone because this could be a very scary time for him, and—"

The sudden heat returning to Jake's eyes took Molly's breath away. He leaned closer, as if he was going to kiss her. "Aw…there it is again."

"What?" Her voice emerged as a soft sigh of need, her lips tingling, waiting.

"Empathy. Compassion."

"I'm trying." Molly blinked, wishing she could just burrow into his arms until all this blew over and it was just the two of them, together.

"I know." Jake brushed the backs of his fingers over her cheek, his expression wistful. "Wonders never cease."

"What do they mean, I can't watch ESPN?" Bobby said, his voice horrified.

"No contamination. That means no TV, no books, no magazines, no nothing." Jake leaned back in the plastic chair beside his friend's bed and scrubbed a hand over his face.

"How about my phone?" Bobby's tone grew desperate. "The screen's kind of tiny, but I could still watch the recaps."

"Which part of 'no contamination' didn't you understand? Sorry, man."

"What am I supposed to do in there while I'm being clean?" Given the slight edge that had crept into Bobby's question, his normally affable friend had clearly taken a turn for the cranky. "She mentioned reflecting, or something, but that's not really my thing."

"How about resting? Enjoying the peace and quiet?"

"That's all I've been doing. Doesn't seem to be working out too good so far."

"Molly will find your diagnosis, bud. I'm sure of it. She's pretty brilliant."

"Molly, huh?" His best friend gave him some serious side-eye. "Since when are you and my new doctor on a first-name basis?"

Jake glanced out the open door and into the hallway beyond. He hadn't meant to let that informality slip, but it was too late to take it back. "We've developed a professional relationship, that's all."

"Professional?" Bobby snorted. "From the sappy look on your face, I'd say it's way more than that. Good for you. About time you got back in there after Kellie."

Jake bristled slightly at the mention of his ex. "Look, I'm just doing my job, and getting along with Dr. Flynn is part of it."

The response was lame, but he wasn't ready to share the things he felt for Molly. They were still too new, too fragile, too tender.

"You should thank me."

"Yeah, right. Thanks for getting me locked in my own private version of hell."

"It won't be any worse than the day we spent in the major general's office after we pranked the sergeant. Remember?"

Bobby's scowl was slowly transformed into a grin. "Yeah... Still don't regret turning that guy into a Smurf. He was a real piece of work."

"Agreed." Jake pushed to his feet and headed for the door. His break time was almost over and he needed to get back to the ER. "I'll check on you later—once they get you moved."

"Okay." Bobby waited until Jake was almost out the door before calling. "Hey?"

"Yeah?"

"Thanks. For everything."

Jake's throat tightened. He owed Bobby more than he could ever repay. "I'm the one who should be thanking you, bud. You know that. Try and relax. This will all be over soon, I promise." Jake pointed to the TV against the wall. "And take advantage of the sports channels while you can."

A busy afternoon loomed ahead, with miles of paperwork to go before he was done. As Jake headed downstairs he still hoped Molly would take him up on his offer of dinner. Her earlier aloofness bothered him, and he missed her more than he cared to admit.

The emotional connection they'd shared since their night together had been stronger than anything he'd ever experienced with anyone—honestly. And, yes, distancing themselves might be the wise move, but, dammit, he wanted to talk to Molly, see her again, spend time with her even if it was only temporary.

Frustrated, Jake pulled out his phone in the elevator and sent her a text.

Dinner tonight? Eight p.m.

Surprisingly, Molly responded before he'd reached his office.

Okay.

Not sure what had changed her mind, but feeling extremely grateful something had, he messaged back, unable to keep the smile off his face.

Pick you up at your hotel.

Grinning wide, Jake shoved his phone into the pocket of his scrub shirt. He knew he was acting like a randy teenager, but it had been so long since he'd let someone close, as he had Molly, and it felt good. It seemed Wendy had been right. Putting himself out there again had given him a new lease on life.

Speaking of his favorite nurse—she stopped him as he passed her desk.

"There's someone waiting in your office." Instead of her usual sunny smile Wendy's expression held hints of anger and apology.

"Who?" he asked. "From your scowl, I'm guessing the answer's not good."

"Hello, Jake," said a female voice—one he'd never expected to hear again.

Stomach nosediving, he found Kellie standing in his office doorway. The woman who'd trampled his heart and his trust—who'd left him behind so fast he still had the tire marks down his back.

"What are you doing here?"

"Work." Kellie's smile was bland. "Can we talk? In private."

Wendy gave Jake a warning look, but he nodded, still in shock. "Uh...sure."

They walked into his office and he closed the door. Kellie settled into one of the chairs in front of his desk, her deep fuchsia power suit neon-bright under the fluorescent lights, her unreadable face made up to perfection.

Jake took his own seat, feeling like quarry avoiding a hunter's crosshairs. "Big news story here in Anchorage, Alaska?"

"Up in Fairbanks, actually. I'm covering the transplant surgery being done at one of the hospitals there by Dr. Roger Flynn."

His phone buzzed and Jake pulled it out to see another text from Molly.

We need to talk.

The tension in his gut knotted tighter. Talking didn't have to mean anything bad. Just because those were the same words the woman across the desk from him had used the day she'd changed the trajectory of Jake's life forever, it didn't mean dinner with Molly would be more of the same.

He set his phone aside. Kellie was his past. Molly, hopefully, might be his future. And, yes, they had issues to work out—like how to deal with the whole long-distance thing—but they'd figure it out together. Life was all about communication.

He coughed to clear his throat. "I don't see what your story has to do with me."

Kellie's smile widened into an insincere affair that only made him yearn for Molly even more. "You're working a case with his daughter currently, aren't you? After seeing the footage of the two of you all over the Internet, I thought perhaps you could provide—"

"I'm sorry." Jake scowled, time seeming to warp around him. "What are you talking about? What footage?"

Surely those old stories about his commendation hadn't resurfaced. They had to be old news by now. And he'd not been anywhere near a TV camera in a year and a half except for...

"Aw... You didn't know."

Kellie's concern only put him more on guard, raising

the hairs on the back of his neck with a sense of foreboding—the same prickling precognition he'd used to get out of the battlefield before a sniper attack.

"I thought it was strange, given your aversion to the press when we were together, but I figured you'd gotten over it since you appeared to be working so closely with Dr. Flynn in the clips." Kellie pulled out her phone, tapped on the screen a few times, then handed the device to Jake. "Take a look for yourself."

The footage showed him and Molly after Dr. Dave's party, both of them grinning as she asked him to go on a whale-watching cruise. His universe imploded as her words from that night echoed through his head.

"I'll make sure they edit you out…"

"Are you two involved?" Kellie asked. "I promise not to mention it in my story."

Wendy knocked before sticking her head inside the office, giving Kellie a disparaging glance before focusing on Jake. "Sorry, Doc, but the patient load is backing up out here. Any chance you can give us a hand?"

Oddly numb now, Jake pushed to his feet and walked to the door, his movements robotic and his smile stiff, all his systems working on autopilot as he struggled to process what he'd just learned.

That footage had been leaked and Molly had never said a word. She'd known about his past, known about what he'd dealt with at his commendation and with Kellie, and she'd still allowed those clips to be released without a word to him. She'd promised to have his shots edited out. He'd trusted her, opened up to her, let himself be vulnerable—and look where it had gotten him.

His chest caved, a black hole forming where his heart had been.

Molly had betrayed his trust—just like Kellie had years before.

We need to talk.

Damn right they did.

Jake walked away without another word to his ex and grabbed a chart from the nearest holder. Tonight he'd meet with Molly and demand to know why she'd lied.

Then he'd close his heart to her and what they'd shared. Once and for all.

CHAPTER THIRTEEN

MOLLY MET JAKE in the lobby of her hotel at eight o'clock
sharp.

After much soul-searching, and anguished hours of
wavering, she'd concluded that telling him about the
leaked footage was only fair, given how close they'd
become. It was in direct violation of what her network
wanted, but she'd deal with that fallout when the time
came. What she felt with Jake was much more important.

As he helped Molly into the passenger side of his
truck the memories flooded back—his taste, his scent,
his touch. His fingers brushed lightly against her skin
and she couldn't suppress an answering shiver. They both
wore the same outfits they'd worn at Dr. Dave's party,
she noticed.

"Where are we going?" Molly asked, nervous energy
suffusing her system as Jake climbed into the driver's
seat, started the engine, and headed toward downtown
Anchorage. She glanced at his strong, tapered fingers on
the steering wheel, remembering the feel of those fingers on her body.

"Ursa," he said, not looking at her, his tone terse.

"As in bear?"

"The food's excellent. Modern American cuisine.
Three-star Michelin rating."

His voice held a chilled edge, but she brushed it off. He was probably tired. They'd both had long days.

"Bobby seems to be doing okay in his clean room," she said, to fill the silence.

"Hopefully you'll find out what's wrong soon and he won't be there long."

He stared straight ahead, no expression, tension evident around his mouth and eyes. Brian had worn that same flat look toward the end. The thought did little to quiet her unease.

"Then you can get back to your life in Chicago and I can get back to giving the ER my full attention again."

And there it was. The inevitable end.

Molly's self-doubts resurfaced, intensified, stung like hell—even though he was right. She'd gone into this affair with her eyes open. There couldn't really be anything permanent between them because of the distance factor, no matter how she might wish things were different.

He wouldn't want to offer her forever, knowing she'd be gone soon, and she couldn't offer him more than she already had either. Not with her show's crazy schedule and chaos at the network. Then again, after she told him about the leaked footage he probably wouldn't want to be with her anymore anyway.

Her chest squeezed and she offered him an easy escape route. "We don't have to go out if it's a problem."

"No, no. We definitely need to talk. About a lot of things."

His definitive statement made the knots in her stomach tighten all the more. Gone was the easy banter they'd shared during the whale-watching cruise and later that evening at the pub, gone the connection and closeness that had grown between them after their torrid night in each other's arms. It seemed they were back to chilly courtesy and wary politeness again.

They pulled up to the curb in front of the restaurant a few minutes later. Red-hued neon highlighted the beige stone exterior and surrounded a huge portrait of a snarling bear. Jake handed his keys to the valet, then helped Molly from the truck, though he let her go almost immediately. She missed the guiding comfort of his hand on her lower back.

Inside, the maître d' showed them to a cozy corner table near a crackling fireplace and took their coats. The interior's wood tones were complemented by plush oriental rugs and cool river rock stone walls. Modern paintings from local artists and sparkling crystal chandeliers completed the eclectic chic ambiance.

A waiter appeared with menus and poured them each a goblet of water. "Would you care for something from the bar this evening or an appetizer?"

"Two glasses of Chardonnay. Thanks." Jake sat back and toyed with his silverware, his expression dour. "What did you want to talk to me about?"

Molly took a sip of her water, still unsure how to breach the topic of the leaked footage and doing her best not to revert to the old patterns of withdrawal and defensiveness that she'd learned over years of dealing with her father.

"There've been some changes at the network."

Jake gave a curt nod but remained silent. He waited until the sommelier had finished pouring their wine before continuing, still not meeting her gaze.

"Such as?"

"They're giving my father his own show."

Jake drank his wine, watching her closely over the rim

of his glass. "Surprised he's got time, what with running the world and all."

Tell him, Molly chided herself, hating the fact that she wasn't braver.

This was her life, her choice, her mess to clean up. She just wished she could've had one more night in Jake's arms before it was all over.

Grief and loss pinched her heart and she squeezed her eyes closed against the pain. Just do it.

After a deep breath for courage, she sat forward. "There's something I need to tell you. About those times when my crew was filming and you happened to be there."

Jake finally met her eyes, thunderclouds gathering in his gaze. "Yes?"

"Well…" Molly swallowed hard against the lump of dread in her throat and forced the words out in a tumble of regret. "Somehow the footage you were in ended up all over the Internet before the network edited you out of it. MedStar's attorneys have forbidden me from saying anything, but I wanted to tell you after what happened between us and—"

"Isn't it convenient how that worked?"

That tiny muscle ticked near Jake's clenched jaw again, the same as she remembered from the night of Dr. Dave's party, when he'd been confronting her father. Not a good sign. Not at all.

"How long have you known?"

Molly winced, not even trying to play dumb. What was the point?

Her heart tumbled to somewhere near her toes and any bit of appetite she'd had was gone, replaced now with the bitter taste of remorse. "Two days."

"Two days." Jake leaned back and crossed his arms,

his expression hard and hurt. "Two days you've known about this and you didn't tell me."

"I wanted to, but then this whole thing with my father getting his own show blew up, and Bobby took a turn for the worse, and the attorneys didn't want me to say anything, and—"

"I trusted you, Molly."

"I know. And I'm so, so sorry. Please believe me. I wanted to tell you, but I wasn't sure how to say it and I didn't want to lose—"

"Jake!"

A brunette rushed up to their table—the same one Molly remembered from the photo in Jake's house. The beginning of a headache throbbed behind Molly's temples, but it was no match for the pain of betrayal clawing through her heart. Had sleeping with her all been part of Jake getting back with his ex? Was that why Kellie was back in town? Had he been seeing Kellie too, the whole time he'd been wooing Molly?

You have no claim on him, remember? her not-so-helpful rational brain stated. That fact did nothing to relieve the ache of loss in Molly's bones.

"Fancy seeing you again so soon, Jake," Kellie said, her gaze locked on Molly. "Aren't you going to introduce me?"

"Molly, this is Kellie Hughes, my ex-fiancée." Jake stared at the tabletop, his expression hard as granite. "Kellie, this is Dr. Flynn."

Anguish swelled inside her. It seemed Jake had reverted to using her professional title.

Molly knew she had no right to feel upset. She'd broken her promises, betrayed Jake's trust, betrayed the fragile bond that had formed between them. Gone. It was all gone now, and she had no one to blame but herself.

Perhaps Brian was right—her father too. Maybe she was just better off alone. Alone and completely driven by her work. Alone and lonely and safe.

Except safe didn't hold the same appeal it once had.

Torn and twisted inside, Molly extended a shaky hand to Kellie. "Nice to meet you."

"You're Roger Flynn's daughter, aren't you?" Kellie's cat-that-ate-the-canary grin widened. "Jake mentioned it earlier today, when we met in his office. I'm here to interview your father. I'll be traveling up to Fairbanks General tomorrow, actually. But since I'm in Anchorage tonight, I thought perhaps you might have a chance to talk with me too, maybe between breaks in filming your show? News just broke about his new slot in Med-Star's fall schedule, right after Diagnosis Critical. Early buzz says it's going to be a big hit. You must be thrilled."

"Thrilled" wasn't the first word Molly would choose. Alarmed, appalled, heartsick—any of those seemed way more apropos. But at the moment she felt as if she was drowning in a big cesspool of recrimination.

Jake stared at her from across the table, his lips tight and his gaze unyielding, most likely detesting her over the leaked footage. Beside him Kellie watched her as if she was some kind of circus oddity—the same look her father's friends had used to give young Molly during her performances at home. As if they could see all her faults, all her foibles, all her flaws. As if they were just waiting for Molly to screw up.

"About the interview," Kellie persisted. "I promise not to take up too much of your time."

"No interview." Molly forced the words past her tight vocal cords. "I'm sorry."

"Too bad." Kellie didn't sound disappointed. "But your

father told me to expect as much. He said you were…different. Now, it's obvious what he meant."

Obvious that you're weird. Obvious that you're awkward. Obvious that you're unlovable.

Why had she ever thought this would work with Jake? Seeing him sitting there with his ex, both so beautiful and poised and perfect, she wondered why he would ever choose someone like her for more than just a casual fling.

He wouldn't.

Molly blinked at Jake as Kellie abruptly walked away, eyes stinging at the realization. She wouldn't cry. She wouldn't. But the harder she tried to stop the tears, the more they struggled to escape. It seemed she'd kept her emotions under wraps too long. Now that the floodgates were open there was no closing them.

"Are you crying?" Jake asked, incredulous. "Dammit, Molly—"

She tuned him out. She'd heard all those taunts from her father too many times to count.

"Stop crying. Tears are for weaklings. Your emotions are your enemy."

Molly knew all that—knew her feelings would only cause her trouble—and still she'd taken the gamble, gone with her gut, chosen a glorious night in Jake's arms over a million days of nothingness in her father's harsh, cold world.

Sniffling, Molly searched her handbag for a tissue and found her phone buzzing with a text from Gladys.

Bobby in RD.

"I need to go." Molly stood and tossed her napkin on the table.

"So that's it, then?" Jake rose as well, scowling, his

eyes glittering with anger. "You're done? We're not even discussing this? You're just going to walk out and to hell with us?"

"There is no 'us,' Jake. There never was. You know that as well as I do."

Molly rushed to the lobby to get her coat while swiping the back of her hand across her wet cheeks, Jake hot on her heels. If this was what it was like to live with your heart on your sleeve, where it could get broken and trampled, then it was awful.

Molly dialed the hospital, waiting anxiously for Gladys to pick up. At Jake's pointed stare, she said, "Bobby's in respiratory distress."

The words emerged more impassioned than she'd intended, but her heart felt ripped out and stomped on. She'd trusted Jake too. Trusted him enough to let him see the real her, opened her heart and soul to him—which had been a mistake. She'd known better than to let him in, let him see her flaws. Honestly, she should be thankful. Thankful that he'd reminded her of why it was better, safer, to keep to herself.

"But he's in a clean room," Jake said softly, his tanned face growing pale.

"I know that." Molly tugged on her coat before pushing outside to hail a taxi, her irritation at herself for being such a trusting idiot bubbling over into her snarky response. "I'm the one who put him there, remember?"

"How could Bobby go into respiratory distress in a sterile environment?"

"Your guess is as good as mine right now."

A cab swerved up to the curb and Molly opened the door. Her cheeks were burning and her eyes felt puffy, but she had to pull herself together so she could save Bobby.

She climbed into the back seat, saying to the driver,

"I need to get to Anchorage Mercy as soon as possible, please."

"Molly, wait!" Jake called from the curb.

"I can't wait, Jake. I'm sorry. Goodbye."

As the car pulled away more tears welled. For the remainder of her time here Molly would have to see Jake as just a work associate—nothing more.

Goodbye fun...goodbye affection. Goodbye love.

Jake stared after the cab, focusing on the red glow of the receding taillights, wondering how in the world this whole thing had ended so horribly. And, yeah, he was fed up. Rightfully so. He was the wronged party. So why did he now feel like as much of a bully as Molly's ass of a father?

Dammit.

He scrubbed a hand over his face and leaned against the side of the cold brick building. Molly had needed him tonight—needed his support tonight against Kellie—but he'd been so wrapped up in his past hurts and bruised ego he'd left her flailing.

Yes, he was upset about the footage. Yes, she should've told him. Yes, he felt betrayed. But as his righteous fury burned away he was left feeling raw and exposed.

Part of him wanted to run after that taxi and make it stop. His past, though, kept him rooted to the spot. After all, he'd allowed himself to trust a woman completely before and look where that had gotten him. Kellie had had excuses, reasons, lies aplenty for why she'd done what she'd done—why she'd left him and run off alone to New York, why she'd never looked back.

Stupid. You're so damned stupid, his brain said. You're an ER doc. Why would a brilliant, successful woman choose you over the bright lights and big city?

It was embarrassing. Shameful. If he had any brains at all, he'd have learned from his mistakes and moved on from Kellie to make wiser choices in his future relationships. Stay away from women who'd only leave him behind in the dust when something bigger or better came along, when the next huge case beckoned.

Why not you? his heart asked. Molly's not Kellie.

And she wasn't. He knew that. They were as different as night and day. Kellie only cared about herself. Molly was selfless and kind and giving. They were different.

Are they? Brain again. Always the cynic.

His mixed reactions made his gut twist.

Still torn, he lingered outside, battling the urge to call Molly and tell her that he loved her, that he would do anything to erase his knee-jerk reaction to the news about the leaked footage and the unexpected and unwelcome arrival of Kellie at their table and beg her forgiveness, but he couldn't.

He couldn't change what he'd done because he didn't want to hurt her. Couldn't promise her something he couldn't deliver. Truth was, once Bobby's case was over she'd be gone and he'd be left to deal with the aftermath alone, as always.

No. They'd both gone into this knowing it was temporary, fleeting.

Still, that was no reason to hurt her the way he had in the restaurant. No reason to lash out and strike all those vulnerable areas of hers just because he knew which buttons to push, same as she did with him.

God, what a mess.

Too late, Jake realized the anger and betrayal he'd felt inside the restaurant had been directed more at past wrongs with Kellie than it had been toward the woman who'd just left for the hospital.

Each time he closed his eyes all Jake could see was Molly's tearstained face, the way she'd shrunk in on herself as Kellie had repeated her father's insults.

Different. Like that was a bad thing. To Jake, "different" sounded pretty damned wonderful.

You're such a jerk.

At least on that point his heart and his brain were united in their sentiment.

Distracted, Jake stalked back into the restaurant and hailed their waiter. Bobby was in trouble and Molly needed him and that was all that mattered.

Ignoring the curious stares of the other patrons, he tossed a fifty-dollar bill on the table to cover their drinks and uneaten appetizer.

"Wait, sweetie." Kellie laid a hand on his forearm as he tried to leave. "I was hoping to talk more—especially since your friend is gone."

"Molly is not my friend." Jake pulled free, then rushed back toward the exit. "She's the most brilliant and exasperating woman I've ever known. And I am not your sweetie. Not anymore."

Kellie kept pace beside him, her gaze narrowed. "You love her, don't you?"

"What? No." Yes. He moved outside and handed his ticket to the valet. "I need to get to the hospital. Go back to Roger Flynn, Kellie. We have nothing left to talk about."

"But—" Kellie said as his truck swerved up to the curb.

"No. Don't." Jake tipped the valet, then started around the front of his vehicle. "I'm over it. Over what happened. Move on, Kellie. Good luck with your career in New York."

"If you think that woman will give up her life and

her show for you, you're wrong," Kellie said, lifting her chin. "She's more like her father than you think. He told me so."

"Molly is nothing like her father. And you of all people shouldn't believe everything you hear." Jake yanked open the driver's side door. "Now, if you'll excuse me, I've got my best friend's life to save. Safe travels."

CHAPTER FOURTEEN

HOURS LATER, MOLLY sat in the small office-slash-observation area attached to Bobby's clean room, going over her patient's chart for what seemed like the billionth time and trying not to think about what had happened with Jake.

Bobby's condition had deteriorated rapidly—so much so that they'd put him on a ventilator and into a medically induced coma to give his poor lungs a chance to recuperate.

The staff had finished re-sterilizing the entire clean room again, screening for all outside contaminates—including testing the rubber gloves and the latex tubing of his IVs. He had no piercings, no implants, no metal pins in his body of any kind. Even the sterile solution flowing into his veins to keep him hydrated had been analyzed for allergens. Nothing had been found.

It didn't make sense.

Molly took a deep breath and stared at the documentation. The only other possible source of the inflammation was an autoimmune disorder, but they'd already screened for those too—multiple times—and the tests had all been negative, as had his bloodwork.

Meaning they were right back where they'd started.

Speaking of right back where you started…

Ugh. Molly's mind filled with images of Jake's angry expression, his ice-cold stare, the way he'd sat there while his ex-fiancée had spewed her father's hurtful words and done nothing.

Logic said being this upset about Jake not caring for her was silly. One whale-watching cruise followed by a night of mind-blowing passion did not a true relationship make. No matter how badly she might have wished it were otherwise.

But her beloved facts and analysis were of little comfort tonight.

Groaning, Molly put her head down on her arms atop the small desk. More tears stung her eyes, though she refused to let them fall. She'd gone from one extreme to the other during her time here, and in the process had blown any chance of a future between her and Jake.

Molly pulled a tissue from the box beside her as moments of their time together flickered across her mind like a sappy movie—the whale-watching cruise, their first kiss in the workout room, the evening at the pub when Jake had all but dragged her home to make love with her.

Gone. Those things were all gone and she was back in her lonely hospital fortress with only the monotonous whoosh and puff of Bobby's ventilator to keep her company.

Frustrated, Molly tipped her head back and rubbed her eyes.

Bobby's case. That was what she needed to concentrate on now—not her disastrous love life.

Think, Flynn. Think.

The next step was to do one last full-body CT scan. Go over the films inch by inch to see if they revealed anything previously missed. That would also keep her busy for a while, and stop her from obsessing over her monumental screwup with the man she loved.

She reached for the phone to call Scheduling, then halted. A voice echoed around her—deep, rich, tinged with sadness.

"Hey."

Jake.

Molly looked around quickly to see where he was, but she was alone. Then she glanced at the small speaker for the PA system nestled into the wall beside the desk. He was talking to Bobby next door. She rose slightly to peer over the sill of the glass window separating the two rooms.

Jake stood near Bobby's bedside, dressed in a head-to-toe white hazmat suit. Only the upper third of his face was visible through the clear plastic shield in the hood, but the regret in his gaze was evident as he took Bobby's limp hand in his gloved one.

"I'm so sorry, bud. After all those missions in Kandahar this was never how it was supposed to end. Never. Thank you for saving my life, for shielding me when that IED went off. With all those Taliban creeping through every crack and alleyway and rooftop, armed to the teeth, there's no way I would've made it if you hadn't been there…"

His words cracked and his brave façade crumbled.

"I'd be dead. If it wasn't for you I wouldn't be here today, and for that I owe you more than I can ever repay. You don't like me to bring it up, but you are and always will be a true hero."

Molly sat back, new memories flooding her mind about the case—Bobby's comment to Jake about thinking he had to watch over him. Bobby's hallucinations about people in the walls and ceiling.

"Thank you for saving my life, for shielding me when that IED went off…"

Improvised Explosive Devices were constructed by terrorist cells and made of cheap materials—metal canisters filled with nuts and bolts or ball bearings, packed tight with explosives. She reexamined Bobby's initial history and physical, taken in the ER.

Activity engaged in prior to dermatitis—polishing team trophies.

Nuts, bolts, ball bearings, trophies—they all had one thing in common.

Metal.

She grabbed the phone on the wall. "Radiology? This is Dr. Flynn. I need to schedule Bobby Templeton for a full-body CT scan."

After giving the technician her patient's information, Molly rushed out into the hallway and nearly ran over Jake, who was removing his hazmat suit.

"I know what's wrong with Bobby."

He froze, eyes wide. "What?"

"A metal allergy. I've got him scheduled for a full-body scan in half an hour."

"But they've already done multiple scans and found nothing." Jake frowned, tossing the disposable suit in a nearby biohazard bin. "Why would something show up this time?"

"Because this time I know what I'm looking for."

Molly's words rushed out in a jumble of excitement, her heart pounding with the thrill of discovery and the fact that Jake wasn't glaring at her with cool contempt anymore.

"Where was Bobby positioned during the IED explosion?"

Jake's gaze narrowed. "You were eavesdropping?"

Guilt prickled Molly's cheeks. She stared at the center of his chest because she couldn't meet his gaze, knowing how he felt—or didn't feel—about her. It would hurt more than she could stand.

"I'm sorry I violated your trust. I'm sorry about the leaked footage and about overhearing your private conversation with Bobby. I'm sorry for everything—more than you'll ever know. But if I'm right we can save your best friend's life."

"Molly, I…"

Jake moved closer—close enough for her to catch his warm, comforting scent, mixed with the Betadine he'd used to scrub down with earlier, and her knees wanted to buckle from the weight of what she'd lost with him. He lifted his hand as if to caress her cheek, then let it fall to his side as he stepped back again, his expression unreadable.

"One more scan. But if you don't find anything it's over. Bobby lives out his last hours in peace."

Molly gave a small nod. "I'll do everything in my power to save him. I promise."

"Right flank."

"Sorry?" She frowned, meeting his gaze as the elevator doors dinged open.

"You asked what position Bobby was in when the IED exploded. He was leaning over me, with his back to the bomb. Since he was wearing Kevlar armor on his upper body, I'd say your best bet to find something would be in the right flank area."

Four hours later Jake sat in his office, staring at the same patient file he'd had open since he'd walked in. He'd long ago finished his documentation, and things in the ER had never been slower. The quiet was enough to drive him bonkers. He'd considered going upstairs to Radiology, to see what Molly had found, but given the current strain between them he'd probably only end up saying or doing something else he regretted.

And when it came to Molly…boy, did he regret.

He regretted reacting like an ass when she'd finally told him about the leaked footage. Regretted sitting there while Kellie repeated Roger Flynn's vile insults, knowing how awfully Molly's family had treated her for her differences. Regretted not rushing to Molly's defense and begging her forgiveness.

Sighing, he rubbed his tired eyes and slumped in his chair, too exhausted to stop images from the past few weeks from flooding his brain. Molly standing up to him at that accident scene. Her surprisingly strong punches in the workout room. Their first kiss…

God, that kiss.

She was all heat and light and sweetness—the way she'd cajoled him out of his depression after that gunshot victim passed away. The way she'd given herself so beautifully to him when they'd made love…

He didn't deserve her. Probably never had.

Worst of all, Jake had known what they had was fleeting, and he should have treasured it even more because of it. Instead he'd thrown it all away, because he was too damned scared of trusting and getting his heart shattered again.

And in the end, that was exactly what had happened anyway.

Cursing his own stupidity, Jake switched on his computer to check his emails.

His web browser loaded. To one side of the screen was a scrolling list of top news stories—the state of the economy, the latest forest fires in California, some celebrity's mega-million-dollar birthday bash in Dubai.

Near the bottom of the feed, one headline caught his eye: Sparks fly between reality TV doc and ex–war hero over star hockey player's treatment.

Curiosity got the better of him and Jake clicked on the link. It took him to one of those tabloid websites that wrote the most salacious articles possible. This one suggested that there was more to his and Molly's working relationship than medicine. Not a lie, but not their business either.

He scrolled farther down the page. The article went on to question Bobby's notorious dating past and his puck-bunny groupies. Near the bottom were several screen shots—Jake and Molly outside Bobby's room, staring each other down like a Mexican stand-off, both of them caring for Bobby during his seizure, both of them after Dr. Dave's dinner party, discovering the yohimbe tea.

His heart ached and his chest squeezed—and that was when he knew the truth. The truth was he'd fallen hard for Molly Flynn, despite all the reasons why he shouldn't. Despite all his well-crafted barriers and walls. She'd crushed them all with just a smile, an awkward ramble, a kiss.

His phone rang and Jake answered, distracted. "Ryder."

"We found it," Molly said, her tone triumphant.

"What? Where?"

"A bolt, about one point four millimeters, near his right iliac crest. Tiny, and deeply embedded in scar tissue. Easily missed. I'd like to schedule Bobby for surgery as soon as we get him stabilized."

"Uh…yes. Yes!"

Jake squeezed his eyes shut, trying to take it all in.

Bobby would be okay. His vow was fulfilled, his debt repaid—all thanks to Molly. "Have them call Dr. Minor. He's the best ortho guy in Anchorage."

"Okay. Bobby's going to be fine!"

Molly's optimism had bolstered Jake's listless spirits. He wanted to reach through the phone line and hug her tight. He wanted to kiss her silly. He wanted to drop to his knees and beg her to take him back.

Instead, he managed a gruff, "Have the staff call me once he's in Recovery."

"Of course."

Jake stood there for several seconds after the call ended. Bobby would be okay. Bobby would be okay, and Molly would leave, and life would get back to normal.

He should be happy. "Normal" was what he'd worked so hard to achieve.

So why, then, did normal suddenly seem like the most awful thing in the world?

CHAPTER FIFTEEN

"SURPRISE!" A GAGGLE of enormous hockey players barreled into Bobby Templeton's room, some carrying balloons or gifts, all wearing the Anoraks's trademark yellow and black jerseys.

Molly and her crew stepped aside. They'd just wrapped the final shots for the episode and Neal wanted to get some last candid footage of her patient making a full recovery.

It had been a week since the surgery to remove the bolt, and Bobby's condition had improved dramatically. So much so that he could be released in a day or two.

One of Bobby's teammates—a huge man with a shaggy black beard and a gold tooth—leaned over and gave Bobby a bear hug, slapping him so hard on the shoulder it made Molly wince.

"Dude! You had me worried."

"Me too," Bobby said, accepting another bruising hug from yet another teammate. "You guys won't believe the sh—" He glanced over at Rob and his camera. "The stuff they did to me. Put me in isolation, probed me, gave me enough isotopes to make me radioactive."

"Whoa!" the team said collectively.

"I know, right?" Bobby said, clearly loving the spotlight. "It was so bad."

He looked over at Molly and winked, and she couldn't hide a smile.

"Do you need anything?" the team's coach asked his most valuable player.

"Nah." Bobby pushed himself up straighter in the bed. "I'll be better once I get out of here and back home again."

Back home. The words were bittersweet for Molly. Usually at the end of a case she couldn't wait to get back to Chicago, but not this time. There was no one waiting for her and nothing but chaos at the network.

At least she'd come to find some clarity about her situation. In the wee hours of the morning, unable to sleep, Molly had taken a hard look at her life. She'd begun Diagnosis Critical because she'd wanted to make a name for herself outside the glare of her father's spotlight, to escape his bullying and prove she was strong and capable. She'd done all those things and it was time to move on. She'd had enough.

As the sun had risen over the snowcapped Chugach mountains Molly had realized something else too. She'd come here to cure Bobby, but she'd ended up curing herself. It was time to stand up to her bully of a father and put an end to his control over her life. She was who she was and it was time to stop apologizing for it and start embracing it.

Here in Anchorage, for the first time, she'd found people who respected her, patients who needed her, and the most gorgeous scenery she'd ever beheld. But, more than anything, she'd found Jake. He'd taught her to embrace her differences, to open up and experience things she'd only ever dreamed of prior to this trip.

For that, and for so many other reasons, she loved him.

Even if he would never feel the same or forgive her for breaking his trust.

She glanced over and saw him leaning against the doorframe of Bobby's room, his gaze guarded. He hiked his chin toward her and gestured at the hall.

"Be right back," she said to Rob.

"Go get 'em, Mol." Her cameraman grinned.

Molly followed Jake down to the door of the meditation chapel, attempting to fill the awkward silence by stating the obvious. "Bobby's doing well."

"Yeah," Jake said, facing her once they were alone in the hall. "About what happened—"

"It's fine."

"It's not fine." Jake watched her from across the span of a few feet, but it might as well have been a few miles, given the distance between them emotionally. "I owe you an apology."

"No, you don't. You had every right to be furious about that footage. And the things Kellie repeated from my father weren't anything I haven't heard before."

By tonight Molly would be on a flight home to Chicago. Anchorage would be nothing but a dot on a map. And this man she loved with all her heart would move on with his life and she'd move on with hers.

The words hurt, but Molly forced them out anyway. "You trusted me and I betrayed that trust. And I'm so, so sorry." Blinking hard, she took a step away. "Now, if you'll excuse me, I have some paperwork to finish."

"Wait." Jake handed her an oblong white object. "Here."

"What's this?" Molly frowned. "Is that a smiley face?"

"It's an Inupiat piece—a carved walrus tooth."

"Oh." She held the precious treasure, still warm from

his body. "I can't take this, Jake. I'm sure it means a lot to you."

"It does." He reached out and tucked a stray lock of hair behind her ear. "You do too."

Molly tried her hardest, but nothing would hold back the tears. "Jake—"

"C'mon. I want to show you something."

He ushered her into the chapel, where Neal was setting up one of the monitors they used in the production room. Jake guided Molly into a seat before the screen then took the chair beside her.

"I can't go any longer without telling you I'm sorry too. Sorry for overreacting and sorry for not standing up for you at the restaurant. You've changed since coming to Anchorage Mercy, Molly. But I've changed too. Because of you."

Sniffling, Molly chuckled. "Yeah, I've changed into a blubbering wreck."

"No, you've discovered the loving, caring woman lurking inside you." He cupped her face, his thumb stroking her cheek gently. "I always knew she was in there, waiting to emerge."

Her heart pinched at his sweet words and more tears flowed. "The problem is, since I've started crying I don't know how to stop it."

"I've got an idea how to fix that, Bolt."

Jake leaned in to kiss her. Before their lips could meet, however, a quick knock sounded on the door, followed by Dr. Dave and Rob shouldering their way inside.

"Ah, Molly!" Dr. Dave said, his jolly blue gaze darting between her and Jake. "Gladys said I might find you in here. I'm not interrupting anything, am I?"

Squeezing Jake's hand, Molly shook her head. "No, no. Please have a seat."

"What I'm about to say may come as a surprise," Dr. Dave said. "But Anchorage Mercy is starting a new Diagnostic Medicine program soon and I'd like to put in your name for the chief director position."

Molly looked from Dr. Dave to Jake, then back again. She hadn't given much thought to the next step in her career. Hadn't even mentioned to her crew that she was leaving the network.

"Wow. I'm flattered."

"What about your show?" Jake asked.

"Yeah, what about the show?" Rob and Neal stood beside the small group. "Something you'd like to tell us, Mol?"

She cringed. "Sorry, guys, but I decided last night that Bobby's case is going to be my last episode of Diagnosis Critical. I've been wavering about signing on for another season and…" she snuggled closer to Jake and smiled "…I've decided not to renew."

"Aw…" Rob and Neal hugged her, then each other. "Congrats, you two."

"Being here in Alaska has helped me realize a lot of things—not the least of which is that I need to get a life." Molly smiled. "One of my own choosing this time—not one based on what anyone else thinks I should want or to prove myself to someone."

"Right. Well, then…" Dr. Dave headed for the door. "Please give my offer careful consideration, Dr. Flynn. I think Anchorage Mercy would be a great fit for your skills."

"I'll give you an answer by the end of next week, Dr. Dave. Thank you."

"Have a safe journey home," Dr. Dave said on his way out.

Except Anchorage felt way more like home than Chicago ever had.

In a rare burst of spontaneity, Molly rushed over and yanked open the chapel door, calling into the hall after Dr. Dave. "Forget waiting. Yes. I want the job. Put my name in, please."

"Marvelous! I'll call the board this afternoon and let them know," he said from near the elevators. "You can stay with Sara and me until you get settled here. No worries."

"Thanks again for everything, Dr. Dave."

Molly stepped back into the chapel, where Jake and her crew waited.

"Well, I guess that's it, then…"

"I'm glad you're sticking around, Bolt." Jake came up to her, slipping his arm around her shoulders and pulling Molly closer. "But you have other living options too."

"I do?"

"Yeah." He flashed that sexy half-smile that made her knees go all tingly. "You can move in with me, if you want."

A fresh wave of tears flooded her eyes and she didn't even try to stop them this time. "Yes, I want," she said, grinning through her sniffles. "I want to so much it hurts."

"Good." He kissed her quickly. "Then we've got lots of plans to make, Bolt. But first there's something you need to see."

"Dr. Ryder taped a special ending for the episode and we thought you might like to watch it before it airs in a couple of months," Neal said.

"Really?" Molly gave Jake a disbelieving look. "I thought you hated being on camera."

"I do." He cuddled her tight to his side again. "But I'm willing to make sacrifices when it comes to you, Bolt."

"We ready to roll?" Rob asked, holding the remote for the flat screen. "Neal and I have a flight to catch tonight."

"Let's do it," Molly said.

The screen flickered and Jake appeared, tapping a little microphone pinned to his scrubs. "Is this on?"

"We're ready," Neal prompted on screen. "Can you state your name?"

"Dr. Jake Ryder."

"And what's your position at Anchorage Mercy?"

"I'm the Head of Emergency Medicine."

"Tell us how it was, working with Dr. Molly Flynn."

"At first it was…tricky. At least for me. But we became a great team."

"Do you believe in her unorthodox treatment protocols?"

"No, not always. But I do believe in her. She's the most brilliant physician I've ever met. Molly has a huge heart and a wonderful capacity to see what others can't. She's truly special." Onscreen, Jake's voice roughened with emotion. "I feel honored to know her and I'm so grateful for all she's done here."

"Okay, Dr. Ryder. Anything else you'd like to say?"

"Yes." Jake looked directly into the camera. "The local Inupiat tribes have a saying: We are forever remembered by the tracks we leave. Molly, your footprints will always stay on the hearts of everyone here at Anchorage Mercy. Especially mine."

The screen went black once more.

"Oh, Jake," Molly said through more tears. "I love you."

"I love you too, Bolt." He meant the words with every fiber of his being.

Rob started packing away the gear, grinning from ear

to ear. "Just make sure we get invited back for the wedding, okay?"

Jake snorted. "Like we'd get married without the crew that brought us together!"

"I thought Bobby brought us together," Molly said, frowning.

"Him too, Bolt." Jake laughed, then pulled his phone from the waistband of his scrubs. "Oops. I need to get back to the ER. Looks like we're getting slammed again."

"Want any help?" She pushed to her feet beside him.

"Sure." Jake took Molly's hand and headed for the door, asking the guys, "When's your flight?"

"Ten thirty tonight," Neal said. "When are you flying back, Mol?"

"I got my flight changed to tomorrow morning."

Jake's heart stumbled. That meant they could have one more night together.

They waved to the guys, then headed to his ER. Jake grabbed the first chart from the queue and perused the history and physical before handing the file to Molly.

"Oh, Bolt. You'll love this one."

"Why? Is it difficult?" she asked, frowning at the notes.

"No. Just the cutest couple ever."

"I thought that was us?"

"You're right. It is us."

He bent to give Molly a quick kiss, then noticed Wendy watching them. She gave Jake two thumbs-up before rushing off to assist one of the residents.

"Ready?"

"Ready," Molly said, and they walked into Trauma Bay Three together.

CHAPTER SIXTEEN

Eight weeks later...

"Do I LOOK OKAY, Bolt?" Jake asked Molly as they stood in the grand foyer of the Drake Hotel in downtown Chicago.

Honestly, Molly wanted nothing more than to whisk him off to a room upstairs, strip off his tailor-made suit, toss him on the bed and make love to him until they were both senseless with ecstasy. But first they had to face Martha's dreaded baby shower extraordinaire.

And Molly's father.

Leaving Jake behind in Anchorage had been the hardest thing Molly had ever done, but she'd had things to settle here in Chicago. She'd resigned from the network, sublet her tiny apartment on Lake Shore Drive, gotten all her things packed and had a proper send-off with Rob and Neal.

All that was left were her farewells to her family.

Those would come today.

Later tonight she and Jake were flying back to Alaska on the red-eye to start a new chapter together. Dr. Dave had pushed through the hospital board's vote and secured her the job of Head of Diagnostic Medicine at Anchorage Mercy, so Molly had been busy telecommuting—signing contracts and hiring staff—and she couldn't wait to assume her new post and start seeing patients in the new facilities the hospital had revamped for her department.

It was like a dream come true. All thanks to the support of the man beside her.

"You look devastatingly handsome," Molly said, smoothing Jake's tie and giving him a quick kiss.

Then, hand in hand, they walked into the hotel's French Room.

Molly had done her best with the decorations, given her limited time and her mother's constant nitpicking, but as she saw the place now she thought the pretty silver and gold streamers complemented the elegant room's pastel green silk wall coverings and the swirling indigo patterns in the custom carpets.

Above, crystal basket chandeliers shimmered, and deep blue satin damask draperies covered the windows overlooking Lake Michigan in the distance. Over a hundred of her parents' colleagues and Martha's friends milled about in the space, chatting or snacking on obscenely expensive lobster and caviar hors d'oeuvres.

"Wow," Jake whispered. "This is quite a spread."

Molly snorted. "Only the best for the Flynns."

"It's about time you two got here." Her mother rushed over.

"Traffic," Molly said, though the real reason for their tardiness was the fact that neither she nor Jake had wanted to leave the cozy little love nest they'd made in their hotel room at the Ritz Carlton on Lakeshore Drive.

"I still don't understand why the two of you didn't stay here at the Drake with the rest of us," Phyllis Flynn said, looking around. "Though you did a decent job on the decorations."

"Thanks. The shower hasn't been my top priority."

Her father joined them, tumbler of whiskey in hand. "Daughter of mine, it's not too late to renegotiate with the network. Though you'll have to take a subpar slot. They've given me your old one."

Molly took a deep breath to relax her tense muscles. "I won't be returning to the network. We discussed this. I've got a new department to run in Anchorage."

"Your loss." Roger Flynn gulped down his drink. "Such a waste—stuck out there in some hospital on the prairie." He narrowed his icy green gaze on Jake. "I blame you for this."

Jake squeezed Molly's hand. "I gladly take full responsibility, sir."

"No. This was my decision. No one else's." Molly squared her shoulders and raised her chin. "You made my childhood a living hell—but that's over. Starting today, you don't matter anymore. I've got a new life, and a man who loves me just the way I am. I don't need you or your bullying, or your opinions about my life. Not that I ever did."

Roger Flynn shook his head, his expression brimming with disapproval. "Love makes people idiots."

"You're wrong," Molly said, an edge of steel in her tone. "Love makes people human. And unconditional love makes them exceptional. Perhaps if you'd loved me without conditions our relationship wouldn't be what it is today."

"Don't be ridiculous." Her father's scowl darkened. "Why do you think I pushed you so hard all those years? I did it because I loved you—because I saw your enormous potential and wanted you to become all you could be."

"What a crock of—" Jake started.

"I've got this." Molly stopped him, turning back to her father. "The only thing you love is Roger Flynn. You constantly nag and push and force everyone around you to breaking point—and if they snap then you call them weak. I'm sorry you consider me such a disappointment, but I'm through trying to live up to your ideals. This is my life, and I plan to do what makes me happy and fulfilled. That includes running my own department and spending the rest of my days with the man I love. And if you or anyone else can't accept that, please keep it to yourself, okay?"

Her mother huffed. "It isn't polite to raise your voice at a party, dear."

"Maybe not, but it's not polite to make other people feel small either," Molly said, staring at her father in a silent battle of wills.

She'd spent her whole life trying to please this man, trying to earn his love and respect. She'd be damned if she'd back down now.

Roger Flynn finally looked away, hailing a passing waiter for another whiskey. "Well, at least you'll be bringing some much-needed expertise to that wild frontier."

Not quite an apology, but Molly would take it. "I'm looking forward to introducing your theories on halting viral disease progression through enzyme inhibition."

Her father watched Molly over the rim of his glass. "Make sure you give me credit."

"Of course." Molly gave a curt nod and took Jake's hand again.

"Sis!" Martha waddled over, her gait more ungainly as she neared her due date. She was still dressed to the nines in designer maternity wear, with her doting investment banker husband hanging off her arm. "I was hoping you'd be the baby's godmother."

Molly was a bit shocked. "I'd be honored…"

"Good luck in Alaska." Roger Flynn walked away before anyone could respond.

"Call me once you get to Anchorage, dear, to let me know you're safe." Her mother gave Molly a quick air-kiss before bustling off to mingle.

"Can I speak to you outside?"

Jake made their excuses to the expectant parents, then led Molly out into the opulent marble foyer of the hotel. Several paparazzi milled about, looking to snap photos of the many local celebrities attending the party.

Jake pulled Molly into a private little alcove, discreetly covered by plush blue velvet drapes. Her pulse raced. Things had been so magical tonight. Maybe too magical.

But adrenaline still pumped through her system from facing down her father at last, and Molly was riding high on a surge of success. "I can't believe I did that! Did you see his face? I stood up for myself. Me! I did it!"

"Yep, you did, Bolt."

Jake smiled—the lopsided smile that always made her knees go wobbly.

"And I'm so proud of you. I've always respected your amazing abilities as a physician, even if we have differing opinions on some of your treatment choices. But, wow. What you did in there—standing up to that man, that bully, like that. Sweetheart, today my admiration for you and your wonderful heart surpasses everything else. You're incredible, Molly Flynn. Simply incredible."

Despite his impassioned words she didn't miss the flicker of uncertainty in his stormy gray eyes, and a tiny tad of her old insecurity seeped in before she could stop it, dampening her joy.

"What's wrong?" she asked.

"Nothing's wrong." Jake's normally graceful moves

turned awkward as he fumbled in his suit pocket and frowned. "I just…"

"Oh, Lord."

Molly's stomach knotted. This might be Brian all over again. She'd finally stood up for herself with one man, but had her newfound gumption cost her the other? Life as the scared, insecure woman who'd hidden inside her sterile, controlled, unemotional world wasn't possible anymore. She couldn't do that again—not even for Jake. But she'd do everything in her power to make things work with him if he gave her the chance.

"Please tell me you're not going to break up with me. I know I've changed since you met me, and things are different with me now than when we first met, but—"

"What? No. I love everything about you, Molly. Never doubt that. It's just that I've got something for you."

Jake went down on one knee, a blue Tiffany box in one hand. Inside was an adorable penguin brooch, with sparkling onyx eyes and black lacquer wings.

"Oh! Wow!" Her smile trembled with surprise. "It's very…cute."

"I spent all day yesterday picking it out while you were wrapping up loose ends at the network. Penguins are kind of our symbol, right? That day in my kitchen you blurted out all those facts about penguins and how they mated for life. I know they're not indigenous to Alaska, but then lots of people are transplants there. Just look at you."

"No. I mean, yes. It's great." Molly stroked her fingers over the pin, her chest squeezing with tenderness and her eyes stinging with unshed tears. She sniffled. "I love it. Really."

"But you were expecting something else?" Jake narrowed his gaze knowingly.

"What?"

She shook her head as he reached into his pocket again. If life had taught her anything, it was that having expectations—especially of the unrealistic kind—was foolish.

She hugged the little penguin to her chest as tears spilled down her cheeks. "No, no. I love it, Jake. Really. And I love you too."

"Good," Jake said, his smile widening.

This time he pulled out a smaller black velvet box and flipped it open with his thumb. Inside sparkled the most beautiful emerald-cut diamond engagement ring Molly had ever seen. She reached out, shaking, to trace her fingertips over the radiant gem, joyful laughter bubbling and fizzing inside her like champagne.

"Molly Flynn, I love you. Will you marry me and be my forever mate?"

Too much. This man was too much. He was all she'd ever wanted and more than she deserved. Overcome with happiness, she felt some of those old random facts gurgling for escape inside her whirling mind. Molly didn't even try to stop them this time. Jake loved her—really, really loved her—quirks and all. She'd take it—and him—forever and ever. Amen.

Molly swiped away her tears with the back of her hand and blinked down at the dear face of the man she loved, reciting statistics like love poems. "People who marry between the ages of twenty-eight and thirty-two have the fewest divorces."

Jake cocked his head, his expression confused. "Is that a yes, Bolt?"

"Yes!" Giddiness rose inside Molly as she knelt too, cupping his cheeks in her trembling hands. "Yes! I love you too and I'd be honored to be your wife."

"Perfect."

Jake slid the ring on her finger, then pulled her in for a deep kiss.

They didn't separate for a long while afterward. At last Jake pulled away, dusting kisses along her cheek to her ear and whispering, "I'm not perfect and I don't profess to be, Molly, but when I'm with you I want to be better. I want to be the man of your dreams."

She rested her forehead against his and smiled, her heart so full it felt as if it might burst forth like a bird from a cage. "You already are, Jake. You already are."

This time when he kissed her she couldn't wait to get back to their love nest at the Ritz Carlton and celebrate their new engagement properly. There'd be plenty of time to tell their friends and family later. Tonight's celebration was for them alone.

A ruckus sounded on the other side of the blue curtains. Jake peered around the edge before giving Molly's hand a reassuring squeeze and helping her to her feet.

"Looks like another local celebrity is arriving for your sister's party," he said. "This is it, Bolt. If we sneak out now there's a chance we won't cause another Internet sensation."

Molly nodded and held on to him tight, ready for her new life to begin. "Let's do it. I'll follow you anywhere, Jake."

"Yeah?" He leaned back for one last, brief kiss over his shoulder.

Molly smiled as they darted out of the alcove, hand in hand, together. "Oh, yeah."

* * * * *

COMING SOON!

We really hope you enjoyed reading this book. If you're looking for more romance, be sure to head to the shops when new books are available on

Thursday
23rd August

To see which titles are coming soon, please visit
millsandboon.co.uk

MILLS & BOON

MILLS & BOON

Coming next month

THE NURSE'S PREGNANCY MIRACLE
Ann McIntosh

Nychelle tried with all her might to say they shouldn't go any further, but couldn't get the words out. Knowing she needed to tell him the rest of her story battled with the desire making her head swim and her body tingle and thrum with desire.

'Tell me you don't want me,' he said again, and she knew she couldn't. To do so would be to lie.

'I can't. You know I can't. But...'

He didn't wait to hear the rest, just took her mouth in a kiss that made what she'd planned to say fly right out of her brain.

Desire flared, hotter than the Florida sun, and Nychelle surrendered to it, unable and unwilling to risk missing this chance to know David intimately, even if it were just this once. Was it right? Wrong? She couldn't decide — didn't want to try to.

There were so many more things she should explain to him, but she knew she wouldn't. Telling him about the baby when she knew he didn't want a family would destroy whatever it was growing between them. It was craven, perhaps even despicable not to be honest with him, and she hated herself for being underhand, but her mind, heart and body were at war, and she'd already accepted which would win.

She'd deal with the fallout, whatever it might be, tomorrow. Today—this evening—she was going to have what she wanted, live the way she wanted. Enjoy David for this one time. There would only be regrets if she didn't.

His lips were still on hers, demanding, delicious. She'd relived the kisses they'd shared over and over in her mind, but now she realized memory was only a faded facsimile of reality. The touch and taste and scent of him encompassed her, overtaking her system on every level.

Her desperate hands found their way beneath his shirt, and his groan of pleasure was as heartfelt as her joy at the first sensation of his bare skin beneath her palms. His hands, in turn, explored her yearning flesh, stroking her face, then her neck. When they brushed along her shoulders, easing the straps of her sundress away, Nychelle arched against him.

Suddenly it was as though they had both lost all restraint. Arms tight around each other, their bodies moved in concert, their fiercely demanding kisses whipping the flames of arousal to an inferno.

Continue reading
THE NURSE'S PREGNANCY MIRACLE
Ann McIntosh

Available next month
www.millsandboon.co.uk

LET'S TALK

Romance

For exclusive extracts, competitions
and special offers, find us online:

f facebook.com/millsandboon

⊙ @millsandboonuk

𝕏 @millsandboon

Or get in touch on 0844 844 1351*

For all the latest titles coming soon, visit
millsandboon.co.uk/nextmonth